For Anuradha

I

The Underdog Family

OUSEP CHACKO, ACCORDING to Mariamma Chacko, is the kind of man who has to be killed at the end of a story. But he knows that she is not very sure about this sometimes, especially in the mornings. He sits at his desk, as usual, studying a large pile of cartoons, trying to solve the only mystery that matters to her. He does not ask for coffee, but she brings it anyway, landing the glass on the wooden desk with minor violence to remind him of last night's disgrace. She flings open the windows, empties his ashtray and arranges the newspapers on the table. And when he finally leaves for work without a word, she stands in the hall and watches him go down the stairs.

On the playground below, a hard brown earth with stray grass, Ousep walks with quick short strides towards the gate. He can see the other men, the good husbands and the good fathers, their black shoes polished, serious shirts already damp in the humid air. They walk to the scooter shed carrying inverted helmets that contain their outrageously small vegetarian lunches. More men emerge from the stairway tunnels of Block A, which is an austere white building with three floors. Their tidy, auspicious wives in cotton saris now appear in the balconies to bid goodbye. They are mumbling prayers, smiling at other women, peeping with one eye into their own blouses.

The men never greet Ousep. They turn away, or become interested in the ground, or wipe their spectacles. But among their own, they have great affection. They are a fellowship, and they can communicate by just clearing the phlegm in their throats.

'Gorbachev,' a delicate man says.

'Gorbachev,' the other one says.

Having thus completed the analysis of the main story in *The Hindu*, which is Mikhail Gorbachev's election as the first executive president of the Soviet Union, they walk towards their scooters. A scooter in Madras is a man's promise that he will not return home drunk in the evening. Hard-news reporters like Ousep Chacko consider it an insult to be seen on one, but these men are mostly bank clerks. They now hold the handlebars of their scooters and stand in a languid way. Then they kick suddenly as if to startle the engine into life. They kick many times, some even appear to bounce in the air. Eventually, the engines roar and they ride out, one by one, sitting at the very edge of the front seat as if that is the cheaper option. They will return the same way at six in the evening carrying jasmine flowers for their wives, who will wear them in their freshly washed hair, filling their homes with an aphrodisiacal odour and stirring the peace of their fathers-in-law who live with them, those old men who are so starved for flesh that they fondle children, fondle fully grown men, furtively flap their thighs when they watch women's tennis on TV.

At the gates, the fragile watchman stands in a farcical para-military outfit that puffs in the wind, and he cautiously salutes his foe. Ousep nods without looking. That always gets the guard's respect. Ousep turns for a glimpse of the women on the balconies, and they pretend they were not looking at him. On his own balcony on the third floor there is no one.

As he walks towards the far end of the street he is in full view of all the balconies of the four identical buildings on Balaji Lane, in full view of all the housewives and the unmoving old wraiths, who watch with open mouths. Ousep walks fast in the mornings, the little finger of his right hand sticking out as if to receive a signal. From the other gates more scooters emerge. Some of the riders stare at him as if it is safer to meet his eyes when they are wearing helmets, which is true in a way. Women disappear from the balconies munching the final strands of prayer, women appear on the balconies preoccupied with many things. When they see him their eyes rest on him a moment longer to accommodate a quick judgement. Considering everything, considering all that has passed and the way he is, it is reasonable that people should stare at him, but he hates it. They may find it hilarious if they are told this but the truth is that Ousep Chacko is a man who wants to be inconspicuous, who suffers when eyes are on him. But then the fate of shy people is that all their fears usually come true.

As things are, it does not take much to be a spectacle on this narrow tarred lane. It waits all day to be startled by the faintest hint of strangeness passing through. Such as a stray working woman in the revolutionary sleeveless blouse, who has the same aura here as a divorcee. A man with a ponytail. A North Indian girl in jeans so tight you can see daylight between her legs. It is as if such apparitions are a sign that the future, which has arrived in other places, is now prospecting the city. Here now is the final stand of an age, the last time one can profile a street in Madras and be correct. Men are managers, mothers are house-wives. And all bras are white. Anglo-Indian girls who walk in floral frocks are Maria.

That is how the people on Balaji Lane would remember these days many years later. And when they remembered these times they would also remember, with a chuckle, the Malayalee Catholic family, the cuckoos among the crows – the despicable man called Ousep Chacko, his stranded wife who told her bare walls all her reasonable grudges, and their son Thoma, who was weak in maths. What became of them, did they survive the sheer length of life, did they make it through?

And they would remember Unni, of course. They would never forget Unni Chacko. 'Remember Unni?' they would say. 'Did anybody ever find out why he did that? Why did Unni Chacko do what he did?' Nobody would ever mention what Unni actually did. It is such a terrifying word in any language.

Ousep does not want to think of his boy so early, at least not until the first interview of the day. If his mind drifted in that direction he would be lost once again in all its familiar traps, and he would be asking himself the same exasperating questions a thousand times. He wants to think of something else, something inconsequential. But the image of Unni Chacko is already assembling itself in Ousep's head, staring back at his father from a self-portrait. What Ousep sees is a boy with keen narrow eyes, a broad forehead and a high mop of thick hair. A seventeen-year-old cartoonist, an exceptional cartoonist, but too young to accept that subtlety is not always a mask of mediocrity. Like most cartoonists, the boy does not talk much, and when he does speak he is not very funny. Most of the time he is excruciatingly terse, even with his mother, whom he loves for exaggerated reasons – the only way sons can love their mothers.

That is what Ousep sees; beyond this he knows very little about his son. There is no shame in accepting that. No matter what their delusions are, parents do not really know their children. Ousep is just a man who knows less than the other fathers. But he has studied every inch of the sixty-three cartoons and comics by Unni that lie about the house, most of them in a wooden trunk. Sixty-four if Ousep includes one inexplicable comic that has landed by chance in his hands, which he has hidden from Mariamma. Not an easy thing to do in that house. He has hidden it inside the radio. He has to unscrew the back panel every time he wants to take it out.

Somewhere in Unni's cartoons and comics is the clue that will explain everything. That is what Ousep believes. There is nothing else left to believe, really.

Most of Unni's works are comics, their stories told over several pages, through elaborate black-and-white sketches with a sudden dash of watercolour here and there. There is no single theme that unites all his works, and there are no dark superhero stories as people might imagine. But, for some reason, there is a disproportionate number of comics that lampoon the human search for the meaning of life.

In the comic that is titled *Absolute Truth*, a blank white envelope floats through deep space, orbits strange worlds and finally heads towards Earth. When it enters the Earth's atmosphere, the envelope burns and what emerges is another white envelope. It has 'Absolute Truth' written on it. It floats down and falls on an endless field. A bare-chested farmer picks it up, opens the envelope, takes out a sheet of paper. He reads it and starts laughing uncontrollably. He passes it on to his wife who, too, begins to laugh. She shows it to the infant in her arm, who becomes breathless with laughter. The farmer passes the Absolute Truth to his neighbour, who holds his stomach, rolls about his cabbage farm and laughs. The letter changes hands across homes, villages, across cities, across the whole world, leaving people hysterical with laughter at the long-awaited discovery of absolute truth.

In *Enlightenment*, a sage in robes is meditating; he is sitting on a high snowy peak. Seasons change, storms pass, but nothing bothers him. He gets a massive erection, which subsides in time, but the man is undisturbed, unaware of what is happening to him and around him. Mountain climbers arrive with their national flags and leave disappointed when they find someone already on the summit. The sage becomes very old, his beard turns white. Finally, he becomes radiant. A halo appears behind him. He has achieved enlightenment. He opens his eyes looking totally stunned. He screams, 'Shit, I am a cartoon.'

There are very few dialogues in Unni's comics and the absence of prose lends a brooding, abstract quality to his works, especially in one of his most ambitious stories, *Beatles, Crossing*, which is twenty-one pages long. It begins with a red beetle that is standing on one side of a broad black road. The beetle says, 'I want to go to the other side.' And it starts crossing the road. The comic then cuts to the four Beatles performing in various parts of the world, against backdrops of iconic monuments. Everywhere they go there are huge delirious crowds. At one point in the comic there is a question: 'Why Is Ringo Starr Not As Famous As The Other Three Beatles?' Under the question is a portrait of the four Beatles performing. At the bottom of the page is the answer: 'Because He Was Always Sitting'. Could this be true? As the story unfolds, it appears that the Beatles are slowly growing sad and discontent. They come to India and meet holy men, who are always in yogic poses. The Beatles begin to meditate, wear Indian clothes, get into extraordinary yogic contortions, play Indian classical instruments, shit on the banks of a river. But then they become sad and lost once again. They return to England, return to their old lives. And one day, they cross a road, they walk across a zebra crossing. All through this, the red beetle has been making its difficult progress across the same road, narrowly escaping violent death under the tyres of speeding vehicles. The final window of the comic has the triumphant red beetle, who has crossed the road and reached the pavement, which is strikingly identical to the pavement from which he had started his difficult journey. He says, 'I have crossed over to the other side.'

Ousep snaps out of the comic world because he is reminded of something unpleasant, something that vaguely resembles a herbivorous animal's petty fear of life, but he is not sure what has made him think of this. Then he recognises what it is. The sight of three adolescent schoolboys who have just emerged from a gate and are now walking in his direction. One of them has sacred ash smeared on his forehead in three straight lines, as if a cycle has run over him. They are in school uniform – white shirts that are already slipping out of their khaki trousers. They don't walk erect, there is no spring in them, there is no joy. The boys stare at him with meaning; he returns their stares without contempt.

The most foolish description of the young is that they are rebellious. The truth is that they are a fellowship of cowards. It is true anywhere in the world, but the fear of the adolescent boys on Balaji Lane is exceptional. They are terrified of everything, of life, of their future, of friends doing better than them, of falling off their cycles, of big trucks and large men, and beautiful women. The only thing that does not scare them is calculus.

They might have turned out a bit differently if they had not been so retarded by a long torturous preparation for one engineering entrance exam. The day they were born and were diagnosed with having a penis, their fate was decided – to one day take the Joint Entrance Exam. The toughest exam in the world, their fathers say. One in a hundred would make it. It has been over twenty years since anyone from the colony has got through. Their fathers tell them every day of their lives, sometimes holding a leather belt in their hands, that the JEE alone will decide their lives because it will eventually take them to America on a full scholarship. On a street where every boy knows that his future rests on a single test with multiple-choice questions, it is appropriate that the four identical buildings here are named A, B, C and D.

As the three boys pass Ousep, he hears one of them ask, 'Tan 2x is equal to?' The other two answer simultaneously in a burst of triumph, 'Two tan x by one minus tan square x.'

$$\sim$$

THE BOY SEES Ousep walking towards him and turns his face away, like a wounded lover who truly does not wish reconciliation. Sai Shankaran, a close friend of Unni, according to general consensus, waits for his bus every morning at the Liberty bus stop. The last few weeks, Ousep has come here almost every morning to torment him. Sai claims he has revealed all that he knows and has nothing more to say. But Ousep does not believe that, he wants to break him. That should not be very difficult. Sai was seventeen when he was slapped by his father in front of his friends for playing cards. He is twenty now but it appears that he is still a boy who can be slapped around by an older male.

Sai stands in his spineless way, young but antiquated, studious but not clever, a thick steel watch on his wrist, his oiled black hair combed in the good-boy hairstyle. He looks like the past of an old man.

He failed all the engineering entrance exams that he had taken, and scored just eighty-nine per cent in the twelfth standard board exams. So he endures the terrifying ignominy of studying physics in just another obsolete arts and science college where Jesuit brothers and blind people go to study English literature. He is in the final year now, but, still unaccustomed to failure, he goes through life like a ghost and probably avoids all the cousins and friends who go to engineering colleges. Sai will learn to be happy again one day, he will even imagine that he is not worthless. He does not know it yet but the simple fact is that he will make it. Ambition is the capacity for unhappiness and Sai has a lot of that to pull through.

And one day he will land in the United States, just like almost everybody else from his class. And one evening he will meet his old friends at a vegetarian restaurant. When they run out of things to say, someone will say, with a gentle smile, 'Remember Unni Chacko?' And through the silence that the name will cast he will tell himself that Unni Chacko may have laughed at him once upon a time but as things stand, Sai has won. And Unni had long ago lost.

Sai and Unni, taken together, must have been an odd sight. Sai, always tense, toiling, afraid that he is a moron and groomed from childhood to believe that intelligence is purely mathematical ability. Unni, handsome in a careless way, and passing through life with the lethargy of an artist. It is hard to accept there was any love or respect between them. That any two men in the world have real affection between them is itself a myth, chiefly of the two men. But Sai and Unni, especially, are impossible friends. One must have used the other.

'I am here,' Ousep says. Sai's head is already turned away, so he cranes his neck and looks beyond the horizon to stress that he is not interested in talking. 'I hope you've changed your mind, Sai. Hope you've something more to tell me.'

This is how it goes every morning. Ousep talking, Sai silent. 'I hate doing this, Sai, I hate bothering you like this, but I have no choice. I know there is something you're not telling me.'

Sai's chest heaves, he shuffles a bit and makes an exaggerated gesture of putting his palm over his eyes and trying to divine the number of a bus that is approaching. But it appears that it is not his bus, and he makes another dramatic face of great dismay. The city is full of terrible actors. That is what historians never say about Madras, it is filled with hams. The bus arrives fully packed, and spilling a swarm of tiny starved young men who would not have made it this far in life if it had not been for all those free vaccinations. Dozens of them, some in trousers, many in lungis, are still dangling from the doors and windows. Two cops in plain clothes who have been waiting on the road take the sticks they had hidden in the back of their shirts, and start hitting the legs of the danglers, who now try to surge into the bus, screaming and laughing.

The commotion passes and there is reasonable quiet for the moment. Just speeding vehicles, and their horns. 'I heard something yesterday,' Ousep says. 'You, Unni and Somen Pillai went to meet a nun who had taken a lifelong vow of silence. You didn't tell me about this. See, this is what I mean. There are some things you didn't tell me. Why, Sai? Why didn't you tell me?' Sai remains silent, as expected, and cranes his neck again. 'Why would three boys go to meet a nun who does not speak?' Ousep asks. 'Say something, talk to me. I am meeting her tomorrow. What must I ask her?'

Sai's stoic silence is a clever strategy. It does frustrate Ousep and make him feel silly. Or is Ousep imagining things? Maybe it is not a strategy, maybe the boy has truly told him everything that he thought was significant.

'OK, don't tell me anything, Sai. Just tell me how I can meet

Somen Pillai. Take me to Somen Pillai. That's all I ask. Somen Pillai.'

A look of immense relief comes over Sai. His bus has finally arrived. He tells Ousep, without affection, what he has said before. 'Why have you started probing again? What happened?'

'Nothing has happened.'

'People say you've found something. That's why you're hounding all his classmates again.'

'They don't know what they are talking about.'

'I hear you have been trying to meet everyone.'

'That's true.'

'Why are you doing this now? Why now? After three years. Why?'

Why now? Why now? That is what people ask Ousep every day.

'Just give up,' Sai says. 'Get on with your life. That's all I can say.'

Sai wades through the layers of damp bodies on the footboard of the bus, and makes his way in. He will squeeze himself safely between the men, feel his wallet at all times, and take great care to ensure that he does not brush against the women because he is precisely the sort of harmless fruit the ladies in the bus wait to slap and punch and stab with the sharp end of their floral umbrellas for the times when they are touched and poked, the elastic of their underwear pulled and released like a catapult by the flying squads of college boys who board the packed buses just to do that.

There is an untitled comic by Unni about one of these squads, which shows how they do what they do, and how much they enjoy it. The comic ends in the distant future of the five boys of the gang. All of them are respectable men who go home every evening to a loving traditional wife and two adoring children.

After Sai's bus leaves, only a young woman and her little daughter are left at the bus stop. The woman and the girl have yellow faces from a turmeric treatment the previous night to make them fairer. The daughter is playing a private game. She pats her mother's buttocks and runs away giggling, returns to pat again and run a few feet. She keeps doing it. The mother stands looking in one direction, hoping to see her bus. A man appears and stands behind the woman. The daughter stops playing the game now, and she begins to toy with a chocolate wrapper she has found on the ground. The man gently pats the woman's back. She thinks it is her daughter, so she stands there without any expression. The man pats her again and looks away. He pats her at short intervals, and finally he lets his hand stay on her. Ousep stares at the scene without opinion, without outrage. A man's hand on a woman's arse and the woman, yawning now, looking at the world go by.

It is a moment that has no meaning. It is as if the tired charade of human life with its great pursuits and history and wounds and deep convictions has collapsed, and the world has been suddenly revealed as a place that has no point, that does not need the hypothesis of meaning to explain its existence.

~

IT IS A misfortune to be in the presence of a writer, even a failed writer, to be seen by him, be his passing study and remain in his corrupt memory. It is like the insult of a corpse on the road by a war photographer. Ousep wonders whether cartoonists are writers, he hopes they have different minds. He is with a lot of them and all of them are looking at him. What do they see? A man with silver and black hair that falls in curls at his nape, and a journalistic French beard. Surely a creative type, like them. Or do they see more than that, do they see a man illuminated by failure, a tragic father who is still probing the life of his son? Should he try to achieve a feeble stoop and somewhat moist eyes, look weak and dependent, make them careless about what they choose to say?

The Society of Amateur Cartoonists meets once a month in the

Madras Christian College, in a portion of a long corridor. The far end of the sunlit corridor frames a huddle of ancient trees that pretends to hide a thick forest within its darkness. Usually, not more than twenty cartoonists attend these meetings but today, because word had spread that Unni Chacko's father wanted to see them, there are nearly fifty cartoonists of various ages, all of them sitting in a crescent on the ground. Ousep is among them, he has refused the offer of a foldable chair. In the small crowd, there are five identical bald Buddhist monks in saffron robes, who look like giant infants. And just two girls, who are in jeans and T-shirt, and they survey the others with the amused look of a newsreader who is finished with political news and is about to announce that the lioness in the Vandalur Zoo has delivered four healthy cubs.

Ousep did not know that his son was a member of such a group until a few days ago when someone mentioned it to him in passing. Unni was in the society for just a few months, he was among the youngest they have ever admitted, but people here remember him in a way that suggests he was important. When Ousep walked into the gathering, everyone stood up and clapped. After the fuss ended and Ousep did not have to nod graciously any more, the president of the society formally introduced him as 'Chief reporter of the UNI'.

Ousep cannot deny that, but it reminds him that he would never be introduced as the greatest writer Kerala has ever produced. When he was young, everybody said that was his destiny. But then the years passed and somehow he did not write his great novel. He decayed in a state of gentle happiness. Or is it just that he did not truly believe he could write a brilliant novel? Many years ago, when Mariamma was still interested in him, she had told him, while sticking a stamp on an envelope, 'Strong people write bad stories.' Why has the comment stayed with him? Was she calling him strong or was it a cruel review of his short stories?

*

OUSEP TELLS THE cartoonists, 'I don't want you to solve the puzzle for me,' which is a lie, of course. 'I want you to tell me what you remember. I want to know Unni Chacko better, that's all there is to this.'

Nobody speaks after that, they stare at him. It is as if he is a wounded presence. But then, slowly, the silence gives way to festive murmurs and even laughter. Through all this, Ousep's eye scans the gathering for the quiet ones, who may know what he really wants to know.

'Way beyond his age,' the president is saying. He is a large man with an enormous paunch and a thick moustache. 'Unni was way beyond seventeen.' The man is probably in his late thirties and Ousep finds it hard to accept that his child used to know such men, grown men, fat men. 'Unni didn't like to get into the conventional superhero-supervillain kind of stuff, you know,' the man says. 'But he created a superhero series. Stunning work, stunning.'

Unni's superheroes, according to this man, did not have any useful powers. They could not fly, they did not have muscles, they did not even wear tight outfits. They wore shirts and trousers, and they possessed silly gifts. The Styleman, for instance, could comb his hair by just moving the skin on his scalp. The Staplerman could staple anything with his fingers. These heroes somehow valiantly fought equally ridiculous villains. Ousep has not seen the series, it is not among the collection at home. There were probably several works that Unni destroyed for some reason.

'I remember a single-panel cartoon by Unni,' a pleasant boy with affluent skin says. 'It has an old woman telling her old husband, "Let's go to a restaurant for dinner tonight and talk about you, you and you."' There is mild laughter, like a passing breeze.

A delicate silence falls as people decide what they want to share. Someone begins to giggle. It is a slender effeminate boy with a jovial face. He says, 'Unni had a very serious problem. He had this artistic objection to the love symbol. He said it doesn't look like a heart, he said it looks more like a red arse.' Everybody laughs but soon a debate erupts over the red heart. Some like the symbol, they think it is a stroke of genius on a par with something called the Smiley. But others take Unni's side. They do see it as a red arse. As the debate collapses into a good-natured commotion, the jovial boy stands up and threatens to take off his clothes to prove his point. Everybody begs him not to do it. Some cartoonists throw nervous glances at Ousep, probably to check whether they are being disrespectful, insensitive maybe. So Ousep maintains a sporting smile. The jovial flexible boy bends forward, raising his arse in the air. 'Look at it from this angle,' he says, and runs his long thin hand over the shape of his haunches. 'See, can you see, my bum is the symbol of love.'

As the debate continues, Ousep whispers to the president, who is sitting beside him, and asks why the two girls have nothing to say about Unni. 'They joined us long after Unni stopped coming here,' the president says. 'They don't know him but they have heard of him. Everybody has heard about him. We talk a lot about Unni.'

It appears, at least for now, there is not a single girl in Madras who knows Unni well. How unfortunate it is for Unni that he does not live in the extravagant memory of an infatuated young woman.

There is a full-bearded young man in the gathering, who is somehow isolated from all that is going on, but he has been staring at Ousep for a while. He looks away when Ousep catches his gaze. 'Who is that?' Ousep asks in a whisper. 'That bearded boy in the T-shirt which has a cow's skull on it.'

'That's Beta,' the president says. 'It's his pen name. Nobody knows his real name.'

'Beta as in alpha, beta, gamma?'

'I think so. Yes. I am surprised he is here. He does not come often. Mr Chacko, if he says anything about Unni, don't mind him. Something is wrong with him.'

Soon, the cartoonists forget Ousep, which is a good development. They are still talking about Unni but they are talking among themselves and not putting on a show any more. They have even stopped throwing glances at him, except Beta, who stares like a child. Ousep listens with full attention to what the cartoonists are saying, though he has heard versions of all this before, many times – Unni's theory that the unfortunate are not as miserable as the world imagines. That urchins, the handicapped, orphans, prisoners and others are much happier than people think. And that language is a trap, that a dark evolutionary force has created language to limit human thought. That writers are overrated fools. That all religions came from ancient comic writers. And that the ultimate goal of comics is the same as the purpose of humanity – to break free from language.

There is now a sudden silence as if everybody has finished talking at once. And it appears that nobody has anything more to say. But then a feeble voice from somewhere in the last row says, 'He read my mind, he actually read my mind.' It is a boy with expensive rimless spectacles. He tries to laugh to convey that he does not really believe in the paranormal.

Ousep has heard this, too. Unni's classmates have told him about his son's rumoured ability but Ousep has met only three before this day who have experienced it first-hand. The cartoonist here is the fourth. The boy says, 'He asked me to think of a number. I thought of a number and he guessed it. Simple.'

'Do you remember what the number was?' Ousep asks, though he is certain that the answer is 'thirty-three'.

'Interesting question,' the boy says.

'Do you remember the number?'

'I would never forget the number,' the boy says. 'It was thirty-three.'

As the evening grows, the silences stretch longer, and the cartoonists clearly have very little left to say. Ousep asks, 'Does any of you know who Somen Pillai is?' The cartoonists shake their heads. Nobody knows Somen Pillai here.

The silence that follows is long and decisive. The society looks restless now, they want to leave. Some boys are wearing their bags around their shoulders, ready to stand. How long can people talk about a seventeen-year-old boy, really? The president grabs the chance to raise his oversized black pen and he says, 'Unni Chacko.' The cartoonists raise their pens and repeat, 'Unni Chacko.' The president makes a squiggle on a sheet of paper and gives it to Ousep. It is a caricature of Unni, which is very good considering the fact that it was made in just seconds. Others stand in line to hand their quick squiggles to Ousep. In most of these comic portraits, his boy has acquired angelic wings and a halo. One has him sitting in the clouds, looking bored. That breaks Ousep's heart. To imagine the eternal boredom of his child. He wishes there to be no eternity, he wishes that even for his foes.

Beta is not part of the queue of cartoonists who are handing in their tributes. But he stands leaning on a fat, ancient pillar and looks on. When everybody is done with their tributes, Ousep holds the thick bunch of papers in his hand and walks to Beta.

'What is your name?' Ousep asks.

'Beta.'

'What's your real name?'

'What's real about a name?'

'Why are you not Alpha?'

'Because I am Beta.'

Some of the cartoonists who are leaving look with passing curiosity at Beta, who does not meet their eyes. He appears clever and formidable, the type of bearded young man who would call himself Alpha. But he has restive eyes and they throw suspicious glances at distant objects. He is now staring at the five monks who are walking away down the lawns in a swarm of college girls.

'I feel you want to say something to me,' Ousep says.

'Yes,' Beta says, returning his steady gaze to Ousep. 'I've something to say but it is nothing important, is that all right?'

'That's all right. I am not here to dig out important things.'

'That's not true. You're here to solve the puzzle.'

'I am here to understand my son better.'

'As you say. I won't argue with you,' Beta says. 'I remember once when I attended one of these dumb meetings, Unni told me that he was working on a graphic novel. He had an idea but he didn't know how to get into it.'

'What was the idea?'

Ousep takes a moment to realise that Beta has launched straight into the story. Many thousands of years ago in the history of man, a great darkness has fallen. The war between good and evil has ended. And it has ended with the complete triumph of evil and a total, irrevocable extermination of good. Evil is cunning, it quickly splits itself into two – into apparent good and evil, so that mankind is under the delusion that the great conflict is still raging and it will not go in search of the truth.

'So all that we think is good,' Beta says, 'love and art and enlightenment, and all that we think is the pursuit of truth is actually a form of evil. That was the idea. He had to work characters into it. Make something out of it.'

'It is a good story.'

'It's an idea. It's not a story. He had to find the story.'

'It is a good idea.'

'It's a lousy story,' Beta says. 'In a story, good has to triumph over evil. You cannot start a story by saying that good is finished for ever. You have to give good a chance to defeat evil in the end. That's the con. That's the structure of every story in the history of stories. Every storyteller has to work within this con.'

'That's true,' Ousep says. 'That is very obviously true. I am so glad I am talking to you.'

'I don't think Unni was working on that comic,' Beta says. 'I think he really believed that.'

'Believed what?'

'What I just told you. It was not a comic. I think he really believed that good was destroyed thousands of years ago, and evil split into two.'

'Why do you say that?'

'Unni was like that. He used to tell me, "What if the meaning of life was realised ages ago by early man, the whole business of truth settled, and the world today is merely a post-Enlightenment residue?" I think that's why he was very interested in delusions.'

'Did you say "delusions"?'

'Yes. He said every delusion has an objective, and the objective of a delusion is not merely to colonise one brain but to transmit itself to as many brains as possible. That is the purpose of every delusion, that is how a delusion survives, that is how it succeeds. By spreading, maximising its colony, like a virus. According to Unni, any philosophy that can be transmitted to another person is a delusion. If two people believe in the same idea of truth then it is a delusion.'

Ousep feels silly asking a young bearded man this but it is a reasonable question in the circumstances. 'So what is truth, then?'

'Truth is a successful delusion.'

'According to Unni?'

'That's what he said.'

'Do you know who Somen Pillai is?'

'You ask this again. Who is that?'

'He was in Unni's school, his class. His closest friend, everyone says.'

'Never heard of him.'

'I do feel silly asking this, Beta, but I can't help it. Why do you think Unni did what he did?'

'Why have you started digging again, Mr Chacko?'

'I never stopped.'

'Is that the truth?'

'Yes.'

'I have no idea why Unni did that, Mr Chacko. I am sorry. I know that's why you are here.'

And so it goes every day. People have a lot of things to say about Unni Chacko, they show his world as a surprisingly large place, but nobody can explain his final act. Ousep wonders whether anyone truly knows why his son died, if a day will ever come when he finally solves Unni.

That a mystery must have a resolution is obviously not a requirement of nature. It is, in fact, another deceit of writers. A plot device, like the idea of a beginning, a middle and an end. In the real world, are mysteries usually solved? What are the chances? Was there ever a person in this world who went in search of an answer and actually found it?

Ousep has been searching for three years, since that Saturday when he had returned to his office after the Chief Minister's lunch. He found almost the entire staff, more than twenty of them, standing near his desk, in a huddle. When they saw him they grew nervous, he could see. They stared at him. He stopped a few feet away and looked at them with his hands on his hips. It is a moment that comes to every person in the world. It may come as a phone call, it can arrive through a stranger at the door, or it can happen this way – when you return to your desk to file a quick report, people stand waiting for you. And someone gathers the courage to say, 'Your son is dead, Ousep. He fell from the terrace. That's what your neighbours say. They say he fell.'

When Ousep reached the hospital he saw Thoma standing outside the gates with a neighbour. Ousep was mad with relief and joy. Obviously, there had been a mistake. The boy was very much alive, Thoma was alive. But for some reason the boy was standing outside the hospital gates. Then, for the first time in his life, Ousep went numb with raw fear. Could it be Unni? But how could it be Unni? Only little children fell, wasn't that true, only children died falling. And if there was a person in the world who was sure of his every step it was that boy. Minutes later, in the morgue, Ousep saw the corpse, the still, cold body of Unni Chacko, a boy of seventeen. By evening people were beginning to tell him the most absurd thing he had ever heard.

Unni had jumped from the terrace, head first. Of all the people in the world, Unni. Why, Unni? Nobody still has a clue. After three years, nobody has a clue.

These are the facts, they are not disputed. About three years ago, on 16 May 1987, Unni Chacko left home in the morning after working all night on a comic. He was gone for nearly four hours. Nobody knows where he had gone. At noon he got a haircut. When he returned to Block A, he played cricket with the boys. He bowled, he did not like to bat. Then he decided to go home. He took the stairs. It is not clear what happened next. He must have reached home, which is on the third floor, the highest floor, but nobody saw him on the stairs or going into his house. His mother was not at home, she had gone to attend a prayer meeting. His younger brother, Thoma, was at home, but fast asleep in his room. In all probability, Unni reached home. The house is never latched or locked in the day, so he could have entered without ringing the doorbell. About twenty minutes after Unni took the stairs, he was seen on the terrace. According to six eyewitnesses – three boys on the terrace of Block A and three women in Block B who had a clear view – Unni stood on the railing, composed and in control. He stopped for a moment, crossed his hands behind his back and plunged down. He fell on the concrete walkway that runs beside the playground. He died instantly, people say. He did not leave a note. His death came weeks after the school board exams in which, as it turned out, he had somehow scored seventy-eight per cent. He had no intention of going to a regular college, but he had plans, the boy had many plans. In six weeks he would have turned eighteen.

Ousep did not know it then, but Unni told a lot of people that he was a Hindu, an atheist Hindu, whatever that means, but he went the Christian way. The funeral mass was in Fatima Church. That was the first time Ousep had entered a church in over two decades. The coffin moved down the aisle towards the altar on the arms of strangers. Ousep walked behind them, hugging the shoulder of the boy's mother, both slowly passing through rows of empty pews. How strong, the legs of dumb parents, how strong. The strangers placed the coffin in front of the altar and left. The lights went on, the fans that hung from the ceiling on long white stems came to life. The silence was so deep that he could hear the hum of the tube lights. Mariamma sat on the floor beside the coffin. She took her son's lifeless hand in hers and rubbed it slowly. Ousep stood beside her, with his hands on his hips, wondering what he must do. What does a father do at the final mass of his son?

A short, stout man in a white cassock walked to the coffin and stood with his hands joined at his crotch. After a few moments he said, 'You must be Ousep Chacko.'

'Yes.'

'I've never seen you before.'

'I never come here,' Ousep said.

'Eventually, they all come. Isn't that true, Ousep? The high and the low, they all come. Your wife is a good woman. She is a pious woman.'

'She is.'

'She is like a child.'

'That's true.'

'I want to tell you something, Ousep,' the man said softly, taking Ousep a few feet away from the coffin. 'We are in the temple of truth but we are also men of the world, we are practical men. I am hearing things about how the boy died, you know people talk. I don't want to know how he died. It does not matter. As long as he is truly dead I will bury him. But what we say is that it was an accident. We will say that today and we will say it every day.'

'As you wish.'

'The boy, he was a good boy deep inside. But he was not normal.'

Ousep looked carefully at the priest. A fifty-year-old virgin, a fully grown man in a white gown who believed that he was an elf who connected God to man, this clown thought Unni was strange.

'Ousep,' the priest said, 'some boys wander far. There is nothing we can do about it. They wander too far.'

There was a flicker of triumph in his narrow eyes. It was a triumph Ousep would see often, in the days to come, in the eyes of other men.

The priest left and in a few minutes appeared at the altar. He told the empty church, 'We are here today to remember Unni Chacko, son of Ousep Chacko and Mariamma Chacko. A child of only seventeen. Such a pure child that God has taken him to heaven. Unni was a very talented and bright boy. He was a good person, and everybody loved him.'

That was it. The story of Unni Chacko's life as told by an imbecile to an empty hall.

The priest wiped his mouth, and said his prayers with slow tired movements, throwing glances at the walls and the floor and the empty pews. For a moment his eyes rested on Mariamma; they stayed longer than he had intended and his face slowly changed from blank to disturbed, and he began to pray in a distracted way.

Ousep looked at his wife. Her lips were curled into her mouth, her head tilted, her eyes glaring at the giant crucifix on the altar, and she wagged a finger.

~

MARIAMMA CHACKO BITES her lip with a ferocity that makes her head tremble and her eyes look interested. She stands facing the bare yellow wall and she wags her index finger. She tells the wall, in a quivering voice, about Ousep's mother and his nine sisters, all unforgettable cows whom only the soil and weather of Kerala can produce. She gets into this state sometimes and when she is this way she loses her sense of the world around her. But there is something about the hum in the air, and the way it stirs the peace of noon. It is now clearly the murmur of men and it does not have the joy of a road accident. The voices are faint and meek as if the men are trying to achieve silence, which is impossible in Madras if more than one person has gathered at a place. As the hum grows, Mariamma's rebuke of the wall becomes softer, she begins to whisper. Finally she gives a snide nod, relaxes her muscles and is even mildly embarrassed by what she has been doing. She licks her lips and listens carefully.

The murmur reminds her of Unni. The truth is that everything reminds her of Unni and she only invents the special connections. But the murmur does have a haunting presence in her memories because the worst day of her life had begun this way – with the whispers of men that she had first thought had nothing to do with her life. That Saturday, after the prayer meeting, she walked home with a branch of stolen bougainvillea in her hand. When she went down Balaji Lane people gaped at her from their balconies and windows, and she thought it strange because people did not look at her any more. When she was at the gates of Block A, she saw a crowd that looked her in the eye. A deep human silence spread, and she could not feel her legs any more. A woman took her by hand and said that they must walk to Ajanta Hospital.

The moment Unni's head hit the ground, what was she doing? She has thought about this many times. She hopes it was not the moment when she was trying not to laugh as the prayer group raised its cries to the heavens, or when she approached one of the ladies for a loan, or when she tried to smile in shame as her request was being politely declined. She hopes he had not fallen when she was in the prayer group because she is not proud of what she does there. She is the spy of the parish priest, the mole who brings him news about the Catholic sheep that are increasingly flocking to Pentecostal evangelists. That is what Mariamma does in her spare time, and she does it because the priest waives the school fees, instructs the Sacred Heart Family Store to give her anything she wants on credit as long as she clears the dues every two months.

She hopes she was doing something dignified when the last sigh of breath left the lungs of her child; she hopes she was walking back home like a good mother, thinking about what meal to cook for two boys who ate so much.

When Unni was a little boy he was deeply interested in getting married. He was just five then and he was willing to wait till he reached the legal age but not a day more. He was so desperate to be married that she often used it to get her way. 'Unni, if you don't brush you teeth I won't get you married.' That was enough to send him running to the bathroom. How did that boy grow so strong?

He spoke a lot about death but not in a dark way as people now claim. One morning he stood in the doorway of the kitchen, bare chested as he always was when he was at home. He had red spots all over his firm athletic chest because he was the type whom mosquitoes would bite. He told her that he had had a very funny thought. As he spoke he ran his thumbs over her forehead, a habit he had picked up when he was around seven, believing that the lines on her forehead were worries and that he could make them vanish by straightening the creases. 'People want to be happy, don't they?' he said. 'They are desperate to be happy, aren't they? But look at how many things have to go right in a person's life for that. Your spouse has to be all right. Your children should not die before your time. And their grandchildren should not have polio or something. They, too, should not die young, of course. And their children, and their children, even if they come after you are long gone, they have to be all right. Everyone has to turn out fine. So many lives have to turn out right. What have you started, Mariamma Chacko, do you realise what you have started by having children? A whole line of humanity that would not have appeared without you. Surely, things would go wrong somewhere?'

And he said something strange. 'But still, if I die, imagine I die,' he said, 'you would be sad, I know. Of course, you would be sad.

But not as deeply as people would presume. In this world, it is very hard to escape happiness. That's how it is.'

The boy thought too much, he was full of ideas. And he told her everything. He was not like the other boys, he did not treat his mother as an idiot who made food. He loved talking to her.

Sometimes he would say, 'Come, let's find the meaning of life.' And he would hold his chin and look at the floor, pretending to be in deep thought. After a few seconds he would shake his head and say, 'No, couldn't find it.' And they would laugh, always laugh.

Other days he was more serious about these matters. He told her that there were people who walked among them who knew something, something very important, but they could not explain. He really wanted to believe that. If he heard of a person who behaved in an extraordinary way he would become very curious, he would try to find out more, even loiter near their homes. That's why some people thought Unni was a bit odd himself.

He told her about a man who lived not very far away. He was a good man, an ordinary man. A good father and a good husband, which were terms that were used very often in her house, as a rebuke, a longing or satire, depending on who was talking. The man returned from work one day, he had his dinner as he always did, played with his children and went to bed. He had two children, a girl and a boy, which emphasised his normalcy. Next morning he told his wife and children that he was going away for ever, that he could not explain why he was going away. He left in his nightclothes taking nothing with him, not even his toothbrush. He never came back.

Unni narrated these stories as if he had a faint idea where such men were going and what they hoped to do with the rest of their lives. Some days, she saw Unni standing on the balcony, looking carefully at everything around him. He told her there were rogues among the birds, too, who went against the natural flow of life, who behaved in unexpected ways. It is a clue, he said, and he said that with a shy smile. 'Something is going on, Mother.' Maybe he was just a boy who liked to look at life around him and he invented the mysteries to grant a greater meaning to an idleness that was not tolerated any more in the new nervous city where a boy had so much maths to learn. She told him, 'You must look, Unni, you must just stand and look at life for hours. If you were born in a village as I was, you would not need a reason, you would not need the high infidel thoughts that are not sanctioned by the Pope.'

There was so much peace in her boy. That was why the mosquitoes drank from him. He slept without moving an inch, like a corpse.

The murmur of the men rises. Mariamma pats her sari, and goes to the kitchen balcony to see what has happened. The commotion has naturally charmed all the women of Block A to their tiny balconies, where the sun is unbearable at this time of day. In normal circumstances they appear here at noon only to hang their secrets out to dry. This is the rear side of the building and there is an imagined discretion to all activities here, unlike at the front, which apparently faces the world.

As she is on the third floor she has a good view of the doctor's house in the neighbouring plot, which shares a wall with Block A. It is a small independent house with a proud woman's rose garden. Its door is wide open and all around the jute doormat that says 'Welcome' there is lots of footwear, chiefly male footwear. Several men are standing in the garden and talking among themselves with their arms folded. The signs are unmistakable but the women of Block A decide to ask what has happened anyway. They lean over the balcony railings, hold their chests to keep their saris from falling and whisper their queries. The men walk down the garden towards the common wall as if they are about to urinate, which is not beyond them. They look up and whisper to the women what has happened. And the chatter of women begins, which drives away the sparrows.

The women stand on their balconies and discuss the matter with the women on the other balconies. Some of them lean dangerously, with half their bodies in the air, to speak to women directly below, who in turn are twisted around their spines as they look up. They speak diagonally too. They also peep through the windows of their neighbours to announce the news to the old, who are probably lying in their hard beds and begging to know what has happened. And word soon spreads that the smart young doctor has been found dead in his chair, his Walkman attached to his ears, a feeble music still coming from it.

Those who live on the ground floor of Block A, whose view is hindered by the wall, have moved to the homes that are on the higher floors. They may have gone without any clever ruses. Just rang the bell, and walked to the view in brisk gloom.

Word now spreads that the doctor, whose age they had never known, was forty-two years old. It is somehow appropriate that the age of such a fine man must be an even number. Late in the morning, when his wife had left home to go to the market, there was nothing wrong with him. He seemed fine. When she returned after an hour and rang the doorbell, there was no response. She peeped through a window to look inside and found him sitting in his chair with his eyes open. He was not moving. She tossed a brinjal at him, which hit him, but he did not react. She ran to a neighbour for help, and soon several men appeared outside her house. They broke open the door.

This is how it happens, always. Every now and then, they hear these stories, which are all the same. The wife would ring the bell and the door would not open. It would soon be broken by the neighbours. Inside they would find, in poses that are generally granted only to the living, the corpse of a man who was in the middle of a routine. In fact, the children know these stories too, and their greatest fear is that they will return from school one day and find a lot of footwear outside their door.

A hush falls; it appears that something important is about to happen. The women wait, but nothing happens. So the murmur returns, and word spreads that someone has gone to fetch the doctor's only child, a girl of fourteen, who was at school. She would not be immediately told about her father's death. She would be led out of her classroom on some other pretext so that she does not faint or wail on the streets. She would soon appear at the mouth of the narrow lane that leads to her house and she would walk down the path unaware that her life has changed, wondering why so many people are standing on their balconies and staring at her. She would be here soon, in a sky-blue pinafore. And everybody would get to see a rare spectacle – of a girl who is about to learn that her father is dead.

Women from the other three blocks of Balaji Lane have begun to arrive, and the swarms of housewives on the balconies of the higher floors begin to swell. Chairs too must have come out because some people have now lost their height. One woman sombrely hands carrots to another woman on the next balcony. The chatter grows and the air is filled with the little things they know about heart attacks. There is probably no Tamil word for it yet. They say it in English – Heart Attack. Some who are prone to eloquence call it 'cardiac arrest'. In the buzzing hive, Mariamma stands alone. Nobody speaks to her.

She wonders why a woman would go to the vegetable market in this unearthly heat, why would a woman go to the market at noon? She looks carefully at the porch of the dead doctor's house. There is no bag there, no vegetables. A woman returns from the market and rings the doorbell. Her husband does not respond. She peeps through a window and finds him sitting in a chair motionless, his eyes wide open. What would she do? She would drop the bag. If her purse is in it, she may take it out. That is acceptable. But she would leave the bag there. And she would scream for help. But nobody heard a woman scream. It was the time of day when one could hear even the sudden wind from the aged in other houses. Even if she had run quietly to the neighbours, being a slim, refined woman and all that, where was the bag? Neighbours broke open the door, and as she ran in she took the vegetables inside? Or, later, as she was wailing beside the corpse of her husband, the neighbours took the bag in? All this is against human nature. But then Mariamma asks, 'Mariammo, what are you suggesting?'

Mariamma is not suggesting anything. She is just thinking. As a girl who grew up far away from the city, in a forest of rubber trees on a giant hill, she remembers the time when men were strong and they moved like alluring beasts. When a man died young those days, in mysterious circumstances, people looked carefully at his wife. Now, things are different, nobody is surprised when a man goes young, people have given a name to such a death.

What she is actually getting at is a question she has asked many times. Will Ousep Chacko die this way one day? Of natural causes? She would return from church on a quiet Sunday, and she would ring the doorbell and he would not answer. And the door would be broken down, without much damage hopefully, if it were broken along the lock. She imagines Ousep dead, lying on the floor, his eyes wide open. She remembers the advertisement for a sunflower cooking oil – 'A Gentleman's Cholesterol Is In The Hands Of His Wife'. But then Ousep Chacko is not a man who can be killed by oil. He does not eat much. He smokes a lot, though, which may have thickened his blood, or thinned his arteries, she always forgets which of the two happens. A man's heart can also be arranged to stop if he is given a good sudden fright. But she knows it would take a lot to damage the pastoral heart of that man. He is made of red earth and Malabar air.

She walks to the bedroom and has a good look at Ousep's chair. She sits on it and feels the strain of her body on its legs. This is her only hope, but she has to be very patient, which she is.

She snaps out of her thoughts, asking herself the startling question, 'Mariammo, what are you thinking?' She is obviously not a murderer, she is just a housewife with exaggerated notions about herself. She does write occasional book reviews under the name 'Gabriel' for a women's weekly, but still she is not a bad person. Also, it is important that Ousep lives, at least for now. If anyone can solve Unni's death, it is Ousep. He has found something significant, she can tell. But for some reason he is keeping it from her.

The doorbell gives her a jolt. She is surprised to find six women from the other blocks, standing in line like penguins outside her door. They say that the other balconies are full, can they come in? They must be desperate to ring Mariamma's doorbell. Nobody comes to her house any more. Out of habit, she wonders whether the women are hiding enchanted coins and nails and needles in their saris to plant them in her house and bring doom to her family, as Ousep's relatives used to once upon a time. But then that is a laughable thought. Nobody is jealous of the Chacko household any more.

The murmur outside grows louder, and it excites the women at the door. They look to their right, at the stairway, which goes up to the gloomy terrace door, but that door is now kept locked at all times after what Unni did. Mariamma asks the women to come in. They rush to the balcony to see what has happened. She does not stand alone any more, she stands in the huddle of women on her balcony like the other women on theirs. Mariamma, finally a host.

They can see the doctor's daughter now. 'Bindu or something like that,' one of the women says. The girl walks down the narrow lane towards her home. She is in a blue pinafore, her hair tied in a red ribbon. She walks with a man who is holding her schoolbag. She smiles at an acquaintance, but she is clearly confused. She looks around at the silent people on the street, who are standing without meeting her eyes. She looks up at the rear balconies of Block A, at the swarms of unmoving women who stare back at her. The girl's face turns serious. She opens the short gate of her home and sees the whispering strangers in the garden. She begins to walk faster. She stops for a moment when she sees the mass of footwear outside the front door, and she runs in crying.

~

IN THESE CIRCUMSTANCES, as he listens to the beatings in the next classroom, Thoma Chacko feels a liquid gloom in his groin. He considers how hard it is to be a bright person. He imagines the sheer length of human life, the many years ahead of him. He is twelve, he has a long way to go. Will Thoma make it? Unni had always tried to reassure him, he even said maths was about to get a lot easier. He said the Home Minister, who is responsible for happy homes, would soon pass a law changing the value of pi from 3.14159 to just 3, making it easier for all Indian children to calculate the area of a circle. That was what Unni said. But then it was probably a lie, like the many other things he used to say.

Every day, Thoma tries to improve his mind, but he does not possess the Power of Concentration, he is a Wool-gatherer. He would stare at the open textbook for hours and be distracted by the pain of the parallelogram, which is slanted for ever. His nails scratch the page to straighten its tired limbs. It affects him, the great arrogance of the Equilateral Triangle, the failed aspiration of the octagon to be a circle, the eternal suffocation of the denominator that has to bear the weight of the unjust numerator, the loneliness of Pluto. And the smallness of Mercury, always a mere dot next to a yellow sun. In this world, there is no respect for Mercury.

Every day, Thoma tries to memorise Interesting Facts but his head is porous. There are only two impressive facts he knows. For some reason they have stuck in his head – the full form of KGB, which is Komitet Gosudarstvennoy Bezopasnosti, and Pelè's real name, which is Edson Arantes do Nascimento. Every day, Thoma hopes a miracle will occur and Mythili Balasubramanium will ask him, 'Thoma, what does KGB stand for? And I wonder if Pelé is his real name.' But miracles do not happen in Thoma's life, even though he is Christian.

The thought of his bleak future brings the apparition of a woman to his mind. She has black decaying teeth. It is his future wife, a fate foretold to all the boys who are not very clever. But when he becomes a man he wants a pretty wife. She would have long braided hair, she would be in a red cotton sari, and a tight blue blouse, and she would be somewhat scared of him. On the days of sorrow she would put her nervous head on his shoulder and cry, inaudibly, and just for a few moments, not long. He would never beat her, he would speak to her with respect, he would treat her well, he would never penetrate her.

But would she find Thoma handsome? Is Thoma handsome? Like Unni? It would be really wonderful if there was a canvas tent where a boy could go in unnoticed, probably wearing a mask. Inside, a panel of men and women would ask him to remove his mask. They would inspect him carefully and pass the verdict – handsome, or not handsome. Thoma wishes there was a way he could solve his doubt for ever.

There is a calm, methodical beating in the next room. An occasional thud, like the sound of a dictionary falling on the floor, followed by a brief silence, as if for appreciation. Then another bang, the unmistakable sound of a hand landing on the bent back of a boy who has failed in science or maths, or both. Sometimes the blow is soft, sometimes hard, depending on how much flesh there is on the boy. Thin backs are louder than fat backs but the pain travels longer through the fat. There is now a loud blow, a sad grunt and silence after that. The silence grows longer than expected. It does not end. Thoma is sure that H. M. Dorai is done with the Eighth Standard and is now walking towards the Seventh. The time has come. Thoma stares hard at the desk, he does not look around, but he can sense that the other boys have stopped moving. They wait.

It is improbable that Thoma will be thrashed today because he has not failed in any subject in the monthly tests. Somehow he usually manages to pass, barely pass, but there is always a chance that something can go wrong. They always pick on something he has written in the tests. Mistakes that he does not fully comprehend. For example, his answer to the question: 'If the base of the triangle is 3.87 cm and its height is 5.13 cm, can you find its area?'

'Of course I can,' Thoma had written.

A slap for that, he does not know why. Then there was the laughably easy question, 'Which living thing makes its own food?'

Gloria Miss had caned his palms several times. 'Not Mariamma Chacko, you idiot, not Mariamma Chacko. Which living *thing*, which living *thing*? Is your mother a thing?'

The correct answer was plants, she said. Which is absurd.

Science is hard because it cannot be fully understood, it can only be accepted, like catechism. Maybe he should become a writer. But writing is hard, too. As a writer, Thoma must write like this: 'He faced the western winds'. But how would Thoma know if a wind were a western wind? It terrifies him, that even writers must know a set of facts, that even writers must have information. Thoma does have information, but it always turns out to be wrong information as opposed to right information, which is useful.

'What is the opposite gender of ram?'

It is amazing that every single person in the class had got the answer right, as if everybody had copied from a single source. 'Ewe'. That was the answer. 'Ewe'? How do people in Madras know such facts? Thoma's answer was 'Sita'. He received several slaps for that.

The boys wonder why H. M. Dorai has not arrived yet. Then they hear a loud thud in the next room. He is still there. They exhale in relief and that makes Gloria Miss laugh because it is inevitable that he will come, there is no escape. She is standing in front of the class, smiling, nodding her head. She is standing with her arms folded, so her breasts are bulging out of her blouse. He feels sorry for her because everybody knows she has breasts. It must be shameful. How do women go through life?

H. M. Dorai steams in, rearranging the air somehow. The stillness and the silence of the room collapse and in their place there is now a new stillness and a new silence. He looks as if he does not have much time and he knows what he must do. He has mad eyes, his gleaming black hair appears to tumble off his head as comic tides. And he has no arse. He places his thick cane and other things on the table and reads out eight names from a piece of paper. The boys rise and go to the door. They stand there, looking serious. He has chosen only those who failed in both science and maths. He rolls up his sleeves. 'Attention,' he says. 'And the special guests of the evening are . . .' He calls out a name. The boy marches, swinging his arms, lifting his legs high, chanting, 'Left, right, left.' He is crying now and his 'left, right, left' sounds like a song. He stops in front of H. M. Dorai and bends his back. Dorai circles his hand on the boy's back, and lands a hard blow. The boy stomps his leg, salutes, shouts 'Thank you', and walks back to his seat. H. M. Dorai calls out the next name. When he is finished with all the eight special guests, there is a Silence of Anticipation. He should go away now but Thoma knows something is wrong. Dorai's eyes had rested on him for a brief moment, and when they wandered away they had taken his image with them. That is not good.

Dorai takes his things from the table, and looks straight into Thoma's eyes. He snaps his fingers and says, 'Come with me.' He stands outside the class and waits. Thoma goes to him. Dorai puts his face very close to Thoma's.

'Thoma,' he says. 'Your father called me yesterday. Do you know why?'

'I do not know, sir.'

'He is asking questions about Unni. I told him I've nothing more to say. Your father is asking a lot of people about Unni. Why?'

'I don't know, sir.'

'Why is he asking questions about Unni, why now?'

'I don't know.'

'People tell me that he has found something about Unni. Do you know?'

'I don't know, sir.'

'Are you sure?'

'I have no information,' Thoma says.

Mariamma opens the door for Thoma with an absent-minded smile that holds him in its affection for a moment before she drifts to the other people who are not present. They exist in another time when she was young and people were so important to her that she still remembers everything they told her. She answers them back now, after all these years, and they probably respond to her, wandering alone in their vast rubber forests in a faraway place, smiling at her memories sometimes, returning her scowls sometimes.

Unni told Thoma that their mother had a Condition, and that it had a name, as if the fact that it had a name was very good news. Thoma has forgotten the name Unni had mentioned. It had sounded important, though very male. 'It is not a serious condition, Thoma, a lot of perfectly happy people have it.'

She is in the kitchen. Her sari is hitched up on one side, the hem bunched into her waist, and Thoma can see a long sliver of her bare formidable thigh. So much of a woman's legs he sees only at home. Mariamma, her lips curled into her mouth, wags a finger at the overhead cupboard. 'Annamol Chacko,' she says, summoning once again Ousep's mother. 'So you didn't like my tea. You and your nine dumb daughters, you sit and whisper among yourself and giggle at my tea. You say to thin air, "This is a cup of tea made by Mariamma, this is the tea made by an economics postgraduate." And all of you laugh.'

She sees Thoma staring at her and first smiles in embarrass-ment, then bursts out laughing. Her sudden happiness fills Thoma with a Sense of Wellbeing. Other days, her voice is loud and it trembles in the air like a wail; she takes the full Christian names of Ousep's mother and all his nine sisters, and on rare occasions she talks in a formal way to her own mother and someone called Philipose. When she is that way, her lip is curled in, head tilted upwards, and her index finger wags. And she is unmindful of everything around her. Unni could change her mood just like that, make her laugh and extricate his mother from the Torments of Memories. Unni would crack a joke, and she would reclaim her pretty face from the angry scowl, and begin to shake with laughter. But Thoma does not have the gift.

His mother surprises him with a packet of cashew nuts, and says, 'The doctor, Thoma, the man with the rose garden, he is dead. It was a heart attack.' They sit facing each other across the dining table and eat. She does not place the cashews in her mouth as economics postgraduates normally do, she flings them in. Unni used to call her 'Village woman'.

As a girl, she tells him as if she has never told him this before, she used to walk down the banks of a narrow silver stream with her friends, collecting fallen cashews and pebbles, and when the laps of their skirts could take no more they used to throw away some of the cashews. She cannot accept now that she has to actually buy cashew nuts.

She repeats things. That is her nature. 'Hunger is the best side dish, Thoma.' And when he is desperately studying on the morning of an exam, she will say, 'This is what you do, Thoma, you study just hours before a test. When you are about to shit, you search for your arse.' She used to tell Unni almost every day how big boys should behave with girls. Boys must not harass girls, must not Pass Indecent Remarks, must not stand too close to girls, must not stand too close to even little girls, must not touch them. All that has stopped, of course, because Thoma is too young for the lessons. There is something else that she does not mention any more. When she heard that the child of a working mother had got hurt by falling or was hit by a bicycle or knocked down by a cow, she would gather Unni and Thoma and say, 'See, this is what happens to the children of working women. You are safe because your mother is always around, don't ever forget that.' With Unni gone, she has lost the right to say this any more.

'How come we are eating cashews?' Thoma says. 'Sacred Heart

Family Store won't give you cashews without taking money. It is not an Essential Commodity. Did you pawn another bangle?'

'I don't have any more bangles to pawn.'

'Did you sell your blood?'

'No, Thoma. A lot of women came to our home to watch the doctor's house. And they decided that they wanted to phone their husbands, they wanted to know that their husbands were all right. They gave me a rupee each. When a man dies in the neighbourhood women think of their own husbands. I too had a long loving thought about your father.'

'So I am eating cashew nuts because the doctor died today.'

'Yes.'

'Strange Are The Ways Of The World.'

'Strange are the ways of the world, my boy.'

'The Lord Moves In Mysterious Ways.'

'The lord moves in mysterious ways.'

Thoma goes to stand on the rear balcony and watch the doctor's house. There is a crowd outside the main door, talking softly about the death as if they don't want the dead man to know that he is gone.

He eyes the balcony to his immediate left, which is just three feet away. There is nobody there, but she may appear any time, tossing her hair and holding a clip in her mouth as she normally does. He can feel his heart hammer against his chest.

When girls toss their hair and hold clips in their mouths, when they run their hands down the back of their skirts before they sit, when they shift a lock of hair from their face and stuff it over their ears, or cover their mouths when they have to laugh, when they do these things that have no name, and when he hears a female chorus sing 'I have a dream', Thoma's chest fills with ache and he wishes them well in life. Is there a movement in his body that can fill a girl with such love? Do women long at all for men the way men long for women? The cold fear inside him at the sight of Mythili, are they capable of such agony inside them, do their throats go cold and do they feel a deep wandering sorrow?

Mythili Balasubramanium arrives the way he had imagined, tossing her abundant hair, bunching it high above her head as if she is about to pull herself up by her hair. And she is holding a clip in the scowl of her mouth. She has large clever eyes. Sometimes she draws her eyes standing on her balcony, making each eye bulge and underlining it with a fat pencil as if to say, 'This is my eye, here is my eye.' She does such things, including rustling her hair, only on the rear balcony. Her mother does not let her stand on the front balcony if her hair is not tied. She is still in her school uniform – green pleated skirt and white shirt with frills at the chest. She is much older than Thoma, she is sixteen. Like most people she does not have any respect for him, he knows that. He is after all from a weird, sullen home, the home of Unni, whose name she does not utter any more, though she used to be very fond of him. At the time of Unni's death, three years ago, she was just a harmless little girl.

Thoma gathers the courage to say, 'I am having cashew nuts.' She does not react, it is as if she has not heard him. He is about to repeat what he had said when she turns and leaves. He stands there, shamed. A familiar gloom fills him. As Unni used to say, 'Thoma, you are feeling low right now, as low as a dachshund's balls.'

Thoma goes down to play and he is soon a part of a cricket match that often forgets he exists. A boy from another colony is setting the field and he, very rudely, tells Thoma where he must stand. Tony is a Sri Lankan refugee. How can a refugee tell Thoma where he must stand in his own country? But Thoma keeps his mouth shut, the refugee is much older and stronger. Thoma is more infuriated when Tony lifts his head and looks up. That is what all grown-up boys here do once every thirty seconds, all the boys on the playground, on the boundary wall, on the lane outside – they keep looking up to see if Mythili is watching. Her balcony has long become a shrine that pulls boys and men from faraway places. They come to strut up and down the lane for her. Even the Roadside Romeos come, with their hair wet, in their best clothes, all of them wearing dark glasses. They come on foot, cycles and motorbikes. The times she appears on the balcony, it is as if a circus bell has rung and the clowns below must now begin to perform. They start doing stunts on their bikes, the slum boys do Michael Jackson's Moonwalk, all this as if it is not a performance but their Fundamental Nature. The boys of the colony, too, become brisk and happy in her presence, they run fast, bowl as furiously as they can, insult each other, harm small boys, talk aloud about intelligent matters – words like 'perestroika' and 'GATT' fill the air. They do this with swift glances upwards to check whether she is still there. But Mythili usually stands in an unseeing way, or she just vanishes. Mostly she never appears.

Thoma is unable to concentrate on the game, his mind wanders. Eight girls of his age are sitting on the wall and chatting. Padmini, in a rare careless moment, spreads her legs and he can see her red underwear. She sits that way talking, and he is hypnotised by the sight. He is unable to look away even though he knows he is committing a crime. Now that he has seen her this way, will she ever get married?

When the sun sets the children vanish, except Thoma, who wanders around the playground. The twilight fear comes to him and he hopes that the night will pass without incident, which it never does.

He decides to delay going home by walking up and down the three stairwells and listening to the other homes. He likes to know what happens in the other homes. Once he heard a man scream at his son for scoring ninety-five per cent in maths. 'Where is the five per cent, where is it, where has the five per cent gone?' Then, something happened that made the boy cry in total fright. The man's voice said, 'Here, these are your clothes. Take this money. Leave the house at once and go search for the five per cent. Come back only when you find it.' The boy begged his father to let him stay. Thoma sat on their doormat and laughed, holding his stomach. Some days he heard the cries of friends whose fathers chased them with a heated spoon because the boys had not scored well enough in the tests. This was rare, though. Usually the boys only got belted. In the middle of one such lashing, a man said, 'The only system that matters to an Indian?'

'The decimal system,' the boy answered.

One hard lash, and a boyish grunt.

'The only system that matters to an Indian?'

'The decimal system.'

But, most of the time, there were happy voices, families sitting together and talking and singing and laughing in the fragrance of their unattainable meals.

Thoma cannot ignore it any more, the fear grows in his stomach. Another night that he must endure. He goes home thinking of what Unni used to say, mimicking their sports coach: 'Fight, Thoma, put fight.' He used to say that when Thoma was trying to study maths at dawn, or when he walked to the stumps to bat at number eleven, or when he was learning how to ride a cycle. It is now Thoma's anthem. Fight, Thoma, put fight. He likes it because it says what he must do but does not mention the outcome at all.

He has to first make a confession to his mother, and he chooses the time when she is doing the dishes in the kitchen. He stands near the stove and numbs her mind by mumbling many things, including the National Pledge and the first two stanzas of 'Lochinvar', and finally he arrives at a prayer, which is a form of silence to her: 'Our father in heaven, hallowed be your name, I saw Padmini's undies. Your kingdom come, your will be done, on earth as it is in heaven.'

Mother does not turn from the plates, but as far as Thoma is concerned he has confessed.

In an hour Thoma is pretending to be asleep in the bedroom that he and Unni used to share. His father will come any time now. Thoma remembers a Tamil proverb that had once startled him with its simple truth – 'You can wake up a man who is asleep, but not the one who is pretending to be asleep'. And that is what Thoma tries to do every night when his father comes to wake him up. But he never manages to pretend long enough. He always rises, but today he decides to lie there with his eyes shut, come what may. If he is pulled, dragged or kicked, it won't matter. Thoma will lie like a dead dog.

Unexpectedly, he has fallen asleep. He is woken by the distant wail of his father's gifted voice: 'Good evening, dear bank clerk bastards.' Ousep is probably at the gates of the block. Everybody must have heard it, but fortunately Ousep had screamed in Malayalam and they do not know Malayalam. But then Ousep repeats the greeting in Tamil. Thoma feels the familiar shame. He hopes Mythili has not heard it, he hopes she is fast asleep. There is a long terrifying silence, for about five minutes. He hears the main door open. He is home. His mother, as always, comes to Thoma and says, 'Be strong, Thoma, don't be afraid. I am here. What am I, Thoma? Tell me what am I?'

'You're the Rock.'

'Yes, I am the Rock.'

He hears his father scream, 'Where is my beloved wife, the beloved daughter of a rubber pirate?' Thoma knows she is sitting in a corner of the kitchen floor, near the stone grinder. That's where she sits in these circumstances. Ousep is standing in the hall, pointing to various objects and asking, 'What is this? What is this?' Then he falls quiet. He is now probably in his room, sitting at his desk and writing his own obituary as he usually does.

There is the sound of a loud crash. He has flung the Best Writer award again, the silver angel on the wooden stand. Father received the award from the Kerala chief minister many years ago, when he was very young. He was famous then, his mother says. She says that when the award first came home the silver angel was looking straight ahead, but as Father kept flinging her, the lady's neck kept bending. Now she looks up at the roof, somewhat heroic.

Thoma can hear him grunting, he is walking down the hall, he is approaching the bedroom door, but then he walks past, into the kitchen, and it appears that he has gone to the rear balcony. Thoma hears him scream, 'Doctor, I hear you are gone, Doctor. Is that true? You asked me a question a month ago. Sorry I could not answer you then. Here it is, though. It is watery. You bastard, my stools are watery. Is that the question you ask the great Ousep Chacko when you meet him for the very first time? How are your stools, Mr Chacko? Moron, how are *your* stools today?'

Thoma feels an irresistible urge to laugh, but then he hears him screaming at his mother – 'Buffalo woman,' he says. Thoma wants to be by her side but he is afraid. Ousep has never hit his mother, but what if he finally decides to? Unni was brave. Thoma does not remember a single moment when Unni was nervous or shaken. He never pretended to be asleep when Ousep came home drunk. In fact, when their father stood too close to their mother, seething like a fool, Unni would stand between them. Ousep would push him away but Unni would always regain his position, fists clenched. Unni usually went about life at a leisurely pace, his movements slow and gentle, but when he was angry he became alert and menacing. Sometimes Thoma got the feeling that there were two people inside Unni.

One night, Unni slapped his drunken father. Ousep just fell to the floor as if he had no strength in him and he did not rise. His head began to bleed but he lay there quoting from *King Lear*. Unni calmly put a thread through a needle and stitched the cut on Father's forehead. A whole week after that Unni looked a bit sad, and he did not meet anyone's eye in that period.

Thoma hears heavy footsteps approach, the door opens, he gets the sweet sugar-cane smell of liquor. Ousep is very close, probably standing right next to him. Thoma is on the floor, lying on his stomach, his head buried in the pillow.

'Get up,' Ousep says. 'Get up, my idiot son.'

Mariamma walks in. She does not say anything, yet. The Rock waits.

'Get up,' Ousep says.

He lifts Thoma's head by the ear and holds it that way for a few seconds and then drops it. But Thoma pretends to be dead. Ousep pokes his back with his finger. 'Get up,' he says. Mother decides to scream, she has had enough. She wrestles with Ousep, saying, 'Leave him alone, leave him alone.' So Thoma wakes up, he is afraid his mother will get hurt. Ousep leads him out of the room.

Thoma sees his father walk in front of him, swaying unsteadily, his hair like Einstein's halo, shirt dirty and wet, trousers sagging. This is not the man he sees in the morning, the strong, tidy and fragrant writer, his long hair neatly combed, so elegant and handsome, who reads four newspapers in three languages with such indestructible clever eyes that Thoma feels scared for the reporters whom his father is reading. In the mornings the man looks exactly like the Great Ousep Chacko of his mother's fables.

In Ousep's room, the noose is ready. It is his lungi, which is dangling from the fan, his chair placed ceremoniously under it. Ousep kneels on the chair and pulls himself up. He puts the noose around his neck. Thoma sits on the floor, by the wall, with a paper and pen. He has already written the words, 'The Obituary of a Failed Writer'. Mariamma watches, leaning on the bookshelf.

Ousep says, in a calm, serious way, 'The Obituary of a Failed Writer.'

Thoma pretends to write.

'By A Staff Reporter,' Ousep says. 'A man was found hanging from the ceiling fan in his house.'

For some reason that brings a terrifying burst of laughter to Thoma's chest. He holds it, but then his mother, too, begins to chuckle.

'. . . Enquiries reveal that the man's name is Ousep Chacko, the greatest writer the Malabar coast has ever produced, greater than all the no-talent effeminate bastards who masquerade as writers today.'

Ousep loses his balance somewhat and he wobbles for a moment on the chair. Thoma is shaking with laughter now. He begs his mind to bring sadness to his throat. He tries to think of Unni, but it is his brother's comic that appears in his mind. It is set in a beautiful park with four children sitting on the swings. Among them is Ousep, hanged by the neck with his own lungi, swinging happily with the children.

'You bastard, Thoma, you find this funny,' Ousep says, gently touching the noose. That makes Thoma burst out laughing, but in the hysteria of a deep terror he is also crying. Mariamma comes to him and leads him out of the room by his hand. They go to the other bedroom, laughing, wiping their tears. 'Now sleep,' she says. 'You have school tomorrow. I promise he won't come here again. He is done for the night.' And she shuts the door.

Mariamma leans on the bookshelf in the bedroom she has not shared with the man in years. He is still standing on the chair with the noose around his neck. She inspects the chair. It has grown weak over time but a chair never collapses like a table. That is the true nature of a good chair. At best, it becomes lame, it tilts. That won't be enough to kill Ousep. She can go and snatch the chair right now from under his feet. It would be a perfect murder. She has considered it before but she is not very sure about the strength of the lungi or even the fan. Ousep is heavier than he looks.

'Ousep Chacko is survived by a wife, who is a buffalo woman, and an idiot son. His elder son Unni Chacko died three years ago in mysterious circumstances.'

'Get down,' she says. 'And go to sleep.'

Ousep removes the noose, somewhat gloriously, as if it is the garland of his fans, those garlands he used to receive when he was much younger. She helps him off the chair. He drags his chair back to the table.

'Why are you looking so sad, Mariammo?' he says. 'Don't look so sad.'

'I am not sad.'

'The secret to happiness is not to have any expectations from people.'

'I know that.'

'Especially from the people who matter most to you.'

'I know that, too.'

'Go away, go.'

She leaves quietly. He changes, turns off the lights, bangs the door shut, and goes to sleep.

Mariamma stands facing the large portrait of Unni in the hall. She runs her hand over its surface, though he seems more lifeless when she does that. He surveys his mother with a knowing smile. He has her beautiful nose, her skin of high pedigree, her colour. He has his father's high forehead. Some people think Unni was arrogant, which is not such a bad thing, not as bad as people make it out to be. But people have their way of thinking. So they have a faint triumph in their voices when they speak of Unni's death, his fall from the height. It is such a defeat, it seems, to die.

There is nothing that she understands about his death. People say something must have happened in those twenty minutes when he was home, or something must have happened on the stairway. Or maybe he got a phone call. Maybe he saw something. But what could have happened, really? Nothing makes sense. Some people say he was not normal, he was drifting towards dark thoughts, he was too clever for his age.

In the days that followed Unni's death, his father tried his best to find out what had happened. He spoke to almost all the classmates and friends of Unni, but in the end nothing could explain what the boy had done. And Ousep gave up. 'Some boys don't make it, that's all there is to it,' he said, and closed the chapter.

So what has happened now? What has landed on Ousep's lap? 'An unexpected message,' he tells the walls in his drunken moments, 'provided by the unnatural level of incompetence of the Indian Postal Department.' He does not say anything more, she has asked him several times, she has even asked him through crafty whispers during his deep sleep, but he does not say what he has found. Whatever it is, it has made him knock on doors again, he is asking questions again.

There is only one clue that Mariamma holds, and she knows it is not as insignificant as Ousep imagines. Unni left without leaving a note for his mother, he left without explaining his action to her.

She turns off the lights and wanders in the hall, wanders in the darkness, feeling the peace of the quiet, imagining that she sees the same emptiness that Unni sees. What is so great about the light that falls on the world, what is so great about what we see that a woman must mourn her son? But then she cries.

She wakes up early in the morning, to the fragrance of para-disiacal breakfasts and the long whistles of steam from the kitchens of happy people, and the monologues of children memorising their lessons. And Subbulakshmi's morning chant from a thousand bad radios, which sounds like a medieval woman's list of complaints in Sanskrit about the men of her time.

~

THOMA AND HIS mother tiptoe into Ousep's bedroom. His lungi is still hanging from the fan as a noose. Ousep is sleeping fully naked, his mouth slightly open, legs spread wide. They can see his large luminous testicles, which look rough and industrial. 'Like something the Soviets have made,' Mariamma says. She covers her man with a bedsheet, muttering, 'He has no shame even when he is asleep.' Thoma wonders whether one day his own organ will be so large, and assume this weird asymmetric shape that has no name even in Euclid's geometry. He is too shy to ask his mother whether this is the fate of all men.

He has seen his father this way many times. He goes into the bedroom often to see whether he has had a heart attack. Lots of fathers have gone in their sleep, and Thoma is afraid that his father, too, will go that way. When Ousep is asleep he looks dead. He does not move and you have to concentrate on his stomach to see if he is breathing. Thoma's mother, too, goes often to his bed to check if the man is alive. She usually stands with her hands on her hips, and stares, waiting to see a hint of breath in him, or a toe move.

That was exactly how the three of them had stared at Unni's body when it lay in the hall under a white shroud. They stood around him for an immeasurable amount of time, in a deep hopeful silence, and waited for him to wake up any moment and burst out laughing. He really did look as if he was just sleeping. They waited, until the hearse driver came and rang the doorbell.

Ousep rubs his nose. He is alive, today. Mariamma climbs on a chair and removes the noose. An hour later Thoma stands with his schoolbag strung on his tense shoulders. He wonders how many people heard the commotion in his house last night. Probably everyone. He stands facing the front door, too ashamed to open it and step out for all to see. But he has to endure the shame, as he does every morning. 'Fight, Thoma, put fight,' he says. And he opens the door.

2

How To Name It

THERE ARE THINGS Mariamma tells Ousep, looking him in the eye and addressing him in the third person, which has a stinging literary quality to it that reminds him of what they used to say in his village – all wives are writers. His favourite is her description of the way he walks in the morning despite the shame of the previous night. 'As if he is going to collect a lifetime achievement award from the President.' It is true, that is how he walks in the morning. With healthy strides, feet landing with purpose, head held high. But he is more aware than she imagines of his disgrace. She may laugh if he tells her this but the truth is that, as he irons his shirt this morning, smoking two cigarettes at once, what is on his mind is an old question. Can he be a better person, a responsible man, a good father? Is it so hard to be all that, to be regular, to be everyman?

Through the bedroom window he sees her marching towards the gate in her thin rubber slippers, going somewhere earlier than usual. He does not remember ever seeing her from this distance. What happens to men when they see their wives from afar? Mariamma looks like any other person in the world. Small, harmless, unremarkable, which she is not. It makes him feel oddly triumphant that she does not know he is watching her – Mariamma, up to something, going about her day, resolute and solitary.

She is not part of the sisterhood here. She is not included in their evening chatter, no one tells her gossip. Women do not call out her name, they do not wait at the gates for her to come down so that they can go to the market together. No one gives her recipes. She is only a subject of their compassion, which is a cowardly form of self-congratulation. She makes them feel they are better than her. They pity her for her man, for the loss of her child, for the way she walks along the road talking to herself, scowling sometimes, smiling sometimes. And her poverty, who can understand her poverty?

She owns many volumes of hardbound books. Those she reads with great relish, though she moves a finger beneath every line as if she is a semi-literate, which she is not. She has a telephone. She has the glowing fair peel of the high class, she is an economics postgraduate, and in her demented moments she evokes the name of Milton Friedman to complain to him about the imbecility of socialism. Yet, in that house, the life of Colgate is squeezed out of it until it is a flat strip of thin tortured metal. Then it is violated by toothbrushes and even index fingers for several days. The brushes are not thrown away until almost all the bristles disappear, and after the brushes do die in this autumnal way, the two post-graduates and their son use their fingers to clean their teeth until Mariamma somehow makes new brushes appear. Soaps are used until they go missing in the crevices of the body. Ousep has seen the strange sight of Mariamma staring at an empty oil bottle left standing inverted on a frying pan.

She said, without turning, 'The last drop, Ousep Chacko, is not a literary hyperbole in your home. Apparently, it really exists.'

'How grotesque this looks, Mariamma Chacko. I thought you had more class.'

That made both of them laugh, their laughter rising in pitch in competition, neither willing to stop and grant victory to the other.

The foam sofa in the hall, which is shrouded by an old bedsheet, has a giant secret hole in the centre. The landlord, who arrives every month and screams for his rent, was invited in by Mariamma only once; she made him sit on the sofa, and as he sank into the hole she laughed. Other men come asking for their money, including an enormous red-faced Afghan moneylender in his Pathan suit who twists Thoma's hand only partly in jest. And there is a sad book salesman who begs to be paid for the books he delivered five years ago – a complete set of William Shakespeare, all the great Greek tragedies, fifteen volumes of the *Encylopaedia Britannica* and the best English short stories from an innocent age when short stories were really stories.

The Chackos are poor because Ousep is poor and too proud to live within his means, not because he drinks. People who do not drink do not understand drunkards. He does not have to buy his drinks, he has many friends who want to buy him liquor. That is the quality of drunkards, they have a lot of friends. Because what men find most endearing in other men are their tragic flaws. That is why alcoholics never run out of friends. In the light of day, Ousep is too strong, too clever, a solitary man. But when night falls he belongs to all men.

He takes the screwdriver, opens the back panel of the long-defunct radio, and removes the folded sheets of paper. This is Unni's final comic, he finished it the morning he died. It is called *How To Name It*.

Ousep has not been able make sense of the comic. Only Mariamma would be able to decipher it for him but the problem is that she plays a significant part in it, she is a part of the riddle, which is bizarre. She is probably hiding something about the boy, something important. But why? If Ousep is going to show her the evidence that implicates her in the mystery of Unni's death, then he has to do it when the time is right. She is a crafty woman. But he too is crafty. Equals, that's what they are. To each other their only equals.

Three years ago, after Unni died, Ousep had set out to find an explanation. Through the memories of the people who knew the boy, he discovered a son whom he had not imagined. Unni Chacko, who appeared to possess a superior detachment, apparently also had an unnatural curiosity about the world around him, as if he could see something extraordinary hiding in plain sight. In the days that immediately followed the boy's death people opened up to Ousep and told him what they knew. But nobody could explain why Unni did what he did.

They said, in their lame ways, he had dark thoughts, he spoke a lot about death, he went to the funerals of people he did not know to see the faces of the newly dead and draw their portraits. Friends insisted that Unni must have had a deep secret grief though he never showed any signs. Behind the light on his face there must have been an ordinary sorrow. Find his sorrow and you would find his reason, that was what they implied. Even now, people want to believe in the theory of Unni's sorrow because that is what they want his death to be about. The tragic defeat of the unusual, and so the triumph of the normal.

This is how people resolve suicides – by considering it a consequence of unbearable grief or by manufacturing motives. Or through the inordinate importance given to the final note of the dead, which is usually only a confused half-truth.

There is something comical about a suicide note, the only known penultimate act of a living thing, and Ousep is glad that Unni had the artistic arrogance not to succumb to a cliché. But Mariamma does fear that the boy must have explained himself on a piece of paper, which might have got blown away. It is a reasonable fear. Ousep has always marvelled at the confidence of people, in their final moments, leaving a note behind in the complete faith that it would be found by the intended recipient.

But the truth is that every suicide remains a mystery for ever because the only perpetrator, the only person who really knows all the fragments of the motive, is gone. That was why Ousep had to give up three years ago. He had tried hard to piece together the circumstances of his son's death but in the end he had to accept that he would never succeed. But about six weeks ago, something happened.

Ousep was going down the stairs when he saw the postman walking up holding an envelope in his hand. It was a strange sight to see the postman so early in the day, and without his sack. The man was holding just one object, which was a large envelope. But Ousep would not have thought much of it if he had not seen the name on the envelope – Unni Chacko. The postman then told him the story of this mail, which was among the twelve letters he was returning that day to various homes in the area.

Three years ago, some boys had thrown firecrackers into the postbox attached to a lamp-post on Pasumarthy Street. Most of the letters were burnt. But some were only slightly damaged and they lay in a cardboard box in the post office, until a new manager there finally decided to return some of the letters whose senders' details were still legible. So, three years after Unni had posted a letter to someone, it was coming back now. But that was not extraordinary in itself.

On the front of the envelope was Unni's name and address, probably written by a clerk in the post office who had put the boy's mail inside a fresh envelope. The front of Unni's original envelope was badly damaged, its top half almost entirely gone, so nothing of the recipient's details had survived. But the bottom half of the envelope was intact. Here Unni's name and address were written in his distinct extravagant hand. Inside the mutilated envelope was a bunch of papers that were in good condition, as if nothing had happened, like Unni's face when his lifeless body returned from the morgue.

What Unni had posted was a comic, fourteen pages in all, not including a covering note written on a page torn in half. It is a brief scribble that does not address anyone. The note says: 'Just finished it this morning. I know you will do it for me.' The note is dated 16 May, the day Unni died.

The comic begins with a giant portrait of a smiling, bald, middle-aged man, whom Ousep does not know. He is a tough, rustic man. He is sitting in his armchair, on the porch of his home, in the shade of a jackfruit tree. The setting is clearly a village in Kerala. Unni was born in Kerala but was brought to Madras when he was still an infant. He had not visited the land since. He had no reason to because his parents had slowly broken away from their large complicated families, much to the relief of almost everybody involved.

The bald rustic in the comic now stops smiling and slowly turns serious, as if he has seen an apparition. He is clearly terrified. He begins to run. He runs down a winding path, through a forest of rubber trees. He falls down and looks increasingly terrified as the apparition approaches him. The comic then abruptly cuts to the Egmore railway station in Madras. Someone, probably the narrator, who is not shown but from whose point of view the entire story is being told, boards the train and travels through the night. The next morning, the train passes through the green hills and the ancient villages of Kerala. Finally, it reaches the Kollam station. The narrator, who is still invisible, now takes a crowded bus, then walks down the narrow paved lanes of a village. There he meets several people, and in some of the frames the characters are obviously talking because there are dialogue bubbles, but the bubbles are blank. Unni probably thought he would fill them in later, a future which he denied himself. The villagers lead the invisible narrator to the banks of a stream. The narrator, finally, approaches the house that was shown at the beginning of the comic. But the bald rustic man is not sitting in his armchair on the porch. There is no one here. A large, amiable, middle-aged woman appears. Something strange happens next. There is the image of a giant bra as a suspension bridge that spans a wide river, linking two mountains. The comic then returns to the amiable middle-aged woman. She leads the invisible narrator into the house, gives him or her a cup of coffee, shows a wall where there are several photographs of the bald rustic man. Then she takes the narrator through the house, through the long dark corridors and empty rooms and finally a storeroom, which is filled with jackfruits and bananas. She points to a bulb on the high ceiling. The next panel, the penultimate page of the comic, has a giant image of the bald rustic, now looking benevolent. This man clearly exists somewhere, he cannot be a work of fiction because his eyes have the certainty of a creature that has seen life. The man is smiling and peaceful, and he is giving a thumbs-up sign, which is uncharacteristic of his age and place. But he is evidently a man who has won, won something. The final page is shocking. It has a dramatic colour portrait of Mariamma standing on one leg, the other leg raised as if she is about to leap, and her right hand is pointing upwards. Her blood-red sari is hitched up and folded at the waist, exposing a bit of her thighs. Her thick black hair is flying in tumult. Her lips are curled in and her eyes are wide and angry. She is placed like a trophy on a wooden stand that has inscribed on it a string of Malayalam letters that make no sense.

Obviously, the comic needs prose to convey its meaning. It even has blank bubbles for dialogue and narration. Unni's works usually are not so dependent on prose.

So, what happened on the day Unni died? He completed the visuals of a comic, posted it to someone, went somewhere for three or four hours, got a haircut at noon at St Anthony's Hair Stylists, as confirmed by the barber. He returned home, played a bit of cricket, went up the stairs, and twenty minutes later decided to die?

The intended recipient of the comic remains a mystery. And what is the meaning of the final window of the comic – Mariamma in full tumult? The covering note, which shows no hint of affection, suggests that the recipient is a male, but Ousep is not sure. Maybe it was meant for a young lady who told Unni that her fat unhappy mother reads all her mail.

From the day Unni's mail returned, Ousep began to haunt the same boys he had interviewed three years ago, and some newer ones. He does not tell them about the mail, he lets out only stray hints. He wants to be careful with the information he holds until he fully understands what was going on in Unni's life.

The boys Ousep had met three years ago are almost men now, they are around twenty. That would be Unni's age if he were alive today. Twenty. A handsome young man whose narrow, interested eyes might have surveyed the world with restrained amusement, a young artist with the opaque seriousness that cartoonists usually possess. Unni Chacko, if he had allowed himself to live, would have grown into a formidable man.

Ousep thinks of the day ahead, the strangers he has to meet. He finds it tiring to talk to people. That has always been his flaw as a journalist, his secret weakness. It makes him uncomfortable, especially when he is not fortified by good rum, to stand in front of a person, to be seen, judged. How nice it would be if he could sit in the confession box of the Catholic priests, behind its ecclesiastical mosquito net, and listen to the old friends of Unni – those intimidating new men who are boys one moment, adults another moment. Some have fully grown moustaches even, their voices have changed, and there is something about their manliness that makes his heart ache for Unni. Unni, who will never shave, who will never stuff his wallet in the back pocket of his jeans with all the preoccupation of a man. What is it about life that even Ousep Chacko believes it is a lottery?

On his way out, he sees Mythili Balasubramanium going down the stairs. Does she know why Unni died? He has asked the question many times but without conviction. The way she is now, with her adolescent reserve, and circumspect walk, and breasts whose time has begun, it is easy to forget that she was just a child when Unni died. That child still survives as a dark portrait by Unni. In the portrait she is in a coffin, her large interested eyes shut, her hands clutching an unidentifiable flower that is resting on her chest.

Almost every day, all through her entire childhood, until the day Unni died, she spent a lot of time with the two boys. She was Mariamma's imagined daughter, Unni's assistant, Thoma's matron. She used to pretend to be frightened of Ousep, she would never meet his eyes. Some days, in the mornings, she would stand outside his room and peep in, and when his head turned she would run away. But when he managed to meet her eyes and smile, she always returned the smile. She did not hate him as others did.

But that was then. A little girl who probably believed all fathers must be nice.

The girl whom he imagines this way is a bit younger than the one in the coffin. She was twelve or thirteen when Unni drew her in the Album of the Dead. In the black diamond coffin, she lies in a blue frock that reaches to her knees, her hair is tied in two flying plaits by red ribbons, and she is wearing silver anklets around her wrists, as she used to then because her mother did not let her wear them around her ankles. Her mother said Mythili was too young to wear anklets. Even now the girl is not allowed to wear them. Mythili's mother, like the mothers of all daughters, has the same porno-graphic eye as men. They see sexual omens in anklets and skirts and flowing hair and long earrings that nod in the wind. They imagine, correctly, that the sex of their daughters is hidden in innocent places, as the soul of a vampire is stored in improb-able objects.

~

IT IS THE first day of the 'fast-unto-death', and not many people have turned out to watch, but if it lasts another two days there will be great crowds on the road – men screaming and laughing, alcoholics singing, women weeping without sorrow, boys hurling stones in the air. But now there is peace, and a deep sullen silence that has the quality of a mishap. Ousep scans the area for a sturdy young man, smartly dressed and not very clever.

Not more than fifty people stand behind the wooden barricades and gape at the ten men on the sidewalk, who are sitting in line on the mats they have brought from their homes. One of them is special, there is a table fan by his side. They claim they will starve to death or until the state government clearly spells out how it plans to protect the Tamils of Sri Lanka. The men are in starched white shirts stitched for the event and *veshtis* that are bunched in a way that magnifies their groins. There is a long silver torch beside every fasting man. The reporters know that the torches contain stuffed bananas instead of batteries, which will be consumed when the martyrs go to urinate.

The fasting men return the stares of the spectators through a distant blank gloom, and when they grow tired of looking sad they take sips of water from plastic cups or join their palms for the photographers. Behind these men, young subordinates stand nervously, as if they are afraid that if they sit they too would have to fast.

Two large muscular goons are setting up a sound system, stringing a Casio keyboard to loudspeakers. The goons are in lungis, which are folded over their knees, and the hems of their long striped underwear are visible. They have a problem, it appears, as the man who knows how to play the keyboard has not turned up.

'Do you know how to play this thing, you motherfucker?' one goon asks the other, somewhat fondly, as he extracts a wire from his sack.

'No.'

'Doesn't matter, motherfucker,' the first goon says, looking at the keyboard without fear. 'You play white. I'll play black.'

The fasting men and their supporters have occupied a fifty-metre stretch on the pavement, between a public urinal and a giant five-storey-high plywood cut-out of superstar Rajinikanth, who surveys the city in golden leather jacket and tights, and dark glasses, his face pink because hoarding painters do not have the courage to paint him black. Vehicles have been diverted from this section of the road, and policemen are lingering on the deserted stretch, as always wondering what they must do to kill time. On the other side of the road, facing the fasting men, a row of crude food stalls has sprung up on the pavement, where reporters and photographers and some of the curious spectators are stuffing hot food into their wide-open mouths.

The voice of Ilango comes from behind. Ousep barely recognises him; he had met Ilango three years ago. How boys grow.

As Unni becomes soil, the sons of other fathers, how they grow.

He is a healthy boy with new powerful muscles and he sways in his own private gale of youthful forces inside him. Somewhat happy, unlike the other vanquished boys like him who go to third-rate engineering colleges. His little exaggerated gestures have a phoney rustic servility about them, as if he is about to ask for a loan. It is tiring just to watch him, and Ousep feels a great relief at the thought that he will probably never meet him again.

'I am sorry I asked you to come here,' Ousep says. The boy puts his hands on his mouth, and says, 'How can you say "sorry" and all that? You are Unni's father. You can ask me to come anywhere.'

'I am working, Ilango. I have to file a story about the fast. That's why I asked you to come here.'

Ilango looks at the fasting men but he has no curiosity about what is happening here.

Ousep lights two cigarettes and leads the boy to a tea stall on the concrete pavement, where they sit facing each other on wooden stools that have unequal legs, a rugged aluminium-plated table between them. For a while they stare in silence at the fasting men on the other side of the road.

'You know why I wanted to meet you,' Ousep says.

'Yes. Please ask me anything you want, Uncle. But I am very curious. What happened? Why are you are asking questions about Unni? I hear you have spoken to almost everybody in the class. I hope everything is all right.'

'Everything is fine. Let's imagine it is not important why I am asking about Unni.'

'I don't know why he did that,' Ilango says, 'I really don't know. After the twelfth standard board exams I was not in touch with him. He did what he did a few weeks after the exams. I heard about it much later.'

'I didn't come for that. I want to know more about Unni. That's all there is to this. Tell me what you remember. When he was in the twelfth standard, the final year of school, just months before he died, that's the Unni I want to know. When he was seventeen, how was he in class?'

Ilango's eyes focus on a spot on the road. He is probably trying to extract something important from his memory, something significant. Everybody wants to tell a good story. That is the problem.

When Ilango speaks his voice has lost all its elaborate modesty. He speaks with a severe fondness for a friend who was shy, who liked to sit in a corner and sketch, but could be interrupted any time. Ousep has heard this many times. The reserve of Unni that yielded to the faintest tug of friendship.

'Unni didn't talk much,' Ilango says. 'I think he liked to be left alone. But if you went to Unni and if you talked to him, he would let you talk. And he would listen carefully, like a girl. He was interested in what you were saying. When you spoke to him you knew he was imagining what you were seeing in your head. And you would wonder, what's so important about what I am saying?'

'Can you recall a conversation?'

'Once I told him about a cat in my street that did not have a tail. He asked me a lot of questions about the cat. How it behaved, how it ran, stuff like that. I don't know why. He asked me if I thought the cat knew it didn't have a tail. How can I know something like that? That was the way he was.'

'Why do you think he was that way?'

'I don't know. I think he liked to collect a lot of information. And he did know a lot of strange facts. Actually, I don't know if they were really facts. One day he told me that the most powerful booze in the world is found only in Kerala. He said it is called Jesus Christ.'

'It's true,' Ousep says.

'Why is it called Jesus Christ?'

'If you drink it you will rise only on the third day.'

Ilango scratches his chin with an open mouth, and looks around.

'Sometimes he did say things that were totally strange, which simply cannot be true,' he says.

'Like?'

Ilango rubs his nose. He is not trying to remember, he is probably coming to a decision. 'One day he came up to me and said, "I know a corpse." I ask him what he means by that and he just laughs.'

'What did he mean?'

'God knows.'

'He said, "I know a corpse"?'

'Yes.'

'What does that mean?'

'I've no idea.'

Ousep is startled by the laments of women. There are about twenty of them, village women, who stand in a swarm on the other side of the road, behind the wooden barricade. They are facing the fasting ringleader, the man who has the table fan beside him. They are beating their breasts and wailing, but they also show the mild wonder of recent arrival. They cry in a distracted way, throwing glances all around, even looking up at the sky, though they know it very well. They are in tattered saris, blouseless, their hair tangled in brown dirt. Most of them are old, some are very young, but in a bestial way. Their wails are composed of the same three words, which probably have no meaning when not delivered in a dirge. They keep kissing the tips of their fingers. It is as if they are begging for food from a man who is fasting to death. But then a woman shows him a banana and it is now clear that they are asking him to eat, they are begging him not to starve to death. They are probably from his village. Someone must have told them that a son of their soil has decided to sacrifice his life for the Tamil cause. So the gang of malnourished women have descended to dissuade this man, whose full belly sits on his lap as if it is something dear to him. He looks at the women with valiant gloom, and their laments grow. He is probably trying to suppress a laugh now, so his face turns more serious. Then, in a masterstroke, he turns the table fan towards the women. In the burst of air the women break into giggles. They try to cry again but their lungs are tired now, and they soon fall silent. They sit on the road and start chatting among themselves.

All this will go one day, this animal poverty, it will vanish. And future generations will not know, will not even guess, the true nature of poverty, which is the longest heritage of man. Shouldn't this be preserved somehow, like old colonial buildings, shouldn't abject poverty be preserved as historical evidence? That is what socialists are trying to do in this country. Everybody misunderstands their intentions. They are noble conservationists who are working hard to preserve a way of the world.

Ousep and Mariamma were socialists once, like all the informed young men and women of the time, slim people in love who thought they knew how to make the world a better place, a place as happy as their beds. But Mariamma was not as naïve as him. One night she told him, her head on his bare chest, her hair all over his face, 'But an idea that overrates human character is bound to fail. Look around, Ousep, in every way of the world, only ideas that do not overestimate human nature succeed.' Ousep quoted her in his popular Sunday column. Not many young journalists could get away with quoting their own wives, but then every odd thing that Ousep Chacko did in those days was heralded as 'Style'. Other writers started quoting their wives in their serious political columns, and that became a brief journalistic trend. Until, inevitably, it became a farce and died.

Ilango is not affected by the women, he sees nothing in what has just happened. But he says, pointing to the women, 'According to Unni those tribals are not as sad as we think they are. They are happy. According to him everybody is happy. And people who are unhappy are only fooling themselves. For someone as clever as Unni it was a weird view that he had.'

Ilango's eyes grow feeble as he quietly sips his tea. He does not speak for a while, then he begins to chuckle. Still he does not speak. Ousep does not push, he waits.

'There was something Unni started doing in the final year of school which he had never done before,' the boy says. 'If a teacher was absent, or during the lunch break, any time the class was not guarded, he would quietly go to the teacher's table, climb on it and stand in total silence, until all murmurs stopped and all eyes were on him. Then he would tell us stories, his own stories. And when Unni told a story . . . now how do I say it? I am not a smart boy. I don't have the words to describe what I felt. When Unni told a story standing on top of that table it was as if there was no other sound in the world. As he spoke you saw pictures in your head, you saw faces, and you could smell things that you did not know had smells.'

This, Ousep has heard many times. The class of adolescent boys falling quiet as Unni approached the table, his smooth athletic leap on to the table, and then his dramatic silence, which infected all and killed the final chuckles. But what is odd is that several boys claim this never happened, or that they do not remember seeing Unni do this. That is strange. An act of this nature would have many witnesses, and it did happen in all probability. Then why would many boys want to deny it? What is even more odd is that the boys who describe Unni's storytelling do not remember any of his stories.

'Do you remember one of his stories?'

'No.'

That was quick.

'You remember the little details of how Unni told his stories, but you don't remember any of the stories that he told?'

Ilango's large, expressive Adam's apple rolls, as if it has become self-aware.

'I don't remember. I wonder why.'

Ousep lights his cigarettes. 'Do you smoke?' he asks.

The boy shakes his head, almost wounded for being asked. 'Why do you smoke two cigarettes at once?' he asks with exaggerated respect in his tone.

'Because three is too much,' Ousep says.

The boy is not sure whether it is a joke; he nods. He looks away for a few seconds, then asks the inevitable question. 'People say you have found something about Unni, is that true?'

'I've always been searching, Ilango, I never stopped. Now I come back to you after three years because I thought age might make you see a few things differently.'

The tea arrives in the filthy hands of a bare-chested waiter, who is humming a film song about the relationship between flowers and honeybees. Ilango drinks in thoughtful sips. And he begins to describe a residential colony, he gives directions on how to get there, which is the Tamilian way of telling a story – describe a place by almost giving its postal address. Several film directors live in this colony. 'Some of them have mistresses,' he says. Ilango pauses in a moment of embarrassment. He feels ashamed for using the word 'mistress' in the presence of a friend's father.

'It's all right, you are not a child any more,' Ousep says. 'We are men. You and I. We are men. What about the mistresses?'

'Unni said that the mistresses always lived on the ground floor. They were never on the higher floors. He used to wonder why. He really wanted to know why. That's it,' the boy says meekly, as if conceding that what he has just said does not deserve the tea Ousep has bought him. 'I know it does not mean anything. Such an ordinary thing, actually. I don't how useful something like this is to you.'

'It's good. It's very good. What I need are bits like these.'

'Really?'

'The other boys I meet, they just don't understand what I want. They try to give me their opinions. But you are a smart guy. You have an interesting memory.'

'Thanks.'

'Did Unni find out why the mistresses are usually kept only in the ground-floor flats?'

'I don't know. But he was sure there was a reason.'

The boy sets his cup down, and wipes his mouth with his fingers. 'What else do I remember about Unni?' he says, and looks lost for a while. He is distracted by a memory, he is probably wondering whether he should give voice to it. He stares at the fasting men without looking at them. Then he makes his decision. 'There is something else I remember,' he says. And he speaks slowly, clearly.

One evening, he is at a friend's house with a few other boys, including Unni. It is a small house with an unpaved walkway that runs from the gate to a high boundary wall. The boys are on the terrace, which is not very high, just about twelve feet above the ground. The gate is locked, but a stray dog slips through the bars. It does not see the boys on the terrace. 'Dogs usually don't look up,' Ilango says. 'Unni used to say that often, I don't know why. Animals usually don't look up.' It wanders in, and goes down the walkway. The narrow path is about sixty feet long, and it is hemmed in by a high boundary wall on one side and the wall of the house on the other. So the gate is its only escape if a situation arises.

Unni jumps down and picks up a stone. He stands at the gate, blocking the dog's path, and flings the stone. The stone is not intended to hit but the dog does not know that. It runs to the back wall and tries to climb but the wall is too high and this dog has probably never climbed a wall before. It stands there with its tongue out, wondering what it must do. Unni flings another stone, which hits the wall. The dog tries to climb the wall again, it slips and falls. It runs towards the side wall, runs in circles, runs towards Unni and then away from him, confused and terrified. It finally goes to the boundary wall and stands facing him, awaiting its fate. The other boys now jump down and pick up stones. Their stones miss, they hit the wall, but the dog is terrified. It makes sounds that are normally not associated with a dog. It leaps at the wall, leaps in the air, it begins to behave like an alien beast. Some stones now hit the dog. It cries, running up and down the walkway. At this point Unni says that they should let the dog go. All go back to the terrace. The dog charges to the gate and escapes. It runs down the road, it keeps running until it vanishes round the bend. That is it. That is what Ilango wants to say.

'How did you feel about it?' Ousep says.

'About what?'

'The dog. The way it ran, the sounds it made, the fear in its eyes.'

'It was terrible.'

'Terrible, yes.'

'There is no other way of looking at it.'

'Is that true?'

'Yes. I don't know what had happened to us. We behaved like urchins who stone chameleons just for fun.'

'Did Unni's stones hit the dog?'

'No. After all of us came down from the terrace he didn't throw any more stones.'

'Interesting that you remember that. A minor detail in a minor incident, after so long.'

'I don't know why I remember that.'

'Did you hit the dog?'

'Just once. I aimed at the wall but the dog got in the way.'

The dog got in the way, he says. A stray dog, probably very ugly, which is a bad thing to be in such a situation, is trapped. It is powerless, comically terrified, almost singing. What would a bunch of boys with stones in their hands want to do? This boy says he aimed at the wall. He only wanted to see the dog react, he did not want to hurt it, he did not want to hear the sound of stone against its flesh and its brief responsive shriek.

'Why do you think he did that, the whole game, why do you think he started it?' Ousep asks.

The boy studies his cup. For a moment there he looks intelligent, the way he looks with unhappy eyes at the cup, the way he lurks in his own silence. He says, 'You used the word "game", why did you use that word?'

'I think sometimes Unni did things just to see how others reacted.'

'Yes,' the boy says, relieved for some reason. 'That's what I think. He had an abnormal interest in how people reacted. It was a game for him. Yes, that's the word.'

'The day the dog was stoned, were the other two present?'

'Which two?'

'Somen Pillai and Sai Shankaran.'

'They were there, yes. Those three were always together. Always whispering and laughing among themselves. As if they were playing a secret game and the others were just fools who didn't know what was happening. Unni had that attitude more than the other two. He could make you feel small and silly.'

There is a surprising strength in the boy's tone now, the impotence of nostalgia is gone, and in its place is the force of contempt, the contempt of a male for a smarter friend.

'People used to say that those three were up to something,' the boy says. The way he says 'those three', it is as if he has forgotten that one of them is Ousep's dead son.

'Those three,' Ousep says in a soft voice. 'What exactly was it about them? What do you think they were doing?'

'It was as if they were a part of something, something others won't understand. Like that day. After we went back to the terrace and watched the dog run down the road, they looked at each other, made eyes, smiled. There was always something going on between them.'

'A lot of people have told me this but nobody is able to say what exactly they were up to.'

'Even I am not clear. They spent a lot of time together just talking, going somewhere, doing things. I don't know what they did. Someone told me they were involved in betting.'

'Do you remember who told you this?'

'No.'

'What kind of betting?'

'I don't know. I think they bet among themselves that some events were going to occur in a particular way.'

'I don't understand.'

'I'm not clear myself. We were not very close, actually.'

'Are you in touch with them?'

Ousep feels stupid for a moment because when he said 'them' he had seen the faces of three boys. But one of them, of course, nobody is in touch with.

'No,' the boy says, 'I've not seen them in a long time.'

'Tell me what you know about Somen Pillai.'

'There is nothing that I remember of Somen Pillai. It's funny, actually. You know, some guys are like that, they are so silent, they are invisible. They don't talk, they don't do anything in the class, they just sit and watch.'

Ousep has heard this before. Apart from the fact that he was Unni's friend, Somen Pillai has no claim to the memory of his classmates. In the ten years that he studied in St Ignatius, there is nothing that he said or did that anybody can recall.

'Have you met him?' Ilango asks.

'Yes, once. Very briefly. I've been trying to meet him again but he is refusing to meet me. Would you know why he would refuse me?'

'Maybe he doesn't like talking,' Ilango says. 'Some boys are like that.'

Ilango wants to leave. He takes one large decisive gulp of the tea, which is surely cold now. Ousep looks at him carefully, now willing to take a chance.

'Did Unni ever send anyone his comics, did he ever post his comics to someone, maybe for a reaction or something?'

'I don't know.'

'Did he have a girlfriend?'

Ilango lets out a shy chuckle. 'I don't know, I was not that close to him. But I heard these Fatima School girls, they used to talk about him, I heard that from my cousin.'

'Really?'

'Yes.'

'Ilango, I know you've already answered this question but I can't help asking this. Why do you think Unni killed himself?'

'I don't know.'

'Can you guess?'

'I don't know. I really have no idea. But since you ask me to guess, I think he was probably not as happy and confident and superior as everyone thought. He was not good at useful things, you know, he was not the type who would have got into IIT or any engineering college. All he did was draw. You asked if Unni sent his cartoons to anyone. Now that I am talking about it, yes, I think he used to send his cartoons to some magazines. But he got rejected, I heard. Got rejected by all of them.'

'His works were rejected?'

'Yes. I heard he sent some stuff to an American magazine called *New Yorker*. And they sent it back to him. Unni said they wrote him a nice long letter, but they didn't want to publish his cartoons.'

'And you think Unni was depressed because of all this?'

'Yes. Just think about it. What would Unni have done with his life?'

'What do you plan to do in your life, Ilango?'

'Me? I am going to become an engineer. Then I will write my GMAT and go to the US. Why do you ask?'

'Just curious.'

'I will work in the US, I will get a Green Card. I have planned out my whole life. I will get married at twenty-eight.'

'Good, good. Any other reason you can think of? Any other reason why he chose to die?'

'I've nothing more to say. The truth is I didn't know him that well.'

'Everybody tells me that.'

'Because the truth is that nobody knew him well.'

'Except those two boys?'

'Yes, except those two. Somen Pillai and Sai Shankaran.'

'Ilango, do you know that the three of them used to go to meet a nun in St Teresa's Convent, who had taken a vow of silence?'

'No,' the boy says with a chuckle, shaking his head. 'I am sure they did many such things that have no meaning.'

A man appears on the road, stark naked, holding a can, and walking as if he is just passing through. When he is sure that all eyes are on him he empties the can over his head. It must be kerosene. He is gleaming now in the sun. He begins to jog, screaming that he will set himself on fire if the Tamils in Sri Lanka are not saved today. He runs through the small crowd asking for a matchbox, scattering the people, who are not sure whether they must flee or stand there and watch. 'Matchbox,' the naked man says as he jogs in large circles. When he approaches, Ousep, with great lethargy, hands him his matchbox. The man ignores him and runs ahead asking for a light. And he looks ecstatic when the policemen finally carry him away.

~

FOR THE FIRST time in his life, Ousep Chacko waits for a nun. He is in St Teresa's Convent, sitting on a wooden bench in the visitors' gallery, which is deserted. There are ghostly echoes in the air, and they have a dark antiquity about them, as if they are from another time, the violent ages when religions were born, when evil finally defeated good, and in an ingenious trick split itself into good and evil.

At the far end of the room is a small door, as if little people live inside. The door is so defiantly shut that it is hard to believe that it ever opens. But it does, without a sound, and six black cassocks emerge and stare at him. One nods to the others, and walks towards him. The others go back in and shut the door. He is all right, they have decided. A harmless man from long ago. That offends him somehow, to be considered innocuous in a fraction of a second by a sisterhood of virgins.

The middle-aged nun is holding a notebook and a fountain

pen. She sits on the bench with him, one foot farther away than necessary. He has not seen her in twenty-four years, but there are still fragments he can see from her youth. He wonders how she sees him now.

She is from his village. He remembers her as a sleepy girl with eight younger sisters who used to walk behind their mother like piglets, passing by his house on their way to the Sunday market. Then she flowered into one of those young girls, their thick dark hair still wet from a long bath, who stood at the bus stop holding college books and giggled at bus conductors who had fair skin. One day, her father decided to make her a nun to save her from poverty. Days before she left for the convent, as she walked down the alleys of the village, men had only one thought, even the pious had only that thought – the wasting of a firm young body so far untouched by any man. After she was sent to the convent, she ran back home twice. But the third time she was deposited in the convent she accepted her fate.

Now she has a vacant peace on her face that does not look like defeat. She is fine, she is happy, they all are. That is Unni's hypothesis – the inevitability of happiness, the persistence of happiness. Happiness as an inescapable fate, not a pursuit.

She was at Ousep's wedding, the only nun present that day, pretty by the standards of nuns, and as famous for fleeing the convent as some legendary girls who had eloped for ever with Hindu men. He has not seen her since. But Mariamma used to write to her and even meet her, probably with the insane caution of a woman encountering her husband's family circle but also with the eager nervousness of a good Christian in the presence of a habit.

The good thing about the nun's vow of silence is that she and Ousep do not have to endure the warming up, and the imagined hilarity of calling each other old.

'You can speak,' Ousep says in a good-natured way. 'Nobody is watching, and both of us know there is no God.'

Her smile informs him that she has already forgiven him. He tells her what he wants. She looks as though she knew he would come for this one day. She writes on her notebook in good Malayalam, and in a beautiful miserly hand. She writes that she will go to a far corner and write down everything she remembers. That is exactly what Ousep wants from everyone. People liberating him from their company, and going away to a far corner and writing down everything they remember of Unni in small precise paragraphs.

She gives a quick written apology for not offering him tea because that is not a privilege she has. She goes about twenty feet away and sits on a bench, which is attached to a desk. After thirty minutes, she gives him a bunch of papers.

Unni Chacko, Somen Pillai, Sai Shankaran – that is the order in which she has named them. He asks her why she wrote Somen's name ahead of Sai's. She curls her lips to suggest the order is not important. She sits staring at the floor. It does not appear that she wants him to leave yet. She writes in her notebook, 'Why did he do it?'

'I want to find out,' Ousep says.

'Can you take a guess?' she writes.

'No. Can you?'

She shakes her head.

'Unni told his friends something very odd,' he says. 'He told them that he knew a corpse. Does it make any sense to you?'

She shakes her head. Then rises, joins her palms and leaves. As she walks away she rubs her eyes like a child.

Ousep reads her memories. About fifteen years ago, she was transferred to Madras from Kerala. She had not taken the vow of silence then. Somehow Mariamma came to know that the nun was in Madras, and she began to visit her at least once a month, and they would chat about the people they knew. At some point she started taking Unni along to meet her. The first time Unni came to the convent and sat here in the same hall, he was probably eight years old. He was 'an extraordinarily beautiful boy with soft, curly hair'. He was probably fascinated by her, he would keep staring. As he grew older, and taller, his visits grew rarer, though Mariamma continued to visit every month. He would accompany his mother only in the rains, to hold her umbrella on their way to the convent. Once when Mariamma came to visit, the nun gave her a note saying that she had taken a vow of silence as her sacrifice to Christ. Mariamma understood that there was no point in meeting her any more, for what use is a silent nun? But, two years later, when Unni was seventeen, he came here with the other two boys. They met her six times, and every time they came unannounced. They asked her many questions but all their questions had only one objective. They wanted to know whether anything extraordinary happened to her because of her silence.

She presumes that they expected her to make startling revelations but she had very unremarkable things to say. 'There is a peace in your chest when you are silent for vast amounts of time, a sweet sadness, but nothing beyond this.' They were very disappointed when she wrote on a piece of paper that she did speak, though rarely, when demanded by the Mother Superior. It was very tiring to write down answers to their questions, and her talking to three adolescent boys did not go down very well in the convent. Eventually, she asked them not to visit her.

'There was something about them, there was the light of God on their faces, but still there was also something odd about them. They were searching for something and it seemed to me I could not show them the path. Unni was relaxed, polite. He asked very few questions but he listened very carefully. I think he was very amused by me. Once he asked me if I was happy. Strange, nobody has ever asked me that question before. "Yes," I told him. Somen Pillai seemed to be a serious boy. He never spoke. I found his eyes very disturbing. He seemed to believe that he knew something deeper about the world than the others. Sai was simple, excited and very curious. He spoke in quick short bursts.'

~

SOMEN PILLAI LIVES in a stout independent house with a pink front. It stands at the end of a narrow mud lane, which is flanked by similar homes. From their dark windows and doorways people stand and gaze, looking bored, expecting a greater boredom to reach them; it is as if they know that the extraordinary does not exist.

Somen's home is one of those houses that have eyes – the guest is fifty feet away, a cheap unchanging blue curtain behind the large front windows moves an inch, and the main door opens slowly, as if much thought has gone into the act. The hosts then emerge to greet or repel. Behind the squat house, tall apartment blocks loom.

After the return of Unni's comic, Ousep has been here probably eight times. And every time, before he can reach the gate, the door would open and Somen's father would step out or the boy's mother would, or the two of them together, or the door would not open at all. When they do appear, they would step on to the porch and stand with their elbows on the short iron gate, and wait for him. But the only thing they have to say to him is that Somen is not home, and that he does not want to meet anyone.

Ousep has met the boy only once – three years ago, a week after Unni's death. Somen, with a mop of accidental stylish hair that rolled dreamily, large moist eyes, a deep dimple on the right cheek and a smile of discomfort, listened with a piercing stare, but when he spoke it was as if he had not been listening. He spoke slowly, carefully, with an inarticulate superiority, as if his thoughts were too complex for words. And he had the same complicated self-regard when he said something as excruciatingly ordinary as 'We were just three friends who lazed around and talked'.

The door opens before Ousep has reached the gate. Somen's parents step out, amble to the gate, looking in many directions, and stand with their elbows on the gate. They do not speak a word but they look conspiratorial, which is what man and wife truly are; when they stand together that is what they are – accomplices.

They have never called him in, and in return they give him their honest shame. They are Malayalees and they know Ousep Chacko as the promising young writer from long ago.

'He is not home,' the father says with a feeble glance from behind thick spectacles. He is in his formal office trousers but is bare chested, and there is a small towel on his shoulders. He is a manager in the Canara Bank, and his wife is a teller in the same branch. She is looking grim right now, as if she is counting cash. A tidy, dignified woman, like most women in the world. She may have never stood even for a moment in her life in any of the gymnastic ways of Mariamma. What is it like to sleep with a calm feminine woman, who does not address the walls?

Ousep is distracted by someone who has appeared at the doorway. The boy's parents panic for a second, they turn to the door and seem relieved when they realise it is just the maid. She is mopping the doorstep, her slim fair back fully bent from the hip. Ousep feels a stab of longing. Her face has an austere diminished beauty about it, as if it is not her place to be any prettier. How could she be allowed to be? A maid in Madras has to be ugly because that is her assurance to the mistress that she will not awaken the egalitarian muscle of the man in the house.

'What must I do to meet your son?' Ousep says.

'Maybe you should call first,' the father says.

'Nobody ever picks up the phone.'

'You say that, Ousep, but that is so strange. We are at home in the mornings and evenings.'

'When exactly is he home?'

'I don't know, Ousep. He has his ways.'

'You say he does not go to college.'

74

'That is what I say.'

'How can a boy not go to college?'

'Some boys don't and that is all there is to it.'

'Something is wrong, I can see that much,' Ousep says.

'You see stories in nothing, Ousep. That is your way. You are a storyteller.'

~

THOMA CHACKO DROWNS his head in a bucket of water and keeps his eyes open so that they become red. He holds his breath and stares at the blurred bottom of the bucket. He imagines a world in the aftermath of a giant sea wave, a world that has been engulfed by the sea as foretold by Unni, he imagines these to be the final moments of his life. His lungs are about to burst but he holds on. How terrifying it is to drown. He hopes a fall from the building's terrace is less painful. The cracking of the skull is a very different form of death, it is faster. Though the best way to die is to be shot in the head. That is what Unni said. 'The explosion of the skull, Thoma, that must hurt but only for a moment. Once the bullet reaches the brain, there is no pain. That is the beauty of the brain. It is the brain that makes you feel every inch of your body, it is the brain that makes you feel pain, but the brain itself has no feeling.'

What might have gone through Unni's mind in the final moments before he jumped, what was he thinking? That afternoon three years ago, Thoma was asleep, but he had sensed the presence of Unni in the bedroom. He knew his brother had walked in, even stayed for a while before leaving the room. He remembers that. That, and an unfamiliar dream in which a woman is screaming, and running away from a giant tsunami. If Thoma had been awake Unni would have sat down on the bed for a chat and even the thought of ending his own life might not have crossed his mind. Everything would have been different. But Thoma had slept.

He wants to know whether making his eyes go red is a good excuse for wearing his father's old sunglasses. It is important that

Thoma finds a reason to wear sunglasses. His mother has just suggested that they ask Mythili Balasubramanium if she will teach Thoma in the evenings, maths especially. They are going to knock on her door and ask. Thoma wants to wear sunglasses when he meets her, she may respect him if she sees him that way. He does look dashing in wet hair and sunglasses, several people say that. They say, 'Thoma, you look handsome right now.' But would Mythili believe that he has got conjunctivitis? Is it absurd to get the Madras Eye on a Saturday? And why does he suffer so much for her? When Unni was alive and they used to spend hours with her, he had thought she was an unbearable, talkative girl. But now that he is what he is, he thinks of her all the time, and the best thing about life and the worst is that she exists.

His eyes almost blood red, he goes to his father's bookshelf and searches for the old green glasses, which are usually left on top of a stack of books. But he can't find them now.

'Why are your eyes red?' his mother asks.

'I've got Madras Eye,' he says.

'You were fine one minute ago.'

'It always happens suddenly,' he says. 'Surely you don't think my eyes would first turn violet, then indigo, then blue and the other colours of the rainbow spectrum before they finally become red.'

'What are the other colours of the spectrum, Thoma? Let's see if you know.'

'I know. I know everything. I just don't tell.'

'Can't you memorise it, Thoma? It is so simple. Just stick inside your thick head the word VIBGYOR. And you'd be able to name the colours of the rainbow any time.'

'Don't irritate me.'

'Someone is angry with his mother today. What are you searching for, Thoma?'

'Where are the sunglasses?'

'I sold them,' she says. 'Come here, let me dry your hair.'

'Why did you sell the glasses?'

'There was someone asking on the church noticeboard.'

'How can you do something like that, how can you take something from our house and go and sell it?'

'I've done that all my life, you know that. All my gold bangles, they have become your shit, haven't they?'

'But you should not sell everything,' he says. 'Some things, you should not sell.'

'How do you think I put food on the table some days?'

'Always ask me before you sell things.'

'I'll only ask you if you're hungry, Thoma.'

They walk out together, leaving the door open. Across the short corridor is Mythili's door. There is something about that door, something arrogant. Another happy home shut to the Chackos. They stand at the door and wait. Thoma hopes Mythili will open the door holding a newspaper and ask, pointing to a headline, 'Thoma, I wonder what KGB stands for?'

'It's been three years since we went to their home,' Mariamma says, the way she usually announces a fact. 'Neighbours right next door, good people, but we have not been here in three years. It didn't strike me until now how strange that is.'

'Obviously they don't want us to go there,' Thoma says. 'Nobody wants us, can't you see?'

'That's not true, Thoma. Mythili smiles at me when she sees me.'

'It's a half-smile, can't you see? She used to love you. Everything has changed now.'

'She loves us still, Thoma. She is a grown girl now, that's all. She can't behave like a little girl any more.'

'Her mother definitely hates us. Elephant woman.'

'Don't say that, Thoma. She talks a lot to me from her balcony.'

'She doesn't talk to you, you talk to her. She just nods and hangs her underwear on the wire. She doesn't even look at you.'

But Mariamma is not listening any more. She smiles at Mythili's coir doormat, thinking of something, probably something entirely unconnected, maybe an unforgettable bird she once saw in her childhood. That is how Mother is. Her mind wanders. But at this moment she does look normal, more tame and womanly than she is at home. She looks prettier this way, even happy and wise. Which she is, though not many people know that.

'Mythili was just thirteen then, three years ago she was just a kid,' she says. 'She is a big girl now, Thoma. A child yesterday, almost a woman today. In the blink of an eye.'

Thoma feels a warm ache when his mother mourns the passing of an age. How time flies. The lost years. Those were the days. He has heard these all his life, but only after Unni's death did something in him stir at the sound of such phrases. The hurting sweetness of memory, it has no name in Tamil or Malayalam. That is what Unni said. But he said there is a word for it in English, which Thoma has now forgotten, a word that sounds like an ailment.

Unni said that there are thousands of Human Sentiments and many of them have not been named in any language. He said every person has at least one emotion that only he or she feels and no one else in the world can even imagine the feeling. 'Even you, Thoma, among the many things you feel there is one that only you can achieve and no other person in the world.'

'I know what it is, Unni, but don't tell anyone,' Thoma had said in a whisper.

'What is it, Thoma?'

'In the mornings, soon after I wake up, my penis grows on its own.'

'My God, Thoma, are you serious?'

'I promise.'

'Thoma, you are one of a kind.'

'I am?'

'You are a mutant, Thoma.'

'What do mutants do?'

'A mutant has abilities other humans do not have. You are a mutant, Thoma.'

It was the happiest moment in Thoma's life, even though Unni did say, 'But it is a talent, Thoma. It is not a sentiment.'

'That's what even I thought, Unni. It is a talent. But I do have feelings that others may not feel. I can smell the earth after it rains.'

'Many people can, actually.'

'Really? There is something else, then. Nobody else can even imagine it. Sometimes when I feel sad, when I think of the way our mother talks to herself, how our father comes home drunk, how we never go out as a family because we don't have any money, when I think of all that I feel a sorrow in my throat, it becomes a ball, and you know, Unni, I actually enjoy it. I like the pain in my throat and like the way tears flow from my eyes. Someone who is looking at me may think that I am suffering. But I am enjoying it, too.'

'Thoma, you are really very different from others.'

'I am a mutant.'

'No. What you told me, that makes you a Unique Person. People go through their entire lives not knowing what is special about them. But I think you've found it at such an early age. What you told me about how you feel, nobody has that feeling, Thoma.'

'Can you think of a name for it? I don't want it to be unnamed. I want people to know that there is such a sentiment.'

'Only the Oxford dictionary is allowed to decide on new words, Thoma.'

Unni went to the phone and dialled a number. 'Is that the Oxford Dictionary Limited?' Unni said. 'I want to speak to the editor, please . . . Sir, good morning. My brother Thoma Chacko appears to have discovered his Unique Emotion . . .'

Thoma was so excited he was jogging on the spot and trying to get Unni's attention by waving his hand.

'What is it, Thoma?'

'Tell him, I am from St Ignatius School.'

Unni said into the phone, 'I am sorry to keep you on hold, sir. As I was saying, my brother Thoma Chacko, a day scholar at the St Ignatius High School for Boys, has discovered an emotion that is unique to him and he proposes that it be named. Yes . . . yes . . . of course. What happens to him is that on some days his sorrow feels like a ball in his throat and he begins to enjoy the whole thing.'

Many weeks later, Unni brought him a pocket Oxford Dictionary that was so new that it was still in its plastic casing. Unni opened it and showed him the word 'Self-pity'.

'That's the word they made for you, Thoma.'

Thoma held the dictionary in his nervous hands and saw with a shudder in his heart what he had done. He had created an English word even though it was borrowed from two existing words.

'They have not mentioned my name,' he said.

'They don't mention names, Thoma.'

'Why?'

'That's the way they are.'

Thoma is not a kid any more, he knows what Unni did, but he still remembers the excitement of the day and he remembers it through a happy scent.

His mother is probably nervous. 'Wonder what is taking them so long to open the door,' she says.

'You've to ring the doorbell,' Thoma says.

'I didn't ring the bell?'

'No, you didn't.'

She begins to shake with laughter, and that makes him laugh too.

Mythili's mother opens the door and is surprised by what she sees. She does not realise it but she is slowly shutting the door. She stares with a fallen face, and if she stays that way for a second more Thoma and his mother will be shamed. She manages a smile just in time. 'Come in,' she says, but she moves back only two feet. She is still holding the door. Mariamma launches one leg in; the other is still outside. The door is ajar and there is no way Thoma can enter.

'He is having his coffee,' Mythili's mother says. The word 'he' from her mouth has always referred to Mythili's father, who is in the hall, minding his own business. Mythili is sitting beside him, on the sofa. She is in a sleeveless pink top that reaches to her knees, and her bare legs are together. She is careful that way, she was always womanly even when she was a little girl. Some girls, they are careless when they sit. They don't know that boys, especially the older boys, are always searching for 'The Gap', they are always on the lookout for it. Mythili probably knows, she is very shrewd.

But she seems somewhat naked right now. It is not just her legs, he can see most of her shoulders and arms. She is this way only when she is indoors. If she wants to go to the front balcony she has to wear other clothes and tie her hair in a ponytail. The thought of Mythili being forced to obey the rules pleases Thoma. He imagines giving an instruction to her and she meekly obeying. That may never happen, but he enjoys the thought.

'I'll come later,' Mariamma says.

'But what is it?' Mythili's mother asks.

'I was wondering if Mythili can teach Thoma for an hour three days a week. He needs help, it seems to me.'

She catches Mythili's eye, and the girl smiles in a distant way, as if she is a stranger. That is unfair. There was a time when she used to shadow his mother, and say that she liked Mariamma more than her own mother.

'But she is going to be very busy,' Mythili's mother says. 'You know the exams are coming.' She turns to her daughter and says, 'You are going to be very busy.'

'Yes, I'm going to be very busy,' Mythili says.

Mythili's mother then steps out of her house and shuts the door. 'There is something I've to tell you, Maria,' she says. She has never been able to accept that Mariamma's name is not Maria. 'The money I gave you two months ago, just two hundred rupees, I know, but it would be nice if you could return it soon. Things are a bit tight right now.'

A jolt of shame runs through his mother. She does not realise it but her lips have vanished into her mouth. She smiles sheepishly at the floor, like a moron. 'I was going to return it in just a few days, meant to tell you that,' she says, and heads back home.

She wanders through the vacant rooms of her house, tossing a ball of crumpled newspaper in the air and catching it with one hand, whispering to herself what she has become. 'Girls who were village idiots when Mariamma was something, they are proud women now and Mariamma a beggar.' Occasionally, her voice rises and Thoma finds it unreasonable that in the middle of all this she should remember his grandmother, who has nothing to do with the day's humiliation. 'I have better things to do, Annamol, than make tea.'

She whispers a question a teacher had once asked her about the gold bullion, and how her answer was so brilliant the class was stunned. She walks this way, up and down the rooms, tossing the ball of paper and muttering compliments to herself.

Thoma imagines a day many years in the future when he would arrive in a black car so broad that it would have to be parked outside Block A, and all the people of the building would assemble on their balconies to take a look at the car. He would emerge from the car wearing dark glasses. His tight white shirt and white trousers and pointed white shoes gleaming in the sun. Then Mariamma would slip out of the car in a sari made of gold. And he would look up at Mythili's mother and throw a huge quantity of notes at her, most of which would somehow reach her third-floor balcony. She would look down at her own belly in shame. Then, for some reason, he would run in slow motion, his hair flying.

Thoma follows his mother as she now walks a bit faster through the rooms, her hands beginning to flay, her fingers stiffening to point at things. The ball of paper falls from her hand. He picks it up and gives it to her. She takes it without meeting his eyes and resumes her march towards another yellow wall. He walks behind her, very close.

'Tell me a story from your village,' he says.

'Later,' she says without affection, as if it were just another voice inside her that had made the request.

He wonders how Unni used to do it. He could make her snap out of her grouses. He had Technique, that was what Unni had, but Thoma is not as smart. He tails her, wondering what he must do to make her laugh. She is slowly getting louder, she is remembering the same old grudges, the subject of her anger is not the humiliation of the morning any more.

She goes to the kitchen and wags a finger. Her lips curl in, her head tilts, her jaws stiffen in the fury of the words that are not coming out of her mouth, and she points a finger at the ceiling. Thoma stands with her, he mimics her scowl and points a finger at the ceiling. Both of them stand this way for a few seconds. Until she relaxes her arm and looks at him with a hand on her hip. And she shakes with laughter. Thoma feels the relief of happiness, and for the first time in his life the air of triumph in his chest. What he had intended to achieve he has attained. That has never happened before. That a motive is followed by its realisation may seem natural to most people but not Thoma. When Unni wanted to draw a cow, he drew a cow that was almost alive. Thoma cannot do that. His cows look like white sofas. When Mythili used to say that she was going to sing a song, she would shuffle a bit, swallow and sing exactly the way she had intended. And long after she stopped and looked shyly at Unni, there would be the silence of joy in the room. But the melodies that play in Thoma's mind, when they come out through his throat, even he does not recognise them. And down there on the playground nobody ever asks him to bowl because the ball can go anywhere in the world. They let him bat only because it does not make a difference to anybody. But today, Thoma had wished to do something, he had a goal, and he achieved it.

Carried away, he continues to stand with his lips curled in and a menacing finger threatening the ceiling. She laughs again, but not as much.

~

MARIAMMA IS WAITING in the dark, her back against the wall, legs spread out straight on the floor, her big toes interlocked. Ousep will come any time, swaying and stumbling, screaming his laments. If she is lucky he will come quietly on the arms of strangers, like a new cupboard. Once, the men had carried him straight into the flat below. That woman had shrieked as they tried to walk in with him. They tried to calm her down, saying that he was not dead, and they asked her the location of his bed. How that woman screamed.

After the incident, which was a few months ago, Mariamma sees a recurring dream. Ousep on the arms of able men being taken into an orderly home, the tidy woman of the house, with jasmine flowers in her hair, opening the door, then screaming in fright and asking them to get out. The men carry Ousep to another home and ask the woman there to show them where his bed is. That woman, too, yells uncontrollably and throws objects at them. They go on this way, carrying Ousep to every home in the world, to be turned away by indignant women. Finally the bearers of Ousep Chacko arrive at the door of Mariamma, who quietly shows them his bed. It is a dream that makes her sad sometimes, but at other times she shakes in her sleep with laughter.

Every time she sits this way waiting for him she feels a familiar fear in her stomach, though what is about to happen is a scene that occurs every night. The rosary moves between her fingers, but her lips mumble other things. One night, a night like this, she would be waiting but Ousep would not arrive. The phone would ring and a policeman would tell her, 'A man has been found dead on the road.'

'Then it is him,' she would say. 'That is how Ousep Chacko would go. Like a dog.'

'What must we do with the body?'

'In his wallet you will find some cash. If you bastards steal it, you and your children will suffer till the very end of time.' That is what she would say, she has enough strength inside her to say that. But when she thinks about the matter more calmly, she decides to exclude the policeman's children from her curse.

But would the call ever come, would Ousep ever fall? Drunkards do live long. They are careful people, especially when they walk on the road. No man has greater purpose than a drunkard.

The thought comes to her, not for the first time, that she could burn him when he is asleep. She could pour kerosene on him and light him up. Men burn their wives all the time and get away with it, don't they? Burning girls, this country is full of burning girls, full of accidents in the kitchen. It is time a man went this way. She tries to think of the details of the plot but it fills her with gloom, which is a type of sloth. She tries to concentrate but as always her mind wanders. She thinks of her hill, the rubber trees, the plantain groves, and the birds that did not have names. She thinks of Unni, from his infant stare to his calm adolescence, and his tireless search for rogues among animals.

When he was six or seven, or maybe younger, she is not sure, he used to pretend that he was blind or that he was deaf. He could play it so well and for so long that she would get worried. The days he claimed he was blind he would walk to school exactly like a blind child, holding her hand all the way and stumbling on things. And when he said he was deaf, he would not flinch even when he heard a sudden blaring horn on the road. Some days his teachers complained about this. But surely he was pretending, it was a game. What else can explain it?

The thoughts of Unni, strangely, remind her of a screwdriver. She wonders why. Why would Mariamma think of a screwdriver? Is it something Unni had told her? And she realises that earlier in the day she was thinking about the screwdriver on Ousep's bookshelf. It is an odd object to find in his room, it was not there before. Ousep is not a man who fixes things, he has probably never struck a nail on its head in his entire life. So why is the screwdriver lying there in the room of a man who never fixes things? Because he wants to dismantle something. But what?

She thinks she has heard him but she is not sure. A moment later his heart-stopping scream eliminates the comfort of doubt. He is somewhere below, probably at the gate. She clenches her fists and mumbles a Hail Mary. She can hear him announce the name of every man in Block A. She goes to Thoma's room. He has heard his father but he pretends to be asleep. She whispers to him, 'Don't worry, Thoma. It is just for a while.'

'Can't we run away?' he says.

'One day, maybe.'

'What are we waiting for?'

'There is a time for everything. We are waiting for the right time.'

'I think we have reached the right time.'

'Not yet.'

'I am afraid,' he says.

'Don't be afraid, Thoma.'

'It's not that simple.'

'Don't be afraid. I am the Rock, Thoma, and I shall never fall.'

She goes to the front balcony, and from behind the limp clothes that are hanging from the wire, she looks. Ousep is standing near the gate, lit by a street light, his hands spread. He is barely able to stand. He is still calling out the names of the men who live in the block. He mentions their name, their door number and where they work. Even in this state the man's memory is sharp. The guard emerges from the darkness in his underwear, hopping as he puts on his trousers on the move. Ousep looks at him and makes a face, holding his chin with his fingers. The guard zips his trousers and stands erect. He is nervous, he does not know what he must do, so he takes his whistle out and whistles. That makes Mariamma laugh. Ousep walks a short distance and picks up a large stone from the ground. The guard looks at the stone very carefully for a moment, and he runs, in a clever zigzag way. He goes to the far corner of the playground, near the swings that are too still. Swings that have no children in them; she cannot bear to look at them for some reason.

Ousep aims at a window, then at another, but he does not throw the stone. 'Sleep, my friends, sleep,' he says as he walks unsteadily to his left, his arms dead, back stooped. His deep voice, whose tremendous strength surprises even her, rips through the sullen calm. 'In your conjugal beds, you sleep. There you commit unspeakable acts. Comical acts. Failed acts. Man does many things with wife as witness. The stories that must not be told. Despite everything, man is safest beside his wife, isn't that true? Who can deny that? Man is safest beside his wife. Far from the treacheries of orphaned women and their wild love. Never stray too far from home, my friends. Quietly, men must pass through life. Great dangers lurk in the paths of men who live like men. Quietly. We must pass.'

Ousep drops the stone and covers his mouth with both hands. He walks with exaggerated stealth in what he believes is a straight line. He looks at the brown earth and begins to laugh. 'Can I tell your dumb adolescent sons something?' he says, looking up at the windows. 'As the semen dries in their hands, can I tell them something? Can I give them some news from the future?' He lets out a long escalating laugh that awakens the crows. 'Boys,' he screams, 'you will become men in the age of women.'

The voice of a man from one of the top floors says, 'Is there a watchman in this place or is it a eunuch that we have hired?' Ousep throws the stone in the direction of the voice. The stone crashes against the concrete. The dissent perishes. The guard appears again in the circle of light, he tries to wrestle with Ousep. In the scuffle he tears Ousep's shirt. Ousep considers his torn shirt and fixes the guard with a severe stare. The guard is terrified but he stands his ground. 'What do you want to see?' Ousep screams. 'Do you want to see what I am made of?' And he tears open his shirt. And it looks as if he is about to take his trousers off. Will Ousep do that?

Mariamma runs into the bedroom, not knowing what she wants to do. She takes the Best Writer award standing on Ousep's table, holds it by the silver angel, and runs to the balcony. She flings it at him with all her strength. It lands a foot away from Ousep. He looks at the award, and at the sky, the award again and the sky. He picks it up and shows it to the world. He says, in a calm voice, 'Once upon a time.'

She goes to sit on the kitchen floor, near the black mortar from where she can see him enter. When he arrives he stands in the hall, holding his shirt and the award, and stares at her. But he does not say anything. He walks to his room and shuts the door.

She sits there, staring at Unni's portrait on the wall and mumbling things. 'I didn't get away, Mariamma didn't get away,' she tells the cat. She is remembering a crime she committed when she was seven years old. She was playing with a black kitten on the riverbank. She buried it in a shallow hole and covered it with soil. She was about to dig it out when she heard someone scream that a girl had jumped into the river to die. She ran to see what had happened. Five strong men swam to the girl and pulled her to the other side of the river. In all the fuss that followed Mariamma forgot about the kitten. It was evening when she remembered. She knew the kitten's mother, she saw the cat every day of her life. 'Mariamma didn't get away,' she says. 'Her son, too, is buried in the soil.'

Her hand rises, a finger wags at the ceiling. 'But Philipose,' she says, 'you got away, Philipose.'

Ousep is slipping into deep sleep; he has a feeble, dying thought, an old unsettling thought that surfaces now and then. There are people in this world who wander through their entire lives searching for meaning, searching for an answer. For all his humour, Unni was probably among them. Could it be that

Ousep, too, is searching, seeking an end that probably does not exist? Is he, too, searching for an illusory truth? Maybe the others are right, the regular people, they are usually right, aren't they? They know the ways of the world better because they are the world. Unni died for the same reason that people usually kill themselves – he was miserable. There is nothing more to it perhaps.

Ousep asks himself why he smells kerosene in his room. The smell approaches and grows strong. Then it recedes and vanishes without a trace. And he is surprised by another question that he asks himself. He wonders what has made him ask this now. He has never asked this before. 'Who is Philipose?'

~

SATURDAY MORNING, THOMA is on the floor of the hall with his mother's thick hardbound books, which are all about Very Serious Matters. As usual, he is searching their pages for a mention of India. Not 'ancient civilisation' or 'second-most populous country' or 'agrarian society', but something clearly complimentary. 'India is full of clever people, who are secretly very rich, and the naked lepers you see on the roads are all actually Pakistani spies. And Indian boys are very handsome, though they do not know that.'

He sees his mother emerge from the kitchen with a blue bucket filled with water. She looks resolute and composed. 'No,' he says, 'don't do it.' She does not do this every morning. 'I must choose the days, Thoma, because of the law of diminishing returns,' she once told him. Thoma does not fully understand the Law of Diminishing Returns, but he knows that she decides to enforce the morning justice only if father has crossed a line the previous night.

'No,' Thoma says, sitting up. 'Don't do it.'

She flings open the door of Ousep's bedroom and goes in. Thoma hears her scream with an evangelical shiver, 'Reform this drunkard, my Lord, my God, he is the lost sheep, and you are the shepherd.'

He hears the explosion of water landing on his father, who rises with a deep moan. A moment of peace, then Thoma sees his mother sprint out. In these circumstances she does not merely run, she really does sprint, her arms oars in the air. Nobody in Madras has ever seen a woman of her age run this fast. 'Thoma,' she says, with a finger pointed at her bare feet as she races past him towards the front door and vanishes down the stairs.

Ousep emerges from his bedroom, tired and fully drenched and very angry, his fist on his forehead. He almost sings to the open front door, 'You bitch, you mad bitch.' And he walks in a daze to the bathroom.

Thoma takes his mother's thin eroded rubber slippers from under the dining table and goes to the balcony. She is standing on the playground, looking up, expectant. He throws her slippers down. She gives him a smile, raises a thumb, and marches to the church.

Other mornings, she tiptoes into Ousep's room, puts her face very close to his and screams the Lord's name into his ears. Or she hides behind the cloth screen and waits until he wakes up to scare him with a sudden howl. Thoma suspects that what she secretly wants is to give him a heart attack so that she can start her life afresh in peace, even if it is in greater poverty.

When Unni was alive she never used to sprint out of the house after the water treatment or the ghost scare. They used to stand together in the hall and laugh with their bodies arched until they were on the floor holding their stomachs. But with Unni gone she is not sure that she is safe. What if Ousep finally decides to hit her? He has never done that but what stops a furious man from losing control?

Ousep Chacko makes peace with the punishment, completes his bath, even shaves. When he walks into the hall, he sees Thoma facing the main door, which is now shut, and whispering to it. The boy has not heard his father. Ousep has a feline walk, unlike Mariamma, who shakes the air around her.

Thoma's fists are clenched and he is looking fiercely at the door. He is mustering the courage to open it and step out, to face the world after the night of shame. His father, almost naked in front of all, drunk and loud and pathetic. 'You can do it, Thoma, you can do it,' the boy is telling himself. 'Fight, Thoma, put up a fight.'

How cruel it is for this sad boy in darned shirt and born-again shorts, and rubber slippers held together by safety pins. How cruel all this. Ousep knows, but then he is what he is, he cannot be a better person. Survive these years, Thoma, somehow hold on. Life is far easier than it seems. A day will come when you will finally grow muscles in your arms, then you can take your anger out. You, too, can slap your father, see him fall. Your father would forgive. And many years later you can tell your woman about him. As you lie naked in the dark you can tell her about your bastard father. With some literary exaggerations, of course. That is allowed, a bit of colour is all right. And she will hold you tight and stroke you gently to heal your rare sorrows. But you must also know this, Thoma, you must accept the inescapable truth. Even an alcoholic gives his son a gift. A precious gift, in fact. You will never ever be a drunkard. That is how it is, that is how it goes. The happiest men in the world are the men who swore that they would never become their fathers. That is how the alpha males became endangered. Their sons decided that they would not become their fathers, they would be decent men, they would not sleep with strangers through the night, they would instead wipe baby shit, they would know at all times the ages of their children and the names of their teachers, they would buy curtains, they would transfer food from large bowls into smaller bowls and put them in the fridge, they will not be their fathers. In a world full of new men who did not want to be their fathers, what chance did the alpha males have? People like Thoma would create a similar world, a world where there is no place for drunkards and others like them. And the wild among men would have to seek refuge in failure to remain truly free.

Thoma is still deciding, he is still not sure whether he has the strength to go out in full public view. 'Fight, Thoma, put fight, put fight,' he is saying. He probably does a version of this every morning when he has to open the door and leave for school. It is a bit like a cold-water bath at dawn – the first mug requires courage, what follows is not so bad. If Thoma can step out into the corridor outside he will endure the rest. But first he must have the courage to open the door. The boy takes a deep decisive breath. And gives up. Last night was probably a bit too much.

Thoma turns to go to his room and he is shocked to see his father staring at him. 'Did Unni ever talk to you about a corpse?' Ousep asks.

'No,' the boy says without meeting his father's eyes.

Thoma now has a good a reason to open the door and step out, which he does. At that moment the neighbour's door opens and Mythili appears in a blue salwar-kurta. Thoma does not look at her, he looks at the floor and runs down the stairs.

'Mythili,' Ousep says on an impulse. He does not remember ever calling out to her. He wonders whether she even knows his name. Somehow that would be flattering. She looks at him with a shy, stranger's smile. What a dignified farce this girl is.

'I want to have a word with you,' he says, walking into the corridor.

'I am going to the library,' she says.

'This will take just five minutes,' he says. 'I have to ask you some questions about Unni.'

Her mother appears, as expected, and stands with her hand on the door frame. She quickly surveys her own breasts as if to confide in them her suspicion of all men. With that bunch of steel keys hanging at her waist she looks the part of the sentinel of her girl's treasures.

'Mythili is going to the lending library,' she says unhappily.

'I need to talk to her,' he says. He tries to lead her into his house. 'Come,' he says, like an innocent respectable man.

She looks at her mother, who glares as if it is all her fault. Ousep tries to achieve the gentle vulnerable stoop and wounded eyes. 'What happened, Mythili? You don't like us any more? You spent your whole childhood in our home.'

'You can talk in our house,' her mother says.

Ousep was worried about this but now that the woman has said it he has no choice. She moves aside for him to walk in, and for the very first time he enters their home. It has the fragrance of all good homes, the smell of steam and herbs and invisible jasmines, and the faint memory of incense. The smell of moderate people. These are people who do everything that they are supposed to do. It is, in fact, bizarre that they have only one child and not two.

The girl's father stands in the middle of the room, maintaining the impassive stare of disturbed authority. He points to a chair. Then he points a finger at his wife, and she disappears. How easy it is for some men. The man now points Mythili to a chair. As she sits, Ousep's eyes rest on her slender body, and her father's hard face registers a passing moment of defeat.

The man sits on the leather sofa and waits. Nobody utters a word for a while. 'You work at the State Bank?' Ousep asks. The man nods.

'Can I ask your daughter some questions about Unni?' he says. The man nods again.

This is the first time a young girl would tell Ousep her memories of Unni. He had always hoped for this but he does not know what he must ask.

'Mythili, it is strange that I ask you this after three years. You were just a little girl when Unni died, so I could not talk to you then. Do you know why Unni did what he did?'

She looks at the floor and says, 'I don't know.' She is sitting at the edge of the chair, her knees pressed together, her back meek and bent. Her nails are painted in a pale colour that certainly has a name. Her large blue earrings are the two hemispheres of the globe.

'I am sure you have an opinion,' Ousep says. 'It seems everybody has an opinion about what happened. But your view is more important because you and Unni were good friends. You spent a lot of time in our home. He spent a lot of time here.'

'I have no opinions,' she says.

'What kind of a person was he, how do you remember him?'

'He was nice,' she says, and waits for the question to go away. But Ousep waits too. She relents. 'He was not serious about anything. He was full of pranks. He used to do a lot of crazy things.' She lets out a chuckle. Finally, the chuckle of a girl at the memory of Unni. He deserves at least this much.

Does she think of him every day, does his memory make her heart ache? Or is she one of those tough pretty girls who would have no time for dead cartoonists? There is nothing about her, at least from what she has shown, that even hints that she attaches any importance to Unni's memory. But if the boy were alive, would they have been covert lovers talking through signs from their balconies in the middle of the night?

'What crazy things did he do?'

'Just silly things.'

'Like what?'

'He would draw me the way I will look when I am an old woman. Things like that.'

'Did you ever feel he was sad?'

'No.'

'So, why do you think he decided to die?'

'I don't know,' she says, still looking at the floor.

'Were you surprised?'

'Everyone was shocked.'

'Were you surprised?'

'That's what I said.'

'Did you see him the day he died?'

'I don't remember really. It was a long time ago.'

That is odd, for Mythili not to remember if she had seen Unni the day he died. But she was thirteen then. From there, three years is truly a vast expanse of time. Also, why should she lie?

'Can you tell me something about him that was unusual, anything strange that you remember, anything extraordinary?'

'Nothing.'

'Both of you spent so much time together, there must be something you can tell me.'

'I was a little girl then and I spent a lot of time with many people.'

'Did he ever talk to you about a corpse?'

She looks up. She has the large amiable eyes of a good person. 'A corpse?' she asks.

'Yes.'

'No, he never said anything about any corpse.'

Her father stands up, and that ends the interview. Mythili rises and walks out of her house. She is going to the library.

~

MYTHILI BALASUBRAMANIUM KNOWS her mother is watching – from the balcony or through a dark gap in the window curtain or from the other places that mothers find. Daughter has behaved in a suspicious manner all morning. A long shampoo bath followed by a bout of general happiness as evident from the humming of a love song, then the sudden decision to go to the library, allegedly. The girl was about to slink out of the house into the light of day without wearing the shroud of the opaque slip over the cheap native bra. Daughter not embalmed as an Egyptian mummy. Why, Mythili?

'It's too hot.'

'When was it not hot in Madras, Mythili?'

'My top is not transparent. So take it easy.'

'Men have X-ray vision, Mythili.'

Also, the visit of the town alcoholic asking questions about a gorgeous boy has shown the otherwise virginal daughter as a girl who might be acquainted with several gorgeous boys, even live ones. So mother will keep a watch on daughter as far as the eye can see. Is she walking with her head subdued, eyes unseeing, hair still in a ponytail, chest deflated?

It is after Mythili leaves the spinal lane of the colony that she feels her mother's ethereal inspection lifting. It is then that she finds the comfort to release her memories of Unni. She wonders what it is that Mr Ousep Chacko has discovered now, why he has started probing Unni's death all over again.

There are many things she could have told Mr Ousep Chacko about his son. She could have told him that she remembers Unni as if it were yesterday. Unni standing bare chested on the balcony like a tribal prince, his body lean and strong, long severe fingers holding a coffee mug. Unni smiling. Unni carrying his brother on his shoulders and drawing a star on her forehead with a black pen. She sees him clearly, she sees him every day. He is carefully rolling a matchstick over her eyelashes to remove a spore. He is sitting with his legs crossed, head bent, hand moving in swift strokes over a notebook, looking up at her occasionally with a serious face. He is looking into her eyes, about to divine a playing card in her mind. He is sitting on the compound wall, and watching the world go by. He is running in the cyclonic rain, in smooth strides, like a wild beast inside a taut expensive skin.

She sees herself, too, as she was then. She is trying to smile at him without showing her teeth. She is showing off. 'Bonjour, Unni, comment allez-vous?'

She remembers the evening when she is walking in the playground. Unni comes from behind and puts his arm around her shoulder, as he sometimes does. Her hawk mother must have seen it or her hawk friends must have told her. Mother walks in concentric circles all evening in the kitchen until daughter returns home. She says, 'Why are you still wearing frocks, Mythili, like an Anglo-Indian?'

'Girls wear frocks. That's why.'

'Only little girls wear frocks.'

'Is that true?'

'And why was that boy putting his arm around you?'

The next day, Mother starts a conversation purely to find a reason to say, 'Unni is like your brother, he is like the brother you never had, Mythili. What a nice boy even though he has insane parents.' Unni as brother is a repulsive thought for some reason, but Mythili keeps her mouth shut. Finally, one morning, in the middle of chopping tomatoes, Mother tells her what she really wants to say. 'You can't go to that boy's house any more. And I don't want him coming here. People have started talking.'

'What are they saying?'

'Doesn't matter what they are saying, you can't go to his house.'

'Why?'

'He has grown like a mountain.'

'So?'

'You are not a little girl any more, Mythili. A thirteen-year-old girl is a child only to her dumb father. You and I know you are not a child.'

But Mythili defies her. She has sat in the Chacko home almost every day of her life, even before her memories began. She has crawled across the short corridor to their door and wailed until Mariamma appeared. She still remembers the day Thoma was brought home, an infant with the odour of a raw egg. She was four. Unni was eight and he was ecstatic at the idea of owning a baby. 'It's like we have got a new TV. For free.' She has eaten with Unni and Thoma, she has slept there some nights, brushed her teeth with the boys. She has listened to their mother tell them the stories of her village, and even the brief history of the Indian rupee. When Mariamma used to get into one of her moods, and Unni tried to make her laugh, Mythili was part of his plots. She has sat with Mariamma on quiet afternoons and tried to understand why she went nuts sometimes. 'I am only a bit more energetic than other women,' she said once. 'If I was in a country where a woman is allowed to run a mile now and then, I think I would be all right.'

Mariamma used to run, a long time ago, when she was an adolescent. She used to run across hills and river bridges and tiny villages that were silenced by the apparition of a barefooted young girl in full skirt running as if an invisible mob were chasing her. Some days, Mariamma used to hear people say, in a good-natured way, 'Run away if you must, but haven't you left your lover somewhere behind?' or, 'It's all right, if your mama does not want you, we will adopt you'. But, eventually, she had to stop running. People talked. Girls had to walk, apparently, holding colourful umbrellas and handkerchiefs in their fists.

Mythili fought every day with her mother to retain her right to go to that house. It was worth it. So what if Unni was almost a man. She even liked the idea of Unni as a man. She still likes the idea of Unni as a man. Or, maybe, what she really wants to say is that she likes the idea of a man as an artist, a man who is beautiful, who is somewhat unaware that he is beautiful, who smells like ginger on very hot days, and whose conceit is that he would never be afraid.

That is a seventeen-year-old boy next door as remembered by a thirteen-year-old girl. At the heart of her memory of Unni is the stillness of time – he is always seventeen, she is always thirteen. Even though she has known him for most of her life, it is Unni at seventeen, Unni in the final year of his life, that is her central memory of him. The boy before that time was a very similar person, as endearing and important but another person. She does not know why she feels that way. She is not sure whether he changed in the last months of his life, changed physically, became a mountain of a boy as her mother accused. Or was it just that Mythili had newly arrived, as a thirteen-year-old, to the outer edges of womanhood? It could be both. Unni and Mythili had come to their own crossings at the same moment in time.

An enduring memory from this time is of ambiguous innocence – a moment on Pasumarthy Street, where in the mornings there is the confluence of the boys of St Ignatius and the girls of Fatima Convent on their last lap to their schools, and with them a swarm of Romeos – malnourished young men, their groundnut arses in tight jeans, all of them in black sunglasses, all of them clones of film actors, saying things, singing songs, offering eternal love, marriage in faraway temples and exactly two healthy children each.

She has walked with Unni down this road for years. She in white shirt and olive-green skirt, he in white shirt and khaki trousers. In time, as they walked, their bodies slowly grew apart by inches. They have walked holding hands, they have walked with Unni's arm on her shoulder, he has carried her in his arms and run the entire stretch of the road, they have walked without holding hands, and finally they have walked with an arm's length between them, as mandated by her mother.

'My arm or his arm?'

'Shut up, Mythili.'

The moment that endures is from the period when they were separated by the phantom arm. She saw a boy by the wayside, a half-naked labourer digging up the pavement to lay pipes. He was lean and powerful, and she could see the ripple of muscles on his abdomen. She thought what a beautiful sight he was, and she thought, a moment later, he has almost the same body as Unni. That made her feel shy and very aware of Unni, and she felt the stab of a nameless longing, but then the moment passed and she was a child again.

By that time, Unni was some kind of a folk hero on Pasumarthy Street, who caused a small flutter among the olive-green pleated skirts walking to school. Even the Romeos studied him through long unhappy drags on their cigarettes. One day a Romeo stared hard at him and said, 'Hero, come here, hero, I want to talk to you.' That made Mythili laugh. 'He just Eve-teased you, Unni,' she said. And Unni laughed so hard, it made her proud. It was the first time she had made him laugh through her own joke.

The seniors in her school began to draw her into quiet corners to ask questions about him, his postal address, his telephone number, the character of his mother. Mythili scrutinised the seniors carefully because if he must have a girlfriend it had to be a girl she approved of. She was unhelpful to the fat excited ones with moustaches, and more generous with the pretty modern girls whose skirts were two inches shorter than the school average. They called him 'cartoonist hottie'.

Mythili is in the Reading Circle Lending Library. She checks the spines of the books on the shelf but what she is thinking is that Unni used to have an account here. She wonders whether there is a register somewhere in the drawers that still bears his name, she wonders what the last book he borrowed was. Did he return it?

She disliked what he read. She used to see the pile of books on his desk and feel repulsed. He never read fiction, never read anything that people generally read. He read a lot about the brain – not just the human brain, all kinds of brains. Even about the future of the brain. His books were a part of his life she did not know much about, the only part of his life that she thought was boring and dreary.

'What is it that you're reading, Unni?'

'This.'

'*Folie-à-deux* by Philippe Boulleau?'

'That's correct.'

'*Vous lisez* Folie-à-deux *par Philippe Boulleau?*'

'*Oui.*'

'It sounds like a French book, Unni.'

'I can't read French, Mythili. It's in English.'

'I know. But what does *Folie-à-deux* mean?'

'The Folly of Two.'

'And what does that mean?'

'It is a neuropsychiatric phenomenon.'

'You look funny when you use big words, Unni.'

'Neuropsychiatric phenomenon.'

'But what does it mean?'

'A mad person transfers his delusion to another person, and both of them begin to see the same delusion. And they mutually corroborate what they see is true. That is the Folly of Two.'

'Do you think that is really possible?'

'All around you, Mythili, is the Folly of Two.'

'"Folie-à-deux." I don't like this word.'

'I was thinking, Mythili. All those syllables at the end of French words, all those syllables that are wasted because they are not pronounced by the French, where do they go?'

'Where do they go, Unni?'

'They join the underground Union of Insulted French Syllables.'

'Really?'

'Yes.'

'What does the underground union do?'

'The syllables try to influence mankind. Over centuries, over vast ages, they try to influence man. They give humans ideas, thoughts, doubts, eureka moments. All this to help man create something, a machine probably, that would have such a name, such a word that all the syllables in the Union of Insulted French Syllables would be included and pronounced. Humans think all of science is their creation, but no, Mythili. The insulted French syllables are the ones who are giving us those ideas.'

'You are mad, Unni.'

'The leader of the union is X.'

'X?'

'Yes, the most humiliated letter in French even today. There was a time when nobody in France used to pronounce it. Don't laugh at X, Mythili. He waited for centuries and patiently fed ideas across many generations. And finally mankind discovered the X-ray. Now the French have to pronounce X. They have no choice.'

'You're mad, Unni.'

'What if I am not?'

When she leaves the library she tells herself that she will go home but she knows where she is going. She walks down the school lane, which is quiet today because of the weekend, turns right towards the church and heads to the churchyard that lies in the scented shade of eucalyptus trees. Nothing unusual about a decent Brahmin girl walking down a narrow path through a pretty ancient Christian graveyard. Nothing odd about the girl casting a glance at one grey tombstone, and nothing wrong at all if she clears a speck of dirt from her eyes.

The afternoon he did what he did, she was having a shower. She heard the faint murmurs of people, then the yells and screams. She turned off the shower and listened to the sounds more carefully. She heard snatches of what people were trying to say, and she began to shiver. She put on her clothes and ran to the front balcony, and she saw Unni lying in a small pool of blood, his eyes shut. Unni, what an idiot you turned out to be.'

3

The Album of the Dead

MARIAMMA CHACKO IN the mornings is a faction of sounds – of furious water colliding with stainless steel, the rain of spoons, the many omens of steam, and the murmur of the huge boulder mortar in which she annihilates grains with inhuman strength. In between, there are satanic whispers about his mother and thick motiveless footsteps outside his door, and sweet lullabies from another time. But it is Sunday morning and the house is in the stunned peace of her absence. She is in the church, her head probably tilted, pious eyes looking up, knees on thin rubber slippers. Or, maybe, she has finally found a way to desert him. Ousep would soon know. At the moment, though, he does not care where she is and only hopes she does not return any time soon. Unni's cartoons are scattered on his desk. In the thick mist of smoke, with two forgotten cigarettes in his fingers, he stares hard at one particular work, a rare single-panel cartoon.

It is a scene in the confession box. A girl in a white dress is on her knees, her palms joined and her head bent. On the other side of the net partition is a sly priest, who is enjoying her confession, as evident from a remarkable bump in his crotch. As always in Unni's works, the characters are carefully drawn, they are very real. So, the aspiration of the cartoon to be a farce fails, defeated by the potent body of the adolescent girl. A girl on her knees, her high heels removed and placed by her side, healthy legs bare, a girl humbled, revealing her secrets, seeking pardon from a man, asking to be punished. Did Unni, too, see her this way? Are sons and fathers stirred by the same thoughts?

The cartoon is part of a series that Unni created in a few intense weeks, probably when he was sixteen. In this period he started going to church. He would sit in the last pew for hours, absolutely still. Some people saw him draw, but mostly he did nothing. His unnatural stillness comes up often in the interviews, though Ousep himself had never noticed that about the boy.

Unni was probably not interested in sketching the giant stained-glass windows or the arches, or the high yellow spire, which is visible from Ousep's desk. The spire does figure in a cartoon, but as a faint rudimentary backdrop. The focus of the scene is an electric wire where nine crows are sitting in line as crows do, their heads turned towards a luminous white dove that is sitting isolated at a distance on the same wire, with an olive branch in its beak. One of the crows is whispering to another crow, 'Kalia has converted.'

Among the other cartoons that were inspired by the church, there is a full-length portrait of a young man standing in the aisle. He is in an extravagant shirt with large flowers on it, and his black trousers have the glow of leather. He is dashing, but looks stiff and uncomfortable. His left cheek is fully puffed. Unni had told a friend that boys from the slums came in their best clothes for the Sunday mass, and they stood in a self-conscious way in the suspicion of their own good looks, rubbing their noses, constantly touching the sleeves and collars of their shirts, and puffing a cheek involuntarily. Some of them used to have their sunglasses on during mass until the parish priest banned them, making an exception only for those who were blind beyond reasonable doubt.

Around this time, a span of about two months according to some accounts, Unni developed an interest in the dead. He had a network of informers who contacted him the moment they got wind of a funeral mass. He would rush to the church, stand near the coffin, and stare at the corpse as the mourners in the pews behind him probably asked each other who the boy was. It was an uncharacteristically conspicuous thing for him to do, and it is not surprising that several people remember seeing his lone figure peering into a coffin. At least once he took his notebook out and attempted to draw the face of the corpse – in that case, an old lady in thick spectacles. A mourner went up to him and asked him to stop. Unni continued to sketch; soon other mourners joined the quarrel, and the priest had to interrupt the service to ask him to get out.

Seeing corpses in their coffins probably inspired his longest work, *The Album of the Dead*. As it progressed he showed it to several friends, who were disturbed by his idea of humour. In the *Album*, he imagined family, friends and other familiar people dead in their coffins.

Every person has a whole vertical page, and there are thirty-two caricatures in all, including a self-portrait. *The Album of the Dead* is his only comic that has been granted its own exclusive book. The portraits occupy only one half of the book; the other half is blank. He planned it as a continuing series that would keep growing as newer people came his way. He even wished to draw some of the people again as they slowly aged. He wanted to frame the passage of time inside unchanging coffins. If he had lived long, as he once certainly hoped, *The Album of the Dead* would have been an enormous work contained in several books.

It begins with his mother, drawn with son's bias. It is a top-angle scene, like the other caricatures. She is lying peacefully in a black coffin, a bit thinner than she is in reality. Her arms are folded over her stomach. There is a solemn dignity about her, which is how everybody is portrayed, except Ousep. He does not emerge very well from his caricature. He is lying in his coffin with his hands and legs hanging out of the box. He is bare chested, and below the waist he is covered by a lungi instead of a white shroud. His left hand is connected to an intravenous fluid system that stands near the coffin. The fluid is in the unmistakable golden bottle of Honeydew Rum.

The humour of the *Album* lies in its entirety, in seeing page after page of people lying in their black diamond coffins. But not everyone found it funny.

Mariamma had seen her portrait soon after Unni had finished it, and she was hurt. She said no son in the world would draw his own mother in a coffin, especially when she was alive. Ousep remembers hearing fragments of the fuss one morning. Long ago, it seems. How would she react if she knew what Unni had told a friend about her? He had told the friend, in the middle of pumping air into a cycle tyre, that if his mother died the same evening he would not be affected. 'I will have no problem using her skull as a pen-holder,' he said. He surely did not mean it. He was probably trying to make a larger point by using the skull of the person he loved the most as an example, but the friend remembered the incident through moral outrage.

'He was a good person, Unni was a good person, but some of the things he said were horrible. His own mother, the skull of his own mother. A pen-holder?'

'Did he imagine her skull as anything else? Or was it only as a pen-holder?'

'No. Only a pen-holder.'

'Are you sure about that? Did he say "pencil-holder" or "pen-holder"?'

'Pen-holder.'

Thoma must have been eight when he was included in the album. He occupies less than half of the coffin. His hair is combed, and his face has an angelic radiance, which he does not possess in reality. Ousep accepts the general hilarity of *The Album of the Dead*, but not of Thoma this way. He feels the fear of losing this one too. When boys want to jump head first, who can stop them?

The others in the *Album* are Mythili from a different time, Somen Pillai, Sai Shankaran, and many of Unni's friends, teachers and neighbours, including Mythili's parents. There are four unidentified people, including a dignified old man who really does look dead. None of Unni's friends have been able to identify these four.

It is a melodramatic coincidence that the final cartoon in the series is the self-portrait – Unni in his casket. And it is natural for his mother to wonder whether this was her deserved suicide note. Did the boy draw himself in the coffin the day he went to the terrace to jump? Is there a message here, a clue that has to be cracked? It is a reasonable thought, but Unni's friends remember seeing the self-portrait months before he died, they are very sure.

Ousep, his chin resting on a palm, looks with affection at the portrait, which has acquired an aching sweetness about it. Unni, with his enormous head and high mop of hair, a clear handsome face, and the austere body of a rustic. This was how he had looked when he was taken to the church in a plywood coffin.

She has not returned yet, though it is time. What if she never returns, what if she has somehow found a way to desert him? But that is unlikely. Where will she go? Everybody wants to flee, but for Mariamma to flee her home, a lot must happen.

First, some socialists have to die. And the nation that they destroyed has to go to the very brink with all its reserve dollars slowly vanishing, a slide that has already begun. With no money left for imports, the government would do what Mariamma has done all her life. Pawn gold to buy oil. The surrender of gold would be a humiliation the whole nation would understand and the new young men would then craftily use the moment of collective shame to convince the old obsolete men that they have no choice but to open up the Indian market to foreign companies. In the liberation that would ensue, Thoma would have to play his cards right. Then he could take his mother somewhere far away and put her in a beautiful new house. For a woman to flee, a lot must happen.

So, in all probability, she is still in the church, together with the maids, the dandy slum boys and the other new converts who attend the Tamil mass. She prefers the English mass, but she feels too small when she stands among the rich. They in their sparkling ironed clothes and happy fragrances, and she in a tired old sari and rubber slippers. After mass, she will go to the confession box to perplex the priest once again by refusing to tell him her sins, demanding instead that she be handed the penance anyway. She will correct him if the punishment is too harsh or too mild, and help him arrive at the correct number of prayers she must utter. It was Unni who had discovered this about his mother. The undercover misanthrope could somehow charm the most insignificant information from the hearts of people. He would have probably solved his own death in no time.

Ousep shuts the *Album* more violently than he intended and puts it on top of the pile of cartoons on his desk. He stares without hope at the haphazard array of lampoons that grudgingly tells the story of a boy. He considers getting the other works from the wooden trunk and going through all of them one more time. He may spot something, a simple clue that was always in plain sight. Are not mysteries solved this way, through a moment of accidental discovery? No one ever solves a riddle by thinking too hard about it.

He opens the back panel of the radio and extracts the pages of *How To Name It*. He goes through the pages, not sure what he is searching for. The familiar scenes pass – the tough rustic man on a rubber farm who begins to run for his life, the journey of the mysterious narrator, the amiable middle-aged woman, the giant bra as suspension bridge over a river, the walk through the woman's house, the rustic man now raising his thumb in triumph, and finally Mariamma Chacko in tumult, standing on the wooden stand, like a trophy, looking up and wagging a finger, her leg raised in a valiant leap.

Ousep goes through the comic again, then again, as he has

done a thousand times. He stops on every page and tries to piece together the story. Most of the panels in the comic have blank spaces at the top, probably for the narration. The dialogue bubbles, when they appear, are all of the same size. Did Unni imagine that every piece of dialogue was going to be of the same length? And why are they blank? The same questions, every moment of Ousep's life.

According to Mariamma, the fact that her son did not leave a note behind for her is a significant decision, even a vital clue. Ousep takes her far more seriously than she imagines. So, he wonders once again, can it be true? Does the absence of an explanation contain within its baffling emptiness a simple message that Unni presumed his parents would be smart enough to see?

$\sim$

THOMA CHACKO STANDS naked in the bathroom and asks himself whether he will remember this moment for ever. Many years later, will he remember this Sunday evening when he was filling a bucket with water? Will he look back across a whole lifetime one day and say to the boy he once was, 'Yes, I remember the moment. You were shorter than the fridge those days. It was a blue bucket, wasn't it? And, Thoma, by the way, if you want to know. You made it, Thoma, you made it. You're very famous and reasonably rich.'

The bucket is overflowing but he does not want to turn the tap off. He likes the roar of water, its ominous terror. In the bucket is the sea, about four kilometres deep. He stirs the water with his hand and makes a furious whirlpool, which leaves a calm eye at its heart. Thoma imagines he is in the eye of a giant ocean whirlpool. Ships and whales, mere specks on the enormous swirling wall of water, orbit him. He feels a deep fear in his stomach and screams.

But what is more terrifying than a whirlpool is a giant wave. Unni said that a powerful earthquake beneath the sea can create a sudden ocean wave one kilometre high. It can appear any time on the horizon. That is why Thoma sometimes looks carefully over the coconut trees and the building tops or as far as the eye can see. Such a wave would exterminate the entire human population. Millions of years later new humans might rise and they might build a new world that would look very different from everything Thoma knows. But the pass mark in science and maths would still be thirty-five per cent. That is what Unni said. It astonishes Thoma, that the human race will always arrive at a cut-off score that he can just about achieve. Unni said that there are many such things in the Universe that nobody can fully explain. For example, even though the sun is many times larger than the moon, they look the same size in the sky. How miraculous it is for a planet to be in a position in space where its sun and its moon appear to have the same size. 'Is there a reason, Thoma?' Unni would whisper, as if he knew the reason.

Thoma looks nervously at the bathroom window; through the iron bars he sees apartment blocks and the tops of independent homes and a distant forest of coconut trees. He looks carefully at the arc of land's end. He has seen something; it seems the horizon has risen, a giant blue mist is approaching. The Bay of Bengal is coming. He screams, jumps into his underwear, remembering through an inescapable moment that it was once his father's shirt. And he runs out of the bathroom. In the hallway he is stabbed by an old fear. Is he like his mother? Will he, too, go through life seeing great spectacles that others cannot see, will he live in the sorrows of the past, will he go through life talking to himself, crying and laughing, calling out the full Christian names of his relatives and asking them the same questions for ever? He can hear his mother in the kitchen, her voice is rising, and her words are beginning to tremble.

He stands in the kitchen doorway and looks as Unni used to. 'Annamol Chacko,' she tells the exhaust fan. 'You and your nine daughters come to visit your son, Ousep, when we are living in Kottayam. I am eight months pregnant with Unni.

Still I make tea for all of you. And you say I am too learned to make good tea. And all of you laugh.'

Thoma has never understood why this moment means so much to his mother. Criticism of tea is hardly a matter that should affect a clever woman like her. But Unni did tell him one day that in the words of some women there is great injustice that only other women can decipher. 'It is not about the tea, Thoma, it is never about the tea.'

Thoma has a hazy memory of his grandmother, who used to visit every summer. He remembers her as a tiny woman with the face of a pony and cruel eyes that had an opinion about all that they saw. And she was usually in a white blouse, shrouded in an expensive white cloth that had a cross pinned on it. Below the waist she was bound tightly by another white cloth that was bunched behind her like a bird's tail. 'Like a hand fan to cool her arse,' Unni said. She used to come by the night train from the village with her silent husband, who carried on his shoulders at least two jackfruits and all the fearless flies of Kerala. For some reason, she always walked ahead of him.

Unni said that their mother's enemy was their enemy, so Thoma decided to hate his grandmother, even though she appeared to love him very much. There was a reason why it was easy for Thoma to dislike her. In the first few minutes of her arrival, Mariamma would cane Thoma's legs for no good reason, then take him inside to kiss him and say she was sorry. She never hit Unni, probably because he was one of those people nobody wants to hit, or maybe she treated him differently because he was older than Thoma. Though, sometimes, she did chase Unni with a broom in her hand, both of them laughing. It disappointed Thoma that his mother, who was usually very kind, would behave in this puzzling manner with him every time Grandmother visited. But Unni told him one day that it was a Village Tradition. One way of insulting the mother-in-law was to beat up your kids in front of her. He was probably right because Annamol was deeply affected by the caning and it could not have been out of love for him. She would look sadly at the floor and weep with an occasional shiver of her nostrils.

Thoma is amazed at the telepathy of women. How miraculous it is for one woman to do something weird and another woman to extract its intended meaning. One morning, his mother told him, 'Thoma, when I am old I'll go to an old-age home so that I am not a burden on you.' Thoma could not understand why she was saying this when there was a lot of time to decide the matter. But then Unni told him, 'That message was not for you, Thoma. It was meant for Annamol Chacko. Mother is hinting to the old woman that she is a bloody nuisance.'

Thoma is a glad he is not a woman. He is not good at deciphering clues and if he were a woman he would go through his entire life missing all the insults hurled at him by other women. Which is not such a bad way to be, when you think of it.

Despite everything, Annamol continued to visit every summer of Thoma's life, until he was seven. He would always remember the dawn when he woke up to her terrifying screams. She was in the bathroom by the time Thoma arrived but the door was not locked. He opened the door nervously and the sight of an old woman wailing at the mirror was so terrifying that at first he did not see what was wrong with her. Then he realised that most of her hair was gone. Someone had cut her long silver hair when she was sleeping. The whole day she sat in a corner, her head covered, looking wicked, holding her broken hair in her fist. Father was not in town that day. He was in Sriharikota to report the launch of an Indian rocket. Mother was silent that day, but not unhappy. Finally, Annamol told her husband, 'I want to leave.'

The old man was sitting cross-legged in just his underwear, a lit cigarette in his hand, elbows resting on his thighs, and his whole body glistening with his own sweat.

'I want to leave,' she said again.

'India is about to launch a rocket,' he said.

'That's all very nice, but Annamol is happy to take a train,' she said.

'You don't understand, woman, the government says that people should remain indoors because the rocket can fall anywhere.'

So Annamol left in the night, after the newsreader announced that the rocket had fallen safely into the sea. When she was at the door she raised a hand and flung a fistful of air at Mariamma. 'I curse you,' she said. 'As I cry, so shall you.' Mariamma looked up at the ceiling and mumbled a Hail Mary. Grandmother stared hard and she said in a whisper that had the hiss of a snake, 'Mary can't save you. Just because men like virgins, it does not make them gods.'

Mariamma looked at the ceiling again and she whispered, 'My Lord, my God, there are Protestants among us, it seems, forgive them their sins.'

Thoma has not seen his grandmother since. She was not present at Unni's funeral. None of the relatives had come. The funeral was a day after he died; there was not enough time for people to come from Kerala.

Thoma wonders whether on a vast field far away Annamol wags a finger at a jackfruit tree and accuses his mother of cutting her hair. Grandmother probably still does not know the truth.

It was Unni who had cut her hair. He was just fifteen then but he was brave, he was always brave. The night Annamol left, he said with terrifying hatred in his eyes, 'Justice for our mother, Thoma. The worst thing that can happen to a person is a tragedy that is also funny. And that has happened to Grandmother.'

Every time Mariamma spoke to the walls, Unni used to listen very carefully, usually standing out of sight, staring at the floor, hands on his hips. When Thoma came to him to chat, Unni would raise a finger asking him to shut up. It was very important to Unni that he heard every word that she uttered. It was as if he were trying to piece together a riddle from the strands of her many conversations with herself. Some days, when Mother seemed particularly disturbed, he would go to her and crack a joke about the way she was or stand beside her and imitate her perfectly. Or he would make her tell him the family stories that lurked behind every grouse, and she would become very happy as she told him her stories. Sometimes she would laugh in the middle of her tales and say, 'You are like a daughter, Unni.'

He once pointed out a fact that Thoma might not have figured out on his own. It might appear that their mother's grouses were endless and the persons who once harmed her numerous but the truth was that there were not more than a dozen names she uttered, and against every name she repeated the same set of two or three incidents. It comforts Thoma, that there are not too many bad things that happened to his mother when she was young. And that if you had the time to do the maths you could actually arrive at the exact number of grouses she has. He hopes there is a way he can calm her for ever and make her a woman, like any other woman, who does not talk to the walls.

Mariamma is bit louder than usual right now and he knows that everybody on the floor and even below can hear her. At some point, as always, she catches him looking at her. She wipes her tears with his fingers and lets out an embarrassed chuckle. Swings her arms in the air like a wrestler before a bout, and says, 'I was just exercising, Thoma. Don't worry. I'm just letting off some steam.' She begins to march like a soldier now, swinging her arms. 'Left, right, left, right,' she says, trying to make him laugh. She gives up, leans against the kitchen counter, and smiles in an ingratiating way. She probably wants him to leave so that she can let off more steam. Thoma decides to make her laugh. He feels a cold fear in his throat because what he is about to do is risky. He has never tried this before, though he has thought of it many times.

'Jesus is sitting with his disciples for the Last Supper,' he says.

'What did you say, Thoma?'

'There is a really foul smell in the air. Jesus looks a bit worried. He says, "Tonight one of you will betray me."'

Mariamma searches for something on the floor. Thoma is surprised that his mother has lost interest in his joke so fast.

'Judas gets up holding his nose and says, "It was Jesus, it was Jesus."'

Mariamma finds the broom in a crevice above the gas cylinder.

'You didn't get it?' he says. 'It was Jesus who had farted and Judas betrayed him.'

'I got that much, you little rat,' Mariamma says, and charges at him with the broom.

He flees, wondering why the joke sounded so funny when Unni used to tell it. Mariamma runs behind him, screaming, 'That's all this house needs, another God-abusing fool.'

Thoma runs to the bathroom and shuts the door. He screams from inside, 'I was only trying to make you laugh.'

'I don't need help to laugh, I don't need help to cry. Don't you know that?'

'I won't try again.'

'Open the door.'

'No.'

'I have put the broom down.'

'No.'

'What you should be doing, Thoma, is having your books in front of you. We have to do something about your marks.'

'I pass in all the subjects all the time, don't I.'

'That's not enough, Thoma. That's not enough. You have to score in the late nineties. Otherwise there is no hope for a boy in this country. I ask you again, do you want to become a writer?'

'No.'

'Then what do we do about your marks, Thoma? I can't afford tuition. I can teach you but I am not good at teaching kids.'

'I don't understand anything when you teach me.'

'So what do we do about you, Thoma? Come out, first.'

'I will work hard. Don't worry.'

'I was thinking, Thoma. Maybe we should ask Mythili again.'

'Don't do that. She has not come here since Unni did what he did. She has become like the other people. She does not like us any more.'

'Don't say that. Nobody dislikes us.'

From the way her last sentence ends Thoma realises that she is probably crying. He begins to cry, too. Both of them stand on either side of the shut bathroom door and cry as silently as they can.

'Why did Unni do it?' he asks. 'Of all the people in the world, Unni.'

'That's what even I ask myself every single moment of my life. Of all the people in the world, Unni.'

Thoma opens the door and steps out. He wants to stand next to his mother and hug her with one hand, without feeling her breasts, the way Unni used to hug her. But then Unni was tall and strong. He would hug her with one hand and lift her off the ground.

'Don't cry,' he says.

'You don't cry,' she says.

'I've stopped.'

'Then I've stopped, too.'

'What is it that Father has found? People say he has found something about Unni. He is meeting Unni's old friends again.'

'I've heard,' Mariamma says. 'But your father is not telling me anything yet.'

'Why isn't he telling us?'

'He is not telling anyone what he has found, that's my guess.'

'Why, do you think?'

'I don't know. But sooner or later he has to tell me. Your father wants to tell me. He is just waiting for the right time.'

'You really don't know why Unni did what he did?'

'I don't know, Thoma. I don't know what got into Unni that day.'

'People say he had a lot of sorrow in his heart.'

'We know that's not true.'

'Will I become like him? Will I decide to jump off one day?'

'Don't talk like that, Thoma. Have you ever felt like doing something like that?'

'No.'

'Tell me the truth.'

'I am telling you the truth.'

'Now don't think about all this. These are not happy thoughts.'

~

THE DAY HER son died she was woken up at dawn by a dream. She does not have the gift of reading meanings in her dreams but she believes it was an omen. At least that much respect she expects from the supernatural. What she had seen was a memory from her childhood, an uncorrupted memory without any magic or the other inventions of sleep. An old wound that does not have a clear perpetrator, like the other wounds of childhood.

She was twelve years old when it happened. She was sitting in a coracle with her mother, both of them looking away from the potent groin of a man in a loincloth who was rowing the boat. She remembers the man only as a pair of powerful dark legs; from the waist up he was merely sky. The stretch of the river was wide. It was calm and forbidding, and the air was still. She wanted her mother to speak, say something loving or even ordinary because of what had happened earlier in the day, but this was not a woman who talked to her children unless it was essential. She was a farmer not given to small talk, who managed a vast land almost by herself because her husband was a good-natured simpleton whom everybody tried to fool. So she was the one who walked among the bleeding rubber trees and monster rocks, heckling labourers, murdering serpents, and some days driving away sand poachers by raising a sudden army of young men. But she did not speak much to her children, daughters especially.

Mariamma was being returned to her foster home down-stream, to the ancient blue house of her mother's sister. She was only two when she was donated to the aunt because her mother had eleven other children to feed. Mariamma was the youngest, and by the time she had arrived her mother had probably grown tired of pretending to love so many. Mariamma visited her mother once every two months. She was happiest when she was with her, and every time she had to leave, as she walked down the hill to the banks of the river and sat in the coracle that would take her to her guardians, she was miserable.

The bank approached, and behind the raised coconut grove the tiled roof of her foster home was now visible. The boat headed towards the high stone wall, startled as always by the submerged rocks. It stopped a few metres from the steep flight of red stone steps that led up to the rear of the house. She struggled to get out of the boat. The black legs, they might have had hands too, but they were not allowed to touch her. She waded through the water with footwear in hand, and jumped on to the foot of the moist steps. When she turned to look at her mother, the boat had already left with her. Mariamma waited; she hoped her mother would turn back at least once to look. She stood there as the boat slowly floated away so far across the river that a human face had no meaning.

A girl waiting on moist stone for her mother to look back just once — that had happened many times. But what she saw in her dream was a particular day. How could her mother not turn back and look, just look, on a day like that? Some things that even good people did were beyond comprehension. That was the thought in her head when she rose that dawn. But how foolish she was to think that was sorrow. In a few hours she would know what grief really was. Unni would be dead, and the next day she would see him lowered into a hole. And watch without anger as two labourers chatted among themselves while they shoved fresh soil on his coffin. And she would walk back home feeling strangely empty handed. That is what she remembers the most about the evening – a feeling that her hands were empty.

But, on the last morning of Unni's short life, her grouses against her mother seemed very large to her. She stood in the kitchen, thinking, triumphantly, how different she was from her mother, how much she loved her own children, and how fierce her love was. She would never abandon them. That was a right only children had. When she crossed the main roads with them she always held their hands tight and sprinted. Unni would burst out laughing. He was almost a man but he would let her hold his hand and run across the road. He was never embarrassed. That was another odd thing about Unni. His lack of shame. He was not ashamed of his home, of his mother. If he had been ashamed she would have forgiven him, but he was not.

As she was standing there in the kitchen, she might have said something aloud, though she does not remember what she might have said. The voice of Unni made her jump. He looked at the wall and muttered something to it, wagged a finger at the ceiling and whispered, 'Mother, you abandoned me, Mother. Mrs Leelama John of Baptist lineage, you abandoned me.' He imitated her so well; the tilt of his face, the pout of his lips, the shudder in his voice were all perfect. How could she not laugh?

He must have been lurking around the doorway as he usually did, waiting patiently to hear everything she said, everything she did. He had been working through the night on a comic, he said. He had almost finished it but he was not getting something right. He asked her to pose for him, he wanted her to stand in her furious way, her sari hitched up, her face breaking into a menacing scowl and a finger pointed upwards.

'Are you drawing me?'

'Don't ask questions early in the morning. Just stand that way for thirty seconds. That's all. I need to just look.'

'I've better things to do, Unni.'

'Just twenty seconds.'

She tried to stand the way he wanted but she would start giggling.

'I can't do it, Unni. I find it ridiculous,' she said.

'Just ten seconds.'

'You can't make fun of me this way. It is not funny beyond a point.'

'I am not making fun of you. Trust me.'

'I am not doing this, Unni.'

He held her hand in his and studied her fingers. 'Do you like your fingers?' he said.

'I think they are pretty. As good as yours.'

'I have good fingers?'

'Yes you do. They are long and strong and one can trust them.'

'I wonder why fingers are so hard to draw,' he said. 'So tough, so tough.'

'That's because you don't really believe they are important. That's why you can't get them right.'

He looked at her with his narrow teasing eyes, in son's condescension. Then he went away to his room without a word. That was the last time they ever spoke. Two hours later, when she left for mass, he was still at his table. She thought what a beautiful sight he was, how calming it was to see a creature so young and gentle and clever. He did not have the quick movements of the other adolescents. Even when he was not working, he could sit still for hours. That is how she remembers him – through his paranormal stillness.

She wanders around her home remembering that morning once again, and the last time she had seen the force of life in her child. Whatever it was that Unni was drawing, it has gone missing. She has searched the house a thousand times, and she probably searches for it every day without realising that she is looking. Her search is always futile but it yields many other things – small photographs of serious people she does not know, several buttons, letters to her family on the giant hill that she had not posted for some reason, and the replies that came anyway, several little keys.

She has asked Ousep on several occasions what has happened to make him start looking for clues again. He never answers. It is to get him to talk that she finally told him one morning, two weeks ago, 'The day Unni did what he did, he was working on a comic. I know that, I saw him. He was up all night trying to finish it. But what he was working on is missing. I know it is there somewhere in this world, but it is not in this house.'

Ousep looked at her with interest, which is rare when he is sober, but he left for work without a word. Two hours later he called on the phone and asked her an odd question. 'Do you know if Unni had finished the comic? You said he was working on the comic, but do you know if he had finished it?'

'There is no rice in the house,' she said. 'There is no oil. There are no vegetables. Not one onion.'

She heard him exhale. 'Woman,' he said, and let out more air. 'Did Unni finish the comic or did he plan to finish it later?'

'I can't go to the store any more,' she said. 'The man in the store is a good Christian. He is a convert but he is a good man. But even a good Christian cannot do charity beyond a point. We owe him too much money, he is not going to give us even a single grain until we pay at least a bit of the outstanding.'

Ousep was probably in his office, so he whispered, 'You are a horrible woman.'

'What does it matter if Unni had finished the comic?' she said.

'Just answer my question.'

'I don't know,' she said. 'But in a way, that comic has ended, hasn't it?'

~

IT IS A hot morning, and the day is lit as if it is the afterlife; faraway windows and the metal poles of bus stops glow. Ousep's walk is brisk, even fast, but then he stops. He would always remember this moment, its stab of cold fear. He realises that he does not know where he is going. There is no appointment, there is nowhere to go. He has been walking for over an hour imagining a meeting with a newly discovered acquaintance of Unni. He knows the acquaintance, the face is clear in his head. But the young man does not exist. Ousep does not remember how he ended up on this road. He was thinking about Unni, and somewhere along the way he had started imagining an amiable person waiting to tell him something more about Unni. It is not the delusion alone that scares Ousep. It is the final realisation that he has probably met all the people who knew the boy. He has met many of them at least twice. There is none left to be interviewed, except Somen Pillai, whose importance anyway rests purely on his unavailability. That is how small the life of an adolescent is. A persistent father can get to all of them. What must he do now? Where was he going so fast, what was he thinking? A man who does not know where he is going, what kind of a man is that?

Ousep goes to a bus stop, sits on the aluminium bench. He does not know how it happens, he begins to cry, pressing his wrists to his eyes. Why, Unni? Strangers look at him far longer and more intently than they do when he walks drunk on the road and stops the Madras traffic. He thinks of the time when Unni was an infant and he used to look up at his father and extend his arms. But Ousep never carried him. They would stare at each other in silence and unequal love.

What is Ousep searching for? An honourable reason for Unni's death, a happy reason? The truth?

He realises that there is someone standing by his side. A scrawny man with a file under his arm is holding out a bottle of cold soda. 'Take it, sir,' the man says. The marble-bottle soda, the panacea of Madras for people hit by trucks, stunned by sunstroke, for men who are having an epileptic fit on the road, and even for the dead. It is a bottle that reminds the fallen that something bad has happened to them. Ousep Chacko, finally, a recipient of the soda.

But by the evening he has recovered. His lungs are clear and his eyes clean. He is even happy, and somewhat ashamed of his ordinary everyday happiness, as if fathers of dead sons do not have that crass right.

With nowhere to look, Ousep abandons his investigation as he has done many times before, and sinks into the banalities of city reporting. He eats with apprentice politicians, whispers with disgruntled bureacrats, drinks with cops and friends. He fills his days with work he need not do. He visits crime scenes, covers interminable second-rung cricket matches, attends the lectures of space scientists, who never tuck their shirts into their trousers. He even goes to Koovagam to cover the annual festival of amiable eunuchs. They come in thousands as spectacular brides in glittering saris, stand in long queues to get married to a minor god, offer free or discounted sex all through the wedding night to the hordes of desperate men who have come to stand in for the divine groom. Next morning, the joyous brides become wailing widows in white saris, who break their bangles and pray with eyes shut tight that in their next lives they are born as complete women. But even they are happy, Ousep can tell, they are much happier than people imagine. Everybody is happy, Unni, everybody is fine.

At the Chief Minister's press conference, Ousep asks, out of boredom and disrespect, 'Are you happy?' The Chief Minister, a frail poet who never suffered the indignity of being young, a man with two living wives and several worthless squabbling sons, is puzzled only for a moment. 'Yes, Ousep, I am happy that the Indian government has ceased all military activities in Sri Lanka and that we are not at war with our own Tamil brothers.'

Ousep begins to spend more time with his friends, sitting with them in the cheap bars long after midnight, and together they sing about their own obsolescence, and the approaching end of a type of man, a type of alcoholic male writer. 'We are the last of the real men, the kings of our times. And our stories will never be told.'

But, despite his best efforts, despite doing all that he can to clog his time with mindless things, one morning he walks to the Liberty bus stop to confront Sai Shankaran again. There is something this bastard is not telling, and Ousep wants to break him.

As always, Sai pretends that he has not seen him, but his unhappy face grows tense. Ousep stands with him. For some reason there are more people than usual at the bus stop this morning and they are a small crowd that has spilled on to the road. A yellow autorickshaw skids to a halt in front of the bus stop. The driver searches the crowd without conviction for someone who may want to sit in his auto. His eyes fall on a striking young girl in a dark green half-sari, her oiled hair braided, standing at the front of the crowd and waiting meekly for her bus. The auto driver stares at her breasts and smiles, and slowly squeezes the airhorn, and laughs. She hugs her books to her chest and looks away with a quick turn of her head, like a sparrow, exactly the way Sai looks away every time he sees Ousep. The auto leaves with a laughing man.

'Have you made up your mind, Sai?' Ousep asks. The same pointless question. Sai takes a deep breath. As expected, he does not say anything. He looks into the distance. 'Sai, there is something you are not telling me. I know that.'

Ousep takes the folded pages of *How To Name It* from his trouser pocket and gives it to Sai, but the boy does not accept it. So Ousep unfolds the pages and holds them to Sai's face. 'This was Unni's final comic. Does this make any sense to you?' he says. Sai's large obtuse eyes stay on the comic for a moment but he does not react.

Ousep stalks him every day, boards the bus with him, stands close to him all the way to Loyola College. When Sai returns from college Ousep walks him home. But the whole time Sai maintains his unhappy silence. On the evening of the eighth day of the relentless stalking there is, finally, a scene.

Ousep is walking a foot behind the boy. Sai is going home. He has the walk of a slow cattle. One of those people whose feet are pointed outwards when they land on the ground, and there is something barefooted about him even though he wears shoes.

Sai stops walking, and pants heavily. He has had enough, which makes Ousep glad. 'Look,' the boy screams, 'there is nothing I have to say. Nothing. You have to believe me. Unni died because he was sad. There is no deeper reason. If there is a reason, you are the reason. Think about it. There is no food in his house most days. His mother begs for money from everyone. The only reason Unni made friends was to eat in their homes. His whole schooling was sponsored by the church. His mother is a nut, and his father is an alcoholic who makes an ass of himself every night. And on top of all this Unni was not very good in MPC. He had a useless talent, which was to draw cartoons which were not so funny actually.'

'What is MPC?'

'Maths-Physics-Chemistry.'

'I see.'

'He had no future, he had no hope. So he jumped. It's time you accept it. Three years have passed. You've got to accept it. Go and take care of your other son before he too jumps off the building.'

'Sai, all I want to know is this. What is it that you, Somen Pillai and Unni used to do together?'

'For the last time I am telling you. Nothing. We were just three guys who used to chat about this and that.'

'What did you chat about?'

'Nothing, nothing.'

Sai walks away. Ousep shadows him until the boy reaches the gates of his building, where the guard has been instructed not to let Ousep in.

〜

OUSEP IS AT the bus stop next morning. Sai arrives in a few minutes, pretends that he has not seen him, and stands at a distance. Sai, the error in nature's trial and error. Ousep does not go to him as he usually does. He stands where he is and stares. Sai is probably thinking of the great abbreviations that define his life – GRE, GMAT, CAT. Without exams that have multiple-choice questions his life would not move, without them he does not understand himself. Even to accept that he is a worthless piece of rag he needs the exams to inform him.

You must see this, Unni. In a world full of Sai Shankarans, you would have become king, if only you had waited. Look at Sai, he does not know why he lives but he lives, and he lives because he does not know why he must die. He will go on this way, doing his little things, enjoying the little victories, adopting morals invented by other people, secretly supporting the ideologies of third-rate men, and at dinner time quoting the philosophies of the extraordinary whom people like him have never allowed to live in peace. How can you, Unni, let Sai Shankaran guard your secrets, let him keep a fragment of your memory in his dim head where he waits for it to rot away?

⁓

MYTHILI DOES NOT deny that she has made an extraordinary request but must her father begin to tremble and yell out for his wife? 'How are you bringing up your daughter?' he says.

'What did she do?' Mother says, faking wifely fear, spreading her sari over her 36Ds.

'Ask her yourself,' he says, and goes to the bathroom with the newspaper, as if the key to good upbringing is having a quiet fatherly shit.

Mother wears her peacemaker mask. She is enjoying this. Something to do.

'What did you tell your father?'

'I want to go to the Marina beach tonight with Bindu and Gai.'

'Why?'

'To see Olive Ridley.'

'Who is he?'

'Olive Ridley is a turtle.'

'A turtle?'

'Endangered.'

'Why must you go to a beach at midnight to see a turtle?'

'The turtles swim in from the sea and walk on the beach at midnight to lay eggs.'

'Why are you interested in turtle eggs?'

'We have to ensure the eggs are safe. Or Olive Ridleys will become extinct.'

'Do boys, too, want to save the Olive Ridleys?'

'Yes.'

'Mythili, just think about it. You. Midnight. Marina Beach. Boys. How could you even ask your father?'

Mythili storms out of the house, which is a moment of comic rebellion because it contains within its drama the indestructible promise that she will return before the sun goes down.

She has to take a walk to release her rage. The option of shutting herself in her room is not available any more. The latch on her door was removed after Mother complained to Father that she was spending long hours locked up in her room. After Father removed the latch with a screwdriver, Mythili started blocking the door with her table. So Father held four sizes of screwdriver in his hand and said, 'If you continue doing this I will remove the door.'

Maybe Mythili should find a sweet boy and fall in love, and have plentiful foreplay in vengeance. She decides to go to the Circular Road, gather two friends and discuss the matter walking in large circles around a park filled with cheap bougainvilleas.

But right in front of her appears a familiar sight that puts her off boys for the week. A tall lanky thing, must be around fifteen, is flanked by his papa and mama, and they are going someplace important, probably to a temple somewhere far away. He is much taller than his parents but they are, at this moment, giving him a good shaft up his arse. The boy is silent.

Father says, 'What is ninety-four per cent, what is ninety-four per cent these days? That, too, in maths. In Madras. What is ninety-four per cent? How can you come home and look into our eyes after doing something like this?'

Mother says, 'You are not working hard, look at all your friends, how hard they are working.'

Father says, 'And your JEE scores. What's happened to you? Do you want to go to IIT or not? Do you want to go to America or not? That is the decision you have to make. Do you want to rot here?'

'Do you want to be a failure?'

'You don't have the option of failure.'

The boy will not be a failure, Mythili knows. She has seen the generations before. The boy will make it. As his father has said, he does not have the option of failure. He will crack at least one entrance exam, and he will one day have a nice house in a suburb of San Francisco, or in a suburb of a suburb of San Francisco. He will find a cute Tamil Brahmin wife and make her produce two sweet children. He will drive a Toyota Corolla to work. And there, in the conference room of his office, he will tell his small team, with his hands stretched wide in a managerial way, 'We must think out of the box.'

Her future husband must be something like this boy who is walking ahead. He would have endured the same endoscopic bamboo up his arse, and emerged more resolute about cracking life. Her husband, her man, he is probably somewhere in Madras at this very moment. She wonders what he must be doing right now. Is he sitting at home, with a pile of IIT study material and a calculator on his desk? Does he, too, call his calculator 'Calcy'? Is he taking breaks to jerk off thinking of Silk Smitha. What are you doing right now, my lord?

Would he measure up to Unni? That is a question she does

not want to ask, she does not like it. She wonders whether Unni will always haunt her. Or will she forget him in time, will he become just another tame memory? As of this evening what she believes is that she will always remember him through the myths of a thirteen-year-old girl. And the men who will come her way, men who will be dull software engineers by the laws of probability, may not have a chance when set against Unni Chacko.

A surprising memory comes to her. She has not thought of this moment before. Since Unni died she has remembered him through the same set of images and events. It is as if the shock of the day had wiped clean many of her memories of him. But now and then some scenes come back to her and she wonders why she is being made to remember those ordinary moments, especially this. Even when she was thirteen, when it happened, she had not considered it important. But now that she remembers, now that she is older, she wonders whether there was more to it. What she remembers is an evening in his house. She has been there for a few hours but Unni is busy at his desk, his bedroom door shut. So she is in the hall, sitting on the floor with Thoma and teaching him how to mix watercolours to create other colours. At some point she realises that Unni is standing in his doorway and watching. She smiles at him.

'What are you thinking?' she says.

'I was thinking, you may never see what I see.'

'What do you see?'

'I see things that are very beautiful. And I was thinking, Mythili will go through her entire life without ever seeing what I see. Mythili will never know what she is meant to see.'

'You are mad, Unni.'

'What if I am not?'

~

THOMA CHACKO WAKES up earlier than usual and tries to understand what has happened to him. His head is fully tilted to his right, as if he is looking at the world with affection. He walks dreamily to the kitchen, feeling like the ghost of a boy who has been hanged, who is searching for his mother to tell her what they have done to him.

His mother is washing the dishes, her sari hitched up well above her knees. She stops for a moment, stands absolutely still, the lid of the pressure cooker in one hand and a wet scrub in another. A smile crosses her face as her hand circles the bottom of the lid very slowly, and she sings a lullaby.

It is dawn and the world is otherwise still. The lullaby is sweet and sad, like all lullabies. It was Unni who introduced him to the true nature of lullabies. 'If you listen carefully, Thoma, you will realise that a lullaby is a sad song. That is the secret of the lullaby.'

'Why is it sad, Unni?'

'I cannot tell you, Thoma. You're too young. But I have information that when mothers first began to sing lullabies they did it to mourn the birth of their babies. It was a tradition. Some people will tell you Thoma, lullabies only sound sad because they are sung softly to lull babies into sleep. But the truth is lullabies are sad because they are meant to be sad. Do you know something, Thoma, even today in some African tribes, lullabies and funeral songs are the same.'

Now that Thoma is older, he knows that when people want to con you they bring in the African tribes. Unni, especially. But as he stands this dawn listening to his mother, how can he deny that there is a stirring sorrow in the song that he hears, a song that is among his earliest memories. When she finally sees him she says, 'What's wrong with you?'

'My neck is broken,' he says.

She approaches him with her strong open arms. 'You've got a crick in your neck, Thoma. It's nothing. Let us fix it the village way. One swift jerk of your head and you will be all right. You won't feel a thing.'

He screams, 'It is not a sprain. I promise you it is something more important.'

She looks at him carefully and gives him the benefit of doubt. She used to be very confident about her ways once, but after Unni's death she has become unsure of all her opinions about the world.

She grabs the coconut-oil bottle from the shelf and before Thoma can react she pours some of it in his raised left ear. There is nothing he can do but just stand there as if his ear is a vat. He never lets her do it normally, but this morning she has grabbed her chance. 'Too much wax in your ear, Thoma.'

'Do we have any money to go to the clinic?'

'We must go to the clinic, Thoma. And for that we must first go quietly into Iago's chamber.'

They tiptoe into Ousep's bedroom. His lungi hangs from the fan as a noose. He is sleeping fully naked, his mouth open, legs spread wide, his balls lying on him like an extraterrestrial pet. She covers him with a bedsheet, and they stand there and stare at him. There is no sign of life in him, his breath is imperceptible, his eyes are half open. But then a toe wiggles, which makes Mariamma and Thoma leave his bedside.

She gently opens the table drawer and extracts Ousep's thin leather wallet. She pouts her lips at Thoma, which means there is some cash in it. She usually does not steal money from him because he gets furious and creates a big scene when he finds out.

They walk to the hospital, which is on Arcot Road, not very far. The coconut oil is still in his ear because there is no way he can move his head to empty it. 'Let it stay there for a while, Thoma,' she had said when they left the house.

On the way she gets into one of her moods. She holds Thoma's hand in a fierce grip and starts marching furiously, thinking of her old foes, her lips curling into her mouth, her eyes looking insanely at the road. Occasionally she wags a finger in the air. She does this in short bursts. She will mumble something, eat her own lips, wag a finger, and the next moment she is all elegant and sharp, her eyes alone preoccupied, lips smacking in preparation for the next bout. One man who is walking in their direction almost jumps in fright when she suddenly chews her lips and wags her finger. There are not many people on the road fortunately because it is still very early in morning, but the few who pass them by look at them curiously.

Thoma endures the shame, his head tilted, his left ear filled with coconut oil. Now and then, he tells her softly to behave like a normal person but she ignores him. There is a moment when her head, too, is fully tilted, and she raises her right arm as if she is doing a warming-up workout. People look at them in incomprehension. A woman and a boy going somewhere, both their heads fully tilted. Nobody knows why.

In the Sai Poly Clinic, there are only three doctors at this hour and they are busy with an emergency case. Thoma and his mother do not want to know what the case is, they wait for a while and decide to leave. They walk back home, the way they had come – Thoma's head almost horizontal, Mariamma in occasional fury.

That night, Thoma is woken up by his father to write his obituary. Mariamma says, 'Leave him alone, his neck is broken.' But she has decided not to fight. Thoma follows his swaying and stumbling father to the bedroom, where there is a noose ready and hanging from the ceiling fan, and a chair below it. Ousep takes his position on the chair and puts the lungi noose around his neck. Thoma stands with his head tilted. They stare at each other. 'Bastard,' Ousep says. 'Are you making fun of me, you bastard?'

'My neck is broken,' Thoma says.

Ousep tries to step down but he is pulled back by the noose. He extricates himself, gets down, and takes Thoma by his hand. 'I will take care of you, my son, I am your father.'

So Thoma walks to the Sai Poly Clinic once again; this time he is led by a man who can barely walk. It is late in the night and the long straight road to the clinic is deserted, but occasionally a taxi or an autorickshaw passes by and people stare at the strange sight of a drunken man leading a boy with a tilted head. Thoma wants to cry. In the morning, he goes somewhere with a mad woman, in the night with a drunkard. What a life, he says. He feels a ball of warm sorrow in his throat.

When they reach the clinic, the guard sees the state Ousep is in and will not let them in. Ousep throws his press card at him and says, 'Do you know who I am?' The guard screams to another guard inside, 'A man here has forgotten who he is. Is the psychiatrist on duty?' And the guards laugh. Ousep threatens to call the Chief Minister. The guard says, 'Call the President.' Ousep shakes his head at Thoma and says, 'This moron does not know the President has no powers in this country.'

Eventually, the guard wins. So they walk back. This time, Thoma has to lead his father, who stumbles many times, he can barely stand. They go this way down the abandoned road – the boy with the tilted head leading the drunkard.

Thoma sees two shadowy figures approach. An urchin girl of his age is leading her drunken father. As their paths cross, Thoma and the girl look at each other, and they smile as if to give the other the strength to survive the times. Many years later, Thoma would think of her and he would hope with all his heart that she, too, has somehow made it across.

Thoma leads his father carefully to the stairway of Block A. Ousep is too drunk and sleepy to scream, which is a blessing. They walk quietly up the steps. Ousep stops. 'Thoma,' he says, 'do you hate your father?'

'No.'

'Don't hate me, son. There are people in this world who set out to make an omelette but end up with scrambled eggs. I am just one of them.'

They resume their walk up the steps. They walk in silence. When they are about to reach the landing on the third floor, they see a strange sight. Mythili walks across the short corridor, like a midnight ghost, towards her door. She throws a look at

Thoma but does not say anything. She slips into her home and shuts the door.

'Did that happen, Thoma?'

'Yes.'

Ousep studies the front door of his house carefully, and he looks up at the short flight of steps that leads to the terrace door, which is locked. Just for a moment he looks strong and clever, the way he is in the mornings.

4

Gentleman's Cholesterol

THE TRUE NATURE of sorrow is boredom. Ousep Chacko is more sure than ever as he stands on his balcony, in the stillness of the humid Saturday evening. The good husbands too are out on their balconies, half naked, their sacred white threads running between their loose undeniable breasts. Their wives keep serving them biscuits and coffee, lemon juice and water, or they disappear after obeying orders and appear with newspapers, bank passbooks or other objects that still belong to men here. Some couples are having long conspiratorial conversations as couples do. On the ground below children are playing a hectic game that is making them delirious. Can people really tell the difference between normal children and abnormal children? That somehow reminds him of the type of people who can tell the difference between good poetry and bad poetry.

Thoma is among the happy kids who are now running like a fleeing mob. Even in Thoma's world, some days are good days. Late adolescent girls walk in packs from one wall to another, throwing sideway glances at the big boys sitting in line on the compound wall. In another time, an evening like this, Unni would have been among the boys on the wall, sitting quietly and returning the looks of the girls.

Boys of Unni's age in the colony are of two kinds, without exception since the exception is dead. The dejected, who failed to clear the JEE but have managed to enter the best of the second-rung engineering colleges, and the irreparably damaged who attend third-rate institutes, some of them in faraway gloomy industrial towns. The irreparably damaged flock together. They walk without the spring of life, their spines have lost their pride, and there is no light in their eyes. They become alert when they hear words like 'idiot' or 'fool' or 'stupid'. Even when these descriptions are not about them, the words land painful blows in their hearts. The eight boys on the wall today are of the flock.

They are distracted by a girl who is walking down the road. Unni used to call her 'Typewriter' and that is what they call her here even now. Books pressed to her chest, oiled hair tied in a single fierce braid, she walks down this road every evening. She walks in great discomfort, as always, to the sounds of her silver anklets, with a distraught smile of excruciating shyness, her head bent, her baffled eyes gaping at the road, fully aware of the boys on the wall, boys on their balconies, boys behind windows, all the boys in the world. She loses authority over her tense legs often and she veers to the side until she reaches the very edge of the road, sometimes a compound wall, when she gets mildly alarmed and veers to the other side, like the roller of a typewriter.

The boys on the wall, the men and women on the balconies, even the old who can see far, laugh as they see the girl go round the bend. She is a passing moment of joy. Like the Chackos, she makes people feel they are better.

After she vanishes, a numbing dullness returns to the world. The boys have nothing to laugh at, nothing to do. On occasion their heads lift for a swift hopeful gaze at Mythili's balcony, where there is no one standing right now.

She used to stand on her balcony and call out for Unni. Some days, when she was in the mood, she would yell out his name several times in the different accents of the elders in the block. Unni would then walk across his father's bedroom with his tired arrogance, without fear or respect, and open the narrow door that leads to the balcony. He and the girl would then chat standing on their balconies, sometimes for over an hour. Unni usually said very little, she did most of the talking, chiefly complaining about her friends or teachers. Sometimes she whispered things about her mother to him and giggled. That was then, when she was allowed to talk to men.

Ousep decides he has had enough of the humid evening, he must now head somewhere affluent and have a quiet drink, maybe more. It is an inevitability that masquerades as a decision. That is the way of a drunkard. He grants himself the dignity of choice, as if there is another option. But then is there really any choice in the world; could it be that every human action is merely an inevitability masquerading as a human decision, life granting dignity to its addicts through the delusion of choice?

He is about to leave the balcony when he spots something at the far end of Balaji Lane. He is unable to understand what is happening but everybody else appears to know what is going on. There is a stranger walking down the lane, a young man whose features are not clear. As he passes the other blocks, boys stop playing and stare, boys stand on the walls and stare. Girls appear on the balconies rolling their hair and look. Men and women point to the young man and talk among themselves, nodding their heads. There is a small swarm of boys, short and tall, who are now following the young man. The news has just gone around Block A. The children run out to the lane, many climb the compound wall and stand on it to get a better look. The big boys too are standing on the wall. The entire length of the wall is now lined with boys of many heights standing and looking to their right. The balconies fill with people. The young man approaches in his swarm. He is unaffected by all the attention. And it is now clear what is in his hand – a red basket filled with vegetables. Miraculously, the apparition enters Block A. Even more incredibly, it speaks to Thoma, who is visibly dazed as he clumsily climbs down from the wall.

Ousep now recognises the young man. He was in Unni's class. Ousep met him once, three years ago, weeks before the boy became a celebrity. Balki had not just made it to IIT, he was ranked all-India second in the JEE, second among over a hundred thousand candidates. The meeting with him was very brief and largely useless, and Ousep decided that there was no point in meeting him again. But now it appears that Balki is coming home for some reason. Thoma, who has suddenly assumed the glow of importance, is leading the star. The swarm vanishes into the stairway tunnel. Is this the breakthrough Ousep was waiting for?

He keeps the front door open and waits. That draws Mariamma's attention; she looks puzzled. She waits with him. When she sees the crowd of boys at her door she begins to tremble. 'What happened, what happened to my boy? Is Thoma all right?' she sings. When she finds Thoma in the crowd she puts her hand on her heart and pants. Thoma leads Balki into the house. The swarm does not come in but it does not want to leave. A boy asks, nervously, 'Balki, do you believe in God?'

'Yes,' Balki says in his surprising baritone.

'What a coincidence. Even I believe in God.'

'OK, all of you,' Balki says. 'Thanks. Now I need to speak to Unni's parents alone. Bye.'

And they leave reluctantly, including Thoma. Balki shuts the door and faces Ousep and Mariamma.

Ousep tries to understand what has come home. Balki is tall, his shoulders broad, and everything in the house has shrunk in his presence. He has a large head, and a long, full neck, which is far more uncommon than people imagine. His movements are brisk and devoid of cultured caution, and his unfocused eyes gape without respect as if the Chackos have borrowed money from him. And he is chewing gum.

Mariamma holds the boy's hand and tells him something about the passage of time. Then, for Ousep's benefit, she mumbles a confused but flattering biography. He was always a genius, apparently. She says she has known Balki from the time he was a little boy.

'We have met,' Ousep says. 'Briefly, a long time ago.'

'Three years ago,' the boy says.

Mariamma touches the boy's cheeks with the tips of her fingers. 'Nobody visits us any more, Balki,' she says. 'All his friends have stopped coming. One by one, they stopped. Then one day, guess who turns up.'

'Who?' the boy asks.

They stare, confused. 'You, of course,' she says.

'I see. I don't easily understand this style of speech.'

She feels his face again. Balki is not embarrassed, he even bends a little to make it easier for her to cup his face in her hands. 'I don't mind being touched now,' he says. 'When I was little I did not like being touched, I would scream if anybody touched me. Unni used to put his arm around me. I used to hate it but I grew to accept that it is a sign of friendship.' He hands her the vegetable basket. 'Look what I've got for you. The vegetables are for you. I brought them from my house. My mother said, "Take some vegetables for Unni's mother." I told her, "I must take fruits." But she said, "Don't be modern, Bala. Take vegetables. It will make her happy."'

'She's right,' Mariamma says.

'My mother asked me to bring the basket back.'

'Will you eat here, Balki? I can make a quick lunch for you.'

'I cannot eat in a house where meat is cooked,' he says in his precise inoffensive way.

'Oh, we don't cook any meat here,' she says throwing a bitter chuckle at Ousep. 'Meat,' she says, and shakes with genuine laughter.

'We don't harm meat, son, by bringing it here,' Ousep says.

Balki looks at them in incomprehension. 'I don't have much time,' he says, 'I have to leave as soon as I've spoken to Unni's father.'

'Is it something important?' she says. 'Tell me, Balki, do you know something about Unni?'

Balki's eyes have been darting to the framed black-and-white photograph of Unni on the wall. They stay on the portrait now.

'He looks so young,' he says. 'When was this taken?'

'Just a few months before he died,' she says. 'It was a

passport-size photograph. We blew it up as much as we could. That's why he looks a bit pale in it. My boy was not pale at all, you know that.'

'He is so young, which obviously he was when he died. But in my mind he is a man, like me. In my mind, he is ageing with me. But in that photograph he is just a boy.'

He goes up to the framed photograph for a closer look at Unni, who stares back with a knowing smile, as if he knew this moment would come. Balki, unexpectedly, joins his palms and shuts his eyes. A deep silence grows. Ousep uses the opportunity to point to his wife's blouse, which is torn at the armpits. He tells her with a violent motion of his hand that she must disappear inside. But she stands there defiantly, even begins to imitate his actions. Ousep considers flinging his slippers at her. Balki opens his eyes after nearly a minute.

'I think of Unni every day,' he says.

'What is it that you want to say to us, Balki?' Mariamma asks.

'I have to talk to Unni's father. I have to speak to him in private.'

Ousep leads him to his room, and shuts the door in Mariamma's face. He shows the boy to a chair across from his desk, which is by the open windows that frame the tops of a sea of coconut trees and the terraces of blue and pink and white homes, and the distant yellow spire of Fatima Chruch. He lights up two cigarettes and tries to look relaxed, even flaps his thighs. The boy is probably amused to see a man smoke two cigarettes at once but he does not say anything.

Ousep wonders what the boy wants. Nobody comes home with a story to tell unless he has a motive. Sometimes, the motive is the story. Ousep points to the church spire. 'Unni is buried in the grounds of that church.'

'I know,' Balki says, 'I've visited his grave twice.'

'Were you at the funeral?'

'I didn't know for a week that he was gone. Most of his classmates didn't know.'

'We buried him a day after he died.'

'I hear you are meeting them again, his classmates, you are talking to them.'

'Yes.'

'They are stupid,' Balki says, as if it is an unremarkable fact. 'Most of them, they are very dumb. Did you find them dumb?'

'They are like anybody else.'

'Exactly. People are generally dumb. They are small petty animals, who want to do their small petty animal things. Unni was smart. I liked him.'

'You were friends?'

'I don't know,' Balki says.

'What does that mean?'

'I don't know, that's what it means.'

'After his death, I came to meet you in your house,' Ousep says. 'I remember you were very surprised when you saw me at the door. You were probably unhappy to see me.'

'I was surprised, not unhappy. I was a bit confused, I could not understand why you were asking me questions about Unni. I didn't know then that Unni's death was not an accident. I heard it from you first, and you revealed it to me towards the end of our conversation when you felt I was not saying anything useful. I remember your words. I will always remember those words. "Unni jumped. He knew what he was doing." I could not believe it. It didn't make any sense. After our meeting I went to meet some boys from the class and they told me exactly what you had said. Two days ago I met someone at the bus stop. He told me that you are meeting Unni's friends again, you are—'

'I am embarrassed to interrupt you, Balki, but it is important that I say this. Unni's mother is the curious type. As you can see, if you look under that door, she is standing right behind it. With her ear stuck to it. I am not saying this in a metaphorical way, Balki. She really is standing there with her ear stuck to the door. You have a loud booming voice, and both of us want to be discreet. I don't have a radio or a two-in-one that works. So we may have to speak softly.'

'I understand.'

'Softer than that.'

'Is this better?'

'Why do you want to speak to me and not her?'

'I want to speak to you and not to her. That's all there is to it.'

'What has Unni told you about his mother?'

'Nothing much really. But I got the feeling that he was very fond of her.'

'He was very fond of her, which is not unusual.'

'I want to know,' Balki says, licking his lips, 'what have you found out about Unni?'

'Nothing at all, to be honest.'

'Nothing?'

'Does it surprise you?'

'I expected it. But why have you started investigating his death now? After three years, why now?'

'My health is bad, I may not last very long. I thought I must solve the only riddle that matters to me before I begin to sink.'

'People say you've discovered something.'

'I've heard that too.'

Balki stares at Ousep with a hint of mistrust. 'Is your heath bad in a specific way? Do you have a terminal disease?'

'It's never that simple. There are things a drunkard knows about his body. Most of Malayalam literature was about that until women started writing.'

Ousep tries to achieve a wounded smile, anticipating the discomfort of compassion in Balki, but the boy is all business. 'You don't have much time, then,' he says. 'Do you have a hunch about Unni at least? Are you following a particular line of investigation?'

'Balki, why are you here?'

'I am here to help you.'

'Then help me.'

Balki looks with great concentration at the surface of the

desk. He takes his time to form the words. 'Unni had ideas, powerful ideas. He believed something is going on all around us. Have you heard about that? He told the whole class this, he said something is happening and if we looked carefully we would be able to see it. He believed that something very ancient has survived and that it lives among us. Has anybody told you this?'

'What was it that he thought was going on?'

'I don't know.'

'Could it be that he had got obsessed with an idea – the great awakening, everything-is-an-illusion, rubbish like that? It happens to some adolescents. They usually come back to their senses.'

'I don't think he was talking about those things,' Balki says.

'Why not?'

'Somehow I feel that the person who thinks he has discovered the absolute truth will not be someone known to me.'

'Why couldn't Unni just say what was bothering him?'

'I don't know. I think he could not explain it. I think he only suspected that something was going on, he was not sure. Then one day he saw something, and that somehow meant that he had to die. It is possible that the reason why he died is linked to what he knew, what he discovered. Does that make sense to you?'

'No.'

'It doesn't make much sense to me, either.'

'Balki, we don't have to sit here and try to figure out why Unni chose to die. That would be mere speculation. What we must do is talk about him, talk about him without a motive.'

Balki nods; he toys with the marble paperweight on the desk. He looks around the room, at the bed behind him, and at the bookshelf in a corner, probably searching for a spine he recognises. He even looks at the ceiling fan, for some reason. When he finally speaks he remembers Unni in a neat, chronological way.

Unni and Balki entered the St Ignatius Boys' High School the same year, when they were six. Balki's first memories of Unni are of a boy who was not exceptional in any way. Unni was a

143

moderately gifted student who was not considered bright until many years later. Balki, on the other hand, was always a clever freak, and for that reason he did not have friends. Even the teachers hated him. But he had Unni, who put an arm around his shoulder, who took him by his hand to include him in the games that the boys played. When Unni was eight he gave Balki a memorable reason why they were friends. He said that Balki reminded him of his mother. Two days later Unni would explain, without being asked, 'My mother, too, is very smart, but a bit nutty.'

When he was around ten, something happened to Unni. Ousep has not heard this before. He is not sure whether the boy's mother knows about this. At least twice in the classroom he held his head and doubled up in pain. On both the occasions he got back on his feet in seconds. And on both occasions he told his teachers that he had felt his brain move, as if it was changing shape within his skull. Balki is not surprised that no one from their class has told Ousep this. 'It happened a long time ago and people have very ordinary powers of retention. People usually remember what happened to them, and not the world around them.'

Around this time, there was another development. Unni began to spend a lot of time by himself in a corner of the playground. He would sit in a hypnotic trance as if he was watching something captivating before his eyes, and he would not hear people right next to him calling out his name. He would stir back to life only when shaken, and he would behave as if nothing had happened. He claimed to have no recollection of what he was thinking about or what he saw in his mind.

It is possible that these are ordinary events whose significance is exaggerated because Unni chose to die. Children do strange things, which are usually forgotten because they turn out all right. Most of them, at least. But some don't make it, do they? Everything else about Unni, when he was a little boy, was unremarkable. Ousep does not like it when Balki uses the word 'ordinary'. But then he knows what Balki means. Balki means 'ordinary'.

When Unni was around fourteen he began to draw

outrageous caricatures of his teachers, which quickly became an underground sensation in the school. Soon, he found legitimate fame when he released what was probably his first comic story. It was drawn in watercolours over six pages.

Ousep lights up two more cigarettes, and as the first cloud of smoke leaves him he asks with a sporting smile, 'You actually remember the number of pages?'

'Six pages. Held together by a safety pin,' Balki says.

'Could the number of pages have been five, or seven?'

'Six,' Balki says.

'Do you remember the story of the comic?'

'Of course.'

The comic begins with a boy, who is probably fourteen, as old as Unni was then. The boy is going somewhere. A man is walking ahead, holding something in his hand. A bus goes out of control and hits the man from behind. The man's wallet, oddly the object that he was holding in his hand, flies into the air and lands near the boy. A great crowd gathers quickly around the man, and they block the boy's view. The comments of the crowd fill the air. 'Is that his face?' 'Is that his ear lying there?' 'There is something white coming out of his head.' The boy picks up the dead man's wallet and walks away. In the wallet is some cash. It also has the address and the photograph of the owner. The boy spends the cash and lives happily for several days, but then he begins to see the dead man in his dreams. Later, he begins to see the man in his waking hours, standing in unexpected corners and staring hard at him. Finally, unable to bear his own hallucinations, the boy decides to return the money he had taken to the family of the dead man. He steals some cash from his grandmother's cupboard, puts it in the wallet, and goes to return it. He reaches the door of a flat and rings the doorbell; he waits. When the door opens the boy is shocked because it is the corpse from his hallucinations who is at the door. The boy is so terrified that he is unable to move. The man sees the wallet in the boy's hand and he begins to thank him for his honesty. It turns out, the man's pocket had been picked earlier that week, and it was the thief who had died.

The comic, which was untitled according to Balki, passed from hand to hand for days. Jealous boys went about revealing the twist in the tale to those who were yet to read the story, but Unni's fame rested not only on the story but also on his exquisite images. The comic finally reached a teacher, who decided to stick the six pages to a wall outside the Principal's office. Small crowds of boys, and on occasion parents, gathered every day to read the comic. The success of Unni's first comic must have created a small stir in the house, but Ousep was kept out of it all. He cannot blame anyone for that, but he does wish that he had been told about Unni's first ever comic story and what a hit it was in the school. Ousep would have put his hand on his son's shoulder and told him, honestly, 'It's a great story, Unni, I am proud of you.' And Unni might have smiled in his shy way, shy but fully meeting the eye.

Around this time, Unni became immodest about his erections. Balki reveals this without any embarrassment or even an inflection in his steady voice. At the end of the class of an English teacher who was slim, whose sari was not tamed, and whose deep navel showed, Unni would sit in his place and invite all to feel his hardness, which in general opinion was so extraordinary that many refused to believe it was a part of his body. Unni was crafty, he was magic. Some said he was trying to pass off a raw plantain as his penis.

'What did you think?' Ousep asks.

Balki says in a severe way, 'How could it have been a plantain? People are so stupid.'

Nothing about Unni when he was fourteen even hinted at what he was to soon become, except for a brief comment one evening. After the final bell, the two boys were walking down the second-floor corridor from their class to the stairway. From that height they could see many streams of children emerging from their classes and joining a sea of uniforms, all going home.

'So many people in this world,' Unni said, 'so many many people. Nature has to keep making billions of people so that by pure chance, finally, one person will be born who will make it.'

What he said appeared nonsensical and Balki did not think much about it. 'Two years later Unni asked me if I remembered that moment, if I remembered what he had said. I said "yes". And Unni said, "There is a reason why you did not forget it."'

'But what did he mean when he said one person will make it?' Ousep asks.

'I didn't ask him.'

'Why didn't you?'

'At that time I didn't know he was going to die. So I didn't attach too much importance to everything he said. But I can guess what he meant. He probably meant that the birth of every human is nature's blind shot at achieving something grander. It constantly fails but by producing billions of people nature is improving its chances of attaining a mysterious goal.'

'Does it make sense to you?'

'If you eliminate that bit about nature having a goal, what Unni said is just a layperson's description of the theory of evolution. Nature keeps producing millions and billions of nearly identical organisms for ages, then something happens to one creature by chance and a new species is born.'

'But that's not what Unni was talking about. He said, in your own words, one person will make it.'

'That's what he said.'

'What exactly did he mean?'

'We will never know.'

The door bursts open, startling Ousep and the boy. Mariamma walks in with a calm phoney smile, carrying two cups of coffee on a plastic tray. She sets the cups on the desk and lingers. Ousep glares at her but she decides not to meet his eye. So he walks her out of the room, shuts the door on her again and latches it.

Balki sips his coffee, ruffles his hair, lets out a deep yawn, squeezes his penis for a moment as if to unknot it, looks in the direction of the church spire. Ousep waits without a word, flapping his thighs. Balki, too, begins to flap his thighs. They sit this way in silence, flapping their thighs.

Balki pulls the *Indian Express* towards him, and begins to read. He turns the pages, even folds the paper and gets down to reading a short item about a flyover that will soon be built. He takes far too long to finish the article, and it occurs to Ousep that the boy is probably here to say something and he is not sure whether he should. He is making up his mind.

When Balki finds his voice again it is as if he had never paused. But it is not clear whether this is what he has come here to say or whether he is just buying time. 'Nobody noticed it at first,' he says, 'but when Unni was seventeen he began to transform. We had just entered the twelfth standard. I don't know how much you know, some bizarre things happened in the class.'

Most of the boys in the class had been together from the time they were children and the twelfth standard was a fore-boding that was lodged in their minds all through the years of their childhood. Innumerable times, on good days and bad, they had sat together and wondered what would become of them when they sat the inescapable board exams at the end of the twelfth standard. They spoke in whispers about the fathers who had killed themselves in shame because their sons had failed. And when they finally entered the last year of school they were filled with the deep melancholy that was seeded in them long before their memories began. The time had come. That was what everyone in Madras told them. The time had come. Their fates would be decided in a few months in the board exam and in the toughest engineering entrance exams in the world. Every teacher, even the language teachers, told them that they were 'at the crossroads of life'. The maths teacher acted out what could happen to them down every road leading from the crossroads.

Every boy in the class became increasingly obsessed with his study material, except Unni, of course. He spent his free time drawing the portraits of boys engrossed in solving sample problems, their desks filled with fat books and their fingers tapping the Seiko calculator. This is what they did most of the time. They did that even in the sliver of time between classes, and during the lunch break, and in their homes as well, into the night and at dawn.

It was inconceivable that anything could distract them. But Unni did something in the class one day that made almost everyone go crazy for over ten minutes. It is only now that the boys talk about the incident freely, according to Balki. And they talk about it only among themselves. But even now, no one fully understands what exactly happened or how Unni got everyone involved in the moment of madness.

'There were thirty-two boys in the class when it happened,' Balki says. 'Everybody saw it, everybody was a part of it, but nobody can explain it. Has anyone told you about Simion Clark?'

'No.'

Balki begins to rock gently in his chair. 'I was sure nobody would have told you this. Maybe they didn't want to say anything bad about Unni to his father. People are so small. The way they think, they are so small. Or, maybe, they are still afraid. They still want to believe it never happened.'

'But what happened?'

Balki drags the paperweight in a circle over the desk, but thankfully he stops. 'Let's say you want to commit a crime,' the boy says, 'but you know there are going to be witnesses, what do you do? How do you go ahead with the crime when you know that there are going to be witnesses?'

'How?'

'You make the witnesses participate in the crime. What happens when the witness is also the accomplice? There is silence. That is how Unni guards some of his secrets long after he has gone. That is why you will never know everything he did. And that's one of the reasons, I guess, why nobody has told you the story of Simion Clark.'

~

SIMION CLARK WAS an Anglo-Indian physics teacher whose sudden appearance in the cheap cement corridors of St Ignatius had all the enchantment of a Rolls-Royce passing through a narrow Madras lane. Simion was a legend even in his time. He sat erect among the dark slouched rustics in the staffroom, he was much larger than all the men in the school and he was large in a way that made those who were smaller than him look like gnomes. He was lean and fit compared to the other teachers, who had been irreparably starved in their childhood; his perfect shirt was tucked inside fitted trousers while the polyester shirts of his colleagues, some days, showed white deltas of old sweat. And the way he pronounced 'screw gauge', 'Ptolemy' and 'relativity', it was as if these were words of his invention. He played the guitar and the piano, and laughed at the harmonium. And he always sang a sad Spanish song during school festivals. He bowed his head to the lady teachers even though they looked like his maids. But he had darkness within. He was merciless with the boys, even by the standards of St Ignatius. He slapped and caned them, hit the soles of their feet with a rod, and landed thuds on their bent backs that echoed, and when they cried a smile quivered at the edges of his lips.

Unni was thirteen when Simion arrived and was taken to every class as a showpiece by the headmaster, whose own English had become confused and tortured in the presence of the new exotic teacher.

Simion began to walk down the school's corridors, enjoying the deep fearful silence he cast all around him. Sometimes he stopped and surveyed the boys in a class through the window, waiting for a wrong move, a conversation that was not in English, a shoe that was not black enough.

In Simion's class, naturally, nobody spoke. If anybody coughed, the boy had to say, 'Excuse me, sir,' which imposed considerable pressure on the boys to control their coughs, which sometimes transformed into loud alien yelps. It was inevitable that Unni and Simion would clash, but strangely Simion never hit the boy, or even spoke to him. The day of conflict came four years after Simion had arrived at St Ignatius. Simion was at the height of his powers. Unni was seventeen.

The class began the way it always did. Simion's entrance was preceded by a nervous calm. Into the familiar silence he walked and settled in his chair, the axis of his upper body slightly tilted as always. He arranged his things on his desk and flipped the pages of a book. There was an absolute stillness in the room, which was not unusual. A physics teacher facing the twelfth standard in any school in Madras would normally have some of the powers of God. In the case of Simion Clark, he was God.

So all hearts stopped when Unni stood up and walked to the blackboard. 'I did not understand what was happening,' Balki says. 'What was Unni doing?' Simion raised his eyes and looked at the class, and slowly turned to his right, where Unni was standing. Unni stood facing the boys for a while. Then he started singing a comical song, which sounded a lot like Simion's Spanish song. The song was brief. Unni then went to Simion's desk. 'And it happened. Unni slapped him. Simion did not move. He sat there looking at Unni without an expression on his face, as if he had expected it. Unni slapped him again and withdrew his hand into his trouser pocket.' That was Simion's style, that was how Simion slapped the boys – with a quick movement of his hand and a ponderous withdrawal of the weapon into his pocket. Unni kept slapping him in this manner. Simion now stared at a distant spot on the wall and endured the slaps. Unni went to the door and shut it. He faced the class and said, 'Your turn.'

'Nobody moved, naturally. We were too shocked. So he dragged a boy called Kitcha to the head of the class. Kitcha was an idiot who was routinely thrashed by Simion. The guy begged, "No, Unni, I don't want to do anything, Unni, no, Unni." But when Unni put him in front of Simion, Kitcha suddenly began to look menacing. Simion swallowed. I clearly remember that. It was the moment, at least for me, when the myth of Simion Clark was broken. He looked afraid and fragile. I think Kitcha saw that too.'

Kitcha kicked Simion's legs, and looked at himself in disbelief. He was so scared he lost his mind. He went berserk. He slapped and kicked Simion a few more times. Now something even more bizarre happened. A few boys stood up, ran to the head of the class and joined Kitcha. They slapped and kicked Simion. Unni was standing near the door and watching carefully. It was strange that Simion did not move from his chair. Just once he spoke and that was to say, 'Please don't.' Now everyone was going crazy. Almost everybody in the class was around his table. 'I saw a boy jogging up and down in the aisle screaming, "I want to, I want to, I want to hit the bastard."'

Someone then went up to Simion and spat in his face. That showed an option for others who did not know how to hit a person. They went to his table and spat on him. Most of them had probably never spat at a target in their lives and they ended up spitting on themselves. 'Spitting on a person is more difficult than it seems. I sat there watching all this. I don't know what happened to me. I could not control myself. I went and punched him on his ear. Just once. It was the first time I had hit someone. I don't know why I did it. It was a magical moment.'

The whole class was now around Simion. Some punched him, many spat. His eyes were still fixed to that spot on the wall. Then, suddenly, his body began to shake, he bit his lips and started crying. The beatings stopped. Unni went back to his seat; that made everyone go back. Simion did not move. He was bleeding from his nose. He took out his handkerchief and wiped himself, all the spit and a trickle of blood. And he got up from his chair and left.

'We went to the door and saw him walk down the corridor,

then across the playground below, all the way to the gate. He did not pick up his things from the staffroom. He just walked away, he left, just like that. No one ever saw him again.'

The boys were delirious and, naturally, they wanted to discuss what had happened, but Unni refused to be drawn in. Every time someone asked him a question he would put a finger to his lips. It was as if he was saddened, even ashamed, by what had happened.

By the end of the day, a rumour was spreading through the school that Simion had hanged himself from a fan in his house. Only Unni's class knew what might have been the cause and they decided, without having to discuss the matter, to guard their secret. None of the teachers had any social contact with Simion. They did not believe they were good enough to be his friend. They did not know where he lived, where he came from. The administration tried to reach him but all his details in the school records turned out to be false. The phone number he had provided belonged to a parish in Thambaram twenty kilometres away, and his address simply did not exist. He was obviously not what he said he was. Simion Clark was probably not his real name even. With his affluent bearing and British English he had secured a job in the school with ease and worked there for four years. Nobody knew why he had lied about who he was or what it was that he had hoped to achieve. He remains a mystery even today.

'Do you think he is dead?' Ousep asks.

'Nobody is sure,' Balki says. 'That is the scariest thing. The moment we heard that he had died something happened inside all of us. We felt sick and afraid. We were regular guys. We had been trained by our parents to fear anything that was remotely dangerous or abnormal. And now suddenly we were responsible for a man's death. That is why nobody talks about Simion. We suspect we killed him.'

'Why did Simion endure all that? He just had to leave his chair to get Unni expelled from school.'

'That's exactly what we wanted to know but Unni refused to tell us anything. Anyway, after we heard of Simion's death we didn't want to discuss that man. Everybody decided to forget about him and get back to work. When you are preparing for the JEE you focus. You don't play cricket, you don't watch TV, you don't even masturbate. Abetting suicide is simply out of the question. So we wanted to just forget about what had happened.'

'Is he dead?' Ousep asks again.

Balki, surprisingly, removes a cigarette from Ousep's fingers and takes a drag. 'Is this disrespectful?' he asks.

'Do you want a cigarette?'

Balki shakes his head, inserts the cigarette back between Ousep's fingers and says, 'If nobody knew where Simion came from or where he lived or what he was, then I wonder who first received the news that he had died.'

'Precisely.'

'Precisely.'

'Do you think Unni started the rumour?' Ousep asks.

'It achieved exactly what he wanted. Simion became a secret,' Balki says. 'It was in everbody's interests to keep him a secret.'

'Why was Unni doing all this?'

'We come back to the original problem. Why did Unni do everything that he did?'

Balki arranges the newspapers on the desk in a neat stack. He gazes at the church spire, nods his head almost imperceptibly at a private thought, gapes again at the objects in the room. 'Or,' he says, 'Simion is dead and I am trying to fool myself into believing that Unni started the rumour. Everyone else who was present in the classroom that day thinks that Simion is dead. The rumour was very strong when it began.'

'Did Simion have a scar on his face?' Ousep asks.

Balki, as expected, considers the question strange. 'No,' he says.

'Any cuts, any old wounds on the forehead, on his lips?' Ousep asks.

'No,' Balki says. 'Why do you ask?'

'Just curious. Was he always a physics teacher or was it something he became later in his career?'

'I have no idea,' Balki says. 'Your questions are strange.'

'They are.'

'Do you know someone who might be Simion?'

'No,' Ousep says, which is the truth. But there are many Simions
in the world. They have scars from old injuries, and they like
labs. Ousep knows where to look.

He thinks of the time when Unni had influenced a gang of
boys to almost kill a stray dog by pelting it with stones. Simion
Clark reminds him of that mongrel, who probably still lives.

After the disappearance of Simion, a myth grew around Unni.
Some boys said that he had paranormal powers, that he could
control the actions of others, that he could read minds, that when
they stood close to him they felt a magnetic pull. It was around
this time that he walked into the class one morning, sat in his
place and waited for a moment of silence to say, very softly, as if
to himself, 'Something is happening around us.' Ousep has heard
of this moment from several boys and all their descriptions are the
same.

Unni looked disturbed. Nobody had ever seen Unni that way
before. He was abstract and incoherent when he tried to explain.
Balki says, 'It was as if he had seen something. He said things
are not what they appear to be. Everything that we know about
the world is wrong, everything is a lie. Nature guards a dark
secret, a secret that would stun us if we knew it, and it guards
it in incredibly clever ways. He didn't make sense but as he was
talking I felt such a cold fear in my heart I turned to look
behind me. It was a strange thing that I did. I looked back to
see if there were any danger coming towards me. Why would I
do that? What is even stranger is that I saw three other boys
look back, exactly the way I did. We didn't know why we did
that.'

A few weeks later Unni started telling stories standing on the teacher's desk. 'Has anybody told you about his stories?' Balki asks.

'Yes. But some deny this ever used to happen.'

Balki laughs; he leans forward and asks in a teasing whisper, 'Those who did not deny it, did they tell you what his stories were about?'

'They said they don't remember.'

'That's what I thought they would say.'

Balki releases a hiss of air from his lungs. 'You have met so many boys from our class, you went to them as the father of a dead boy, not just any dead boy but Unni Chacko. Yet they hold back information because they are afraid, they are afraid of everything they were, everything they are. People are such cowards, people are so pathetic.'

Ousep realises why he has been feeling hopeful in the presence of this boy who has a reasonable contempt for the world. It is the misanthrope alone who has clarity. By standing outside the huddles of man he sees a lot, and what he often sees is the evidence that people are not as smart as dogs think they are. And he wants to see it time and again. In the fog of ambiguities and mysteries he desperately searches for truths because truth usually shows humanity in a poor light. Balki and Unni are similar in that way. Unni, too, was exceptional, he was strong, so he did not need to belong. Unni, too, stood beyond the bonds of people because that was a good place to stand and watch. And Balki does not want to concede that such an endearing foe of the ordinary was ultimately defeated by the world. For that is what Unni's death is until proven otherwise, a defeat. Balki would do all he could to take Ousep closer to the truth.

The boy says, 'What is more important than Unni's stories is what happened in the days that preceded them.' After what Unni did to Simion, he exerted considerable power over the class. When he spoke people listened, when he asked a question they answered. And, for some reason, he slowly influenced many of them to confess to their sexual acts and fantasies. 'Those days we had more fantasies than acts. He asked me, too. I told him I have nothing to say. Then he asked me, "Have you ever committed a sexual crime?" I said, "No." He looked at me in disbelief. That was the only time I thought he looked dumb. Did he really expect all schoolboys to be rapists?'

After Unni had collected all the confessions he could, he converted them into true stories that he would deliver from the teacher's desk. 'That's what he did, those were his stories.' He protected the identity of the boys but gave broad hints. He described the setting and the characters involved in great detail. 'Now, these were true stories, sex stories,' Balki says, 'stories of the boys in our class. Some really dark stuff was coming out. I was very surprised by the kinds of things boys did. Everybody was hooked, they got addicted to the stories, and everybody tried to guess who was who.' Some begged Unni not to reveal their confessions, which were told to him in good faith, of course. They feared they would be identified. But Unni assured them they were overreacting.

'His first story was about a boy whose identity we could guess through the descriptions. He had molested the servant maid when she was sleeping in his house. She did not complain because she feared she would be sacked. So he did it again. Some stories were sad and infuriating, some were funny. There was one about a boy who used to take his own sister's school uniform, put it over a pillow and do things to it. Another guy took a pomegranate from the kitchen, made a hole in it and made love to it, and actually returned it to the kitchen.'

'Were there any stories in which the protagonist was probably Unni?'

'No.'

At some point in the final year of school, Balki had distanced himself from Unni. He says that in an uncharacteristically obtuse way, with a hint of lame pride about his decision, about his discipline, the way some people would say, expecting a compliment in return, 'I don't eat meat.' 'There was something about

157

him,' Balki says. 'There was something going on inside his head, obviously. And everything he said, everything he did, somehow affected me. He distracted me. And the exams were just a few months away. So I thought it was best to keep away from him. He didn't care, actually. He probably didn't even notice. He was the star, I was just the brilliant guy.'

Unni was increasingly drawn to the shadowy Somen Pillai, and the unremarkable Sai Shankaran. The three spoke in whispers in class, they were rumoured to meet in Somen's house every evening, they went places together, they had a mysterious purpose. They were on to something, everybody said. Ousep has heard this many times in different forms.

This answers a question Ousep has been waiting to ask. Why did everyone describe Somen and Sai as the closest friends of Unni and not mention Balki at all? The Unni that everybody remembers is the indecipherable boy of seventeen, and it turns out that in this period Balki was not around Unni.

Balki dismisses Sai as an idiot who was perpetually unhappy because he was afraid that he was an idiot. 'You know the kind of guy who would not play chess with you because he is afraid that he would be exposed? That's Sai. Actually that's most guys in the world, but you know what I mean.'

Somen Pillai, on the other hand, is more complicated than Ousep had imagined. He had first walked into St Ignatius when he was six, the same year as Unni and Balki. Through a huge expanse of time, his entire boyhood, Somen sat quietly in his place, spoke only reluctantly, did nothing memorable – he never ran, never played, never sang, never danced or acted in a play, and he barely managed to pass every test. He hopped from year to year in a shroud of silence and insignificance. There is a Somen in every class, in every room of the world where men congregate – the quiet one whose opinions are never known. Wherever he exists, he creates a dim corner out of his space. It is not surprising that when Simion Clark was being assaulted by the entire class, Somen was the only student who did nothing.

He sat in his place, in his safe corner. In the ten years that they were together in the class, Balki does not remember a single conversation that even mentioned Somen in passing.

'But he is the key,' Balki says, 'Somen Pillai is the person who knows what happened to Unni in the months before he died. The question "Why did Unni do what he did?" has an answer. I think Somen Pillai knows the answer.'

'What about Sai?'

'I think the other two used him as an errand boy. Sai might know something more than he lets on, but I don't think he is important. Somen Pillai is the person who can help you.'

'I can't find him.'

'I've heard.'

'How do I meet him?'

'I don't know.'

Balki rubs his eyebrows, glares intensely at the desk. Unexpectedly, he rises. He says, 'I have to go now.' But he stands there, lingering, which is odd. He pouts his lips and stares at Ousep, who decides to say nothing, but he gets the sense that it is important not to take his eyes off the boy as he struggles to make a decision. There is nothing Ousep can do but wait.

The boy, finally, makes the decision.

'I've something to say,' Balki says.

Ousep points to the chair; the boy lands hard on it. He looks nervous and his breathing is perceptible. He appears his age now. 'I've to get it out of my head. I think I trust you, I don't know why, but I trust you. I have to say it now or I'll never say it.'

'Tell me, Balki.'

'Unni used to wander in the night,' Balki says, 'late in the night, sometimes he would get back home at dawn. You may know this.'

Ousep knows, though he learnt about this long after the boy died. Unni did it only on some nights. He would wait for his father to come home, wait to stand with his mother, and for the storm to pass, and Ousep to fall into his bed. When Unni

159

began to slip out of the house at midnight, or sometimes at dawn, he was probably fifteen, a time when he was still a child in many ways and was fragile enough to be saddened by the ways of his father. His mother tried to stop him but she had no control over him. According to her, and she says it in an accusing way, Unni walked in the peace of the night to relieve his pain, to be far away from home and to dream of his future, his whole life that lay ahead, which made him happy. But in time he began to enjoy walking down the abandoned lanes and seeing his world emptied of the tame people and replaced by another kind who did not belong to the day. He told his friends about what he saw, the long stretches of time when absolutely nothing happened, nothing stirred, then the appearance of beautiful eunuchs in bridal splendour, and the solitary women going somewhere with a smile. And how he was questioned once by cops and how they turned respectful and offered to drop him home when he spoke to them in English.

'I had been hearing the night stories of Unni for months,' Balki says, 'and I was curious to go with him into the night. Like the boys of my type in Madras I was brought up as if I was a girl. I was not allowed to step out of the house after dark. So, when my parents decided to go to a wedding and leave me alone in the house for a week, I decided to wander with Unni one night and see for myself what he had been talking about. I took my father's TVS50 and we went all around Madras. We were breaking the law but the cops did not care. I realised the rules were very different late in the night. We were passing along a dark narrow lane under the Arcot Road flyover when we saw something strange. A woman in a red sari was lying on the pavement. I wanted to know why she was lying there but I didn't stop. I went straight ahead but Unni asked me to go back. So we went back, parked the TVS and walked to where she was lying. Unni squatted very close to her. So I did the same. All we could do was stare. She was a young, slim woman. Not very pretty or anything but not bad at all. We could smell liquor. She had probably got drunk and passed out. She was a prostitute, I think. I have never seen a prostitute but if a woman is so drunk that she has passed out on the road she must be a prostitute. Unni said, "Do you want to squeeze her breasts?" That's what he said. I had never touched a woman's little finger before, as in touched it in an impure way. But now all I had to do was extend my hand and I could squeeze a real woman. "Have you done this before?" I asked Unni. He said, "No. They usually don't lie around like this."

'I was not sure if I should do it but I wanted to. Very badly. I could see her legs. I wanted to do things to her, I was desperate. I was not in control. "Do it," Unni said. I shook her shoulder and said, "Excuse me, madam, wake up, please." Unni burst out laughing. He knew that I didn't want to wake her up, I just wanted to touch her. I tried to wake her up by touching her stomach, her arms, her legs, and finally I stopped pretending. I squeezed her breasts. She started mumbling something, I could not understand what she was saying but it was something very sad. We fled. That's it. That's what I wanted to tell you.'

'When you said you got your father's TVS50 out that you were breaking the law. What did you mean by that?'

Balki looks baffled, probably because he was expecting a deeper question. 'It was my father's TVS50.'

'But it's not illegal to ride your father's TVS.'

'I didn't have a licence,' he says.

'You said, "We were breaking the law."'

'Neither of us had a licence.'

'Did Unni squeeze her?'

'No. That's the whole point. That's the way he was. He wanted others to do things, so that he could watch.'

Balki rubs his face with his fat palms. 'What I did, was it wrong?' he asks. 'Did I molest a woman?'

'Yes.'

Balki raises his voice. 'But she was lying on the road and I was so desperate.'

Two weeks after the incident, unable to contain his guilt, Balki went to the Kodambakkam police station and confessed. The inspector called several of his men and asked Balki to repeat his confession. And they laughed at him. They said he should be sentenced to death by hanging, and they tried to chase him away. But Balki stood there, he insisted that he be punished. So they let him write down his confession, which he wrote in Tamil. They said they would get in touch with him. But he never heard from them.

'In your confession, Balki, you obviously gave your name and your address?'

'Yes.'

'And the names of the other two?'

'Yes.'

Balki stares at Ousep unpleasantly. He rises, but then decides to sit down.

'I am sorry, Balki, I didn't mean to trick you. So, that night there were three boys on the TVS50, not two. Isn't that true?'

Balki does not answer. He toys again with the paperweight.

'No cop in Madras would fine you for riding a moped without a licence. You know that, Balki,' Ousep says. 'The only way you can break the law in the night is by having three people on that thing. Who is the third boy in the comic?'

'I cannot tell you that. It would be unfair to that person.'

'But you wrote his name in the confession you gave to the police.'

'Yes. I had gone mad. I don't know why I did it. But that was a long time ago. I am sure that piece of paper no longer exists.'

'It exists in the police files. That is the nature of papers and police. I can retrieve it for you if you want.'

'How will you do that?'

'A reporter has his ways.'

'I don't want you to do anything. I want to forget the matter.'

'I understand. But, Balki, I've run out of people who will talk to me. I want to know the name of this person. He may want to cooperate with me if he knows I have this information.'

'Then this is going to disappoint you. It is not someone you have not met.'

'Who is it?'

'It is not fair to reveal his name.'

'That's all right. Be unfair, for Unni's sake.'

'You've met him before. So what use is this?'

'He may want to talk at length now.'

'You're going to twist his arm now?'

'I may try and persuade him.'

'That would compromise my identity.'

'Yes, but to a person who already knows what you have done.'

Balki looks at the church spire and tries to make a decision. He does not take long. He says, 'It was Sai.'

'Thank you, Balki. I have one more question. Did Unni ever talk to you about a corpse?'

'Yes,' Balki says, still preoccupied with his guilt. 'But I think he was just fooling around.'

He has not recovered from his confession. He does not want to talk about anything else now. 'Unni had this theory,' he says. 'According to him every man, even a regular decent man, has harmed a woman at least once, or will in his lifetime. He really believed that for some reason. I used to argue with him that such statements are plain moronic. I think he made me do that thing on the road so that he could prove his point.'

'You don't have to take everything he ever said so seriously.'

'But he turned out to be right, isn't that true?'

'Don't whip yourself,' Ousep says. 'Men do things. We can't help it. That's all there is to it. As you will discover in time, Balki, the primary choice every man has to make is whether he wants to be himself or if he wants peace.'

~

THE EIGHTEEN WOMEN and the clean-shaven evangelist are on their knees, in a tight circle around a small golden cross. They raise their hands and sing 'Praise the lord'. The woman whose house it is sings the loudest and the other women are careful not to eclipse her voice. Mariamma Chacko does not want to raise her hands because the underarms of her blouse are darned, so she raises her head in compensatory devotion.

This Sunday she will report what she has seen in the room to the parish priest to further milk him and also reconfirm his fear that the light of his authority has been diminished by the more energetic Protestant evangelists. But she must admit that there is something to his fear, there is something eerie about what is happening to the Catholic women of the Kodambakkam circle these days. The daily mass in the church does not satisfy them, they want more than the soft hymns, the sermons and the murmurs of prayers. They want what the young hallelujah evangelists make them do, they want all that dancing and clapping and screaming. And the evangelists are drawing more and more women into their fold.

The evangelist who is with them this afternoon is famous for converting hundreds of Hindu villagers, stunning them with a blessed white powder that makes the sick feel better. It is surprising what crushed paracetamol can do to parched, starving people. In his spell, the Catholic women of Kodambakkam, too, are now trying to convert their servants and the slum women, and anybody they can find.

How is it that an ordinary man can cast such a spell on women who are far cleverer than him? She wonders whether Unni was right, after all. He told her once, during one of his biblical moods, 'Truly I say unto you, Mariamma. The fundamental quality of a delusion is that it is contagious. The very purpose of every delusion is to transmit itself to other brains. That is how a delusion survives. On the other hand, Mariamma Chacko, truth can never be transmitted, truth can never travel from one brain to another. Movement is a quality of delusion alone.'

'What nonsense you talk, Unni. Are you saying that if two people believe in something it simply cannot be the truth?'

'Absolutely, Mariamma Chacko, you're a very clever woman.'

'So there is only one person in the world who knows the truth. And that is you?'

'Truly I say unto you. Truth is not consistent. It changes from brain to brain. The truth of every neurological system is unique and it cannot be transmitted. It cannot be told, it cannot be conveyed, it cannot be searched for and found.'

'Unni, do you want some coffee?'

When she returns home and is about to open her door she hears the phone ring. That is unusual because the phone does not ring at this time of the day. By the time she reaches it the phone has died. She wonders why she is afraid. Thoma is in school. What can happen in school? Did he fall down the stairs? Someone poked his eye with a divider? The phone rings again and she grabs the receiver. 'Hello,' she says. A man's voice at the other end says, 'Is this Mariamma Chacko?'

Is it that call, then, the call she has wished for many times? Now that it has come she does not want it, she wants it to go away. She may have sent some prayers up in her weak moments but surely God has the sense to know which of a woman's prayers he must take seriously.

'Is this Mariamma Chacko?'

'Yes.'

'I am calling from GG Hospital. Ousep Chacko has had a heart attack.'

It is several moments before she speaks. 'Is he all right?' she asks.

'Can you come down to GG right now?'

'Is he all right?'

'The doctors are still with him.'

'Is he all right?'

'I don't know. Please come immediately.'

Long after the line goes dead she stands holding the receiver. The first time she saw him she had felt her cheek with her fingers. She had a stain on her face from brushing against a raw hill mango. The black stain from the milk of the mango would take a month to go, and what bad luck it was that the fine young man who had come to the hill to seek her hand should arrive at this time in her life. Not that she adored him at first sight. The truth is she was disappointed. He was in a cheap shirt, with many things in its sagging pocket, and in rubber slippers. But then his name was known to all in her village, and probably everyone in Kerala who read short stories. A poor writer, but still a writer. Which girl back then would not have wished to marry a young writer?

Thoma Chacko always knew that this is how it would be, this is how the news of his father's death would be broken to him – that the day would begin like any other day, that he would be in school and his mother would suddenly appear looking like a maid, pretending to be calm, and take him away to a hospital without revealing much. But he would never have guessed that when the day he feared the most arrived he would be in a purple velvet frock.

It is the dress rehearsal of the school play and he is in the main hall. He is, as usual, an extra, but this time a female extra, one of the many girls in frocks waiting with their right hands on their left elbows for the king to arrive. Rufus Sir has told all the lady extras that they must stand with their legs together. 'That's how girls stand,' he says. Everybody knows that Rufus Sir enjoys beating up boys when they are dressed as girls. So Thoma does not let his mind wander, he does not want to give him any excuse.

When Thoma hears her the first time he knows that he is not imagining it but he pretends that he has not heard her. He can see his mother standing at a great distance, in the doorway, with the headmaster. She has dressed in a hurry and he is surprised how cheap she looks. 'Thoma,' she says again.

As he walks down the large empty hall and the strong, grim figure of his mother approaches, Thoma is sure that his life is about to get worse. 'Thoma, where is your uniform?' she says.

'It is in the class.'

'We don't have time, you have to go this way.'

'What happened?'

'Your father has had a heart attack. He is in the hospital.'

She tells the headmaster, 'I rushed out of my house without taking any money. Would you have a hundred rupees for the auto? I have to go to GG Hospital.'

'I have nothing, madam,' the man says. 'And the office deposited all its cash in the bank in the morning.' He screams to the assembled cast, 'Does anybody have a hundred rupees? It is an emergency.'

There is silence.

Mariamma takes her son's hand and walks. Thoma hears a boy whine, 'Sir, that is my sister's frock he is wearing. I have to take it back today.' They walk at a steady pace towards the school gate. There is an auto waiting for them outside. The driver looks annoyed. 'You can't make me wait that long,' he says, 'this is not your car.'

They ride in silence. Thoma allows the gloom to fill him, he sees his father in the mornings, when he is a clever, elegant man. Thoma is proud that his father is not an ordinary person on an old scooter. He is not a bank clerk carrying a lunchbox to work, he is not just anybody. His father is a journalist. When important things happened in this country, Ousep Chacko used to be there, taking notes. He appeared on TV once, very briefly, to say something about a politician whose name Thoma has forgotten. Everybody saw him and everybody said, 'Thoma, we saw your father on TV.'

'Is he dead?' he asks his mother.

'They won't tell me,' she says.

'He is dead, isn't he?'

'I don't know, Thoma.'

His father had a complicated relationship with their Mustaang TV. He tried many times to take it away and pawn it. Some days, when he was about to set out for work, he would stop and stare at the TV for a long time, making an elaborate plan in his head. Then he would lift it from its stand and take it to the door with great care as if it were a fallen child he was taking to the hospital. But he would always return it to the stand, smile at Thoma and pat his face. One day his father brought a muscular man along who carried the TV away in a tight hug. Ousep was about to follow the thug but he stopped in the doorway and looked at Thoma. 'We are just taking it for repair, Thoma,' he said. The TV never came back. But at least his father had the heart to lie. It is the sweetest memory he has of his father. It was a moment of love, who can deny that?

His father wanted to be left alone most of the time. Some fathers are like that. But Thoma knows that there were times when his father wanted to be included in the antics of Unni and his mother. Thoma is sorry today that his father was never allowed any easy entries into family life. Unni and his mother knew how to punish him and they always did.

Thoma remembers a Sunday afternoon from a distant time when he woke up from his nap and began chatting with Unni, who was working on a comic. Unni did not say anything, which was not unusual. When he was working he did not get distracted. But Thoma was so annoyed at being ignored he said, 'Can you hear me?' Unni did not turn. Thoma tried to distract him, even poked him a few times, but Unni could not see or hear or feel his brother. Thoma began to suspect that he had become invisible. When he rushed to his mother to confirm it she, too, could not see him or feel him. But he could see that she was trying not to laugh. Was it a prank? It was natural that Thoma would consider his father the ultimate test of his invisibility. He stood at the door of his father's room and mustered the courage to sing a song, but Ousep could not hear him. Thoma kept inching into the room and finally stood in front of his father, but Ousep looked right through him. Thoma put his hand on his open mouth and ran outside screaming, 'I am gone, I am gone.' Unni was watching this from the hall. He hugged Thoma and told him that it was just a prank. Thoma was so relieved he laughed insanely, his eyes still wide and terrified, which made his mother hold her stomach and shake with laughter. Ousep stepped out of his room to laugh with them and be included; after all, he had figured out the game from the commotion in the house and had played along. But when he appeared they went inside in a huddle to laugh privately. Thoma is sorry they did that.

The ride in the auto is long and slow. Thoma looks at the harsh light of day outside, an incandescent plane in the sky, vehicles going somewhere, men hanging from the window bars of buses, people laughing, waiting, running. He hopes his father is still a part of all this, he hopes Ousep Chacko will walk again, with his brisk morning strides.

Finally, his mother asks the driver to stop. Thoma is confused. They are not at the hospital, they are outside an apartment block.

'You said GG Hospital,' the auto driver says.

'I have to go and fetch someone,' she says.

'You have to come back fast,' he says. 'This is not your car.'

She takes Thoma's hand and marches into the concrete entrance of the building. The watchman decides not to stop them, possibly because Thoma looks like a flamboyant modern girl going someplace important with her maid.

'Where are we going?' he asks.

'Thoma, it is like this. There was no money at home and I rushed out in a state. So we have no money for the auto.'

'What are we going to do?'

'We must do what we have to do,' she says.

They go to the rear portion of the building, climb the wall and jump into a quiet lane on the other side. 'What we are doing is wrong, Thoma, but we didn't have a choice,' she says. 'Jesus knows.'

As they walk swiftly down the back lanes, hand in hand, throwing nervous glances at the autos passing by, Thoma sees men looking at him in a way he has never seen them look. They are not trying to make up their minds, they are sure he is a girl. They look at his chest, at his crotch, at his arse. They are looking at him as if he is an ancient familiar foe from whom they would like to take something. Thoma feels humiliated. They look at him and spit unconsciously. He is reminded of what Unni had said. 'I have done research, Thoma, a lot of research over many weeks. Men in Madras spit all the time but the chances of them spitting when they see a young girl are seventy-eight per cent higher than when they are not looking at a young girl. When they see a girl they don't even realise they are spitting.'

When they reach GG, the huge reception hall is crowded, and they stand there wondering what they must do. His mother asks a nurse something in Malayalam. The nurse then leads them to the lift. In the lift she gapes at him.

'I am a boy,' he says, 'I was rehearsing for a school play.'

'You are a very beautiful boy,' she says, which makes Thoma happy despite the circumstances. She leads them to the longest corridor he has ever seen. He is stunned by the affluence of this place and he is proud that his father somehow managed to land here and not in some dreary government morgue.

The nurse consults with other white frocks and takes them through a network of clean beautiful corridors. 'He is in 401,' the nurse says, 'that's the one.' As they walk down the final corridor, his mother clutches his hand.

They are almost jogging now, which makes the nurse jog, too, though she does not want to. She opens the door of 401 and takes them in. Thoma has not seen a more luxurious room. Everything is white and expensive and there is a deep elegant silence in the air. How can anybody have the heart to die in a place like this?

He sees his father lying in a green gown on a thick comfortable bed. There are some wires shoved up his nose, which must mean that he is alive. The nurse studies a bunch of papers hanging from his bed. 'He is all right,' she says. 'He is all right, Mariamma. He is very weak but he is going to be fine. He is going to be asleep the whole day, though.'

His mother begins to cry but she has no desire to go and touch her man. Thoma wants to hold his father's hand but feels too shy to perform an act of love. 'Who brought him to this expensive place?' his mother says.

'His office people,' the nurse says. 'He was in his office when it happened.'

'Who is going to pay for all this?'

'His office, from what I can see. Mariamma, don't you worry. You can go home this evening and come back tomorrow morning. He is not going to wake up before morning.'

More nurses come in, all of them fully grown women in white frocks. Like Thoma and his father, they too look as if they are extras in a bad play. A fat doctor walks in smoking a pipe. He studies Mariamma and figures that she is not important. He mumbles that her husband almost died, and he goes away. The nurses follow him, leaving Thoma and his mother alone. They stand together in discomfort, looking at the ceiling and the walls, as if they are in a rich stranger's home.

Ousep's trousers are hanging on the wall. Mariamma extracts his wallet and a bunch of papers, which are neatly folded. She arranges the papers and searches for a place to sit. But something about what she is holding makes her freeze and she forgets to sit. It looks like one of Unni's comics, but Thoma has never seen this one before. His mother looks disturbed as she turns the pages. When she comes to the image of a man giving a thumbs-up sign, she drops the comic in shock, or maybe the pages just fell for no reason at all. She is a person who drops things. She picks up the comic and looks carefully at the man. When she reaches the final page, Thoma is surprised to see a giant image of his mother in full flow.

'What's this?' he asks.

'I don't know,' she says.

She takes all the money in the wallet but leaves the comic behind. They take a bus back home. It is when they walk through the gates of Block A and all the boys who are playing begin to laugh that Thoma is reminded of his dress. He looks up at the balconies, at the men and women who are standing there. They do not laugh. They probably know about the heart attack and they wonder what has happened. Thoma is reminded of the time when he and his parents had returned from the church. It was a day like this. They had gone somewhere as a family and returned one person short.

He looks up again to check whether Mythili has seen him in this condition but there is only her mother standing there. As they walk up the stairway, doors open and the women step out. They ask Mariamma what happened and they hold her hand and ask her to be brave. Later they come to his home, one after the other, with hot food and fruit and coffee. Even Mrs Balasubramanium comes with many things on a plate. His mother puts it all on the table, and at some point in the evening, when they hear another doorbell, she says, 'This man should have a heart attack every day.' And they have a good laugh.

5

Philipose, Philipose

OUSEP IS NOT dreaming, he is sure about that, even though he is asleep and what he sees is a world in which Unni is not dead. Unni is not dead because he is not born yet. The world before Unni Chacko, according to Unni Chacko himself, 'is the strongest evidence to support the ridiculous hypothesis that life will continue as usual after I am dead'.

Mariamma is young, beautiful and has been married for three months. She goes through these days with somewhat exaggerated glee, like an amateur lover. When he cracks a joke she runs away covering her mouth, she serves him food with a flourish of her hand, cleans his ear with too much care, as if she is repairing a watch. She lives with him in a large house that smells of red earth and bananas, and is surrounded by high palms and plantains and jackfruit trees. It is the office accommodation of *Weekly* in Kottayam. He is among the brightest journalists in Kerala, and the youngest columnist anyone has ever known, whom politicians and bishops visit. Priests quote him in their Sunday sermons, even Protestant priests. Publishers, who have read his hugely popular short fiction in the Sunday magazines, beg him to write a novel.

Mariamma enjoys her new life, she sings love songs to herself, names the calves born in other houses, reads anything she can find. She translates *One Hundred Years of Solitude* into Malayalam. Small portions actually, and she does it out of love for the great Marquez. Her translation is good but there are words she skips; she says those words do not exist in Malayalam. He tries to think of synonyms to impress her but she is right, those words do not exist. And some objects in Marquez's story remain blank gaping spaces in her prose.

She forces Ousep to go to church with her every Sunday; they walk together in their best clothes on narrow, wet, winding roads, talking and laughing, and fully aware that neighbours are watching from their windows – narrowing their eyes, craning their necks, fanning their stomachs, moving their jaws and whispering things to others. Ousep feels vulgar to be so happy in plain sight; he feels as if he is walking through a famine eating a large fried fish. But then that is how they were, Ousep and Mariamma, young and happy in an unremarkable way. Who would believe it, once they were like anybody else?

She is shameless when they make love, which is often, and when they are this way the air is filled with the calamitous sounds of a woman who appears to be mourning the destruction of furniture. She stops now and then to give precise instructions on how he must proceed. But when they lie spent she turns quiet and melancholic, even bad tempered, and she is the first to leave the bed. That, innocent Ousep imagines, is how women are. He imagines that he fills her with so much tumult that she must retrieve herself in private. He begins to strut around his life thinking that there is something extraordinary about him as a lover, a suspicion he always possessed. How else can a girl collapse so completely in his embrace? When he sees new brides walk with their men he is surprised at how they can be so happy, as happy as Mariamma Chacko. It seems odd to him that other men, the simple men, men who are not writers, they too can make their women laugh, make them glow.

Relatives and friends visit every day, there is much laughter and happy commotion in the house. Some evenings, white Ambassador cars with red lights on top are parked outside their home. The Deputy Collector asks Mariamma, not entirely in jest, 'Considering everything, how tough the world is on women, would you still like to be a woman in your next life?' She gives a gentle tilt to her head and asks, 'And what is the other option?' There is an explosion of laughter in the room.

Too much happiness, she tells Ousep. She says it with a hint of fear in her voice. She is sure that some visitors, his relatives especially, leave behind enchanted things to bring doom to their home and end their joys. She is right, she finds black coins and chicken bones hidden in the nooks of the iron gates of their home. There are things written on them, threads tied to them. She laughs because she is not superstitious. She collects them and puts them in a box. One day she finds a copperplate with inscriptions buried in the land that runs around their home. Another day she discovers a vial of dark oil in the grounds. She collects them all, keeps them safe, as if they are precious relics of human nature. Which they are, in a way.

Ousep goes to work around noon every day; Mariamma stands at the gate and watches him go down the red-earth path that runs in the shade of immortal trees. He looks back several times and they laugh always at their juvenile love. They are the couple who would stretch their arms and run towards each other in a sunflower farm, though they have never done that.

Ousep has stopped drinking. It is a tradition among Malayalee men to stop drinking after marriage. But slowly, like the rest, he resumes with small innocuous nips. Mariamma does not mind because she is yet to know him well. She has not seen him on buckling knees, seen him sway like a fool or on the arms of other men. But there is a lot about her that Ousep does not know. She too has abandoned something that really cannot be given up.

The first time he hears the voice is at dawn. He is stirred from his sleep by the unfamiliar sound of a woman's deep whispers that break into soft howls and more whispers – 'Just a girl, I was just a girl, Mother, a girl can tell her mother some things, can't she?' Ousep follows the voice, which leads him to the kitchen doorway. He sees his young wife standing with her lips curled inside her mouth, her head tilted. Her finger wags. Nobody has told him that she becomes this way sometimes. It is now clear why the rubber merchant had given away his daughter to the son of a pauper farmer. He was not mesmerised by Ousep's prose as he had claimed. He had found a fool. But what Ousep feels at that moment as he stands outside the kitchen is a wounded affection for his woman.

Mariamma is studying the burnt bottom of a large aluminium vessel and she is saying, 'You could have said something, Mother, just anything. So what if the boatman heard?' She is shocked to see him in the kitchen doorway. She is so ashamed she begins to cry. He asks her why she is this way. He will ask her the same question in the months to come and, on occasion, in the years to follow. She will tell him that she was always this way, she will tell him that she cannot help it. 'But I am not mad, I am actually a happy woman,' she will say. She would try to control herself, be the girl she was in the first light of marriage but she would slip into the trance every few days, especially when she imagines she is alone.

In time Ousep would stop loving home, he would become the other men, the men who sink into the company of other men, the veteran husbands, the men who drink late into the night with their friends, the men with frail thighs who have never played football but talk about football, and at other times about the superiority of Marx over Keynes, and about the unattainable prose of the new Spanish writers.

Mariamma knows he has changed. She tries to make her home as beautiful as possible, she wakes up at dawn and grinds things in large stone boulders, stands sweating in the charcoal fumes of the kitchen and cooks for hours so that she can watch him eat like a boy. She tries to be happy enough so that she does not enact the moments from another time. She makes love to him in the mornings. But Ousep has gone too far the Malayalee way. In the mornings he does wish to be a good person, a decent man, but in the nights he returns as a corpse. She becomes bitter and angry. To punish him she takes the tailoring scissors and chops off the sleeves of his best shirt. They have a big fight. He holds his amputated shirt and calls her names, which makes her cry. He returns that night drunk. She chops off the legs of his best trousers. He continues to return drunk and she continues to cut his clothes. She stops cleaning the house, leaves things lying around, puts things in disorder, arranges the furniture in crooked ways.

Ousep's tiny avian mother has been waiting to torment Mariamma by right, but he has never let her stay in the house for too long. She smells trouble in his home, so she is persistent, says she wants to live with her son, her great writer son for whom she has toiled all her life, milked buffaloes on so many dawns. Eventually he gives up and the woman comes and straightens the furniture, cleans the house, cooks for her son. His nine parasitic sisters too move in, one after the other, to harass the weird girl who talks to herself. They insult her, treat her poorly in her own home. He does not know how he allowed it but he does not deny he did – he does nothing as they torture his wife every day. Those petty women, he let them do all that. She suffers in silence but she does not forget. Their full Christian names enter her insane monologues, she repeats what they tell her, hangs their memories on the wall and asks them pointed questions. Even now, after all these years, she says almost every day, 'You got away, Annamol, you got away.' That is at the heart of Mariamma's lament, the grouse against all who committed crimes against her and got away.

Mariamma abandons her proud rationality. She throws away the enchanted items, she calls a controversial Catholic priest to purify her home, who utters things in Sanskrit. But nothing changes.

Ousep and Mariamma are not ethereally fused any more, they drift apart, but when they attain a distance between themselves, from where they cannot always hear the other but they can still see, they drift no more. They begin to orbit each other, like two equal planets that cannot let go. The distance separates them in their bed too, but there are times when they collide, searching for flesh.

The night Unni is born, Ousep comes fully drunk to the hospital, he goes to the wrong ward and abuses the baby in the crib, calls it an ugly monkey. The new mother screams for help. Men and women hold him by his arms and carry him to Mariamma's bed. He mumbles something to her but leaves without seeing the baby.

Around this time he gets a lead from an altar boy that the powerful archbishop is a paedophile. Ousep chases the story for months, convinces several boys and parish workers to speak to him, promising them anonymity. When he finally files the story, the editor, a venerated old man, calls Ousep to his office and asks him the identity of his unnamed sources. Ousep is reluctant. 'I am not asking you to give it in writing, Ousep,' the editor says. 'Just tell me who these people are. Their names would dissolve in air. I've a right to know, you have a duty to tell, it is journalistic tradition.' Ousep reveals the names. The story is then killed. The archbishop had long known of the story, and had been waiting patiently to learn the names of those who had ratted on him. Ousep gets drunk one night and tries to break into the archbishop's residence to beat him up. He loses his job in disgrace. To his surprise, he finds himself unemployable. He has suddenly acquired the reputation of being an arrogant, uncontrollable young man, who fabricates stories. There are tales about him in the newsrooms, most of them exaggerations of things he has said and done under the influence of alcohol. The men who were waiting for Ousep to fall, who include some friends, ensure that he will never rise again in Kerala. He finds a modest job with the United News of India, moves to Madras, and begins to live in the midst of austere vegetarians.

~

NOT FOR THE first time since he was brought here, he wakes up and accepts that he is in an impressive hospital ward and that he has not slept on a better bed than this. He is probably heavily drugged; everything around him is in a tidy white haze. He enjoys his own physical frailty, which reminds him of a sleepy rainy day, enjoys the fact that he is being cared for by strangers to whom he owes nothing, especially money. His body is too feeble even to think, he is filled with what has to be deep serenity, and he is worried that he has been transformed into someone better. Is this clarity? Is clarity a single transparent thought or is it the absence of thought? Was Unni right after all – could it be that thoughts are truly the corrupt dominant species of the world that have colonised man, relentlessly mutating into increasingly complex ideas and making him do things so that they can finally intrude into the material world as marvellous objects?

Ousep loves the drug the hospital has given him, but then his palm circles his hairy chest, which means what he needs now is a small nip.

The white door opens and an almost beautiful nurse enters the ward holding a pen over a notebook as if she knows what she is going to write but will not do so until she sees it with her own eyes. Unlike the older nurses she does not seem lampooned in the starched white frock and white stockings. She looks forbidden and unattainable, even important. As the door shuts behind her, there is something deeply carnal about the decisive click of the knob. It is the first time in years that he has been alone in a sealed room with a young woman, and he feels he must do something inappropriate. The eyes of the nurse fall on different objects in the room, including him. She makes some quick notes in her book and leaves.

He does not know whether it is night or day, or how long he has been here, lying like a transvestite in this ridiculous green gown, but he decides to stay awake and wait for Mariamma. He has a feeling that she is somewhere around, she would not leave him alone in a hospital ward. There is a lot that they have to talk about – that is, if she is willing to answer his questions.

He sits up in the bed and leans his back against the massive pillow. He tries to remember when exactly he had seen the apparition. A few hours ago, days ago? He is not clear what had woken him up at that moment but when he was awake the first thing he saw was Sai Shankaran standing in the doorway of the ward, meek and harmless, his hair wet and immovable as always in the mornings. Even as a sudden apparition, Sai was incapable of giving a fright. When he finally walked in, the room was filled with the smell of Lifebuoy soap.

'Have you come to kill me, Sai?'

'No,' Sai said in a way that turned Ousep's jest into a reasonable question.

'Sai.'

'Yes.'

'Will you help me urinate?'

Sai looked terrified. So Ousep lied. 'I was just kidding.'

The boy picked up a stool from the corner of the ward, sat a foot away from Ousep's bed, and said, 'I didn't come here because you blackmailed me.'

'I did no such thing, Sai. You're imagining things.'

'But what did you tell me at the bus stop? You said the cops would come to my home and ask me questions. You said I have to now mention in the US visa form that there is a police complaint against me.'

'I was only trying to protect you. I was only trying to inform you of the possibilities so that you are on your guard.'

'I didn't come here because you blackmailed me, I want you to know that.'

'I believe you, Sai.'

'I know what I did to that woman in the road was wrong. I don't know what happened to me. I am ashamed. I am ashamed because I am an upright person. I am a moral person, I believe that every man should touch only one woman in his entire life. I believe in morality.'

It occurred to Ousep that morality was probably the invention of unattractive men. Who else does it benefit really?

'What made you come here, Sai?'

'I thought, what if you died, what if you died without knowing the real Unni? So I thought I would come here and talk to you. I owe Unni that much. So I don't want you to think I am here because I am scared.'

Sai gaped without pride or hope but in his large dull eyes there was also unhappy compassion, which was not a good sign. Ousep was expecting fear.

'I will tell you everything I know,' Sai said, 'but in the end what will be clear is that I may have hidden some things from you but I was not lying when I kept saying that there was no deep reason behind Unni's death. He wanted to die and that is all there is to it. He killed himself for the same reason people always kill themselves. He did not wish to live.'

He fell silent for a while. Then, as if he had remembered something painful, his nostrils vibrated, his lips trembled, his eyes blinked several times. He blew his nose into his ironed handkerchief and licked his lips as he waited to gather his thoughts.

'Why are you crying, Sai?'

Sai slouched his back and looked all around the ward. 'What is everything?' he said. 'What is all this? What is life, what is space, what is finite, what is infinite?'

Through Sai's mouth, philosophy was revealed in its true form – as a bunch of dim questions asked too early in the life of science. The boy fell silent again. And when he found his voice he spoke about himself, which was surprising. Sai, truly, had come here to talk.

Like Unni and Balki and many others in their class, Sai was enrolled at St Ignatius when he was six. He was a dull student, and his father believed that a thrashing with a leather belt every now and then would solve the problem. The man had the habit of holding his son's report card in one hand and the belt in the other, and reading out the scores aloud and whipping him. On occasion, he chased little Sai around the house with a heated serving spoon. Very often the spoon found Sai's body, usually his arms and thighs. Like many other boys of his age, Sai eventually grew up into a fragile adolescent who was beaten up at home by a man who was shorter than him and was progressively getting shorter.

'I was so miserable,' Sai said, rubbing his nose and looking away. 'I was so unhappy my hair began to change, it began to curl.'

'Your hair?'

'Yes. For a few months when I was sixteen, I was so stressed, my hair became very curly, like a black man's hair. Unni used to call me Pubic Hair.'

The whole decade in school, until the very end, Unni did not mean much to Sai. Even after the Simion Clark incident, Unni was at best a curiosity, until the day he walked into the classroom and said that reality was not what it appeared, that something was going on, that everything people believed to be true was a lie.

Sai described Unni's nervous declaration and his account was consistent with everything Ousep has heard before about the day. Unni must have spoken for less than a minute but something happened to Sai, something powerful went through him, it was as if a dangerous idea that was lurking in the darkness inside him had been shown a luminous light. 'The first emotion I felt was fright and I don't know why I looked behind me,' he said.

Ousep wonders what it was about the moment that made such a lasting impression on so many boys. Its impact appears to have been out of proportion. He tries to imagine the scene, which has now been narrated to him by so many. All the accounts are the same except for Unni's exact words, which will never be known. They all begin with how Unni walked into the classroom just before the first bell was about to ring. Did Unni plan it that way – to wait till everybody was seated and appear at the very end in a conspicuous way so that all eyes would be on him?

By the time the event occurred, Unni had stature, which was important to what was about to happen. Unni was many things. He was a storyteller, he played football as if it were important, he bowled with furious pace, and he had subdued a powerful sadistic teacher in an extraordinary fashion. It was such a person, not just anybody, who had walked into the class that day. And he told them, with fear and nervousness in the place of his indestructible cool, that there was something lurking out there in the world around them and that he might have seen it from very close. Ousep concedes that there is probably enough in the scene, and in the background of its protagonist, to make it an unforgettable moment.

By the time the incident occurred, Sai had long abandoned the idea of religion. 'God did not make any sense to me,' he said in the proud self-congratulatory way of young atheists, 'I could see that life was merely an accident.'

Ousep waited for the inevitable sentence, the line that drags atheists back into the fold of religion without their knowing, the line that usually goes like this – 'But I believe in a force.'

Sai looked intently at the floor and said with the sparkle of epiphany, 'But there is a force, I believe in a force.'

The idea of an accidental life insulted God, and that comforted Sai, but it did not explain everything to him. He spent hours looking up at the sky. 'Day sky, night sky,' he said to show how comprehensive his study was. Thinking about the infinity of space made him go crazy for several hours every day. He imagined there was something deeply cerebral about his new obsession with the question 'Where does space end?' He often thought about why there was something instead of nothing and what exactly was the meaning of human life on a speck of dust at the edge of just another galaxy.

'So that was my life. Deep thoughts, belting by my father, very deep thoughts, more belting. I led a double life. The universe inside my head sometimes, other times red rashes on my arse.'

Ousep yawned to conceal a laugh.

It was in that period of gloom that Unni walked into the class one morning and said that something mysterious was going on. 'An inner eye opened inside me,' Sai said. 'How can I explain what happened to me? I felt as if I could see for the first time in my life.'

He realised in an instant that all the philosophers he had read, all the religions, even Einstein, even J. Krishnamurthy, were saying the same thing in different ways – there is a shocking truth hiding behind the world that we see, behind the ordinary days of our lives. God is not a lie but some kind of an abridged version of this reality, a beginner's course that has been misunderstood.

Trapped in the trance, Sai thought he had become enlightened and that the full details of the universal truth would enter his head by lunchtime. When a teacher asked him a question in class he remained silent, even smiled peacefully. He was thrashed by the man. 'Yet another son of an illiterate farmer who had converted to Christianity in exchange for a bicycle or something. He kept slapping me but I could not speak. That made him go mad. He said, "Sai, say one word. One word and I will let you go. At least say A, B, C, D with the mouth that the Lord gave you or I am going to kill you today."'

Despite the beating Sai was unable to extricate himself from the moment. But when the day ended he had recovered. He realised he had not become enlightened. He asked Unni the meaning of what he had said in the morning. Unni told him that it was an insane moment and that he did not wish to speak about it. He said it was dangerous to talk about those things. That, naturally, made Sai even more obsessed.

For several days he begged Unni to explain. Unni said it was not a matter that could be explained, but that there were clues everywhere.

'Unni told me, "Sai, have you ever wondered why animals don't look at the sky? There must be a reason, there is a reason."' Unni showed him a series of portraits he had drawn of various mammals looking up at the sky. Unni said, 'I drew these to show how weird it is for us to see animals looking up. They never do it. Why?' Sai begged him to explain but Unni said that language was not the medium through which to understand these things. 'He said, "Language was created by nature to guard its secrets not to reveal them. We are trapped in language. Even thought has become language. That is what nature wants, Sai. It has given us language because it has hidden the truth somewhere else."'

'Nature is the enemy?' Sai asked, in a whisper.

Unni said, 'You won't believe it, Sai. When you see, you won't believe it.'

Sai began to spend hours by himself trying to guess what Unni seemed to know. He shadowed Unni, called him up several times with questions, came to his house, sat beside him in class. In time Unni loosened up a bit. 'One day he told me, "Try walking on the streets without looking at girls, just do not look at them, do not look at their bodies. Don't ask me why, just do it."'

Sai stopped looking at young women, including some of his teachers. When he saw women on the road he would lower his gaze and walk on. 'Like a woman.' In packed buses he would shut his eyes. When young mothers spoke to him he stared at his toenails and answered them. He began to look at the world differently and the world, too, seemed like another place. A world without women is a very different world.

One afternoon on the stairway of the school, Unni came from behind and whispered into his ear, 'Now it is time for you to stop masturbating. Just quit it right now. Don't go home and send out one last spurt. Start from this moment. You will begin to feel a powerful force inside you. That will take you to the next level.'

It was a surprisingly candid revelation by Sai to the father of a friend. Ousep saw a motive in this. The boy probably wanted to convince him that he was withholding nothing, and he was building this myth through the facility of sexual confession. Was Sai a cunning bastard, or was he just a boy who had dropped his guard?

Sai's imaginary fornications were the only happy moments in his life. 'But I stopped. Just like that I stopped because Unni said I must stop.' Within weeks, he went crazy. He began to have enormous erections that lasted for hours, even powerful sexual desires for his own mother, whom he had not considered a woman before. He stopped looking at her, too, which confused everyone at home. Finally, his father held the leather belt in one hand and pointed the other at his wife. 'Look at her, Sai, look at your mother.'

In the middle of these upheavals, he cycled every evening to Brilliant Tutorials for the JEE classes. The exam was just months away but Sai's practice scores, not surprisingly, were getting worse. His father began to belt him almost every day now. That made Sai think more deeply about the meaning of life and Unni's secret.

Unni, by now, was often seen in the company of Somen Pillai, even on Sundays. It was a new association by all the accounts Ousep has heard, and Sai confirmed that. Somen Pillai, the lonely insignificant boy whose voice was rarely heard in class, who had no talents, who never used to even run, became an enigmatic figure all of a sudden. Now that everybody was looking at him more closely they agreed that there was something wrong with him. His walk was unnaturally slow, and there was an unfathomable smile on his face. 'There was something about him.'

That is the most exasperating quality of everybody's memory of Somen. They are sure that he was not normal but nobody is able to fully explain what exactly was wrong with him. 'He had a way of not being there even when he was there. He did not move much, never drew much attention to himself. He rarely spoke and when he did speak his sentence construction was a bit weird. I cannot explain beyond this.'

Sai let himself drift into the company of Unni and Somen Pillai. They did not resist. He walked with them, ate with them, sat on the steps of the Fatima Church and listened to them talk. 'They spoke mostly about Hindu gods, which was a surprise to me.'

In the world according to Unni, Hinduism was a giant comic created over centuries by great artists who encoded within their cryptic stories meanings within meanings. But the demons and the gods with several hands and animal-headed beings were not outlandish metaphors. According to Unni, they really existed and they exist even now, they live among ordinary people. What was Unni trying to say? Surely he did not believe this? Was he just trying to muddle the minds of fools? Is it now time for Ousep to accept a fact that has long been staring him in the face – that his son was an anarchist, who plotted against the people around him with the modest means available to a seventeen-year-old?

One evening after school, on his way to the twilight JEE coaching class, Sai turned his cycle into the narrow mud lane that led to Somen's house. He had never been to the house before. As he approached the gate he could see Somen and Unni framed by the foyer's giant window. They were playing chess. Somen, who did not look surprised, let him in and went back to the game. Sai sat with them and watched the game in silence. He could see that their level of play was high, far beyond his. 'It was very peaceful to just sit there and watch two guys who were not interested in any entrance exam in the world play a great game.' Somen's mother appeared briefly to give them something to eat and left them alone for the rest of the evening. At some point Somen and Unni decided to stop the game. They noted down the positions of the pieces in a notebook, which held several scribbled chess notations from past games.

They went to the terrace and talked about ordinary things.

Teachers, cricket, people they knew. 'Nothing deep.' After it got dark, Somen walked on the narrow ledge with his arms stretched out. He slipped, almost fell. He turned to Unni and they laughed as if it was a great joke. Later, there would be many times when they would treat death as something funny. When they saw a funeral procession in the road, a body being taken for cremation, they would giggle.

Sai began to meet them every evening. On the terrace, Unni and Somen showed him the open window in the neighbourhood through which he could see a very old man try, for hours, to achieve sex with his old oiled wife, who hit him and kicked him to save herself from certain death.

The three boys went on long walks or on Somen's scooter, at which times Unni showed Sai the weird people he knew – a short, brisk man who worked in Canara Bank, who locked his extraordinarily beautiful wife in the house every morning when he left for work. An architect who had suffered a head injury and after that started drawing flowers that do not exist on earth. A middle-aged woman who had the ability to open the dictionary at exactly the page she wanted. A scientist who was part of a team that was researching the desire in homeless madmen in Madras to direct traffic.

Unni and Somen then introduced him to the nun who had taken the vow of silence. Later, they took him to a slum in Choolaimedu to show him a very old man with flowing silver hair, who walked along the narrow unpaved lanes humming in the Carnatic classical style, pointing his finger at the lumps of human excrement deposited at short, equal intervals on both sides of the alleys, his pitch dramatically increasing or decreasing depending on the size of the shit. People stood outside their huts and watched without anger or amusement as their own shit determined the music of the wandering hummer.

'I thought Unni and Somen were trying to tell me something,' Sai said. 'I thought they would soon explain everything to me.' But that did not happen, and as the days went by Sai began to get impatient. He kept asking Unni, 'When are you going to show me how to go to the next level?' Unni never answered the question. He would laugh and maintain a knowing silence. But Sai was relentless. One day Unni asked him, 'What do you want me to say? What is it that you want to know?'

'What is everything, what is the secret, what is going on, why does the universe exist?' Sai said, which made Unni and Somen laugh hard. But later that evening, as Unni and Sai left their friend's house together and walked down the narrow lane, Unni whispered, 'It is dangerous, Sai. We must not talk about such things.'

'Why?'

'Because it is dangerous.'

'Why is it dangerous?'

Unni did not say anything for a while. They had left the narrow lane when he spoke again. He said, 'Somen is trying to get his hands on a bit of *Mycobacterium leprae*. Do you know what that is?'

'No.'

'It is the bacterium that causes leprosy. Somen wants to become a leper, he wants to sit on a roadside without fingers and toes and die the most painful death. He wants to beg to survive, he wants to destroy every bit of ego in him, he wants to crawl on the road, Sai. Why would a boy want to do that? Because ego is what stops us from seeing. What you want to see, what we all want to see, is not easy to achieve. That is the thing about this path, Sai. The path that we are seeking does not pass through beautiful Himalayan mountains, the path does not take us to tantric sex. It passes through unimaginable pain and misery. Have you wondered why I meet Somen so often? Because I want to ensure he does not harm himself. That is why I come here. But you know what is the scariest thing of all? I don't know why I am stopping him. I know what he wants to do to himself is the right thing. That is what is scary.'

Sai was so terrified and confused by the moment that he ran

away at a full sprint, he just ran and ran. But, after a week, he returned to Somen's house because he could not resist being with them. As the weeks passed he felt that Somen and Unni were beginning to transform.

'Many times they would just sit without uttering a word, sit like that for hours. One day, Somen told me, very softly and with great sadness in his voice, "Sai, some days I want to go to the terrace and scream, just scream, 'People, can't you see, can't you see?'" I asked him what exactly did he want the world to see, but he and Unni just looked at each other and they did not say anything. A few days later, I saw Somen with a large, very sharp knife. He kept patting his wrist with the edge of the knife. He did it gently in the beginning but slowly the knife started landing on his wrist harder and harder. I got so scared I ran to the door. That made them laugh.'

One evening, Unni told him that the Superman comics contained many secrets, which could be understood only if he practised the Superman pose – the flying pose. 'He made me lie on the floor, on my stomach, with my arms stretched and head looking up. It was tougher than I thought, but I lay like that for God knows how long. When I could not bear it any more, I got up and went to find them, they were on the terrace. They burst out laughing when they saw me.'

In time, Somen started asking him to go and buy groceries, post letters, drag his scooter to the mechanic, even clean the ceiling fans with Somen's mother trying not to laugh. 'They treated me like a servant. Can you imagine that? The exams were just a few weeks away. The board exams, JEE, the regional college exams, all the exams were just a few weeks away and here I was cleaning ceiling fans.'

When his servant phase began, Sai was reminded of the kung-fu films in which Zen masters made their disciples perform all kinds of menial labour. He imagined that he was being drafted as a disciple. He thought Somen and Unni were trying to break down his ego so that he would begin to see the world through their eyes. So he endured all the humiliation and hard work without resisting. But, finally, some events helped him escape from their grasp.

On the Marina beach one Sunday evening, Unni and Somen started swimming, and kept going farther out. Sai sat on the sands and watched. Slowly, he began to get nervous. People on the beach started gathering to watch until they could not see the heads of the two boys. Sai sat there and cried. An hour later a fisherman's catamaran arrived with the two boys, who looked peaceful. 'I heard the fishermen say they had never seen anyone swim so far out. By the time they found the boys they were too tired to even move their arms, but they were floating on their backs and laughing. Unni told me later that they knew this part of the sea well, they knew that they would be rescued by one of the many fishing boats that were going home.'

A few days later, they did something more dangerous. 'They told me that they wanted to show me something and took me to a railway bridge near Perambur.'

It was a single-track rail that ran over a canal, an isolated spot where nothing much happened for hours and then, suddenly, a train hurled past at full speed. Sai shuddered visibly when he recounted the incident. They convinced him to stand with them on the track and wait for the train to arrive. They stood in a tight line, in a huddle, holding each other's waists.

Unni was in the centre. He was holding Sai's waist tight. 'I didn't know how strong he was until that moment, he had an iron grip.' The game was simple – they had to stand waiting for the train, let it approach them and they would jump off just a moment before it hit them. Sai stood looking at the horizon, waiting for the train. But nothing happened for a while. Then he heard the train's horn. He shut his eyes, clenched his fists and waited. He could hear the horn grow louder and louder, and then the sound of the train on the track. He opened his eyes, but he could not see the train. It struck him then that it was coming from behind. When he turned to look, the train was just a hundred metres away. 'I wanted to jump off but Unni was holding me so tight I could not free myself. He and Somen were laughing. I started hitting Unni but he did not let go. I thought I was going to die with them. I thought they had come here to die.' Sai shut his eyes, he could feel a great breeze on his back, and then he remembered flying. Somen and Unni were on the side of track, rolling on the rocks and laughing. Sai was too stunned to even move.

That was the moment he ended the friendship. He stopped going to Somen's house. He ignored them in class. 'They didn't care. They didn't ask me why I was not talking to them. They just didn't care. I did not speak to Unni after that. When I heard that Unni had killed himself I was not surprised. Have you wondered why you have not been able to meet Somen Pillai?'

'Why?'

'Can't you see?'

'No.'

'Because he is dead.'

'And his parents are hiding the fact? That doesn't make any sense.'

'There is a good chance his parents don't know. Maybe he just vanished one day and they don't want to admit that their son has gone mad and abandoned them. I think his bones are at the bottom of a canal under a railway bridge.'

'You say that, Sai, because you wish it. If I meet Somen Pillai and he talks to me I'll figure out how much you've not told me. Isn't that true, Sai?'

Sai let out a sad chuckle. 'I've told you everything. Except one bit. And I am going to tell you that now. If I had told you this before you would not have let me talk about anything else.'

Sai was right because what he had to reveal, very simply, was the fact that Unni's final comic, *How To Name It*, was meant for him. The only thing Unni hated about cartooning was filling up the dialogue bubbles with text. He found it tedious, probably the reason why he usually devised stories that did not need prose. But, apparently, several of his comics did need text and for that he used Sai as mule. What Unni used to do was finish his comics leaving the bubbles blank, and write out the story on a piece of paper.

'I was supposed to read the story and make a rough draft of the storyboard and show it to him for approval. He would make a lot of corrections and I would write another draft and another until it was good enough for him, then I would sit and carefully fill up the bubbles in capital letters. But many times, after I finished, he would just tear up the comics and throw them away. He was not happy with most of his work.'

Sai then asked how Ousep had got hold of the comic. As Ousep was explaining the boy did something outrageous – he collected his cheap shoulder bag from the floor, stood up and looked set to leave.

'Sit down, Sai.'

'I have to leave.'

'Really?'

'Yes.'

'How were you supposed to fill in the dialogue bubbles when you didn't know what the story was?'

'I knew the story. He had written the story and given it to me but got down to finishing the comic only weeks later. I never saw the comic, until you showed it to me.'

'Sit down, Sai, we have just begun.'

'I know what you're going to ask me.'

'What am I going to ask you?'

'You are going to ask me, "What is the story of the comic, where is the story of the comic?"'

'Where is the story?'

'I gave it to Unni's mother this morning.'

A soft moan may have escaped Ousep's lungs. 'Why would

you do something like that, you idiot? You go and give something that I have been searching for to that woman.'

'Because the story is about her. It is a private matter from her life. I have a duty to the memory of Unni to protect his mother's past.'

'Wait, wait, wait, Sai. Wait right there.'

'Unni's comic was about something that concerned his mother. I will not tell you what it is about. You must ask her yourself.'

'Sai, you're making a mistake. What's the story?'

'I can't tell you.'

'But he told you. So his father can surely know. What was it?'

'Unni said that his father must never know because that is what his mother wishes.'

'Sai, sit down. Sit down and tell me more.'

'Do you know that Unni went missing for three days?'

'No. I didn't know that.'

'You didn't know anything that happened in that house.'

'Why did he go missing? Where did he go?'

'Why is the comic so important to you?' Sai asked, walking back a few steps.

'Because, a few hours after he posted the comic to you, he was dead.'

'And you think there is a connection?'

'Obviously.'

The way Sai looked, it killed something inside Ousep. The honest compassion of a fool, how humiliating that is. 'Is that why you started probing his death again?' Sai said. 'Is that why you did everything you did in the last few months? Because you found this comic? I feel sorry for you. The comic has nothing to do with why he died. If Unni's mother ever tells you what the story is you will understand what I am saying.'

'Tell me the story, Sai.'

'I have to go now. I've told you everything I know and everything I can say. I don't want to see you again. You and Unni and Somen. I am done with all this. I am an ordinary person, I want ordinary things. I don't want to know the truth. I don't want to see beauty. I am just another boy in Madras who wants to escape to America.'

~

FOR THE REST of her life Mariamma Chacko would tell herself that it was a mistake to let Unni know what had happened to her when she was twelve. For all his swagger he was just a child, and as his mother she should have protected him from himself. But then Unni had been persistent. He had pieced together many of her monologues and figured that at the heart of her indignation was an incident in her childhood. He asked her almost every day what had happened. He was relentless, and in a moment of weakness she yielded. They sat on the kitchen floor and she told him about that day. A happy twelve-year-old village girl without a grouse, that was how she had begun, that was how she had described herself.

She is in her village, walking down the south stream at the foot of the hill towards a giant rock from where the half-naked boys dive into the water. She has walked alone on the banks many times and it is an unremarkable part of her life. She cannot see the rock yet but it will appear after the bend in the stream. There is a familiar stillness all around her and she tells herself that she likes the peace of the hill more than the fuss of the big cities. She sees someone approach, a young man with smooth fox-like strides. When he gets closer she realises it is Philipose, a man who is described in at least eight villages as the 'talented young man'. He reads from the Bible on Sundays, sings in the choir, organises boat races, heads protest marches to the collector's office and demands black-tar roads for the rubber hills. She smiles at him. Unexpectedly, he stops and starts talking to her. She smells liquor on him, so she begins to walk away. 'Wait here and talk for a while,' he says. She says she has to go. But he holds her hand and says, 'Why are you in a hurry today?' She tries to extricate herself from his grip but he holds her tight. She begins to scream. He covers her mouth with his palm and pushes her down on the ground. His hands begin to grope her, tearing her clothes. She struggles but he is too strong. She manages to poke his eye with a stone. As he howls, she screams, too. People run towards her. Philipose flees. Nobody chases him. 'It is Philipose,' they say. 'It is Philipose.'

Mariamma is taken to her mother by seven women who have shrouded her in a bedsheet. They walk up the hill. Her mother stands at the top with her hands on her hips, and waits. She has heard the news. Mariamma is happy to see her mother. But the moment she is handed over, her mother slaps her in front of everyone. 'Why do you strut alone on the banks?' she says. She takes her in and asks her, 'What did he do?' Mariamma does not know how to answer that. She does not say anything. Mother inspects her, and looks relieved. 'Such things happen when girls are not careful,' her mother says. 'Don't think too much about it.'

The same evening, they sit in the coracle and go to her foster home. Her mother has nothing to say to her, not a word. Mariamma is dropped on the bank. She wades through the shallow water and reaches the steps. When she turns back, the boat and her mother have already gone some distance. Mariamma stands there and watches long after the boat has disappeared. She does not know how long she has been standing there. She is finally surprised by a pall of middle-aged women in white who are returning from a funeral. They look at her as if she is a strange animal.

'What is wrong with you, Mariammo?' one of them says.

'Why do you ask me that?'

'You were talking to the river.'

This happens several times in the coming weeks. People start-ling her and telling her that she has been talking to herself. They begin to say, Mariamma is behaving in a funny way. That is what they say. But about Philipose, they still say, 'the talented young man'.

Unni was furious. 'Did they punish Philipose? Tell me they did something to him,' he said.

'No,' she said. 'Nobody wanted to even talk about it. My mother, especially. Philipose went on living as if nothing had happened.'

Unni took a glass and broke it on the floor. 'I'll kill him,' he said. It was terrifying, to see the rage of such a gentle boy.

When Mariamma opens the hospital ward door and walks into the milk-white room, she finds Ousep sitting on his bed and staring at her as if he has been waiting for the door to open. She drags a chair over and sits by his side, and sets her bag on the floor. 'I know what you want to know,' she says. And she tells him what she had, until this moment, told only Unni. Ousep listens without a word. When she finishes, he puts a feeble hand on her lap.

'Why didn't you tell me?' he says.

'I didn't want to tell you. You were my happiness, when I married you. I wanted to forget all that was old.'

'You should have told me,' he repeats like a fool.

'I told Unni, I don't know why. I should not have. He was disturbed for many days. He started talking like me. "He got away, didn't he? Philipose got away." One evening, Unni did not return home. I waited but he didn't return. I called all his friends but nobody knew where he had gone. You came home drunk, did your usual things and went to sleep. But Unni was not home yet. Next morning I got a call from him. He said he was in Kerala. He said he was going to confront Philipose.

I started screaming at him, but he put the phone down. He returned two days later. He told me what had happened. The comic that you have been guarding, Ousep, that is what it is about. It is about Unni's journey to meet Philipose.'

'And what happened when he went to meet Philipose?'

'How did you get that comic?' she asks.

He tells her.

'Is that why you started meeting his friends all over again?' she asks.

'Yes.'

'The comic does not explain why he died, Ousep.'

'I know that now.'

'What you must search for is what I have told you before. Why Unni did not leave a note behind for me. That is what you must chase.'

'But what does that mean? If Unni did not explain his death to you, what does that mean, Mariammo?'

'It's obvious. I thought you would know. I thought you understood.'

'No, I don't understand,' Ousep says.

'Unni thought I would come to know why he chose to die.'

'But you don't?'

'I don't. You go and find out what is it that my child thought I am supposed to know.'

She digs into her coir bag and takes out sheets of paper that have been stapled together. Ousep can see Unni's extravagant handwriting on the pages. She hands them to him. 'This is the story Unni wrote about his journey,' she says. 'This is the story of the comic. This is exactly what he told me when he returned from Kerala.'

The story that Ousep holds in his hands is not the clue he thought it was. But his hands are not steady as he begins to read the account of Unni Chacko, who is on his way to confront a man he has never met before. The story of a seventeen-year-old boy who is about to meet a man who had molested his mother many years ago, when he was young and she was just a girl. A man called Philipose.

~

How To Name It
BY UNNI CHACKO

Philipose, Philipose.

I have heard your name many times. I have heard your name from the time I was a child. I have heard it from my mother. This is what my mother says, 'Philipose, you got away, Philipose.' You know my mother. I hope you are human enough to remember her.

For most of my life I did not know who you were. I thought you must be just another relative. But now I know who you are. I am coming to get you, Philipose. Finally, I am coming to get you.

I know the name of your village, I know your family name, I know your house name. I will find you. I know you are still in your village because my mother says men like you never leave. You have your land, a hill full of rubber trees that you got in dowry, and you are semi-literate. There is no respect for you outside your land, Philipose. In the big world outside your village, men like you have no respect, so you live there in your old homes all your lives, eating jackfruits and mangoes and river fish and red boiled rice.

You will see me soon. You will see me from your window, a strong athletic boy walking down the mud path to your house. You will narrow your eyes, you will get up from your armchair, and you will step out of your door and wait for me. You will ask me, 'Who are you, my boy?'

I will not tell you anything, Philipose. I will first punch you on the nose. And you will begin to see Mariamma Chacko in me. And you will run. But you won't go too far. I will hold your neck and drag you through your land and take you to the state highway outside your farm. I will beat you up until all the villagers gather around us and then I will tell them. I will tell them what you did to my mother when she was just a twelve-year-old girl. I will tell them, 'I am the son of Mariamma Chacko and I have come for justice.' I will tell them what you did.

I say this to all the men who commit such crimes. You may think you can get away, but a time will come when the girls will become mothers and they may tell their sons about what you did to them. And their sons, if they are sons like me, will come to get you, will come and beat you up and shame you in front of your own people.

I am seventeen years old, Philipose. You must be over sixty now. You are probably a strong man. I know you work in the fields with the labourers. I know you have big bones and you probably have big muscles. You may have strong sons and strong friends. But I am strong, too. You won't believe it when you see me but there is something inside me, Philipose. But it is possible that you and your sons and your village people will defeat me. There is a chance that you will hold me in your hundred arms, put me on the ground and stand with your foot on my head. But before that happens, I will have told everybody what you did three decades ago to a little girl on the banks of the white stream. I will tell all the women of your village. If you have daughters I will tell them what you did.

I am on my way. I have borrowed money from my friend for the journey. I left home without telling my mother. She would have tried to stop me because she thinks I am a child. But I am not a child. I was never a child.

I am inside Egmore Station. I am waiting on the platform, in front of me is the Quilon Express. I am getting into the unreserved compartment, it is packed with men and women and children. I will sit on the floor and travel this way through the night and all of next morning. I smell piss and shit in this compartment, I smell filth. But I can sit absolutely still for many hours and when I sit that way I am not affected by anything. I am indestructible.

Many people who were sitting on the floor got off in the middle of the night and there is a place for me in the doorway. The thick iron door is fully open and I am sitting on the edge with my legs hanging in the air. The breeze is so powerful that I have to turn away to breathe. I see dark forests and villages and mountains pass. The night becomes day and I see Kerala. Entire villages are rushing past me. I see green hills and wide rivers and narrow black roads. I see red roofs and there is this smell of steam. The women here, their hair is always wet. And all the men have moustaches. Do you have a moustache, Philipose? Do you feel like a man, Philipose? Like a man-man? Do you have a thick bushy moustache, which you rub fondly when you see little girls?

I have reached Kollam. I am here. From the station I call home because I know Mother will be worried. She is hysterical when she hears my voice. I tell her calmly where I am and why I am here. She screams at me. 'Those are bad men, Unni,' she says. I tell her, 'I am no saint, myself,' and I put the phone down.

I am sitting in a packed bus. We are close now, very close to each other. I am in Patazhi, Philipose. Can you believe that? The boy who was born years after your crime has arrived in your village for justice.

I am walking down the narrow roads of the village and everybody is looking at me. They can see I am a city boy. They have so much time to stare. I ask a man who is passing by, 'Where is Valolikal, the house of Philipose K. John?'

He tells me, 'Go down this road, son, and when you see the stream to your right, walk down the bank until you reach a big yellow house. That is where you want to go. But who are you?'

'I am the son of an old friend of Philipose,' I say.

I walk down the long road. People who are standing outside their homes stare at me. People who pass me by look at me as if I am a creature they want to know. They probably know my mother. Her village is not far away. Her stupid old mother still lives but I do not wish to meet her.

I must have walked over two kilometres when I see a gushing white stream. I walk down the bank and I wonder where it happened, where exactly did the crime happen. When my mother was just a little girl and she was walking along the stream. I have walked for over forty minutes by the stream but I don't see any houses here. Where are you, Philipose?

I see it now. A big yellow house on top of a small hillock at the end of the bank. What a place to live, Philipose. A forest of rubber in front and a white stream as your backyard. I walk up the steep path towards the front of the house. Do you see me, Philipose, do you see me coming? Come out, Philipose, step out right now. The door is open but there is no sign of people. I say in Malayalam, 'Is there anybody home?'

Nothing happens for nearly a minute. I wonder if I must go in. Then a middle-aged woman appears. She looks at me and goes and fetches her glasses. And she looks at me as if she needs more glasses. I say, 'Is this the house of Philipose K. John?'

She giggles. 'That's his name but nobody says it like that.'

'Where is he?'

'Who are you, son?' she says. 'Are you from the city?'

'I am the son of an old friend of your man. Can I meet him?'

'What is the name of this friend?'

'Mathew.'

'Which Mathew? The world is full of Mathews. There are more Mathews than Anthonys. I wonder why.'

'Mathew from Kottarakara.'

'I did not know he had such a friend,' she says. 'What is your name?'

'I am Unni.'

'So, Unni, son of Mathew, why is your Malayalam so terrible?'

'I was in Madras for too long.'

'And what does Unni want?'

202

'Are you the wife of Philipose K. John?'

I use your full name, Philipose, because I cannot bear to use any word that would grant you a hint of respect.

'Yes, I am his wife.'

'Can I meet him?'

'What business do you have with him?'

'My father used to be with the Rubber Board and he used to talk about Philipose K. John. They had some good times together. My father is dead and he told me on his deathbed that I must inform his friends of his death personally.'

'In that case, son, Philipose K. John already knows. He is in heaven with Mathew of Kottarakara. My husband died eight months ago.'

I am stunned, Philipose. What do I do now? I don't know what to say, what to do. I just stand there. I came all the way to get you but you've escaped.

Your wife asks me to come in and have a cup of tea. Your wife, she has big sagging boobs. She must wear a suspension bridge as a bra.

She takes me into the house, then into a room, then another room. I don't know where she is taking me. Finally, we enter a dark storeroom. I can see a lot of plantains hanging from the ceiling as if they have been sentenced to death. The floor is filled with jackfruits.

She says, 'I've been waiting for days for a tall young man to come by and change the bulb.' She takes out a bulb from a box and hands it to me. 'Unni, my angel, will you stand on that stool there and change the bulb for an old widow?'

I drag the stool over and stand on it and change the bulb.

'How did he die?' I ask.

'He came home one night in the rains. He had a fever. He had some tea and went to sleep. In the morning I found him dead in his bed. It was a peaceful death. That is how we must go. Peacefully, in our sleep. His face looked so serene.'

So, that's how you went, Philipose. Peacefully, in your sleep.

After what you did to my mother, that is how you went. And I am now changing the bulb in your house.

She takes me into the kitchen, she is looking around the house as if she is searching for something for me to fix before I leave. Cunning old woman. She gives me tea, which has a lot of dead red ants in it. We sit at a table in the kitchen and drink tea. She talks about you with great affection.

'He was a good man, a very good man. He was a loving husband and a good father of four strong sons and two beautiful daughters who adored him. They are all in the Gulf now, everyone is in the Gulf. Who has the time these days for their mother, who has the time for an old woman?

'They make so much money, so that's all right. They want to buy me a car. My husband, too, had made a lot of money. He bought so much land, so much land. If I stand on my land I cannot see its end, Unni. Isn't that a nice way to live? He was a rich man, my husband, but he was a good man. He started eight free schools for poor girls. He funded the college education of hundreds of girls from poor families. Do you know, Unni, the state government gave him an award?'

She takes me to a shelf which is full of awards for the social work done by you, Philipose. There is one award that has a white angel standing on a wooden stand. I cannot read Malayalam, so I ask your wife what the inscription on the stand says. She tells me the award was given by the state government for 'Services To Humanity'. She shows me your framed black-and-white photographs that spread across time. I see you the way you must have looked when you attacked my mother, then I see you as you aged slowly. You look so happy and normal. You look like just another decent man. Then I see you on the wall. A giant photograph of a kind old man with a full mop of silver hair. You are smiling at me, Philipose. I know you are smiling at me.

It is time for me to go home. I hug her, I don't know why. I walk along the stream, I look around as if I am searching for a twelve-year-old girl who might be in danger. I now say what my mother always used to say: 'Philipose, you got away, Philipose.'

You lived a life filled with love, children, wealth and awards. And you died peacefully in your sleep. I was eight months late, Philipose.

When I get home, my mother slaps me hard. She has a powerful arm, so it hurts. Then she hugs me tight. 'That's a bad man, Unni, that's a very bad man. I was so scared.' Then we sit on the kitchen floor and I tell her what happened. We hold hands and we cry together.

'But at least he died, Unni, so that's all right, so that's over,' she says.

I tell her, 'Also, I squeezed his wife's boobs.'

And we laugh so hard, with tears running down our cheeks, we do not know if we are laughing or crying.

~

6

Corpse

THE MOST TENSE moments in Thoma's life are when his mother takes him to the Sacred Heart Family Store, where the enormous bare-chested shopkeeper sits on a sack of rice eating his own jaggery. Mariamma owes him more than three thousand rupees but the parish priest has bought her time to settle the loan. The man in the store does not like seeing her face and he usually pretends that he has not seen her. She stands patiently as he finishes with everybody else. When there is nowhere else he can look, he asks without respect, 'What do you want?' Thoma does not like anyone talking to his mother this way. Sometimes the man says, 'You people do eat a lot.' Mariamma quietly points to what she wants.

Thoma and his mother are walking back from the store, sweating in the afternoon heat, when they see the figure of Mythili Balasubramanium coming their way. Once again in his life, Thoma forgets how to walk. He is carrying two kilos of rice and his mother is holding a coconut in her hand as if it is a shot-put. He wishes he was walking alone, and wearing a tight white shirt and tight white trousers and white pointed shoes, with a Walkman strung to his ears. He hopes she does not see them, which is not an outlandish wish. Nobody ever sees them.

Mythili is walking the way she usually walks, mostly looking down at the road. She has not spotted them yet. He throws a nervous glance at his mother. If she chews her lips and wags a finger he will die on the spot in shame. But she is only looking at Mythili with a loving smile. 'Be normal,' he whispers to her. 'Be absolutely normal.'

Mythili's eyes are still on the road. The way she walks, it is a surprise she even gets anywhere. Thoma is distracted by a sudden movement behind Mythili. A man is walking fast and is gaining on her. He is in a brown shirt and a lungi. As he passes her, he slaps her back. That gives her a jolt. She glares at the man, who now walks ahead of her as if nothing has happened. Then Mythili, too, continues to walk as if it did not happen. But Mariamma stops. She stares hard at the man, who is fast approaching them. He looks nervously at Mariamma for a moment and looks away. 'Normal,' Thoma whispers to his mother, but she is not listening. She holds him in her stare. When he crosses them she flings the coconut at him. It hits his head, falls on the road and rolls away. But the man walks away as if nothing has happened. It is as if he gets hit by a coconut all the time. What is this world, exactly? Thoma wonders. A man slaps a girl's arse, she walks on as if nothing has happened. Then the man gets hit by a coconut thrown by a weird woman, and he walks away without even turning back.

Thoma sees his mother kneeling on the pavement. She says, 'The coconut has rolled into the bushes.' Thoma whispers to her, 'Don't overreact. Get up, get up, she is coming.'

'The coconut, Thoma, it has gone into the bushes. He is not going to give us another coconut even if Jesus Christ asks him to do it.'

'Get up,' Thoma begs.

He decides to pretend that he has not seen Mythili, and when he wants to pretend that he has not seen someone he always yawns for some reason. But Mythili does not walk away. She goes up to his mother and peers into the bushes with her. 'I can see it,' she says. She puts her hand into the bushes and brings out the coconut. She looks fully into the eyes of his mother and gives her a smile. That has not happened in a while. As she walks away he can see she is crying.

'Why is she crying?' Thoma asks.

'She still loves me, Thoma, that's why.'

'So why is she crying?'

'That is how it is.'

In the evening, he and his mother are standing on their rear balcony and watching the doctor's widow below as she waters her roses. Every woman in Block A is keeping a close watch on that lady, who has decided not to wear a white sari as widows do, nor does she have an Usha Tailoring Machine on which widows sew with a sad face. That woman is under a lot of pressure to look sad, and even when she does something as ordinary as watering the plants, the women of Block A begin to murmur about her. Some say, 'But why shouldn't she be happy?', which actually sounds like a reprimand. Mythili appears on her balcony, her hair in a white towel. Thoma has never seen her this way. She looks like a woman. She smiles at his mother, but this time her smile is cautious as if she is a stranger once again.

'I will teach him,' she tells his mother as she hangs the pleated green skirt of her school uniform to dry. 'I will teach him on Tuesdays, Fridays and Saturdays. We can start this Saturday.' His mother and Mythili decide, without asking his opinion, that she must first teach him maths, then they discuss the exact time he must turn up.

Thoma waits nervously for Saturday. He will sit with Mythili, and they will talk. She will know, beyond any doubt, that he exists. The very thought scares him. He hopes, when he walks into her home, she will say, 'Thoma, let me see how much you know.'

'Ask me anything, Mythili.'

'What does KGB stand for?'

'Komitet Gosudarstvennoy Bezopasnosti.'

'My God, Thoma, I can't believe you are so bright. Let me

try another quiz question. It's a very difficult question. What is Pelé's real name?'

'Edson Arantes do Nascimento.'

'Thoma, you are smarter even than Unni.'

In the days that follow, as he waits for Saturday to arrive, he begs his mother not to be too loud when she speaks to the walls, and he prays that his father, who has started drinking again after returning from the hospital, has another mild heart attack. But life is merciless, that is one thing Thoma knows about life. His daily humiliations continue. When his mother talks to herself in the mornings he goes to the stairway to check whether her voice travels far enough for Mythili to hear. At night, when his father screams from the gate, he hopes she is in a deep sleep.

The good thing about school is that Mythili will never know what happens to him there. No matter how well he guards himself, no matter how innocuous his actions are, he often walks into the open arms of humiliation.

He is going down the corridor from his class towards the toilet. In front of him is Matilda Miss, a short, tight woman with no moving parts really. She is walking with quick, hurried steps, which is unusual. As he walks cautiously behind her he spots something – she is leaving a trail of red dots on the floor. He stops to look at the dots and he is stunned. It is blood. He follows her, and the trail of red dots. She rushes into the staffroom, filled with teachers. She goes towards the ladies' room, the trail of red dots in close pursuit. Before she can open the door, he decides to shout, 'Miss.' There is silence. A room full of teachers, most of them men, look at him. He is sure that he has probably saved her life with his timely warning. He points to the floor and says, 'You are leaving a line of red dots, miss.' Everybody looks at the floor and for some reason turns away. Matilda Miss moves one step forward like a little soldier and slaps him hard. What must Thoma Chacko do, what must a boy do to be happy? Will Thoma Chacko ever make it?

When Unni was his age he was cast as Nehru in the Independence Day play, but Thoma is now rehearsing once again to be a nameless extra, just one of the many idiots who roll on the floor holding the national flag as British soldiers beat them up saying, 'Bloody Indians.'

Even a haircut in the saloon is a form of humiliation. The St Anthony's hairstylist, who has an image of the centrally bald St Anthony on his sign, has been instructed by the parish priest to cut Thoma's hair Free of Charge. So, the man there always makes Thoma wait for over an hour and cuts the hair of the people who have come after him. It is when there is no sign of a paying customer that the man asks Thoma to sit in his swivel chair. He never gives Thoma a white apron, never gives him a head massage as he does the others, and never holds a mirror behind him to show him his new haircut from all angles. In fact, when it is all done, he makes Thoma stand in front of him, and whips him hard several times with a short towel, making it look as if he is only dusting him.

An hour before Unni died he had come here for a haircut. Ousep has interviewed the barber many times. 'What's your father looking for?' the man says. 'He keeps coming here to ask me if there was anything strange about Unni that day. I keep telling him Unni did not speak a word but your father keeps dropping in to ask the same questions again and again.'

'Was there anything unusual about Unni that day?' Thoma asks. The man whips him with the short towel harder than he usually does.

Thoma wants to investigate. He wants to ask questions, good questions, trick questions, he wants to probe, extract clues from the minds of people and find the reason why Unni did what he did. But when he thinks about it, he does not know where to begin. It is so difficult to solve mysteries. Will Thoma ever solve a mystery in his life?

~

IN HIS DREAM, which Thoma knows is a morning dream, he is a tall, smart and deadly bodyguard walking with the Chief

Minister down an endless corridor. Terrorists with machine guns appear from nowhere and take aim. Thoma, in slow motion, pulls the Chief Minister towards him and uses the man as a body shield. The Chief Minister is soon riddled with bullets, but Thoma is safe. He wakes up feeling sorry for the old man.

He has a long, nervous bath, washes his hair with soap and wears his best shirt, which was once Unni's. Thoma does not own a pair of trousers. Shorts are all right, he does not mind them, but then he has to sit very carefully when he is with Mythili. If she sees through the gaps in his shorts, sees the old checked curtain of the Chacko household now reborn as his underwear, he will have no choice but to go to the terrace and jump head first.

That makes him wonder whether Unni had actually killed himself out of shame. There cannot be a better reason for a person to die than shame. But it is hard to imagine Unni being ashamed of anything. He was so strong, so superior to everything around him, even though he was as poor as Thoma.

At ten, the ominous maths textbook in his hand, he rings Mythili's doorbell. His mother is watching from her doorway. He whispers to her, 'Go inside.' But she stands there because she is a curious person. When Mrs Balasubramanium finally opens the door, the two women look at each other across the short corridor and they imagine that they have smiled.

Mythili's mother takes him to the door of her daughter's bedroom, where Mythili stands waiting. 'Very bad idea, Mythili,' she tells her daughter. 'You've so much work to do. Why are you taking on this burden?' Mythili glares at her mother, drags Thoma in by his wrist and bangs the door shut. Mythili's hand, he will always remember, is very cold.

She is in a half-skirt and T-shirt, the way she normally is at home. She does not wear such things when she is in full public view. She is a respectable girl, and Thoma likes respectable girls, though he is not sure why. She clasps a hairband in her mouth, and holds her thick black hair above her head as if she wants to lift herself in the air. She ties her hair in a ponytail because he has come – Mythili has performed a set of actions as a reaction to Thoma. He feels a moment of uncontrollable joy around his temples.

She sits on her bed with her bare legs crossed, and asks for his maths book. 'Sit there, Thoma,' she says, pointing to a solitary chair facing her. He senses an affection in her tone. She said 'Thoma'. She need not have used his name but she did.

The last time Thoma was in her room was about three years ago, the day before Unni died. It has not changed since that day. Her windows are covered by a pink floral curtain that he does not remember, but her Godrej steel cupboard with a mirror on it, her tiny wooden desk and cot are in the same positions as before. Her bed is still the same, narrow even for a single bed, as if she should not share it with her own shadow.

She is going through the pages of the textbook carefully, with a smile, as if it is a family album. He has not seen anyone smile at a maths textbook before.

'Mythili,' he says.

'Yes.'

He does not know why he opened his mouth. He had just wanted to utter her name in his mind, he did not expect any sound to come out of his stupid mouth. He has nothing to say, really. She is looking at him now.

'What?' she says.

'Mythili, is it true that the Home Ministry is planning to change the value of pi from 3.14159 to just 3?'

'Who told you this?'

'Unni.'

She puts her hand on her mouth and laughs. Her fingers are clean and slender, and her nails are painted in a girlish colour whose name he does not know. 'Unni,' she says, and when she returns to the maths book he can see that she is somewhat distracted. She has a ghostly smile, which bursts into laughter again. 'Unni was such an idiot,' she says. She turns a few pages, her smile slowly receding. 'You are wearing his shirt,' she says without looking up. 'I remember this shirt.'

Thoma is ashamed, he feels he is going to faint. He says, 'My mother has bought me a lot of shirts but I like wearing Unni's old shirts. You know, an old shirt feels softer than a new shirt. This was not altered. This was the shirt he used to wear when he was as old as me.'

'I know, I know this shirt. You look like him in it,' she says. Her large, serious eyes scan his face and he hopes she does not doubt her own analysis. Unni was handsome beyond ambiguity, and it is a good sign that Mythili sees his brother in him.

'Do I look exactly like him? Or is it fifty per cent? Or is it ten per cent?'

'In a very mathematical mood, are we?'

'I am very mathematical actually. When I think, deep inside my mind, I am mathematical.'

'When Unni was your age he used to look a lot like you. Now that you are wearing his shirt, I feel I am talking to him. It feels a bit strange. But then he had a bigger forehead and his eyes were more narrow, and they were not as innocent as yours. Even when he was a little boy he had the eyes of an old man who has seen it all.'

'You remember so much, Mythili?' he says, and uses his fingers to make a quick calculation. 'When Unni was twelve, you were just eight.'

'Girls remember,' she says.

'That's what Unni used to say. Girls remember everything. I am beginning to forget his face, can you believe that? Some days when I try to think of him I cannot remember his face. I have to come home and see his photograph on the wall. You know where the frame of Jesus Christ used to be, we have a big picture of Unni there now.'

'I remember his face very well,' she says.

'But when he died you were only as old as I am now.'

'I was thirteen, you are twelve. Big difference.'

'It's just one year.'

'Big difference.'

She says they must now stop chatting and focus on the maths. 'Angles,' she says.

'That night,' Thoma says, remembering something, 'my father and I saw you walking to your door that night. Where were you coming from?'

'Nowhere,' she says. 'I thought I heard a sound outside our door. I went to look. I went up the steps to see if the sound was coming from the terrace.'

'You were wearing proper clothes.'

'What does that mean, Thoma?'

'You were wearing clothes you usually wear when you are outside your house.'

'I was outside my house, wasn't I?'

Thoma whispers, 'What do you think the sound was?'

'I don't know.'

'You are very brave, Mythili.'

She shows him her palm and says that there are angles between her fingers.

Thoma wonders whether he is in love with her. Strangely, he has not thought of it before. And the question terrifies him because the fate of love in Madras is neatly divided into four kinds of suicide. Lovers who know that their parents would never let them marry go to a cheap hotel room, get into wedding clothes and eat rat poison. If they elope instead, their parents will consume the same rat poison. If it is only the girl's parents who object to the marriage, then she is most likely to immolate herself. Men who are spurned by girls almost always hang themselves from a ceiling fan. Men very rarely set fire to themselves.

'If there are no angles between two lines, then the value of the angle is either zero or 180. Thoma, idiot, are you listening?'

'Mythili, you think Unni died because of some love problem?'

She makes a fist and knocks his head with her knuckles. How do all the bloody women in Madras know how to do this? He feels humiliated for a moment but then Mythili rubs his head.

He is glad he washed his hair with soap. 'You must listen, Thoma,' she says.

But they do chat about this and that. He has figured out that the best way to get her to talk is to talk about Unni.

'Mythili, do you know the names of all the players in the national women's basketball team?'

'Of course not. Who would know something like that?'

'That's what Unni said. He said nobody would know the women's basketball team. He said when you want to impress someone just make up ten names of girls and claim that this is the Indian women's basketball team. Nobody will be able to check.'

She takes a thick strand of hair that is falling over her face and pushes it behind her ear. 'Unni was always up to something,' she says. 'Remember how he used to read my mind? How do you think he did that, Thoma?'

Yes, he remembers. Unni would ask her to pick a card from a pack and put it back. He would then stare deep into her eyes, as she giggled or fluttered her eyelids in an exaggerated way. And he would guess the card she had picked. He was right every time, and Mythili would be stunned. She would ask him to leave the room when she was about to pick the card, and she would hide the card, chew it or even tear it into many pieces, but Unni would just walk in and guess it right. She even started going up to the terrace to pick the card in private, but Unni always guessed the card. Some days he would pretend that he was unable to read her mind because of too much activity inside her head. But the next morning, when she opened her school bag or a notebook, she would find the card she had picked. And she would shriek so loudly that Thoma and Unni could hear her in their house.

'You think he could really read minds, Thoma?'

Thoma cannot bear it, but he doesn't say anything.

'You know what he told me?' she says. 'He told me that once upon a time in this world there lived a secret race of humans with supernatural powers. They invented cheap magic tricks and spread them far and wide so that people believed all supernatural acts to be just magic tricks. That's what Unni told me. I still remember because I used to think that Unni was one of those supernatural people.'

'I think Unni was good at some tricks. He did not have supernatural powers. I am very sure he had no supernatural powers, Mythili. I think only Pelé is supernatural.'

'Pelé?' she says, spitting out the word. 'From where did you pick Pelé?'

'Pelé is a great man,' he says. 'Do you know who that is?'

'Yes, Thoma, I know who Pelé is. Everybody knows Pelé.'

'He is a genius.'

'Yes, he is a genius.'

Thoma is comforted that he has created reasonable competition for Unni.

'Pelé is mind blowing,' he says. 'Only Pelé is supernatural.'

'But what a dumb name, though,' she says. 'Pelé. How funny.'

Thoma cannot believe it. This is the moment he has always been waiting for but now he feels he is going to faint. This is a miracle. The first miracle in his life.

'Not his real name,' he says softly.

'Pelé is not his name?'

'His real name is Edson Arantes do Nascimento.'

'How do you know these things, Thoma? Not bad.'

'He was a Russian spy,' he says.

'That's rubbish.'

'He used to work for the KGB. KGB is the Russian secret service.'

'I know what KGB is,' she says.

'Usually girls do not know what KGB is,' he says. 'In fact, very few people in the world know what KGB stands for.'

'What does it stand for?'

'Komitet Gosudarstvennoy Bezopasnosti.'

She rubs his head fondly. 'I think you read a lot, Thoma.'

'A lot. I read all the time.'

*

The whole day Thoma wanders down the lanes of Kodambakkam with a Sense of Wellbeing and with sympathy for everybody he sees on the road because Mythili does not know them. He chooses only the short lanes because he fears that if he walks down a long street, Mythili will appear at the other end and he will forget how to walk, and she will know that he is just an ass. In the days that follow he walks up and down his house, from the front balcony to the rear, for a glimpse of Mythili. Sometimes his path crosses that of his wandering mother, and they smile politely as if they are pedestrians greeting each other. He develops a nervous reverence for Mythili's school uniform, which she hangs out to dry every evening. He looks at it only discreetly. The best part of his day is the time before he goes to sleep when he imagines that he is dying and that Mythili, in her school uniform, is crying softly for him, hiding in her bathroom. And the times when he is with her, he tries to distract her from maths by talking about Unni. And when she is not looking he gapes at her, the way she used to stare at Unni when he was not looking – with a blank, serious face.

~

IT IS NOT that Ousep Chacko has abandoned the investigation again, it is just that he does not know how to proceed. After he was discharged from the hospital he resumed the probe, though he did not know what he was looking for any more. He has met everyone who appears to matter, except for Somen Pillai. There is no one else left to meet or to confront. He has met Simion Clark, too. That was a week ago.

Simion Clark turned out to be a tall, fit man in his forties who was at once Caucasian and Indian, with cautious eyes behind square glasses, thin severe lips, hair the colour of dirt, and a pronounced arse. He stood in the doorway unnaturally erect and stared with mild hostility. There was a bit of unpleasantness at first as Simion insisted he was Albert Fernandes. But he slowly relented because he knew his cover was blown and he knew it was silly to defend his position. Also, he was curious.

His flat was small and it was further diminished by three massive leather sofas that faced each other. Simion pretended to be relaxed. It is easier for men with long legs to appear that way.

'How did you find me?' he asked.

'You don't have a scar, Simion, which is surprising.'

'I said, "How did you find me?"'

'Usually men like you in Madras have scars.'

Scars from the times when they were attacked by cruel mobs of men who did not understand their way. The description of Simion as given by Balki had suggested to Ousep a pattern he was familiar with. The descriptions of the others later only confirmed that. Simion was one of those classy men in Madras who liked to be teachers in a boys' school, who were very strict, who inflicted pain, who spanked boys, who liked to teach subjects that needed a lab, where they could meet young boys behind shut doors. And in Madras, men like Simion are accustomed to fleeing. When Ousep began asking around in the gay underground, it turned out that Simion was not hard to find. A gay Anglo-Indian was just too conspicuous in the city. Simion also wrote for the editorial pages of the *Indian Express* under the name of Roy Gidney, tirelessly demanding legitimacy for homosexuality. The man even had a big following.

'I want to know why Unni did that to you in the class,' Ousep said.

'Is that why you are here?'

'Yes.'

'Why do you want to know?'

'I want to know my son better.'

'Why don't you just ask him?'

'Because he is dead.'

Ousep had not expected Simion to be stunned by the news. His farcical composure was gone and there was no strength in him. 'How did that happen?' he asked. When Ousep told him,

Simion looked lost and confused. He went to the bathroom and shut himself in for over ten minutes. When he emerged his nose was red, as if he had had a good cry. He asked Ousep to leave but did not insist. He sat with his hands folded and took several minutes to weigh his options. Ousep had not conveyed any direct threats to make his life hell but Simion was smart enough to see the sense in cooperating.

Simion rose again, and this time he disappeared into a room, probably his bedroom. He did not shut the door. He returned with a sheet of paper and handed it to Ousep. It was a full-length caricature of Simion, a flawed portrait but somehow efficient. There was a touch of Unni in the art but strangely it was a diminished Unni.

'He must have been thirteen when he drew this,' Simion said. 'He gave it to me in the school corridor. I think he admired me as a teacher, I think he did. I am a good teacher, a bit strict, but I am good. I am not strict for the filthy reasons you presume, but yes, I am strict, I care. And Unni at thirteen was the most beautiful thing I ever saw. His face, I will always remember his face.'

Simion was so infatuated with young Unni that he would become tongue-tied in his presence. He was too nervous even to speak to him. He thought if he spoke to him or if he even looked at him beyond a passing glance he would stray. As Unni grew up, Simion could see that the boy was not gay. 'What a shame, what a waste. With that face, that body, what a waste. There was something about him, about the way he moved, that was divine.'

Ousep had longed to hear this, longed to know his son as a subject of unashamed love, but he was offended by the idea of Unni as the sexual fantasy of a man. 'I am not a bad person, Mr Chacko. I try to be a good man,' Simion said. 'In every school I've worked at, I've tried to control myself. And when I was in that school I tried harder than ever. But it is tough for a man like me in a city like this. It is very hard.'

Simion used to take the train to school. He had an old sky-blue Fiat but he took the train because he wanted to travel on a particular morning train, in a particular second-class compartment, in the predetermined tight squeeze of a predetermined corner. That corner was legend in the folklore of homosexuals. In that corner, men stood feeling the bodies of other men like them. Eyes met, affections were conveyed, plans were made, all in great caution because a single bad judgement would have meant a violent attack by outraged men. On good days, virgin adolescent boys in search of male flesh made their way to the corner to see for themselves whether the legend was true, 'if paradise really existed in Madras'. They came to be felt and loved and promised a more elaborate time.

'Such a beautiful creature came one day to the compartment. He looked me in the eye, stood close to me. I felt the tightness of his young body, I imagined him being mine. In the crowd of men I placed my hand on him and I could feel him come to life. But he was nervous, naturally, very scared. When the train stopped at the next station he rushed out and disappeared. He went away, just like that. I knew I would never see him again.'

Simion reached school that morning stirred and insatiate. All morning he was distracted by the apparition of the exotic boy on the train. He was unable to focus on his classes. That afternoon he was in the lab, alone, and wishing the thoughts would go away. He saw a little boy of around ten pass by in the corridor. 'I don't know why I called him in and started talking to him. I don't know why I started massaging his thighs. That's all that happened.'

Unni walked in at that instant, and saw what was going on. He asked the little boy to leave, and held Simion in a steady gaze. 'I could not figure out what he was thinking but it was the most shameful moment of my life. When I was caught like that, it should not have been Unni. I went on my knees and joined my palms and begged him to forgive me. I told him I was quitting the school at that very moment, I accepted that I did not deserve to be a teacher.'

But Unni surprised him. He convinced him that he should

stay. Unni said, 'Things happen. We cannot control ourselves all the time.'

Simion decided to stay. But the next day, when he entered Unni's class, the boy knew what he was going to do. 'I don't know why he did that. My beautiful Unni, I don't know why he did that. I don't know, I really don't know. I think of him often and I ask myself why he was so cruel to me. I ask that even though I deserved it.'

Unni had found his Philipose. That was what it was about.

$\sim$

THE COMIC THAT is titled *Epidemic* begins with the Revolutionary Leader standing alone on the Marina Beach. The man is in a white fur cap and dark glasses, a white shirt and white *veshti*. His feet are bare. There is a blank thought-bubble over his head. He looks silly and clueless, which he was when he ruled the state as a semi-literate film star who had become the hero of the poor even though he did not know how to solve the poverty of other people. He gave free lunches to schoolchildren, and made it legal for two people to ride on a bicycle, and did other such things. But the intention of Unni is not to make the great Leader look silly. *Epidemic* is much deeper than that. The comic acquires an eerie quality as it progresses. In the second panel, the Leader's plump cylindrical mistress, Amma, in a dark green sari, appears beside him. She too is thinking, and she is sharing the same amoebic thought-bubble. The blank bubble, though, has now grown in size.

After the Leader died, which was a few months after Unni's death, hundreds immolated themselves, apparently in grief. Amma got on to the open hearse of her departed lover, which inched through a sea of people. But that was no place for her – the mistress of a man is always in a very bad position, especially on his hearse. She was kicked by several men in full view and thrown off the vehicle. Later, she was molested on the floor of the legislative assembly and hit on the head with a mike. But there is something of the Leader inside her and the masses see it very clearly. She is ascending, she is going to be the next Chief Minister, and in revenge for everything that men have done to her, she often makes them stand in a long line and come to her one after the other and fall at her feet. And the men are happy to do that because, even though many people have tried to inherit the power of the Leader, it is Amma alone who has acquired it, and for some reason she alone is able to transmit it to the people. *Epidemic* is about mass movements as infestations.

As the comic moves on, more and more people are added behind the Leader and Amma – regular, nameless people, the masses. All of them just stand and share the same empty thought-bubble, which grows larger in every frame. *Epidemic* ends with thousands of people massed on the beach, and all of them share one blank thought, which is now a giant white cloud over their heads.

Ousep goes through the comic again, this time very slowly. He hears the doorbell ring. Mariamma is not at home, so he decides not to open the door. It rings again, then several more times. Through the doorway of his room he sees Thoma walk across the hall, hears him open the door, and the sound of him running. The boy appears at the doorway and says, 'He has come.'

The mountainous Afghan in the Pathan suit smiles. His face is almost the colour of blood from the heat and the walk up the stairway. He rolls his sleeves over his enormous arms, his thick powerful legs stand apart in combat stance. In the republic of small male thighs, this is a rare stud.

'So fast, the door opened so fast,' he says, looking down at the boy from his foreign heights. 'Usually, it does not open until I almost break it down. Your wife sees through the peephole, I see through the peephole, all those games happen before the door opens. But today is different. Today is a good day. Maybe you have my money, then.' Thoma tries to squeeze himself between the Pathan and the door frame and escape to the stairway outside, but the man grabs him. 'Where are you going, hero?' He begins to tickle Thoma, who giggles. He pokes the boy in the chest with his fat fingers. Then he holds the boy's right arm in a fierce grip, and raises his gaze to Ousep. He begins to slowly twist the arm. Thoma's body turns as if in a modern dance, and he now faces his father, his arm pinned to his back. Thoma thinks he is laughing, but his face is growing serious.

'Do you have my money, Ousep?' the Pathan says.

'Next month,' Ousep says.

The Pathan gives another twist to the boy's arm.

'I want my money,' he says.

'Come next month.'

'Now.'

Thoma's heels have left the ground and he is on his toes. There is a feeble smile on his face. His eyes keep darting to Mythili's door. He is afraid the girl will open her door and see him like this.

The phone rings, which gives Ousep an elegant reason to wave his hand at the Pathan and say, 'Come later.' But the man wants to create trouble today. He gives one more twist to Thoma's arm. The boy does not pretend to smile any more. The phone rings in a persistent way and Ousep cannot ignore it any more. He goes to his room and picks up the receiver. He pulls the wire to its full extent, stares at the Pathan through the doorway, wags a finger at him and says, 'Hello.' The Afghan is perplexed but he gives another twist to Thoma's arm.

'Hello,' Ousep says again.

'I said you've been asking about me,' the voice of a man says.

'Who is this?'

'Beta.'

'Yes, I've been searching for you. The people at the Society of Amateur Cartoonists don't seem to know where you live or even your phone number.'

Ousep wags a finger at the Pathan again. Thoma is beginning to struggle now, he lets out a sporting laugh and starts hitting the man's powerful arm. The Pathan laughs.

'I don't like it,' Beta says.

'You don't like what?'

'I don't like people searching for me. I will speak to you when I want to.'

'Can we meet?'

'I don't want to meet you because I know I cannot help you.'

'Do you know who can help?'

'I have been speaking to someone who may be interested in talking to you. He does not like meeting people,' Beta says.

'Who is he?'

'Alpha.'

'Really?'

'Yes, really. Alpha.'

'Is he a cartoonist?'

'Yes.'

'When can I meet him?'

'I'll speak to him. I'll ask him if he will meet you.'

'Where does he live?'

'I can't tell you that right now. You have to wait.'

'You say Alpha will help me?'

'I don't know how useful he will be. But he can lead you to the corpse.'

'The corpse?'

'Yes.'

'The corpse is a cartoonist?'

'I don't know,' Beta says, laughing.

'Is the corpse male or female?'

'Strange question. I never thought of it before. But I've never met the corpse. So I don't know.'

'What would the corpse tell me?'

'The corpse would know what you want to know.'

Ousep hangs up and goes to the hall, distracted but ready for the confrontation. 'Let the boy go,' Ousep says.

'We are just playing,' the Pathan says. 'Aren't we just playing, boy?'

'We're playing,' the boy says, giggling like a fool, 'but I want to go now.'

'Not that easy,' the Pathan says.

The appearance of Mariamma startles everyone. Ousep feels a stab of shame. She looks carefully at the giant Pathan as if his face is really at the back of his head. She whispers to him, 'Blade.' Ousep, despite the circumstances, appreciates the literary beauty of her metaphor. That is what the moneylender is, he bleeds his prey through compound interest. 'Blade,' she says, and this time she is menacing and loud.

'What are you doing to my boy?' she says. There is a quiver in her tone and the Pathan knows it is not a good sign. Even Thoma senses it. He looks nervously at Mythili's door, and his eyes plead for his mother to take it easy. He puts a finger on his lips. 'Shh,' he says.

'Leave the boy alone,' she says.

'We are just playing,' the Pathan says.

'Do you hear me? I said leave the boy alone.'

'There is no respect in your voice, madam. That's not how women should be talking to men. I have three wives and a mother. None of them talks to me this way.'

'Leave the boy.'

'Ask your man to give me my money and I'll be gone.'

'You ask him. Twist that man's hand. Not my son's.'

'Any hand that eats my fruit, I will twist.'

'Is that true?' she says. She is panting now. And the next time she says, 'Is that true?' the quiver in her voice is operatic. Thoma puts his finger on his lips and says, 'Shh.'

'Take it easy, madam,' the Pathan says, 'we are just playing.'

'Let me play, too, then,' she says.

'Shh,' Thoma says.

'Let me play this game, Thoma,' she says, and she sprints inside the house, straight into the kitchen. She emerges with a broom in her hand and runs back to the doorway. She stands with the broom raised, ready to strike. Her chest heaves and her whole body bobs as if she is in a boat. She will hit him, Ousep knows.

The Pathan looks at her with fear masquerading as rage. He raises his hand slowly and points his index finger at her. He looks intently at the broom, which now begins to wag in the air. He lets the boy go, and Thoma runs away down the stairs – not that his life on the ground is going to be any better. The Pathan wags a finger at Ousep. 'You meet me tomorrow,' he says, and he goes away, looking back one last time to assess the woman standing at the door. She marches to the kitchen to update the lemon-yellow walls about what has just happened.

~

IT MUST BE Alpha's father. He holds the door as if he wants to shut it. 'We are watching a film,' he says.

'Alpha asked me to come,' Ousep says.

The man rebukes the doormat, 'Who is Alpha?'

'The cartoonist. This is the address given to me.'

'Would you be interested in the name his dumb father gave him?'

'I apologise,' Ousep says. 'I know him only as Alpha. What is the name you gave him?'

The man leaves the door open and goes in. Ousep follows him. The small flat is dim and has the odour of a burp. The man knocks on a door and says, 'Someone has come to see you.' He goes back to his chair and gapes at the TV. His wife, who is sitting with her legs folded on the sofa, rocks on her haunches for a moment, as if she is lulling an invisible baby to sleep. The man points to a chair without looking at Ousep.

Ousep sits with the strangers and watches the film as he waits for Alpha to emerge. It is an old Tamil film, which was revolutionary for its time. He forgets its name but he has seen it before.

It is about a beautiful innocent girl. She does not see men as predators, and is very friendly with them, especially the men on her lane. She plays volleyball with them, even kabaddi, she wrestles with them, she goes to their homes, their rooms. Her sari is always falling off her chest, because she is innocent, and the men are often dramatically stunned by her gaping blouse. One day, she turns sad and mature, she becomes very ladylike. The reason for the sudden transformation is that she has become pregnant. She does not know how that has happened. As an innocent girl, she has only recently learned about the whole plumbing of pregnancy. Her parents, who believe her tale, set out to find out which of her half a dozen close male friends on the lane has impregnated their daughter – those men alone had the opportunity. The parents suspect the girl was made unconscious by one of the men and plucked. Every man they investigate turns out to be a good person, a decent, clean-shaven man with strong ideals, who quotes Tamil poetry, who confesses that there were several situations when he was tempted and did very nearly take advantage of the girl but that he did not commit the crime. In the end, the mystery remains unsolved.

The suggestion of the plot is that one of the men is lying, or even that all of them probably slept with her. And the moral of the story is that women should never trust men, even men who appear to be good people in plain sight. Who can argue with that?

'So you're the father of Unni Chacko,' the sullen voice says. Alpha is a tall, slender boy with long hair and a full black beard. He is in tired jeans and a T-shirt that has 'OM' written on it. He looks a lot like Beta, he has the same restive eyes expressing general contempt, but Alpha is much thinner. 'Look at these people,' he says, pointing to his parents. 'Hypnotised by a box that has moving images. Look at these idiots. These two idiots. Look at them. Like drugged animals.'

The man and wife do not react. They stare at the TV. It is as if every day their son introduces them this way to a visitor. The man looks sideways at Ousep for a moment. The woman rocks briefly. Beyond this they show nothing. Ousep feels an uncontrollable urge to laugh. Look, Thoma, another unhappy home.

'If you want to talk to me, come inside,' Alpha says. He throws a final look at his parents. 'Morons,' he says.

Alpha's room has four visible objects – a cot, a cupboard, a table and a chair. There is nothing else. The walls are bare and his table clean. Ousep studies the boy with overt interest, and the boy appears to be doing the same with Ousep.

'Do you believe in God?' the boy asks.

'No. What about you?'

'Unni was a Hindu, do you know that?'

'Yes, I've heard.'

Alpha pats his chest with a tight fist. 'Hindu,' he says. 'A Hindu understands things that others don't.'

'What does he understand?'

'He understands that everything is a hint.'

'A hint at what?'

'At more hints, Mr Chacko, and more hints.'

'What does it lead to?'

'You've started with questions, which is a good thing. It is good,' the boy says, 'I was about to tell you that we cannot have a conversation. You must ask me questions. I will answer those questions.'

'All right. You, too, can ask me questions.'

'I may not have any questions for you. You are the seeker. What are you, Mr Chacko? You are the seeker. Do not chat. Ask me questions.'

'What do you do?' Ousep asks.

'I do nothing,' Alpha says.

'You must do something with your time?'

Alpha points to a shut drawer. 'A graphic novel,' he says, 'I am working on a graphic novel.'

'That is very ambitious.'

'No.'

'As you say, Alpha. What is the story of your graphic novel?'

'Why do you want to know the story?'

'I am curious.'

'Is it important to you that I tell you the story?'

'No. But I would really like to know the story. What is it called?'

'*Anti-story.*'

'That is the name of the graphic novel?'

'Yes.'

'And what is the story?'

Alpha looks at the floor and does not speak for a while. He is probably deciding whether he must tell the story. The boy, obviously, has psychiatric problems. Why was Unni interested in Alpha? Maybe Alpha is an extraordinary comic artist? Unni and Alpha have nothing in common. But when Alpha begins to tell the story of his graphic novel, it sounds like something Unni might have written.

'In the beginning,' Alpha says, 'as in the beginning of the universe, the beginning of time, there is Story and there is Anti-story. Story wanders through the entire universe searching for a Storyteller who would, as you may have guessed, tell the Story.'

It finds a small blue planet that orbits around an average-sized yellow sun in the outer edges of an ordinary whirlpool galaxy. Story tries out many ways to create the Storyteller and arrives at the idea of the carbon body, and after millions of years of creating and discarding species, it finally invents the human ape. Story enters the human body as a hallucination. The purpose of the human race is to pass the hallucination down the ages, across all of eternity.

Meanwhile, Anti-story gets wind of where Story is and what Story has done. So Anti-story infiltrates the human body and becomes thought, which is so powerful that the human race becomes trapped in thought and is unable to see the hallucination of Story any more. The world is now filled with Anti-storytellers who are entranced by thought and logic and the associated hallucinations that thought and logic together create. Thought takes over the world. But there is something about the brain, some kind of an evolutionary glitch. One in a million brains, by pure chance, escapes from thought and sees the original primordial hallucination and becomes the Storyteller. These people are so stunned by the vision that they isolate themselves for exactly thirty-two days, and when they emerge into the world again something about them has changed. There was a time in the history of man when Storytellers were worshipped by the Anti-storytellers. But the power of logic is so strong now that the world now thinks of Storytellers as mentally ill, so they put them in cages in an asylum.

'So, the fellowship of Storytellers has to come together and find a way to reveal the original hallucination,' Alpha says. 'They have to find a way to tell the Story.'

'So there are many hallucinations that the human brain sees. And one of the hallucinations of the mind is the original Story?'

'You are right.'

'Why can't the Storytellers just stand on the street and tell the Story?'

'The Story cannot be transmitted through language. But Antistory has trapped mankind in language. That's why it is difficult for the Storytellers to tell the Story. They don't know how to tell the Story. They can only see the Story.'

'Why can't a hallucination be told through language?'

'There are many ordinary hallucinations that cannot be explained through language.'

'That can't be true?'

'Can you describe the colour red through language, describe red without using its wavelength or comparing it with other colours of the spectrum? If you cannot describe the illusion of red through language, obviously the highest order of hallucination would be impossible to describe through mere words.'

'Do they succeed, the Storytellers, do they win in the end?'

'I don't know.'

'Are you on the side of Story or Anti-story?'

Alpha laughs. It is a surprising, booming laughter.

'What about you, Mr Chacko?'

'I want the Storytellers to win because that appears to be the happy ending.'

Alpha laughs again, and nods his head.

'Did you and Unni talk about this story?'

'Yes.'

'How did you meet Unni?'

'Beta brought him home.'

'Have you ever met Somen Pillai?'

'No.'

'Alpha, do you know why Unni killed himself?'

'No.'

'Can you tell me what you and Unni talked about?'

'We met only eight times,' Alpha says. 'We spoke about this and that, I don't remember. Yes, we had conversations. But it has been a while.'

'Still, I am sure you remember something.'

'We spoke about many things, things that do not interest people. We spoke about the eye, how the eye sees.'

'How does the eye see?'

'What the eye really sees, the image, is registered at the back of the retina, at the back of the eye, yet what we see, the visible world, is in front of us. How is that possible? Why is sight in front of us and not at the back of the eye, like a thought?'

'Why?'

'Because what we see is a projection of the brain. The world we see is a projection.'

'What else did you talk about?'

'What do you mean, "what else"?'

'I mean what else did you talk about?'

'Just this and that.'

'Can you think of something specific? Like the eye.'

'We spoke about the corpse.'

'Who is the corpse?'

'The corpse is a corpse.'

'I don't understand.'

'You would understand everything if you met Psycho.'

'Who is Psycho?'

Alpha laughs. He repeats the question – 'Who is Psycho?'

'Is Psycho a cartoonist?'

Alpha looks away and laughs hard. 'Psycho is Psycho,' he says. 'He spent a lot of time with Unni. Psycho is different from me. Psycho has conversations. Psycho has very long conversations.'

He writes something on a piece of paper and hands it to Ousep. It says, '4 Anna Salai'.

'Is this an address?' Ousep asks.

'You're a very clever man.'

'What will I find there?'

'You will find a white building with six floors. Go to the third floor. On the third floor, there is a long corridor. At the far end of the corridor is a white door. Behind the door sits Psycho.'

'What does he do, Alpha?'

Alpha laughs and shakes his head. 'You'll understand everything when you get there,' he says.

'Is this his real name? "Psycho", is that his real name?'

'What's real about a name?'

'What's his name, Alpha? You know what I mean.'

'Yes, I do. His real name, his real real real name, his very real, absolutely truthful name, is Psycho. You have to be very careful with Psycho. He is on the side of the Anti-storytellers.'

'Does Psycho know why Unni did what he did?'

'Mr Chacko, you're not listening to me. You have to be very careful when you meet Psycho. You cannot tell him why you are there. You have to invent reasons. You have to be smart. He is a very dangerous man.'

'Does Psycho know why Unni did what he did?'

'I don't think that bastard knows anything. But Pyscho will lead you to the corpse. Only Psycho knows who the corpse is.'

'Who is the corpse?'

'I just told you. Only Psycho knows. I have never met the corpse. All I know is that Unni was very close to the corpse.'

'And what will the corpse tell me?'

'The corpse will tell you everything you want to know.'

~

OUSEP FINDS IT hard to accept what he sees in front of him even though there is no doubt in his mind that he is at the address Alpha had given him. It is a white building with six floors. A giant board over the dark hollow of the porch says 'Institute of Neurosciences'.

In the waiting area inside there are not more than twenty people and they appear to be in good health. At the reception desk three women in starched cotton saris are in the middle of a conversation about a man they do not like. Behind them is a wooden board that announces the speciality of every floor above. The third floor, the board says, is the Schizophrenia Day Ward and Research Centre.

Ousep takes the stairs. Good for the heart, he says. Did you hear that, Unni? Even Ousep Chacko wants to live. On the third floor there is a long, dim corridor flanked by shut doors, river-green doors. At one end of the corridor, which is now behind Ousep, is the gloom of a yellow wall. The far end is dark, but Ousep can make out a broad white door. There is nobody in the corridor but he can hear voices coming through the walls, sudden solitary laughter, a hard object falling on the floor, soft conversations that do not intend to be whispers. As he walks to the far end, a side door opens and three middle-aged nurses in white frocks walk towards him, laughing and talking in Malayalam about bananas, about yellow bananas and green bananas. As they pass him they look at him with suspicion as if he is a patient who has gone astray. That makes him walk more briskly and call on all his daylight dignity.

As the white door approaches, the corridor gets cleaner, and a short red carpet appears and leads all the way to the door. He can see that there is a nameplate on the door and it is so large that it probably says much more than 'Psycho'. When he finally arrives at the door he feels that one part of the Alpha puzzle is beginning to fall into place, but he is still not very sure. The nameplate says:

Dr C. Y. Krishnamurthy Iyengar
DM, FRCP (Glas), FRCP (Edin), FRCP (Lond), FAMS, FACP,
   FICP FIMSA, FAAN
Neurosurgeon, Neuropsychiatrist
Chairman Emeritus
The Schizophrenia Day Ward and Research Centre

Ousep considers the door for a moment. Behind the door, somewhere inside the room, sits a doctor, a grand old man in all probability, a neurosurgeon, a neuropsychiatrist, whom Alpha calls Psycho. From what Ousep has seen, Alpha is not a normal person. The nature of the association between Alpha and a neuro-psychiatrist is not hard to guess. It is natural that the boy would imagine Psycho as an adversary. But then Ousep does not want to dismiss Alpha's warning. He has to decide. Should he reveal to the man the reason why he is here, or should he play?

He opens the door and finds a surprisingly large room, with no windows. In the middle of the room is an ancient wooden desk, and behind the desk sits a small old man with rich silver hair that has been neatly combed back. His head is bent, he is reading something engrossing on his lap, and if he has heard the door open he is not curious to know the nature of the intru-sion. Ousep walks in and stands still. The old man is in a checked cotton shirt that is buttoned at the collar and the cuffs. There are eight fountain pens clipped to his shirt pocket and one small black object, which is probably some kind of a torch. There are three silver medals pinned on the third button. The room is filled with shields and framed citations, most of which contain the unsmiling face of a younger man who has undoubtedly become the person in front of him.

Iyengar lifts his head and is not surprised by what he sees. He does not stare in incomprehension, does not ask any questions. He points to a chair. This is the old man in *The Album of the Dead*, one of the four unidentified characters in the series. Ousep tries to assume an apologetic inferior face that still retains considerable dignity. Iyengar puts the book he was reading on the clean desk. It is the Bhagvat Gita, in Sanskrit. An old philosophical man with a lot of time, which is a good sign.

'Dr Iyengar, my name is Ousep, I am the chief reporter with UNI. I apologise for coming here without an appointment.'

'What is UNI?' the doctor asks, leaning back and looking amused. His voice is deep, but feeble.

'United News of India, it is a news agency, like PTI.'

'I get it now.'

'I am working on a story. A feature story on schizophrenia in Madras. The condition of schizophrenics.'

'The condition?'

'How people with this condition go through life, what is being done to help them.'

'So, Ousep, you are going to write a story about schizophrenics, and what you write will be carried by all the newspapers that subscribe to UNI. Is that correct?'

'That's correct.'

'But this is not news, it is not a current affairs story. As you say, you are working on a feature story, which means it can appear at any time. It can appear in a week, in a month. Is that correct?'

'That's correct.'

'Would it appear in *The Hindu*?'

'That's possible.'

'But you don't know?'

'I don't know.'

'I've never seen a feature story that has the name of a news agency under it. I see PTI stories all the time, which are all news stories.'

'Yes, it is a bit odd but I am very interested in the subject.'

'Why?'

'I just am interested.'

'Ousep, I have a friend. He is a sexologist. Do you know what a sexologist does?'

'Yes.'

'Good. Because I don't know what a sexologist does. He meets a lot of journalists every week. Senior journalists like you, elegant men, smart men, but more importantly they are not young men. They go to his office, just turn up, as you have come here to see me. They tell him that they want to know something about the sexual problems of men and women in Madras. The sexual condition of men and women. They tell him they are working on a story. That's what they tell him. But he knows what they want. They want to get their penises up and they want a free and discreet consultation.'

'I am here for the story.'

'I am not disputing that. I am merely telling you something I know about journalists. Do you have any mental condition?'

'No.'

'Do you suspect that any of your family members has a mental condition?'

'I am not here for a free consultation.'

'You're here to do a story.'

'Yes.'

'And you came without an appointment because I am an old man, unimportant, useless.'

'That's far from the truth.'

'I am sure you interviewed all the bright young neurologists in Madras before coming to me.'

'That's not true. You are, in fact, the first person I am interviewing for the story. You can verify this. You belong to a small, tight community. You can call up a few people and find out.'

'Why am I the first person you chose to meet?'

'I wanted to meet the patriarch first and then move downwards.'

'You wanted to meet the patriarch first and move downwards. All right, Ousep, if that is what you want.'

'Before we start, Doctor, I am very curious,' Ousep says, taking out his scribbling pad and pen from his trouser pocket. 'Why do you carry eight pens in your pocket?'

'Because they are mine.'

'And is there a special reason why those medals are pinned to your shirt?'

'These are medals of honour, Ousep. One is from the American Neurological Association, another is from the American Academy of Neurology, and the third one is from the Indian International Neuropsychiatry Association. I like wearing them. I know how this looks. I know what you are thinking. You think a patient is sitting in the doctor's chair. My patients, they like it when they see me, they like the fact that I don't look normal, that I don't look like one of those people from the other side. They think I am on their side.'

'I see you were reading the Gita.'

'Yes, you see a lot, it seems to me. If you are an Indian, a real Indian, Ousep, you never start reading the Gita. You only reread it. You reread it at different points of your life and you see things you never saw before. It is the greatest subplot ever written. I feel peaceful when I read. I feel good. I am a bit lost these days, Ousep. That's why I am with the Gita.'

'Why are you lost?'

'My wife died three months ago. Have you heard this joke, Ousep? "My love, I feel terrible without you. It is like being with you."'

Ousep lets out a good-natured man-to-man chuckle.

'Do you find it funny?' the old man asks.

'Yes, it's funny.'

'Humour is a form of fact, isn't it? That's why it works. Do you know why we laugh?'

'Why do we laugh?'

'Our laugh evolved from a ferocious face that early man used to make. He made that face when he was not sure if a danger had passed. That face in time became human laughter. We laugh because humour assaults us with a slice of truth and we sense danger. That is the same reason why people laugh in an aeroplane – when there is turbulence and people are scared, they laugh, don't they? Have you ever been inside a plane?'

'Yes, a few times.'

'You must be an important journalist, then. My wife, she had never been inside a plane. Isn't it sad? That a person has died without ever flying.'

'It's sad, yes.'

'Do you know anyone who has died without ever flying?'

'Strange question, Doctor.'

'Do you know anyone who has died without ever flying?'

'So many, there are so many.'

Ousep wonders what Unni would have thought of flying. He imagines him as a smart young man in a serious blue shirt, very preoccupied with something important, strapped in a seat, looking at the world below through the plane's window.

Iyengar rolls a pen between his palms in some kind of an exercise, and says, 'Who were you thinking about?'

'No one.'

'Someone who has never flown?'

'I was not thinking about anything specific actually, Doctor.'

'I was thinking about my wife,' Iyengar says. 'I think about her all the time.'

'You must love her very much.'

'All Tamil Brahmin women of an age hate men. Did you know that?'

'Is that true?'

'That's what my wife said. And she said – you know what she said? – she said she hated me, that she always hated me. Those were her last words. I was a monster, apparently. People look at an old man and they think he is an innocuous fool, that he can be toyed with, that he is an idiot whose time and dignity have no meaning. He can be tricked. But old women, they have a different story to tell, don't they?'

Iyengar, obviously, is no fool. That much he has conveyed. He probably senses that Ousep is hiding something. Ousep wonders whether he must just reveal the truth and get on with it.

'I am such a silly old man,' Iyengar says. 'I've been talking rubbish. Like silly old men. You're here for a purpose. Tell me, Ousep, what do you want to know?'

Iyengar takes his card from a stack on the table and hands it to him. Ousep has no choice but to hand him his own card. The doctor studies it but there is no sign of recollection on his face, no hint of remembering a name from the past.

'Ousep Chacko,' Iyengar says. 'Yes, Ousep Chacko, chief reporter of UNI, what would you like to know?'

'Maybe we can start with an interesting case that you're working on right now.'

'Interesting?'

'A case that has fascinated you recently?'

'I know what you mean. Interesting case. There is a case of two sisters. Would you like to know?'

'Yes.'

Iyengar looks at the empty pen-holder on his desk and says, 'One sister is thirty and the other is twenty-eight. A few weeks ago the two sisters were found almost dead in their house. The milkman found them. Which is strange. Usually, in such cases, the maid finds them, isn't that true, Ousep? The maid knocks on the door, nobody opens the door, she breaks a window and peeps in and there she sees someone lying motionless. Isn't that how these stories usually start, Ousep?'

'That's true.'

'But these sisters, they didn't have a servant. So, it was the milkman who found them. Every day he would drop the milk packets outside their door. Not a very observant man, this guy. He took a week to figure out that the milk packets he had been dropping outside the door had not been touched. He decided to knock. When they did not open, he looked through the window and he saw a leg on the floor, behind a cupboard. He broke open the front door and went in. He found the girls lying on the floor in the kitchen, mumbling something. He got some neighbours together and they took the girls to a clinic. The doctors there soon realised that the girls had almost starved to death. They fed them through tubes, and soon they referred the sisters to the Schizophrenia Centre because the girls were saying that they heard voices. When you hear voices, you come to me.'

The sisters lived alone. Their father had died when they were little girls. And their mother had died a few months earlier by consuming poison because she could not marry off her daughters.

'I asked the girls why they had starved when obviously they had enough money to eat. They said that they had been hearing the voice of their mother and she had been warning them that someone was poisoning their food, a mysterious hand was poisoning their food, poisoning everything. Both the girls heard the voice and the voice said the same things to both of them.

'I had a fair idea what was going on and what emerged did not surprise me very much. The older sister was schizophrenic. The younger one was normal, absolutely normal. The older sister has a history. Right from when she was a child she saw visions, heard voices. She had a special bond with Lord Krishna, who sat on her bed every night and guarded her from Indra, who was trying to rape her. But she went to work like any other person. She worked in a small library. Since she was a bit off, it was hard for her widow mother to get her married. Until the older one got married, the younger one could not be married. So one day their mother decided that she had had enough of this world and decided to die. She ate a lot of rat poison and to be sure drank half a bottle of phenyl.

'The girls sat at home mourning their mother. It is not unusual for two children, in these circumstances, to completely cut themselves off from the rest of the world for a few days.

They were depressed, naturally. Also, society, the world, was responsible for their mother's death. That was how they saw it. So they lost interest in going out of their house. They sat in the house and did nothing. After a week the older sister began to hear voices. She started telling her sister that their mother was saying that she had not killed herself, someone had poisoned her, and that the girls should not eat anything until the danger had passed. The older sister stopped eating and she kept telling the other girl about the voices. One day the younger sister, too, started hearing the voices. The older sister had transferred her delusion to the younger sister. And now they found confirmation of their delusion in each other. It is a classic case of shared delusion. *Folie-à-deux*. The Folly of Two.'

'The older sister has a history of hearing voices, seeing visions?' Ousep says.

'Yes. She is schizophrenic. We are treating her.'

'And the younger one. She is a normal girl but she began to hear the voices.'

'She is absolutely normal to the best of my knowledge.'

'This is strange. Can a schizophrenic person transfer her delusion to a normal person?'

Iyengar looks at Ousep with meaning. It appears to Ousep that he has said something that has given him away, but he is not very sure.

'Happens all the time, Ousep,' Iyengar says, turning his swivel chair to the wall and leaning back comfortably. 'You will have seen it in your own life without recognising it as the Folly of Two. Cases that are not as dramatic as the story of the two sisters, but still cases of shared delusion. Happens a lot in families, especially between husbands and wives. Man keeps losing his job, never survives in an office for more than a few months. He thinks the world is against him, he thinks he is too good for the world. Wife begins to believe that too. He has transferred his delusion to her. They go through life thinking the world is out to harm them, that someone has cursed them, that there is a force working against them. But in reality the guy loses his job because he is not good enough.'

'But this can happen among normal couples, too,' Ousep says. 'A man need not be delusional or have a neurological condition to fool his wife. Maybe he is just an idiot. An idiot who loses his job every few months because he is incompetent, and he lies to his wife about why he loses his job.'

'Yes. But would she believe him?'

'What do you mean, Doctor? Why wouldn't she believe him? If he is a good liar, she would believe him.'

'Can you fool your wife?'

'I don't see your point, Doctor. Husbands fool their wives all the time. Do you dispute that?'

'Ousep, we arrive at an intriguing aspect of the Folly of Two. You have to listen to me carefully. Imagine the two sisters. Imagine the older sister is you. You as in you – Ousep Chacko, who is not schizophrenic. We assume that though I don't know your medical history. So, in the place of the schizophrenic older sister who hears voices, it is you. You do not hear voices because you are not a nut. Now, imagine I ask you to fool the younger sister, I ask you to lie to her about the voices. And you lie to her. You tell her that you have heard your mother's voice and that the voice has instructed both of you to stop eating. You keep saying this to her. You do this for days. Would the younger sister start hearing the voices?'

'I don't know.'

'What do you feel, what does your instinct say?'

'I would be very surprised if she starts hearing voices just because I tell her that I am hearing voices.'

'I have studied this, Ousep. I have studied the phenomenon in this very building. Even if you are the best actor in the world, there is only a very small chance that the younger sister will begin to hear voices just because you say there are voices. You are as persistent as the older sister, you say everything she would have said, you do everything she would have done, but you cannot make the normal younger sister hear voices by lying about the voices.'

'Why is that?'

'Because to fool a person, it appears, you have to first fool yourself. That is at the heart of all human influences. That is why the older sister can make the younger sister hear the voices, and you cannot do that. A delusion is many times more powerful than a lie. The distinction between a delusion and a lie is the very difference between a successful saint and a fraud. Why does one man succeed in convincing half the country that he is God while other third-rate magicians like him fail, or even get arrested or beaten up? Why do some evangelists do better than other evangelists? Rationalists think all god-men are frauds. That is the problem with rationalists. They are not rational enough. The world cannot be conned so easily by frauds. Great god-men are great because they really believe they are holy. And all our gods, Ousep, are not lies. They existed. All our gods, from the beginning of time, have been men with psychiatric conditions. And their delusions were so deep, they passed them on. God and believer were then locked in the Folly of Two, they still are. Sometimes in this equation the god could be a political theorist who is in the grip of a powerful idea, or an economist, a dictator, even a particle physicist. They can influence the world not because they are right, or because they are conmen. They can influence the world because they are deeply deluded. The human delusion has that extraordinary property. It transmits itself. Especially when it does not have to fight a powerful existing myth, a delusion moves from one neurological system to another, it spreads. This is a world that is locked in the Folly of Two.'

In an afterthought, he includes social workers in the list of the deluded. 'Some of them, our living saints, do not realise that they are actually sadists who enjoy watching human misery from very close up.'

His eyes grow ponderous and he smiles as if he has experienced a happy memory. 'A boy once told me something, and he said it in this very room. He was sitting where you are sitting right now. He told me that the very objective of a delusion is to spread, to colonise other neurological systems. That is its purpose. There is no evidence to support this but it does appear sometimes that the boy was right.'

'Who was the boy?'

Iyengar waves his hand in a dismissive way. Ousep decides not to push. He says, 'From what you say, Doctor, it seems a person can pass his delusion to more than one individual. So it is not just the Folly of Two. Is that correct?'

Iyengar is about to say something but stops himself. Ousep knows that his questions are somehow exposing him but he cannot understand how that can be. Or is Iyengar just a dramatic man, a cinematic man, who has learnt to intrigue people with cinematic moments? Ousep would never underestimate the power of Tamil cinema. Madras is full of actor clones, full of acts and moments that people have plagiarised from films.

'Ousep, how did you come here?'

'I don't understand your question.'

'Let me imagine the chain of events. You decide to write a story about schizophrenics in Madras. You decide to meet the patriarch first, as you say. But then you don't know what I am. You have done no research, it seems. Very odd for a senior journalist like you. Don't get me wrong, I am not trying to embarrass you. I am trying to understand the situation that we are in. You wanted to meet Dr Krishnamurthy Iyengar but you have no idea who he is, what he means to his profession. When neurologists think of me, do you know what they think of?'

'I should admit that I've been incompetent in my research.'

'Or you just walked into this building not knowing what to expect, and you knocked on a door. But why?'

'It may appear that way, I admit, but I came here looking for you.'

'I believe that, Ousep.'

'If you're not too offended, and I am truly very embarrassed to say this, can you tell me what you are, Doctor?'

Iyengar laughs like a child. 'Of course, I would love to. Isn't that what I was getting at? My wife always complained that she and I only talk about me. One day she told me, "Let's go to a good restaurant and talk about you, you and you."'

Iyengar laughs again, drinks a glass of water that was waiting for him on the desk. 'All my life I have used the Folly of Two to study mass delusion,' he says. He speaks softly, he is reflective, even proud perhaps. 'That is my rebellion. That is what I am. Why is this important? The society of neuroscientists does not recognise mass delusion as a psychiatric condition. What does this mean? This means, the society of neuroscientists would admit that all evidence points to the fact that God is a figment of man's delusion, yet believers in God, who form most of humanity, cannot be considered delusional. This is a ridiculous position. From the point of view of neuroscience, sanity is a majority condition, and a mass delusion is not a delusion but merely human nature. I don't agree. I have never agreed. What they are saying is that if there is a pandemic and all of mankind is infected, then that must be considered normal and a healthy human a freak. That is rubbish. That is why I fought for the inclusion of mass delusion as a part of neuropsychiatry, but I failed. I was ridiculed. Why did I fight, Ousep? Because I believe that there is absolute sanity, there is a human condition that is perfectly sane. But it is a minority condi-tion, which means, from the point of view of neuroscience, it would be in the spectrum of insanity. Somewhere in this world there are people who are in an extraordinary mental state, an extraordinary state of sanity. And they would be considered odd.'

'What is this state, Doctor?'

'I don't know.'

'So you have not met anybody who is in an extraordinary state of sanity?'

Iyengar answers with a blank face. 'A neuropsychiatrist would be the last person to meet such a being, isn't that true, Ousep?'

'That's true.'

'But neuroscience does recognise the delusion of a group of people as a form of mental instability. There is the Folly of Three, and the Folly of Four and even the Folly of Many, which is sometimes used to describe the mass hysteria in the adolescent girls of a school, or the sort of people and their master who wait for alien contact, or wait for the arrival of The One. But they all come under the basic principles of the Folly of Two. There is usually a primary agent, whose powerful delusion is passed on to the secondary agents, and they start corroborating each other's delusions. They start seeing visions, hearing things.'

'So it is never equal. Two people in the Folly of Two are never equally deluded.'

'Rarely.'

'So there is always a primary and a secondary?'

'Yes. A primary agent and a secondary agent.'

'Alpha-Beta.'

Iyengar nods, drums the table with his fingers, fixes Ousep with an indecipherable stare.

'I am reminded of an old case. Not very old, actually. It is another classic case of the Folly of Two. Can I tell you?'

'Yes, you must, I am grateful.'

'I know you are, Ousep. I know. There were two brothers, they were twins, not identical twins but fraternal twins. When I met them they were in their late teens, which is when these things happen to boys. Adolescence is a very dangerous period in the lives of philosophically oriented males. The brothers, they were cartoonists, very good cartoonists. They showed me their comics. The comics were about powerful supervillains fighting underdog superheroes. Not surprising at all, you will understand why. I don't remember the names of the boys now but I remember what they called themselves – Alpha and Beta. That is how they signed their comics. Strange, because that was what they turned out to be. Alpha and Beta.

'Alpha was schizophrenic. He believed that the early human

race was in the trance of a great vision, which has now been lost. He believed, and he probably still believes, that some people, by pure chance, see the original vision, a vision without thought, a vision of the entire universe that is immeasurably beautiful. Meanwhile the others, almost all of humanity, are trapped in what is generally considered human nature. Some days Alpha heard voices, voices of ancient people who have seen the great hallucination, guiding him, asking him to lock himself in a room for days and meditate so that he can prepare himself to see what they saw. Alpha passed his delusion on to Beta. Beta was not entirely normal but as a doctor I would not diagnose him as schizophrenic. But, under the influence of Alpha, he started believing in the vision. Some days, he, too, started seeing visions and hearing voices. The boys stopped going to college. They started acting weird. Their father forced them to meet me.

'The boys did not like me much. They thought I was with the dark forces, they thought my purpose was to brand people like them mad and lock them up. They refused to meet me but their father kept forcing them. One day Alpha walked into this room and picked up a paperweight and threw it at me. He missed, fortunately. But then he held me by my shirt and started shaking me as if the truth would then spill out of my ears. I yelled like a fool. The peons came and saved me.'

'When was this, Doctor?'

'About three years ago.'

'Was that the last time you saw Alpha? The day he attacked you?'

'Yes, that was the last time. But a few a weeks later something interesting happened. Alpha sent a message through a friend.'

Iyengar opens the drawer of his table and takes out a folder, which contains handwritten letters, short printed notes, medical certificates and yellowing pages from Sanskrit books. He takes out a sheet of paper from the folder and hands it to Ousep. 'Alpha sent this,' he says.

On the sheet is a brilliant caricature of Iyengar. At the bottom of the portrait is the short message – 'I am sorry'. And it is signed 'Alpha'. But the style of the cartoon very clearly points to Unni. Unni's caricatures are austere portraits, he did not exaggerate any part of the face, he was true to all dimensions and there was no attempt at humour. It was as if he found the human face funny enough, so he did not try hard. The quality of the paper, its density and colour, is the same as the pages of Unni's notebooks. Also, from what Ousep has seen of Alpha, he does not appear to be the sort of person who would care to apologise. In all probability, the messenger was Unni and the message was his.

Iyengar asks a surprising question. 'Do you think the portrait was done by Alpha?' Ousep decides to be silent. He realises that the conversation is not in his control any more, it probably never was.

'The friend whom Alpha had sent was a cartoonist,' Iyengar says, extending his hand to retrieve the portrait and carefully inserting it back in the folder. 'I forget the boy's name but I remember his face very well. A handsome boy, there was something about his face, his stare. He was younger than Alpha. He told me he was seventeen.'

The boy starts a conversation with the doctor about the Folly of Two. 'That boy knew a lot about the subject. He obviously had been reading about it. He even knew about my position on mass delusions.'

At some point, the boy tells the doctor about his hypothesis – that the objective of every human delusion is to spread to other brains. Iyengar, naturally, does not take an adolescent's theory seriously enough to offer a scientific opinion, but he enjoys the conversation that follows. 'It was a rich conversation. I enjoyed talking to him.'

The boy asks him whether there is a possibility that enlightenment is just a schizophrenic condition. All the sages who turned into anthills beneath tropical trees in the search for truth, and all the saints and the gods, what if they were just schizophrenics? Iyengar accepts, with complex qualifiers, that he has seen patients who exhibit the enlightenment syndrome, who believe that they are one with the universe, who feel that their bodies are mere vehicles of an eternal condition. Iyengar has seen people who believe they are gods with many hands, demons with many heads, giants of astronomical sizes, even illuminated white doves that speak. He has met men whose dreams contain coded messages from heaven. The boy finds it funny that men and women whose mental conditions have specific names in neuropsychiatry today were, in another time, gods. He finds it funny, and strangely satisfying, that the pursuit of truth is in all likelihood a path left behind by ancient schizophrenics.

'As we were chatting, at some point the boy probably realised that I could not continue talking to him. I had work to do. But he wanted to hold my attention. So he had to make himself valuable. He had researched me, Ousep, he knew a lot about me, he knew what I would fall for. He told me, "Doctor, I know someone with the Cotard Delusion." I was hooked. The boy had me. The Cotard Delusion is a very rare form of schizophrenia. It is also called the Corpse Syndrome. A person with this condition would feel as if he were a living corpse, that he was rotting inside, that he was actually dead and so eternal. It is a strange philosophical state, but also an extreme case of depression, and the only reason the corpse does not kill himself is that he thinks he is dead anyway. I had never directly interviewed a person with the Cotard Delusion. Not many doctors in the world have. And here was a boy in my room who claimed that he knew someone with the condition. Someone very close to him, he said, but did not reveal any details.'

The boy and Iyengar meet several times over four weeks. The boy wants to understand the world of delusions, and Iyengar wants to meet the corpse. They spend hours together, Iyengar even lets the adolescent meet some of his patients. They form a relationship, a bizarre fellowship. Every time they meet, Iyengar asks the boy about the corpse and the boy says that the corpse does not want to meet the doctor yet. But the boy is confident that he will eventually convince the corpse. 'Then one day, the boy simply vanishes. He stops coming. I don't see him again. This was three years ago.'

Iyengar leans back in his chair, crosses his fingers. 'Now, Ousep, I've told you everything you may want to know. Is there something you would like to tell me?'

'The boy's name is Unni.'

'Unni, yes, that was his name. Unni Chacko.'

The doctor leans forward, and asks in a gentle tone, but without compassion or curiosity or fear, 'Where is Unni?'

'He is dead.'

Iyengar nods. 'How did he die?'

'He killed himself.'

Iyengar nods again. 'When was this, Ousep?'

'Three years ago. Sixteenth May 1987.'

'And you have been trying to find out why he died?'

'Yes. One of the people I met was Alpha. He asked me to meet you. He said you would know who the corpse is. And the corpse would know why Unni did what he did.'

'How did Alpha know about the corpse?'

'Unni used to talk about the corpse. He had told several people about the corpse.'

'So the corpse does exist. He was not lying.'

'Yes. He knew a corpse. I was hoping you would know who that is.'

'I am sorry, Ousep. I don't know.'

'You don't seem very surprised by his death, Doctor.'

'In my line of work I have no room to be surprised. But if it is grief that you are actually asking about, I will deal with it when I am alone, which is most of the time.'

Ousep's scribbling pad and pen lie on the desk like the props of a farce. He puts them back in his trouser pockets, which makes Iyengar smile. 'There is something else I want to ask you, Doctor,' Ousep says. 'Unni used to play a prank with people. He would ask a person to think of a two-digit odd number.

The chances of his guessing the number right were roughly one in forty-five. He would always guess the number as thirty-three. That way, by pure chance, he would get it right sometimes. There are people who still think Unni could read minds. They don't remember that he had asked them to think of a two-digit odd number, that he had reduced the odds, they only remember that Unni had somehow read what was in their mind. Why do you think Unni did it?'

Iyengar shakes his head. 'I've no idea, Ousep. But listen, not everything he did need have any relevance to his death. He was an adolescent. He discovered a great prank. There is probably nothing more to it.'

They sit in silence, without any discomfort between them. The old man, too, is remembering Unni perhaps. He puts his elbows on the desk and asks, 'Is there anybody you know who was very close to Unni who appears to fit the description I gave you of the Cotard Delusion? Anybody? Family, friends, the guard in your building, it could be anybody.'

'No.'

'The boy told me that he was very close to the corpse. It is highly probable that the corpse would know something important about him.'

'Can you take a guess, Doctor? Why would Unni kill himself?'

'I cannot, Ousep. I am as clueless as you are. I gather you have interviewed everyone who matters.'

'Yes.'

'Except the corpse?'

'Yes. Except the corpse.'

'And there is nobody you know who could be the corpse?'

'Did Unni ever tell you about a boy called Somen Pillai?'

'No. Who is Somen Pillai?'

'He was Unni's closest friend. But I have not been able to meet him. He does not want to meet me. Every time I go to his house, his parents send me back saying he is not at home.'

'Can you describe this person to me?'

'I've met him only once and that was three years ago. He was shy, he did not talk much. He did not always look me in the eye. That is all I can say about him.'

'You know nothing more about him?'

'All his classmates say he spoke very rarely. When he was in a room it was as if he did not exist, he was one of those invisible types.'

'Was his hair neatly combed?'

'Yes, it was combed.'

'Did he have a hairstyle?'

'Nothing flamboyant.'

'And his clothes? They were clean and smart?'

'Yes.'

'Did he use the word "I" to refer to himself? Was he aware of his self?'

'I don't remember,' Ousep says.

'Did he have plans? Did he have a concept of the future, his own future?'

'I can't be sure.'

'Still,' Iyengar says, leaning back and resting his head comfortably on the chair, 'he could be the corpse. There is a corpse in this boy, I feel.'

7

The Folly of Two

THOMA HAS TRIED everything to diminish Mythili in his mind. He has searched her face for the hint of a moustache, he has imagined her naked and laughed at her shame, he has imagined her on the commode though he does not really believe she would ever do anything as cheap as that. But all his methods have failed and he now accepts that he must quietly suffer his adoration.

'Do you know about the sun and the moon?' he asks to show her his range of interests. They are in her room, she sitting with her legs folded on her bed, and he sitting on a plastic chair facing her.

'What about the sun and the moon?'

'The sun is a thousand times larger than the moon.'

'So?'

'But they are positioned in space in such a way that from Earth they appear to be the same size in the sky.'

'I never thought of it that way.'

'Unni told me that.'

'So what if they are the same size?'

'They are exactly the same size in the sky, Mythili. It is a mystery how they ended up where they are in space so that they look equal in the sky. They are where they are because that is the only way there can be life on Earth.'

'But that is circular logic,' she says.

Thoma pretends he knows what circular logic is, he nods his head.

'I have an Engish teacher,' Mythili says. 'She tells us, "Girls, isn't it amazing that the boiling point of water is exactly one hundred degrees. What a nice round number the Lord has given us."'

Thoma laughs to show he understands. They fall silent, as they usually do. But he knows they have a lot to talk about these days. He does not have to bring up Unni any more, she asks him herself. She is very curious to know what his father has discovered. Thoma tells her the bits and pieces he has gathered from his father's drunken confessions to the ceiling fan, and from what his mother has told him. Mythili's face grows sad when she listens.

She usually lifts her mood by recounting her memories of Unni – most of them unremarkable things, which she greatly exaggerates. Like Unni's mind-reading abilities. 'How could Unni know which card I had picked? Remember, Thoma? I started taking the whole pack of cards to my room, shutting the door and then picking a card. And when I stepped out, Unni would guess it correctly. Then I started going to the terrace like a fool to pick the card. But he would always guess what was in my mind. I have picked a card and torn it into many pieces, too, but he would always guess it.'

She goes on and on as if she really believes that Unni could read minds, and she has this annoying smile on her face. Thoma cannot bear it any more. He tells her, 'It was a trick. He didn't read your mind. Nobody can read minds.'

'But then how did he do it?'

'He didn't do it. He didn't do anything.'

'What do you mean by that?'

'I did it.'

Mythili's face turns serious; she has never looked at Thoma with so much concentration. He tells her, 'Remember? I was always around when you picked the card. I was this little boy whom nobody noticed. I was invisible. That's what Unni told me and he was right. I would be standing right behind you when you picked the card. In your room, on the stairway, on the terrace, I was always around. But you never saw me. Unni taught me how to make the signs to pass the message to him behind your back. Sometimes Unni would pretend that he could not guess the card. Then we would wait for you to go to the kitchen or the bathroom and I would slip the card in one of your books.'

She folds her arms, and looks away with a sad smile. 'I wish you had not told me, Thoma,' she says. 'It was my sweetest memory of Unni.'

Thoma had once promised Unni that he would never reveal the secret. 'Many, many years later, Thoma, she will ask you, "How did Unni do it?" But you should not tell her. You must never tell her.'

'I will not tell anyone, Unni. It is our secret.'

'Our secret, Thoma. Only two people in this world know this secret. Unni Chacko and Thoma Chacko.'

Thoma feels a powerful silence within him. It is not sorrow or shame, or anything as ordinary as that. It is merely silence, there is no other way to describe it. He sees his betrayal of his brother for what it is – an act of pettiness. Thoma asks himself why he is petty and why Unni never was. Unni did not want anything. Unni Had No Expectations from Life. So Unni had no reasons to be afraid. Thoma wants so many things from the world, from people. That is why he is afraid, and that is why he was petty.

Later in the evening, he walks to the churchyard, leans on the bare white trunk of a eucalyptus tree and stands facing Unni's grave, and tells him what has happened. Thoma does not move his mouth when he speaks to his brother. There is too much shame in appearing to talk to yourself, as he knows better than most people. He talks about this and that, updates Unni about their mother and the state of their father. And he describes Mythili to him. 'She is taller than her mother now, Unni. She speaks very softly now, she does not scream, she does not fight, she does not sing, actually she does not talk a lot now. She is not a motormouth any more.'

Thoma remembers the times when he was in the care of Unni, how they walked hand in hand, how they played and how they laughed. How Unni would come steaming in when boys tried to push Thoma around. And he remembers the day Unni took him all around Madras in a suspenseful search for 'the white sugar cane, which does exist, Thoma, somewhere in the city there is a white sugar cane'. They went in crowded buses, and in the train, they walked and ran down the roads in search of the white sugar cane and returned home telling each other that they would set out again to hunt another day.

Thoma stands in the churchyard until it gets dark, and when he leaves he is glad that he does not feel scared to be alone in a place like this any more. He wants to believe in ghosts, he really does hope that in this world there are ghosts.

~

THE CLOSEST OUSEP has come to seeing the future is when he goes down the mud lane to Somen Pillai's house. This evening, too, he knows what is about to happen. Before he reaches the gate the door on the pink front of the house opens and the man and wife emerge on to the porch, whispering to each other. They stand with their elbows on the short iron gate, and wait for him to arrive. Somen's father is bare chested, his mother is in a sari. Ousep can see their bellies. And their deep navels that gape at him as if they are the alert eyes of a long, indestructible tropical marriage.

'Somen is not home,' the mother says.

'Where has he gone now?'

'He has gone to a friend's house and he will be late.'

Ousep searches the windows, searches for the furtive movement of a shadow, for a curtain moving an inch, anything that would give a sign that his quarry is inside, but there is nothing.

The father says, 'You've started coming here every day, Ousep. What has happened?'

'Does he live here any more?' Ousep asks.

'This is his home.'

'I have been trying to meet him for the last six months.'

'We have told you many times he does not want to meet you.'

'Why?'

'You must ask him that,' the mother says.

'That is what I have been trying to do. I've been trying to meet him. But, obviously, you don't want that. You refuse to tell me which college he goes to, you refuse to tell me where he goes every day and what he does.'

'It is not our fault if he does not want to meet you,' the father says.

'Is he in the house right now?'

'We're getting a bit tired of this, Ousep.'

'I met a boy,' Ousep says, 'Sai Shankaran. You know him. He says Somen has run away from home.'

'That's nonsense – you go and tell Sai Shankaran that. Our boy is with us.'

'Sai Shankaran says your boy may have gone someplace to die in peace.'

'Ousep,' the father screams, 'I have sympathy for you because of what happened to your son. But don't wish that on everyone. I am not a drunkard. I feed my family, I keep them happy. My son has no reason to kill himself.'

'Can I come inside? Let's talk.'

'The ceiling fan is not working,' the father says. 'So it is very hot inside. We must stand outside and talk.'

Somen's mother looks incredulously at her husband and goes away inside as if she wants to search for a far corner and burst out laughing. Ousep holds the hand of Somen's father and asks him softly, 'Why are you doing this?'

'What am I doing?'

'Why don't you let me meet your son?'

'You see a deeper story in things, Ousep. Boys these days are busy. They leave early, they come home late. He is twenty, he is busy. And when they don't want to meet someone they just don't meet them. They are young people, they have their own minds. He does not want to talk about Unni, and there is nothing we can do about it. He will not meet you. He will never meet you.'

The man leans forward and whispers, 'Ousep, just give up. Children do strange things when they are seventeen. That's the age of madness. What can we do? Maybe there was a girl. There is always a girl. Move on. Get back to your life.'

'This is my life. Unni is my life. I will be coming back, Pillai.'

Pillai goes back into his house and shuts the door. Ousep tries to understand the home. A home is a person. If you stare long enough at its face you begin to see beyond the façade. It is a small, simple house embedded at the end of the lane in such a way that there is only one point of entry or exit. All the windows are shut, which is strange for a house in Madras, and all of them have curtains, which is not surprising. On the terrace, just about twelve feet above the ground, there are some clothes drying. From what he can see there are no jeans or T-shirts among them. There is nothing on the surface of the house that indicates the presence of a young man.

In the houses that flank the narrow lane there are people standing in the doorways, behind their windows and on the terraces. He goes up to a woman who is standing at her gate holding her infant. He asks her, 'Have you seen Somen Pillai today?' The woman spreads her sari over her chest, toys with her pendant and says, 'I have not seen him in a while. What happened?'

'When was the last time you saw him?'

That makes her think. Four men of four generations emerge from her house and step out to talk to him. They are amiable people, that is the nature of the world. People who do not know him always offer him the option of respect. He is an elegant man in daylight, a man with a greying French beard.

They have not seen Somen Pillai for a long time but they don't remember when they last did. He walks across the lane to another house and asks the same question. 'I see you here often,' an old woman says. 'I see you going to their house. Do you want some water to drink? It is a very hot day.'

'It is a very hot day.'

'My granddaughter says the world will soon become ice. But there is no evidence of that in Madras. Do you think the world will turn into ice?'

'When did you last see Somen Pillai?'

'I see his sister once every three months or so. She comes for the weekend. She goes to a medical college in Kerala. Girls are so smart these days. But the boy, I have not seen him in a long time. Never struck me before you asked. I'd seen him grow up on this lane. I've seen so many grow up on this lane, it did not occur to me that I have not spotted the boy in ages. Maybe he has gone somewhere far away to study. They all go away, don't you know? Why don't you ask his parents?'

Ousep goes to every house and asks. Nobody has seen Somen Pillai in a long time. 'Why don't you ask his parents? They live right there,' a man says, wiping his scooter, which is parked inside the house, near the front door.

'I did ask them but they are not telling me. Something is wrong. I think the boy has gone missing.'

'How can a boy go missing? I heard he goes to Loyola College.'

'That's what they told me once. I've checked. He doesn't go there. He has gone missing.'

'Why are you asking about the boy?'

'He has borrowed a lot of money from people I know and now he has gone missing.'

By the time Ousep reaches the end of the lane it is clear to him that Somen Pillai has not been seen on the lane for an indefinite period of time. It is possible that he has been dispatched to a college in another city and his parents do not want him to be bothered by Ousep. But if that were true the boy would still be visiting home once in a while as his sister does. What Sai Shankaran had said begins to make sense. Somen Pillai has probably gone somewhere to die in isolation. The way Unni died was too conspicuous, setting a relentless father off on a trail. Somen probably did not want to draw too much attention. He wanted to be presumed lost. But why?

Ousep returns to Somen's house at midnight, his walk unsteady, hair tempestuous. This time the house does not see him come. He stands at the gate and asks, 'You can't see well in the dark?' He goes up to the front door and begins to pound it. The lights go on. Somen's father looks through the window. He glares in fury but in a moment turns nervous. The man studies the night outside to see whether Ousep has brought any muscular friends along. When he is reassured that the drunkard has come alone, he opens the door and stands with tight fists, legs parted. Ousep withdraws, walks backwards in kung-fu steps and holds his hand as if it is a cobra about to strike.

'Master, I've come to meet Somen Pillai,' he says.

'What's wrong with you, Ousep, are you drunk?'

'Is he back? Has Somen Pillai returned home?'

'Why have you been bad-mouthing us to our neighbours, Ousep, have you lost your mind? You've been telling everyone that the boy has gone missing. You've been telling everyone that he has borrowed money from people.'

'Is Somen Pillai home?'

'Don't come here ever again. I warn you, Ousep. Don't push me.'

The door shuts, there are sounds of all the latches and locks being invoked. Ousep screams, 'Where is Somen Pillai? Were is Somen Pillai? Where is Somen Pillai?'

Lights go on in the houses on the lane. People stare from their windows. It is a moment Ousep is familiar with, a moment in the night. Lights going on in homes, people peeping through their windows, seeing him in a way they would never have imagined in the light of day, and everybody agreeing without a word that they are better than him. This lane, too, now knows of Ousep Chacko.

He comes back at seven in the morning and stands at the gate to take the house by surprise. Nothing stirs. He waits. That is his talent, he knows how to wait. After about an hour, he sees the maid come down the lane. He is struck again by her face, a face that is hard but very aware of its own frugal beauty. She is probably in her early thirties, middle age for maids, but there is much left in her that a man can see. She does not look famished like the other maids, her breasts are full and proud, and she is fleshy in a shapely way. She must be the queen of her slum. She is an anomaly; women like her usually do not survive as maids. She walks towards him, her head bent, and when she raises her eyes they look with the incurable contempt that all Tamil maids have for men who are not film stars.

'Is Somen Pillai in the house?' he asks her.

She walks away without a word.

'Does he live in this house?'

She rings the doorbell. Somen's mother opens the door and she is startled to see Ousep at the gate so early. She shuts the door in his face. Ousep waits to see how the morning unfolds. The maid leaves in about an hour, which is not unusual. When the man and wife emerge, they are in office clothes. They lock their door, and do not meet Ousep's eyes when they go past him. They walk to an old grey scooter that lies by the side of the lane. The man kicks it many times until it roars into life. His wife sits on the pillion holding his paunch, and they leave.

The large padlock on the front door has a melancholy finality about it. Has Somen really abandoned his parents and vanished for ever? But if the truth is that Somen has gone missing, his parents need just to tell Ousep that. Considering what a nuisance he is, that would be a simple solution to get rid of him. Surely there is no shame in telling Ousep that they have lost their son to philosophy. There is no shame in saying that to Ousep. But they have not done that. In fact, they have insisted that their boy lives with them. Also, there is still the glow of life in their eyes. They do not look like parents who have lost their child.

He returns in the evening but the house does not see him any more. The door does not open, the couple do not emerge to face him. He rings the doorbell several times but there is no response. He can hear the sounds of life inside but the Pillais have decided to ignore him.

~

OUSEP IS IN full view of all the women who are standing on their balconies to bid goodbye to their husbands. He is across the lane, facing Block A, and smoking two cigarettes at once. He looks to his left once again, down the whole stretch of Balaji Lane. The car will appear any time now at the far end.

Men on scooters leave the building, one after the other, giving him cold glances. Some women on the balconies disappear, some appear muttering prayers. The figure of Mariamma, unexpectedly, stands on her balcony. She pulls his shirts from the wire, without affection it seems. She sees him and is, naturally, puzzled. Ousep standing quietly on the road, she has never seen that before. She vanishes inside, but she is probably watching through the curtains.

He sees a woman approach; she walks slowly past him carrying an empty basket. She is going to the vegetable market. He does not know why but he is unable to take his eyes off this plump, unremarkable, asexual woman. Her face is calm and unseeing, and it reminds him of the great peace of failure, the peace of simply giving up.

When the car finally appears, he is not sure whether this is the one he has been waiting for. The man had said it would be black, and the car is black, but it is surprisingly grand and obscene. He has never seen such a car before, and it comes towards him like an object from another time. A scooter that was going in the car's direction veers to the edge of the road and stops because the lane is probably too narrow for the two of them to pass and the scooter has accepted its inferior position. As the car passes, the man tilts his scooter to his left, like a dog about to urinate. Guards from the other blocks run out into the lane to stare at the back of the car. One of them salutes. The car stops near Ousep. The guard of Block A, in his cheap military outfit, points a finger at the steering wheel and laughs in mild confusion, which looks like a type of sorrow. He has never seen a left-hand drive before, never knew such a meaningless trick was possible. Ousep throws his cigarettes away and gets into the back seat. The car smells like another country, which it is, in a way. Krishnamurthy Iyengar, in the back seat, looks smaller than Ousep had imagined. He is, as before, in an oversized shirt that is buttoned at the cuffs, his silver medals pinned on the third button, eight fountain pens and a tiny black torch in his shirt pocket.

'A gift from my son,' Iyengar says. 'It took one year to reach me from America. Chevrolet Cavalier, it is called.'

'I've never been inside anything like this.'

'It is the only car I have, Ousep. I didn't bring this to scare you.'

'I was surprised when you called me.'

'And you would like to know why I called you, of course,' Iyengar says, but he does not say anything else for a while. When the old man had called early this morning he had said, in between coughs, 'Don't have any expectations, I just want to meet. There is nothing more to it.'

The car leaves Balaji Lane and heads towards the Arcot Road. The whole way, people stare as if the Chevrolet is at once a foe and a beautiful woman, which is the same thing in a way. 'I've been thinking of calling you the whole week,' Iyengar says. 'Then I decided that if I am ever going to meet you, now is the time.

Now as in today, this morning. Because I am going to the airport.'

The old man sinks into a comfortable silence once again, so Ousep says, 'I don't see the connection.'

'I am going to America,' Iyengar says, 'I am giving a talk at Johns Hopkins. Then I am going to spend some time with my son and his family. Then my daughter and her family. Because I am a jobless old man.'

'So, you didn't want to wait. Is that what you're trying to say?'

'I don't know.'

'You don't know if you could have waited?'

'What I want to say is that I want to talk to you in the car, when I am on the way to the airport. Yes, that's what I want to say. Because that way I can say what I wish to say and just get rid of you. You may have questions and more questions, but I don't have the answers. I want to say what I have to say, drop you somewhere on the way, and go away.'

'And what is it that you want to say?'

Iyengar runs his fingers through his silver hair, and appears to gather his thoughts, though he has surely had a lot of time to do that.

'Unni told me something one day,' Iyengar says. 'He told me that in the greatest stories of the world there are always opposites – there is the superhero and the supervillain, the good and the evil, the strong and weak. He asked me if the Corpse Delusion had an opposite condition. Are there people in this world who feel very alive, who feel every moment of their days as if life inside them is the greatest force in the universe? People who are hopelessly happy? I told him that for some strange reason neuropsychiatry does not deal with such conditions – it deals with conditions that need a cure. The anti-corpse would not need a cure. The anti-corpse is the aspiration of mankind. And Unni said, "I am the anti-corpse."'

'Doctor, why would a person who is so happy choose to die?'

'It is possible,' Iyenagar says slowly, with unfathomable caution, 'it is possible that Unni Chacko was not what he thought he was.'

Ousep feels an enormous weight on his chest, as if a powerful adolescent boy is holding him in a fierce embrace. 'Do you believe that, Doctor?'

'Or, Unni was everything he thought he was, and we do not understand the happiness of other people. Maybe happiness has nothing to do with life, maybe we are overestimating the lure of life.'

'So what are you trying to say, Doctor?'

'Just this, what I told you. That's all I wanted to say.'

'But what do you make of it?'

'See, that is the problem, Ousep. My opinion is not important. It would be unfair, too. I have not formally studied him.'

'Be unfair. Tell me.'

Iyengar considers his own wrinkled fingers, then his tired palms. He says, 'Many times in my career I have wondered if some of my patients are in my room only because they have seen beyond what the normal brain can see. What I am trying to say, very inarticulately, is this. What if Unni was a person who could see more than others? What if he saw the world in a form that he could not explain?'

'What if he didn't, Doctor? What if he was just deluded?'

'That was what Unni was trying to find out, Ousep. Can't you see?'

'So why did he have to die?'

'I don't know, Ousep. I cannot answer that question.'

They are caught in the morning traffic on Arcot Road, and the car has not moved in several minutes. Urchins who have lost different body parts are banging at the car windows. They are not as miserable as people imagine, according to a boy who once claimed he was unbearably happy and then decided to jump off a building.

'So you've said what you wanted to say, Doctor?'

'I have,' Iyengar says. 'Ousep, before you go, I want to know if you have found the corpse.'

'No.'

'That boy, Somen Pillai, you could not meet him?'

'No. I don't know where he is. Every time I go to his house, his parents tell me he is not at home. I go at odd hours but I have been unable to meet him or even see him. But one of the maids on the lane said something odd. I don't know what to make of it.'

'What did she say?'

'She said that she has heard from someone who has heard from someone else and so on that Somen has shut himself up in a room for over two years. It doesn't make any sense to me.'

'It makes complete sense, Ousep. A corpse is most likely to do just that.'

'Are you saying that the boy has been inside the house all this while?'

'Much longer than that even.'

'And his parents have been locking the door and leaving him inside?'

'Possible.'

'Are you sure about this, Doctor?'

'Go and get your corpse, Ousep. Do what you have to do. I've lost all interest in mine, but go, Ousep, go and find your corpse.'

~

IT IS NOON, and the people who live on the narrow mud lane take in the sight – the town alcoholic and a dwarf key-maker, who is holding three large metal rings filled with hundreds of keys, are going somewhere. To open a door, perhaps.

As Ousep had expected the door is locked. Somen's parents are away at work. The lock looks particularly large in the small hand of the midget key-maker, who is a delicate and dignified man. He makes a sound through his nose and dismisses it as an easy job. He looks up and laughs at a joke he is about to crack. 'What if this is not your house?' He shoves various keys inside.

A frail old man, in a blinding white shirt, appears at the gate. He stands there with his hands joined behind his back, and looks. Within minutes four more old men and two old women appear behind the gate. They stand still, asymmetrically, as if they are in an abstract dance. The key-maker is kneeling on the doormat, scratching the teeth of several keys with an iron rod and inserting them into the lock. On occasion he turns to the small gathering of curious retired people. The crowd slowly grows, and now the housewives too have joined the assembly. The dwarf is increasingly confused and his glances are longer and more frequent. He looks at Ousep with mild suspicion but decides not to understand the situation.

Ousep sees the furious grey scooter at a distance, racing down the lane carrying Somen's parents. As it approaches, Ousep can see that the man is in a murderous rage. When he stops the scooter by the side of the lane, he just leaves the handlebar and charges at his house. The scooter falls with Mrs Pillai still on the pillion. The crowd moves towards her but Somen's father is unaffected. He starts kicking the key-maker, who is now delirious as he fends off the kicks with carefully observed movements of his hands. He points to Ousep and screams, 'I thought it was this man's house.' He manages to run away at a full sprint, carrying his three metal rings. He dashes across the lane without slowing down or even looking back. In fact, he gains speed as he reaches the end of the lane.

Pillai thrusts a finger at Ousep. 'Don't push me, Ousep, this has to end right now. You are losing your mind.'

'Somen Pillai is inside,' Ousep says.

'That's not true.'

'Then all you have to do is show me in and I will believe you.'

'This is my home, Ousep, I decide who will enter this place.'

'Take me to Somen.'

Somen's mother goes into the house crying; she is followed by her man, and they bang the door shut. Ousep looks at the small angry crowd and says, 'Think about it, when was the last time you saw the boy? Where is that boy? What happened to that boy?'

Ousep begins to come here every night, fully drunk. He rings the bell several times but he knows the door will not open. He stands outside the gate and screams the boy's name. He walks up and down the lane, screaming, 'Somen Pillai, speak to me, speak to the father of Unni Chacko.' He is at the gate in the mornings, sober and elegant. He is there when the maid arrives, he is there when she leaves. He stands smoking his cigarettes as Somen's parents appear in office clothes and secure the door with two padlocks. He stands and watches their sullen departure on the old grey scooter. He does this every night and day. He won't stop, this is his final stand.

Thoma's mother says, 'Your father has gone crazy.' Ousep has stopped going to work. He wakes up at dawn these days and goes somewhere, he returns and sits till noon in his room with Unni's cartoons and a magnifying glass, which he runs over the comics. Some days he spreads out all the pages of Unni's comics and cartoons on the floor, climbs on the bed and tries to get a top-angle view. Then he leaves home again. When he returns at night he is as drunk as ever, but he does not stop at giving a speech from the gate. He has started going to some of the homes in Block A, he asks to speak to the boys inside. He wants to know everything everybody knows about Unni. Last week he banged on Mythili's door and fought with her father, who threatened to call the police. He has started wandering around the city at night and raising Unni's friends from sleep. People have started slapping him around. That's what Mariamma says. Some nights Ousep comes home with bruises. Thoma and his mother sit on his bed and clean his wounds, which is strangely the most peaceful moment in Thoma's life. The sight of his father, alive, safe at home, sleeping like a child, and Thoma taking care of him. Something has happened to Thoma, too. He feels stronger. After his betrayal of Unni he is repulsed by the idea of pettiness and fear. He does not ask himself any more whether he will make it across the giant span of life. He knows he will. He sees clearly that he does not have the option to be ordinary.

Thoma has heard that his father has become obsessed with Somen Pillai. At the end of all his wanderings in the night, he goes to Somen's house and creates trouble. Mariamma gets news from the women who live on that lane. Somen's mother herself has come and wept and begged to be saved. Thoma hears this from his teachers, too, who take him aside and ask him what is happening. But Thoma walks with his head held high, he is tired of being ashamed. If this is his life, so be it.

But Mother has had enough. She tells Ousep one morning, 'Stop this or I will kill you one of these days.' He says, peacefully, 'Get me some coffee.'

She has started pouring water on him every morning. That is how he wakes up these days. Right now, she is walking purposefully into Father's room with a bucket. Thoma hears his father's sad yelp, sees his mother sprint towards the door, then his father's tired, drenched appearance. But in time, Ousep is not so surprised any more. Thoma then understands what his mother had meant by the Law of Diminishing Returns. In fact, after Mariamma empties the buckets on him, Ousep does not even yelp any more. It is as if he has employed her to wake him up. He walks briskly to the bathroom and takes his bath. And she has stopped sprinting away after the punishment. She hovers around the house wondering what more she can do to control him.

One night she takes the scissors and slices Ousep's shirt. She cuts its sleeves off and puts it on a hanger in the bedroom for him to see in the morning. But Father is not affected, he does not say anything, though he does hold his limbless shirt in his hand and stares at it for a long time, probably wondering what he should do. By the end of the week she has sliced all his shirts. So, in the mornings now, Ousep sits on the bed and sews his shirts with a thread and needle. She starts slicing his trousers, too, but Ousep has learnt how to sew. He looks like a beggar in rags these days.

Then one morning, as Mariamma is about to empty a bucket of water on him, the phone rings. Ousep wakes up and sees his wife standing with a bucket of water. 'Can you do that after I take the call?' he says. She steps back and lets him pick up the phone.

'Hello,' Ousep says.

The voice on the other end is strong and serene. 'Ousep Chacko?'

'Yes,' he says, sitting up.

'My name is Somen Pillai. Come to my home at six in the evening.'

~

OUSEP WALKS AS if it is morning, with short brisk steps, his little finger sticking out, hair combed back. Ousep Chacko, finally respectable at dusk. The longest day of his life has almost passed in an unbearable wait and the humiliation of sewing his own trousers. As the stout house at the end of the lane approaches, he accepts that he has not walked so steadily in the twilight in many years. The front door opens and Mr Pillai, who is wearing a shirt this evening, stands in the doorway to receive him with a compassionate hand waiting in midair to grab the shoulder of his guest. Ousep goes beyond the doormat for the first time and takes in the small foyer, where two adolescent boys, in another time, used to play chess for many hours and talk about the nature of reality, and on occasion toy with the mind of a fool who had come to them seeking easy answers to borrowed questions.

The hall is dim, its walls sky blue, and there is the smell of soap.

The room has two cushioned chairs and a thin sofa arranged around a low table, a colour TV in a corner, and a dining table, which blocks half the doorway to the kitchen. Pillai leads him to the sofa and sits by his side, very close. In the blue wall that faces Ousep, there are two shut doors. Behind one of them Somen Pillai waits.

The boy's father is not comfortable, his movements are quick and his eyes restless. Mrs Pillai steps out of the kitchen holding a serving spoon; she smiles without warmth and goes back in.

'My boy is inside,' the man says, pointing to a shut door. 'He has been in that room for more than two years. For more than two years, Ousep. He never leaves the room. He does not speak. Not a word, even to himself. Actually, it is good, isn't it, that he does not speak to himself? We send food inside once a day. We are glad that he at least eats. That makes him shit like any of us, which is a good thing. There is a bathroom inside, so he does not have to step out. He bathes. We are grateful for that too. Ousep, do you know why he is this way?'

'No, Pillai, I don't.'

'We don't know what has happened to him,' Pillai says. 'One of these days a yellow halo is going to appear behind the idiot's head. Wouldn't that be nice? Two years ago he told us that he wanted to stop going to college. I had sold some land in Kerala and got him a seat in an engineering college, but he decided not to take it up. He said he wanted to sit in the room and do nothing. I fought, I begged, but I soon realised that I would lose my only son if I insisted. I told him that if he wanted to do nothing he was free to roam around the entire house, watch TV and do abso-lutely nothing. At least I could then tell myself my son had retired early. But no, he wanted to be contained in that room. He told us that if we tried to talk to him, if we bothered him in any way, he would leave the house for ever. So we let him be. We have made our peace, Ousep. This morning, for the first time in two years, he stepped out. His mother and I were sitting where we are sitting right now, and what do we see? We see our son come out of his room. The light went on in our eyes, Ousep, just for a moment. He goes straight to the phone and calls you. For the first time in over two years we heard his voice. Isn't that nice? We must thank you, Ousep. Your trick has worked. You made such a scene every night, the boy has decided to deal with you and be done with it.'

Pillai's body begins to shake, he covers his face with his fat fingers and cries. 'What is it, Ousep? What has happened to our son? Ask him to show one flaw in me, one flaw. I fed him, I loved him, I held him by his hand and took him places, I played with him. I gave him everything. And he decides to shut himself in a room for ever. You talk to him. Ask him anything you want. I know you won't understand what he says. You will go away very confused. Trust me. We tried talking to him when it all began. But after today, please don't come here again.'

'Can I go in?' Ousep says.

Pillai points to the door. 'Don't knock. Just go in.'

As Ousep walks to the door, his breathing becomes laboured, and for a moment he feels giddy. He pushes the door open and sees a young man in a plain white shirt and brown trousers sitting behind a wooden desk and smiling at him. He is much thinner than he was three years ago, which is not surprising. He has a thick full beard, as Ousep had expected. The boy's hair is long, but not as long as Ousep had imagined. He has large teasing eyes, piercing eyes, but they still have some mirth in them.

'Shut the door and latch it,' the boy says. His voice is not deep but it is strong and clear.

Ousep does as he is told, and when the boy points to the vacant chair across the desk, he sits. Finally, Somen Pillai. He does not look mad at all. In fact, this one is going to be tough.

'Are you afraid?' the boy says.

'Why would I be afraid?'

'Sitting alone with me in this room. Are you afraid?'

'No.'

'I will call you Ousep,' the boy says.

'That's a remarkable coincidence. My name is, in fact, Ousep.'

Somen laughs, like anybody else. 'I can call you uncle or sir, or things like that, if you want me to be respectful, but I would prefer to call you Ousep. As you said, that's your name.'

'Call me Ousep.'

'Ousep, you see this window? I have been watching you every time you've come to the gate. I have seen you in the mornings, I have seen you at night. You are more literary in the nights, I noticed.'

'I am sorry for all that I did but I had to meet you.'

'I can see you are not drunk today.'

'You are right.'

'I have not spoken in over two years. I am surprised I am even able to speak. But I think my speech may sound a bit strange.'

'Why haven't you spoken for two years, Somen?'

'You will figure that out as we go. But before we begin I have something important to tell you. You've destroyed my way of life, Ousep. You are a persistent man who has no shame. I thought I should let you ask me everything you want to ask so that we are done with it and never meet again.'

'I can accept that, Somen.'

'It is natural that you would attach a certain importance to the fact that I have refused to meet you for so long. But the truth is, as you will see, I have very simple things to say. The only reason I did not meet you was that I did not feel like meeting you. That's all there is to it.'

'That's reasonable.'

'There is something else you must know,' Somen says. 'In the time that follows you will ask me questions. I will answer them. We will talk. We will have what is called a conversation. I will tell you everything I know. You can ask me anything you want. But at the end of it all you will not know why Unni Chacko killed himself. You will fail in your mission. Because the fact is that I do not know why Unni did what he did.'

'I can accept that.'

'In that case we must proceed. You must first tell me what you know about Unni.'

Ousep wonders where he must begin. And how much he must reveal.

Mythili Balasubramanium stands still on the narrow rear balcony, under the festoons of white undergarments left to dry on the high, discreet wire, and she listens to the voice, as she has done many times in the past. Her head is bent in careful attention, eyes staring at bare feet, hands folded. The voice of Mariamma, as powerful as ever, the voice of a woman trapped in her own play, talking to the walls in her kitchen, talking in whispers and exclamations. What her voice usually says is nothing new, Mythili has heard the same things for years. But this evening she hears a lament she has not heard before.

'Why, Unni, that's what I ask myself, that's all I want to know. Why?'

It is not surprising that Mariamma should say that. It has to be the most important question in her life. But when Mythili imagines that woman standing alone in her kitchen, wagging a finger, begging the walls for the answer, something in her breaks. Mythili shuts her eyes and feels the tears. Is there a way she can end this, lead that woman to the answer she so desperately seeks, and bring the pointless search of Ousep Chacko to a close, a search whose sad little details she hears every night when he howls like a beast from the gates below? Is there a way Mythili can end all this for ever, and let the Chacko household move on?

She leaves the balcony when Thoma comes for his tuition. He is wearing an altered shirt of his brother's, the same shirt Unni was wearing the day before he died. She is surprised she remembers that. They sit in her bedroom as always; the door that does not have a latch is shut.

'If eight men can build a wall in ten days, how many days will two men need to a build a wall three times as big?'

Thoma makes some calculations in his notebook. He is taking

a while. 'Thoma,' she says. 'You look different these days, Thoma, you look sad.'

'I am fine,' he says, 'I am strong. It has the same face as sadness but I am only stronger than before.'

'What happened that you are strong now?'

'Something happened to me.'

'What happened to you?'

'After I told you about Unni's trick, I realised I was just a moron, like most people. I don't want to be a petty moron any more.'

'It's all right. You only told me the truth.'

'Truth is not so important. What is important is that I told you about the trick because I thought I was not good enough. I don't want to be so afraid any more. I want to be strong so that I can take care of my mother and all the people who need my help. I want to be like Unni. I want to be strong.'

He scribbles in his notebook but she can see he is not working on the problem. He says, without looking up, 'And I want to find out why he did what he did.'

'What is it that your father has found?'

'I don't know much. I only know what I hear my father say when he is drunk. I think a few months ago my father found a comic by Unni. The day my brother died he had posted it to someone but somehow it returned after three years.'

'So?'

'So my father thinks that if Unni had posted a comic on the day he died, it may have some clues.'

'What is the comic about?'

'It is a true story.'

'What is the story?'

'Do you know about Philipose?'

'It is a very familiar name. I don't know why it is so familiar.'

'Have you heard that name?'

'Yes.'

'Where did you hear that name?'

'It is a name that has your mother's voice in it. Yes, it comes to me now. I have heard your mother mention his name sometimes. You know, when she gets into one of her moods. I used to think it was one of her relatives.'

'He is not a relative.'

'Who is Philipose?'

'Something happened many years ago, when my mother was much younger. One evening she was returning alone from school, and Philipose attacked her. My mother escaped because she started screaming and people came running. But she was very shocked, and from that day she started talking to herself. She did not tell anybody about this. But one day she told Unni about him and about what had happened. Unni was so angry he took a train and went to meet Philipose to beat him up. But Philipose was already dead. He died of old age, I think.'

'And?'

'That's all. That's how the story ends. I don't like that story.'

She turns the pages of the maths book, and tries once again to make up her mind. There is the bleak quiet of twilight all around. The children have quit their games, the birds have gone, it is as if nothing exists in the world but the two of them in a small room. 'One hundred and twenty days,' Thoma says. She looks at him and sees a flow of events that is now inevitable.

'Mythili,' Thoma says, 'it will take two men one hundred and twenty days to build the wall. That's a lot of time for a wall.'

'Philipose should have killed himself, not Unni,' she says.

'Philipose led a normal, peaceful life, my mother tells me,' Thoma says. 'I don't know if she is angry about that.'

'Thoma, when Unni died, where were you?'

'I was sleeping in my room. I sleep till late morning on holidays because I don't sleep well at nights.'

'Did Unni come into your room?'

'I think so but I am not sure. I think he kissed my forehead, but I am not sure.'

'You're not sure?'

'I am not sure. He always kissed me on my forehead when he saw me sleeping, so he might have done that. All I remember clearly is that I had a dream.'

'What was your dream?'

'I dreamt that a woman was running away from a giant sea wave.'

'Who was the woman?'

'She did not have a face. Does it make sense?'

'Yes, that's not unusual.'

'But she was screaming as she ran.'

'You heard her scream?'

'Yes.'

'Was it a voice you have heard before?'

'I don't know. A scream is a scream.'

～

THE SILENCE IN Somen's room is deep and ordained, and filled with indecipherable meaning. It feels like marriage. When Somen Pillai finally raises his gaze from the floor, he smiles and rotates the index finger of his right hand as if to stir the air.

'You may have realised,' the boy says, 'as you were recounting the many bits of information you have so painstakingly gleaned, you may have realised the problem with your story. What you need is a chronology. When you understand the chronology you understand a lot.'

'That's true, Somen.'

'So let me begin at the beginning. Wouldn't that be nice?'

'Without a doubt.'

'In the beginning, Ousep, there was nothing. There were no stars, there was no space, there was no matter, there was no time.'

Ousep rests his chin on his fingers and tries to achieve an impassive face. The boy bursts out laughing. 'Don't worry. I am just playing with you.'

'I must admit, my heart did sink.'

Somen leans back, puts his arms behind his large head and

277

studies his visitor with a relaxed superiority, which is not very different from the arrogance of doctors when they face their patients. It would be useful to puncture his confidence, see him collapse. Something always comes of that, but for the moment, though, the boy looks formidable as he speaks in his slow scholarly way.

'What I know about Unni is what he told me and what I observed in the classroom sitting in my corner and later in my home, which he visited very often. As you have so competently gathered from your sources, I came to know him well only when we were seventeen, just months before he died. There are many things he did not tell me. But what I know I will tell you.'

It is disturbing for a father, even if the father is Ousep Chacko, to hear the story of his son's childhood from a stranger. He can accept the fact that he did not know the life of Unni the adolescent. But Unni the child is a different matter.

Ousep never hugged his son, never carried him on his shoulders, never took him to the circus or did any of the things that fathers do these days. Like the other fathers from a pastoral time and place, from the golden age of men, he had imagined that he had appointed his wife to do all those things. But now, as Somen speaks of Unni's childhood, Ousep feels a fierce ownership towards his little boy. It offends him that an odd young man in exile in his own room is telling him things about Unni that he did not know. He feels a great desperation inside him to touch his child, hold his little fingers and walk with him, put him on the table and somehow charm out of him the strange world that he claimed he saw in his head.

'Unni was normal most of the time,' Somen says. 'Normal means that the world he saw was identical to what others saw with their senses. Are you offended that I described the meaning of normal to you?'

'I am not offended.'

'Normal is a majority state.'

'That's a reasonable definition.'

'Unni was normal most of the time. But he was born with a condition. His earliest memory of the phenomenon was when he was around five. It probably started much earlier but he realised that it was a condition and that it was odd only when he was five. What happened to him was that there were moments when one or more of his senses shut down. For a few minutes or even an hour some days, he would go deaf, or he would go blind, or both. Sometimes he would lose his ability to tell the difference between faces, everyone would look identical to him. On rare occasions he would not feel anything even if he pricked himself with a pin or hurt himself in another way, which he often tried to do to understand what was happening to him.'

'He was not just imagining all this?'

Somen lets out a gentle infuriating laugh, but he does not react to Ousep's question. He continues to tell his story as if the question is not important.

Unni is not terrified by what is happening to him. As he is just a child he considers it a game. He imagines there is a person inside him, a friend whom he calls Abu, who is playing with his senses – switching things on, switching things off. Unni would shed Abu around the age of seven.

By the time he is ten, something else begins to happen. The sporadic shutdown of his senses continues, but there are also moments when his senses are enhanced. He claims that he can see the textures on the skin of an ant, see the details of people standing hundreds of metres away, claims that he can hear things others cannot hear. But there is nothing special about Unni's sense of smell or taste, which are actually a shade below normal. His nose does not easily differentiate between coffee and tea.

The collapse and escalation of the senses visit him for short bursts of time. There are phases when they occur every day, times when they do not appear for days. He tells his mother about what is happening to him but she finds it hard to take him seriously because he tells her about his condition in a happy, excited way and not as a complaint. In time he decides not to tell his mother or anyone else about his condition. He is happy in his weird state, even eagerly waiting for things to happen to him.

Unni goes through an enchanted boyhood, losing his senses sometimes, seeing more than he is meant to at other times. But when he is around fourteen the condition disappears.

'He became normal. All his senses became consistent. He waited for weeks, for months, but his condition did not return. But his experience left him with an insight that would never leave him, that the world is a charade created by a combination of senses. His was not a philosophical view. It is important that you understand this, Ousep. As I get deeper into the story of Unni, it is natural that you should form your own explanations in your mind, and many times you will imagine that Unni was pursuing an abstract philosophical line of thought. But the fact is that he was merely converting experience into understanding. As a boy whose reality kept changing depending on what was turned on and turned off inside his brain, he could see more clearly than others that reality is merely the myth of the senses. When you do not experience but accept a phenomenon, it is philosophy, which is a form of religion. But when you experience, it is different. An experience is a plain fact, experience is truth.'

Somen Pillai overrates experience but Ousep is not here to argue. He wants to extract all that he can before his situation changes and he is asked to leave. The boy is not as stable as he had appeared when Ousep entered the room. Somen falls silent often, as if distracted by ghostly strands of thought. At times he studies his own hand or his bare feet and looks very surprised that they exist. But when he speaks he is coherent.

'That's why Unni was drawn to cartoons,' the boy says. 'He loved their distortion, their caricature of reality. He could not take the world and its preoccupations seriously. If the world is the myth of the senses then there is something pointless about all arts. Who will you read, what will you write, what music will you listen to, what can move you, what can you adore when nothing is true? But cartoons are different. In a farcical world farce is the true art.'

Unni at fourteen is slowly consumed by an idea. He begins to believe that what has happened to him is a glitch in a subterranean process of nature. In his magical moments as a child, when his senses were enhanced, he had seen beyond what a human is supposed to see. He believes that he has either seen far into the past of human evolution or deep into the future. He does not know which. In him are the remains of an extinct species or the portents of what is to come. He is convinced that nature creates a huge quantity of life so that, through trial and error, through the extinction and the evolution of billions of lumps of flesh over a vast period of time, it will finally attain its goal – a particular kind of neurological system.

'He believed that the aspiration of nature is to achieve a type of brain. And that this ultimate brain is supposed to receive a set of information, which would fulfil the very purpose of nature.'

But, two years later, when Unni is sixteen, he begins to believe that the very opposite is true. That the very purpose of nature, the evolutions it has managed through the vast ages, is to prevent a particular kind of neurological condition. It is as if the system of life is a devious force that does not want any organism to look too deep.

'Ousep, now you are thinking that your son was probably delusional, that he was making up concepts so that the world appeared more and more extraordinary than it was in reality. But then, the fact is that when you begin to see the world more clearly what you first contradict are the very ideas that were once dear to you. Isn't that true, Ousep?'

At some point when he is sixteen, a more powerful version of his childhood condition returns. Unni begins to blank out for short periods of time. 'A few seconds maybe, a minute sometimes, as perceived through the standard measure of time in the material world.'

In these periods, all his senses collapse but he sees flashes in his mind. It is an extraordinary vision, according to him, but he is unable to describe it. He claims that what he sees is the true nature of reality.

'In your mind, Ousep, you are trying to imagine what Unni may have seen. You are seeing a colour. You are imagining a giant black night, or you are imagining a spectacular white sky, depending on your personality type. But these are the myths of storytellers. Unni does not see a black vacuum or a giant white sun. I have not seen what he has seen. I am only repeating what he has told me. He has not told me what he saw because what he saw is meant to be beyond the medium of language. He could not even begin to draw it.

'How convenient, you think. A boy claims to have seen something paranormal, but he is unable to describe it. But is that so hard to accept? You and a dog see a car passing by, Ousep. Now imagine, the dog has to describe the scene to other dogs. It cannot. The dog saw an ordinary sight, even to a dog the moment is simple, but its neurological system has been devised in such a way that it is not meant to convey the thought, it is meant to be trapped in its own communication channels.'

Unni feels trapped in the austerity of human communication, 'he is trapped in language'. He wonders whether there is a way he can convey what he has seen to others. Convey the message that reality is very different from what people imagine. According to Unni, all of nature is a timeless contest between two forces – absolute reality, which is the true state of all matter, and the 'syndicate of life', which does not want its organisms to see the truth.

'Because, if you see the truth, you will be in a perpetual state of ecstatic trance, you won't fuck, you won't sustain life, you won't be desperate to live inside a carbon body. If you see reality you will not want to be a part of the syndicate of life. The purpose of the syndicate is to sustain itself, to exist for ever in the minds of its organisms. Therefore, from the beginning of conscience, it has eliminated any neurological network that has the potential to see nature in its true form. It has done this through a process of natural selection, through trial and error, by rewarding species that are delusional and by terminating species that are awakened. What is left of this process is what you see around you – beings that are programmed to survive and multiply but cannot think too deeply, which includes almost all of humanity.'

'Whose view is all this?' Ousep asks. 'Did Unni say this or is it your view?'

'Both of us had this view, the same view.'

'A shared view of the world?'

'Yes,' Somen says, 'a shared view.'

'But who said it first? Who came up with the expression "syndicate of life"? You or Unni?'

'What is more important is that you understand the rogue brain.'

'The rogue brain?'

'Over the ages, the syndicate of life has exterminated all types of brain that have the capacity to see too much. But now and then, by pure chance, nature accidentally creates human brains that can see more than they are meant to see. So, the syndicate has inserted some safeguards – one of them is that the brain can perceive a lot more than it can describe to other brains through language and visual arts. That way, even if a rogue brain is accidentally able to grasp the truth, it will not be able to describe it. It would start behaving in a manner that would be considered abnormal or unstable.'

'This was Unni's view?'

Somen ignores the question. It is as if he has not heard him, but he looks Ousep in the eye when he speaks.

'The syndicate also responds to the rogue brain by inflicting a condition that is widely known as depression – the idea is to switch off all the delusions of pleasure and make life itself seem so dull and meaningless that the organism will be influenced to self-terminate. The syndicate tries many other methods of quelling the rebellion of potential rogue brains. In most brains, including

283

conformist brains, the system has seeded the delusions of many philosophies and the delusion of enlightenment. The idea here is to satisfy the curiosity of the brain by providing a false sense of intellectual quest. Through philosophy, God and rationality, the syndicate efficiently ensures that the curiosity of almost every neurological system is satisfied.'

Who is left, then? No one, except Unni and Somen?

'But there are rare rogue brains, which are not fooled yet,' Somen says. 'And the syndicate responds through more powerful delusions. In such rogues, the syndicate enhances all the senses and shows a life that is extraordinarily pleasurable. That is what happened to Unni. Soon after he began to blank out and see the flashes of something he could not explain, he also began to feel moments of unnatural power within him. In these moments he would be filled with great happiness and he would see the world in all its colours and beauty. Even a touch of the breeze or the movement of ants would seem to him as if it were a deep experience. Life made him feel every moment it had to offer. He also became supernaturally sexual. He did not tell me much about his sexual cravings, all he told me was that he was filled with the filthiest thoughts, dangerous thoughts, but very pleasurable thoughts.'

But Unni knows what is happening to him. He has seen the other side and he knows that the syndicate of life is trying to delude him. He believes that there are more like him in the world and begins to search for them. He searches among the seemingly normal, and among the mad. He searches for the unnaturally happy and the inexplicably sad. But he finds no one who is like him.

～

THOMA CHACKO STANDS in the doorway of the kitchen and wonders whether it is a good time to make the confession. His mother looks peaceful by her standards, but she is clearly lost in her own thoughts, which is what he wants. She has just returned from the Sacred Heart Family Store and is transferring things into jars and bottles. She takes the one-kilo sachet of sunflower oil in her hand and bites the tip off. This is the best time to confess, Thoma knows, because when she is pouring sunflower oil into a bottle she does it with ascetic concentration. 'Our father in heaven, hallowed be your name,' he says. She does not turn, she is not listening to him. Thoma must do it now. 'Your kingdom come, your will be done, on earth as it is in heaven. I told Mythili about Philipose, I don't know why I did that. Hope I did not do anything wrong. Give us this day our daily bread, and forgive us our debts . . .'

Mariamma stops pouring the oil into the bottle, puts the sachet on the kitchen counter and stares at him. 'What did you say, Thoma?'

'I was praying.'

'What did you say?'

'I said, "Give us this day our daily bread and . . ."'

'Before that?'

'I have something to confess,' he says.

'What is it?'

'I told Mythili about Philipose, about what he did to you, about Unni and Philipose and the comic and everything.'

'Why did you do that, Thoma?' she asks. She is not angry, she is sad and hurt, which is worse.

'I don't know. Did I do something bad?'

'You cannot go around saying these things to other people, Thoma.'

'I don't know what happened to me,' he says. 'She asked me, "Thoma, what has your father found about Unni?" And I don't know why I told her everything I know. Mythili was very angry. She still loves us, she was very angry. She hates Philipose. She said Philipose should have killed himself, not Unni. That's what she said. She still loves all of us very much, I think.'

He stops talking because his mother looks as if she has seen a ghost behind him. Thoma turns nervously to see what has terrified her but he sees nothing. Then she takes the oil sachet and begins to pour its contents into the bottle again.

'What happened?' he asks, but she does not say anything.

After she has put the bottle back on the shelf, she begins to walk up and down the hall. She does not make any violent movements, she does not talk or wag her finger. She is calm, but she is also disturbed. He has never seen her this way. He sits on a chair at the dining table and watches her for nearly an hour. He wonders what it is that he has said that has made her behave in this manner.

She would explain this moment to Thoma many years later, when they stand together facing Unni's grave in the churchyard that lies in the shade of the high eucalyptus trees. She would by then be one of those calm, dignified, affluent middle-aged women who emerged from their long silver cars. 'If one half of your life has been tough,' she would tell Thoma another time, 'the chances are that the other half will turn out all right. As Unni told me once, "In this world, you cannot escape happiness."'

~

'YOU MUST REMEMBER,' Somen says, 'you must remember what I said in the beginning, Ousep. Unni was normal most of the time. And when he was in control of himself, which was most of the time, he was hopelessly in love with all those who mattered to him. Like anybody else. They could affect him and he wanted to be affected by them.'

Unni is seventeen when he finally charms out of his mother her secret, and he is filled with a great rage at the injustice. He wants to punish Philipose. But he can also see the sexual criminality of men as a powerful force of the syndicate. His own body is desperate for women, any women, and there are times when he fears that he could do anything to satisfy it. But that does not mean he will pardon Philipose. He goes to find him but Philipose is gone. Dead after a good life. Unni seethes for days. He feels violent towards all men, he is disgusted by them. One afternoon he finds Simion Clark in the lab massaging a boy. 'He was more than massaging, actually,' Somen says with a giggle. The next day,

Unni dispenses justice to the man. He is somewhat comforted by his action, his desire for vengeance is quenched. And he resumes his search for people like him, people whom the syndicate has chosen to torment through abilities and disabilities, through moments of ecstatic happiness and deep destructive sorrow.

He decides to be less discreet in his search. He walks into the class one morning and reveals the rudiments of what he has seen, what he knows. Something about him, something about what he says, affects them all. Everyone is disturbed, some even feel the transient fright of coming close to a forbidden truth, some are affected in a deeper way, but they are too ensconced in the syndicate to fully see what Unni has tried to show them. There is no one who can fully understand him. Except one. Somen Pillai.

'That moment in the class is when I really looked at Unni Chacko. And I told myself, "I think I know what that boy is talking about." Why do I say that, Ousep? To understand that you need to know something about me.

'I, too, was born with a condition. I was always filled with unreasonable sorrow, even when I was a child in a very happy home. I had no reason to be this way but I was. The world around me seemed bleak and pointless. Nothing interested me. Nothing. I was a corpse. A corpse inside a living body. I thought of killing myself many times but I didn't because I knew what it was to be dead. All my life I have been dead. What's the point in merely shedding the body? That's what I would say every time I thought of killing myself.

'I went through life in silence and a pointless loneliness, wondering what all the fuss around me was about. Then one day, Unni walked into the class and said, "Something is happening around us, there is a secret we must know, everything that we know is false." For the first time in my life I felt the excitement of hope. I thought if there was another reality, maybe I belonged to that, maybe that was what was wrong with me, I was trapped in the wrong place.

'I started talking to Unni. In the beginning, I did not understand many things he said, but we talked for hours. He was trying to tell me something, and I tried hard to understand. He was very interested in knowing how I perceived the world and I told him things I had not told anybody. I told him I was a corpse, and I told him how a corpse sees the world. I slowly began to understand what he was trying to say and I was stunned. It was clear to me that the syndicate had attacked me long before my brain could see the true nature of reality. The syndicate of life was afraid that I would see the truth.

'Being with Unni was bliss. For the first time in my life I felt the excitement of living in this shit decaying body. Unni and I went in search of many people who are considered abnormal. His search for someone like him was also a search for someone like me. Even with the normal people we became very curious about some of their quirks. There are traces of the syndicate's safeguards in all of us. There is God in all of us.

'Sai Shankaran was a lot of fun. We used him to understand how a confused conformist brain really worked. The corpse could finally laugh at the living. That was Unni's gift to me.'

But Unni now increasingly believes that he has been defeated by the syndicate, he feels that the material forces inside him are very strong. He is extraordinarily happy and desperate to live. 'Like a drug addict would be desperate for his drug, Unni was desperate to live.'

He decides to fight the syndicate. He thinks that the exhilaration of near-death will give him the powers to take on the primordial forces of the syndicate. Somen joins him in this fight. They swim in powerful ocean currents and almost drown. They ride Somen's scooter at top speed across busy juctions. They stand on railway tracks and watch trains hurtle towards them. Then, Unni claims that there is a more powerful way to fight the syndicate, a Gandhian way that he says is more powerful than near-death. Near-sex. 'Lying with a naked woman without screwing her.'

The idea comes to him one morning when he is in Somen's house. No one is home but the two of them. Somen's parents have gone to meet their relatives in Pondicherry. 'Sakhi comes home, unexpectedly, because she has realised that one of her earrings is missing. Do you know who Sakhi is?'

'No.'

'Sakhi is our maid. You have seen her. She is very hot.'

As she searches for the earring in the hall, Unni keeps staring at her. He feels a powerful desperation. He is fascinated by how aroused he is and how hard it is for him to restrain himself from tearing her clothes off. Somen tells him, 'Unni, she is broad minded.'

A few months earlier, in the backyard of the house, as she was squatting and washing clothes, Somen had lost control of himself and grabbed her. Not such a corpse after all, this boy. She screamed and ran away, but she did not complain. She appeared the next day as if nothing had happened. When she was cleaning his room, she whispered to the floor that she might consider letting him squeeze her again if he gave her fifty rupees – an offer he accepted. But he was so disgusted with himself that he did not pursue her again.

When Unni hears this, he gets an idea. He negotiates with her and it is decided that, for a hundred rupees, she will sit naked with him in Somen's room for exactly thirty minutes. He promises that he will not touch her. When he emerges after thirty minutes, he feels it is the toughest thing he has ever done. To have a beautiful woman, completely naked, by his side, and keep his hands off her. He claims that the exercise will give them the power to triumph over sexual desperation. Somen, too, tries the experiment. She tries to convince him to pay her five hundred rupees and do what he pleases with her. But he resists, he claims, successfully.

Unni leaves early that day because he has things to do. He borrows thirty rupees from Somen for his haircut. 'That was the last time I saw him. Less than two hours after he left my house he was dead. As I told you right at the beginning, Ousep, I don't know what happened to him. I do not know what happened to him after he left my house.'

When Ousep finds his voice he feels as if it belongs to someone else. Somen says, 'Can you repeat what you said, Ousep? You've lost your voice, it seems to me.'

'Can you guess what may have happened to Unni after he left your house?'

'No, I can't.'

'Why have you shut yourself up in this room?'

'To diminish the forces of the syndicate. I don't want to see or hear the delusion of life. One day I will escape my corpse state and see what Unni saw – the true nature of reality.'

'Somen, what makes you think Unni did not suffer from a powerful delusion?'

'Which takes us to the inevitable religious moment, Ousep. I believe.'

'What do you believe?'

'That there is truth and that Unni saw it. I believe.'

When Ousep had first told the boy what he knew about Unni's life, he told him everything except Unni's association with Krishnamurthy Iyengar. Somen, too, has not mentioned the doctor. In all probability, as Ousep expected, the boy is unaware of that part of Unni's life. It is now time to shake the ascetic. Ousep has nothing to lose. He has a vague idea how this meeting is going to end. It would end, as Somen had put it, in a religious moment.

'Did Unni tell you that he used to meet a neuropsychiatrist? The man's name is Krishnamurthy Iyengar. Also known as Psycho among some cartoonists.'

There is a look of surprise on Somen's face. 'No,' he says.

'Why do you think he did not mention him to you?'

'He didn't tell me everything. He didn't have to tell me everything. He only told me what I needed to know.'

'Unni used to discuss you with the doctor.'

'So?'

'Somen, your condition has a name. It is called the Cotard Delusion, the Corpse Syndrome. It is a rare mental disorder.'

Somen's face cracks into an unhappy smile. 'You have not understood anything I have said, Ousep. I think you must leave.'

'It can be treated, Somen. The pursuit of truth, in most cases, is a mental disorder. Unni knew that. Trust me.'

'As expected, the syndicate of life infiltrates my fortress. As I grow powerful and see beyond the limits of delusion, the syndicate sends its pathetic agent. Leave, Ousep. You are being used, can't you see? You are being used by the dark forces of life to draw me out of my state. Get out.'

'I lost a son,' Ousep says. 'I don't want another boy to die because he did not understand what was happening to him.'

'Goodbye, Ousep.'

'Come,' Ousep says, extending a firm hand. 'Come, Somen. You, too, are my son. Step out of your room.'

'Ousep, the world that you would show me outside is merely a larger room than mine.'

Ousep leaves without a word. When he emerges into the dim hall, shutting the door behind him, Somen's parents rise from their chairs with tired faces expecting a conversation. But he just walks out, into the relief of the night. And he goes down the narrow mud lane, probably for the last time in his life.

~

WHEN HE WALKS into his home he startles his wife, who is leaning on the sofa, with her hands on her hips. She is still emerging from a thought and takes a moment to understand that Ousep has come home, silently, without being preceded by laments.

'Why are you not drunk?' she says.

'I forgot. I don't know how,' he says.

'Are you not well?'

'I am tired. Where is Thoma?'

'He is sleeping in his room,' she says.

Ousep is about to go into his room but he lingers in the hall because she has been looking at him as if he is new. He returns her stare, trying to understand what is wrong with her. She now takes long breaths that she clearly cannot help, her eyes still on him, hands still on her hips.

'What?' he says.

She pants, a shudder runs through her body, but she says, 'It's nothing.' Ousep puts his arm on her shoulder. It is a powerful shoulder that has forgotten how to accept affection. It feels like stone, so he withdraws his hand.

Ousep goes to his room, changes, turns off the lights and goes to sleep. He is tired but it will be just a nap, he knows. And it is just that, a dreamless, thoughtless, shallow nap. As he had expected she wakes him up. He hears her voice say, 'I've something to tell you.'

When he rises, he can barely make out her figure leaving his room. All around him there is darkness, and the world outside is still. He is surprised by the deep, perfect calm of the night. What an assault he must be every night when he disturbs this solid quiet. He wears a shirt whose sleeves he has stitched himself, and he walks into the hall. It is as if he is stepping out to receive the news of another death.

The hall is lit by the kitchen light. She is sitting on the sofa, which is shrouded in the same old unchanging bedsheet. She is at one end. He sits carefully at the other end, trying to remember where the large hole in the foam is, into which their landlord had once sunk. They sit this way, staring ahead, like a couple that is about to be photographed, and are waiting for their joyful sons to join them in the middle. She looks strong, even peaceful. 'Thoma told Mythili everything about Philipose,' she says. 'That's what the boy did today. Then Mythili said something to him. I have been thinking about it all evening. Mythili said, "Philipose should have killed himself, not Unni." That's what she said. That's what Mythili said.'

*

Ousep is too stunned to speak, he just sits there without a word. He feels the same heaviness in his chest that he had felt in Iyengar's car; it is as if he is in the fierce embrace of a powerful boy. He tries to imagine the chain of events that might have unfolded the day Unni died.

Mariamma turns to him, expecting a response, she is not sure whether he understood her. So he tells her, in a calm, steady voice, 'You were right. Unni presumed you would know, he thought everybody would come to know. But the girl chose to keep it to herself.'

'Yes,' Mariamma says, 'she chose to keep it to herself. She was just a child then. But one of these days she is going to tell me. That's what I feel, she is ready to tell me. I'll wait.'

'The day our boy died,' Ousep says, 'he was in Somen's house. He sat in a room with a naked woman. The idea was not to touch her. That was the game, a philosophical game. So, for thirty minutes, a seventeen-year-old boy sat with a naked woman. Then the boy comes home. He comes home in a state, doesn't he?'

And, even though she has not asked, he tells her the story of her son, at least what he thinks he knows.

Mythili sits in the darkness, on her narrow bed, her legs folded under her. She has been trying to make a decision for months. But now she is stronger, and she knows that to be good is to be brave. And Mariamma deserves a bit of decency from this world, especially from the people she loves. Mythili has come very close to telling her. Thrice she has crossed the short corridor in the middle of the night as her parents slept. But every time she stood outside that door, she would lose her nerve and return. But at noon tomorrow she would walk down the ten-foot-long corridor, ring the doorbell and speak to Mariamma. For the first time since Unni died Mythili would enter their house and she would tell the most lovable woman in the world why her son died.

*

Three years ago, Mythili's mother hands the girl a new silk dress to try on. It is real silk, a sky-blue top and a full skirt with silver elephants embroidered on the hem. Mythili stands on the rear balcony wearing the top and skirt. She has let her thick long hair loose. When Mariamma appears, Mythili stands on a high stool to show her the full length of the dress. 'You look like a beautiful lady,' Mariamma says, and sings a brief song in Malayalam. Mythili tells herself that she probably does look beautiful today. She wants Unni to see her this way. But she wants their meeting to be accidental, so she does not call out to him from her balcony as she normally does. She waits for a long time on both the balconies but there is no sight of him. Her mother, as expected, keeps asking her to change because these clothes are new and they are meant for festivals. But then Mother leaves for the temple. She won't be back for over two hours.

It is late morning now. Mythili stands on her front balcony and calls out Unni's name in the many accents of the elders of the block. But he is not at home. It appears that nobody is at home. She waits on the balcony to see whether Unni will appear in the lane below, walking in his languid, arrogant way. She wonders whether he is inside his home, shut in his room and working on a comic, deaf to everything that is happening around him. So she decides to go to his house. She walks down the corridor and opens the door as she has done all her life. There is nobody in the hall. The door to Mr Ousep Chacko's room is open and she can see that there is no one there. The boys' bedroom door is shut. There she finds Thoma sleeping in the bed, but there is no sign of Unni. She decides to wait in the hall and surprise him. She will pretend that she just happened to be in these clothes, by pure chance. She takes a bunch of old *Reader's Digest*s from the shelf in the hall, and sits with them on the floor between the sofa and the two chairs. She lies on her stomach and starts reading the magazines. She is drowsy but she tries to keep her eyes open. If Unni sees her sleeping he will draw a moustache on her again, and that would be very inelegant. But in the gentle, steady breeze, her eyes slowly relent and shut, and she lets herself sleep.

When she feels the hand running through her hair and down her spine and legs, and all over her body, she is not sure whether it is a dream. She cannot deny she has had such dreams before, but then she knows it is not a dream. She gets up with a start and sees Unni staring at her. He holds her in his powerful arms and kisses her. She is so frightened she screams and tries to extricate herself from his grip, and in her struggle, her top tears at the shoulder. That is when Unni leaves her, something in him snaps. She looks at him just for a moment before she runs away. That would be the last time she would see him alive. What she sees in that minuscule moment is Unni standing without meeting her eye, looking at the space behind her with a gentle smile. She has thought of his expression many times and tried to find its meaning. But she does not understand the face.

She runs to her home, into the bathroom. She sits on the floor and cries, she is shivering. She decides to have a bath. She wonders what she should tell her mother about the torn top. She invents many excuses in the bath. That is when she hears the sounds of men, she hears the word 'Unni' several times, and she is too terrified even to guess what may have happened. What an idiot, Unni, what an idiot.

In a few hours, Mythili will tell his mother everything about that day. But what she really wants to tell her, if she is not too shy to do that, is that she is sorry she abandoned her. The day Unni died, Mariamma lost a son and a daughter. Mythili is sorry she chose the comfort of hiding, she is sorry it turned out that way, but now the daughter has returned, and she will always watch over her till the end of her time. That is what she will say. She has the strength to say it now.

*

Ousep has long finished the story of Unni Chacko, and his wife had listened in silence but without any questions. Something about her tells him that she has finally made peace with Unni, she may even believe that his death has been resolved. But Ousep plans his day ahead.

He will wake up early and make a list of people he will meet – all kinds of people, new people. What did Unni see? What did Unni know, what could make a boy so contemptuous of happiness, of his own extraordinary happiness, and of human life, which he considered so trivial that he needed merely one honourable reason to shed it? Ousep will go in search of the answers, he will not stop. A search without an end. What is so terrifying about a search without an end?

Ousep, finally, in the search for meaning. Resolute, even though he does see Unni Chacko in another place arching his body and laughing.

Acknowledgement

The novel led me to several people in Madras, or Chennai as it is now called. It is where I spent the first twenty years of my life. I am grateful it was not a paradise.

Among the people I met were neurosurgeons and neuro-psychiatrists. Some of them were amused to learn that even novelists have to gather facts, but they gave me their days. Dr Krishnamoorthy Srinivas, an unforgettable patriarch with eight pens and a tiny torch in his shirt pocket, Dr Ennapadam Krishnamoorthy and Dr A.V. Srinivasan, have contributed to the novel more than they will ever guess.

I am fortunate to have the unrelenting confidence of the finest editors in the world. Roland Philipps of John Murray. Karthika V. K. of HarperCollins India. Amy Cherry of Norton. Iris Tupholme of HarperCollins Canada. Joost Nijsen of Podium. The novel is a beneficiary of their remarkable eye, and the care of their team, especially Joanne Gledhill of John Murray.

But my primary editor is a person I am besotted with – Anuradha, who was the first person to read the novel, and she began her analysis, as usual, with the words, 'Now don't growl…'

Isobel Dixon of the Blake Friedmann Literary Agency – poet, advisor and accomplice – who gave me my first break has saved me in more ways than I have let her know.

For some reason, my mother Kunjamma and sister Aswathy, the extraordinary women who raised me, found it hilarious every time I called them up and asked them to tell me our family stories. But they always found the time for me. As did Joseph Madapally, a storyteller himself.

But most of all, I thank my daughter Kavya for delaying the novel.